GUYANA
on the RISE

Khalil Rahman Ali

First published in 2025 by Hansib Publications
76 High Street, Hertford, SG14 3TA, United Kingdom

info@hansibpublications.com
www.hansibpublications.com

Copyright © Khalil Rahman Ali, 2025

Khalil Rahman Ali has asserted his right to be identified as the author of this work in accordance with the Copyright, Designs and Patents Act 1988.

ISBN 978-1-0683952-6-0
ISBN 978-1-0683952-7-7 (Kindle)
ISBN 978-1-0683952-8-4 (ePub)

A CIP catalogue record for this book is available from the British Library

All rights reserved. No part of this publication may be reproduced, stored in a retrieval system, or transmitted, in any form or by any means, electronic, mechanical, photocopying, recording or otherwise, without the prior permission of the author.

Produced and printed in Great Britain

Founded in London in 1970, Hansib Publications has played a crucial role in documenting the Caribbean experience and bringing Caribbean perspectives to a wider audience. It is renowned for its extensive catalogue of Caribbean fiction and non-fiction, spanning a diverse range of genres, including historical novels, biographies, poetry anthologies, political commentaries and social narratives. It has also made significant contributions to Caribbean scholarship by publishing insightful works on history, culture, politics and social issues.

Today, Hansib Publications remains a significant force in the world of Caribbean publishing and continues to publish books that reflect the vibrant diversity of the Caribbean region and the global Caribbean diaspora. Its legacy of promoting Caribbean voices and perspectives has made it an invaluable resource for those seeking to understand and appreciate the rich cultural heritage of the Caribbean.

Dedicated to my ancestors who took the courageous decision to migrate from India to what was then British Guiana (now Guyana) as Indentured labourers, and to remain after the end of their Indentureship on the sugar plantations.

To my grandparents and parents who established their businesses in Leonora and Anna Catherina, on the West Coast of Demerara, for the benefit of their families and the local communities.

To my amazing and caring wife, Manjeet, and our incredible daughter, Sonya.

To my dear brother, Nasimul, and loving sister, Razia, and their wonderful families.

To the remarkable people of Guyana and my many relatives and friends there and around the world.

ABOUT THE AUTHOR

Khalil Rahman Ali is a successful Guyanese born author who has travelled extensively around Guyana and many other countries of the world. He has lived, studied and worked in London for several decades, and has retained a very close interest in his homeland. He is keen to see Guyana and his fellow Guyanese achieve their full potential as a leading nation of South and Central America, and the Caribbean.

He believes that Guyana, with most of its rainforest still intact, can show the world how to effectively deal with the challenges of climate change whilst the country is being rapidly developed.

Khalil hopes that this book will inform readers more about the country, its history, its people, and he highly recommends visiting this exciting and fascinating nation.

He is also a keen follower of sports including cricket and football. He loves Indian music, and is an accomplished singer and composer.

PREFACE

Guyana is the only English-speaking country on the mainland of South America. It has become one of the fastest growing economies in the world since the discovery and production of oil offshore in the Atlantic Ocean in 2015. The country is undergoing a progressive transformation from being one of the poorest nations in the Western Hemisphere, towards substantial growth.

Guyana on the Rise is the story of a journey through the country's past, observing the present, and providing views of its future, by a group of Guyanese friends who were the 'Domino Masters of Demerara' and members of the ACES of Anna Catherina, the LIONS of Leonora, and the COBRAS of Cornelia Ida on the West Coast of Demerara.

The quest is undertaken at the invitation of Nazir and Neesha Khan and John and Muriel Charles of Anna Catherina, to Vishnu 'Double Six' Prashad and his family residing in Queens, New York, and Michael 'Histry Maan' Brown and Doreen Brown of Brooklyn, New York, and other longstanding friends living abroad.

The tour group is taken to visit and experience a number of the sites and places across some of the 83,000 square miles of Guyana's ten regions of outstanding natural beauty, great historical significance and struggles for freedom. They acknowledge and learn about the contributions of many Guyanese from all walks of life in building the nation, offer their own observations on the current issues and developments of the country, and express their thoughts on how they perceive Guyana in the future.

The multi-cultural and multi-racial demographic of the country's population, provides great potential but, at the same time, serious challenges such as a racial tension between the two main ethnic groups: those of Indian and those of African heritage. However, there is a strong commitment in the country to bring the people together under the vision of "One People, One Nation, One Destiny".

Can Guyana, 'The Land of Many Waters', and its people emerge from the doldrums to soar high and achieve the goals that prosperity can promise?

GLOSSARY

Abeer: Vibrant and fragrant coloured powders used in the Hindu festival of *Holi.*

Acchar: Hindi word for pickle. Acchar is made of several spices and with fruits including *mango,* lime, *bling bling,* and apple. It is normally used with Indian meals or snacks such as *poulouri* and *baara.*

Agouti: Dasyprocta: A mammal found within the Amazon rainforest. It is of the rodent genus, about two feet long, and weighs between four to eleven pounds. It is smaller than the *capybara* and is hunted for its meat.

Akawaio: One of the nine Amerindian tribes of Guyana. The Akawaios live mostly in the Upper Mazaruni area of Region 7 and near the border with Venezuela. Their population is about six thousand.

Akurio: One of the Indigenous tribes of Suriname which is to the east of Guyana. The Akurios are hunter-gatherers and also known for harvesting honey. Their number has reduced to about forty.

Aloo: Hindi word for potato.

Aloo choka: A dish made of mashed potato with several spices including crushed ginger, cumin, red chilli pepper, turmeric, and salt.

Alhamdulillah: Arabic expression for "All praise is due to Allah".

Amerindian/s: Indigenous People/s of Guyana. There are nine Amerindian tribes or nations in Guyana. The *Akawaio, Arawak, Arecuna, Carib, Macushi, Patamona, Wai Wai, Wapishana,* and *Warrau.*

Aracari: Pteroglossus Erythropygius: A medium sized *toucan* and is resident in the rainforest.

Arapaima: Arapaima Gigas: This is the largest scaled freshwater fish in the world. It can grow to over fifteen feet long and weigh as much as five hundred pounds. The arapaima is called "oma" which means "Mother of all fishes".

Arawak: One of the nine Amerindian tribes of Guyana. They live mainly on the coastland areas and are about sixteen thousand in number.

Arecuna: One of the nine Amerindian tribes of Guyana. They were originally settled in Venezuela and migrated to the upper areas of Mazaruni and Cuyuni Rivers in Essequibo. They are about five hundred in number.

Arya Samaj: A Hindu Reform Movement founded by Dayananda Saraswati in 1875 in Mumbai, India. The Arya Samaj believe in One God, and the texts of the Vedas. They do not perform ritual worship of murti (idols) as is done in Hinduism.

Assalaam O Alaikum: Arabic. Normal Islamic greeting which means "May the Peace and Blessings of Allah (God) be with you."

Awara: Astrocaryum Vulgare: An orange-coloured fruit of the awara palm, and which grows in large bunches. The skin and flesh of the fruit are sweet and leave an orange-coloured stain on the teeth. It is considered to be nutritious and is a rich source of carotene and vitamins.

Baara: A Guyanese snack made of flour, ground split peas, spices, salt, and is fried. It is normally used with a pepper sauce, *chutney,* or *acchar.*

Backdam: A piece of land which lies at the rear (or back) of a place. It is also a built-up dam away from the coast to prevent water flooding the agricultural fields.

Baccoo: A mythical creature of Guyanese folklore which has the power to provide good fortune. It is of small stature and must be "fed" banana and milk or else it will harm the "owner".

Baigan: Solanum Melongena: Aubergine or eggplant or brinjal.

Baigan Choka: A spicy dish made of roasted *baigan* mashed with tomatoes, peppers, and salt. It is normally used as a side dish.

Balata: A rubber-like material made from the sap that is bled from the balata "bullet wood" tree (*Manilkara Bidentata*). Balata is used for craft products and for the core of golf balls. The wood is very robust and used for making furniture.

Banga Mary: Macrodon Ancylodon: A popular freshwater fish used widely in Guyanese cuisine including as fried, stir-fried, curry, or stew.

Baraat: A baraat is a Hindu wedding procession of the groom with his family and friends travelling to the bride's home or the location of the wedding ceremony accompanied by musicians.

Batting Crease: Cricket term. A line from the stumps or wicket which can determine whether or not a batter is out or dismissed by way of a stumping or run out.

Benab: Amerindian structure meaning "meeting place of the people". It is normally round at the base, constructed with local timber, and with a conical roof made of the branches and leaves of the palm. At the centre there is a main pole made of the resilient purple heart timber.

Berbice Chair: An elegant, elongated armchair shaped to allow reclining. It has two long arms which can be folded inwards to allow resting of a person's legs.

Bhaji: Althernanthera Sessilis: or Callaloo or Spinach. Bhaji is a popular green whose leaves are boiled or cooked with spices and used as a dish alongside rice and *daal.*

Black Pudding: The Guyanese version of black pudding is normally made of rice, pork or beef, coconut milk, pork or beef blood, spices including black pepper, nutmeg, salt and cinnamon. The outer casing is made of pig or cattle intestine.

Bling Bling: Averrhoa Bilimbi: The fruit which grows in large bunches on the stems and trunk of the bilimbi tree. It is used to make pickles or *acchar*. It is normally sour to the taste and appears throughout the year.

Bollywood: The name associated with the Indian Film Industry initially based in Bombay, now Mumbai. The Indian Film Industry is also located in several places across India.

Calypso: A song believed to have originated from West African kaiso music. It was adapted and modified in Trinidad and the lyrics are topical commentaries about social and political issues. The most famous calypsonian is Slinger Francisco, known as the "Mighty Sparrow" who was born in Grenada in 1935.

Capadulla: Doliocarpus Dentatus: Capadulla is from the woody vine and used to make tea or other drinks believed to cure impotence. The leaves of the vine have anti-inflammatory and anti-bacterial properties.

Carib: One of the nine Amerindian tribes of Guyana. They are settled in the Pomeroon and North West Essequibo including alongside the Cuyuni, Barama and Barima Rivers. They are about fifteen thousand in number.

Cassareep: A dark brown cooking sauce made from continuously boiling the juice of the *cassava* until it is caramelised. It is the creation of the Amerindians of Guyana and is commonly used as the main ingredient of *pepperpot*, a famous Guyanese dish.

Cassava: Manihot Esculenta: Cassava is also known as manioc, yucca, and mandioca. It is an edible starchy tuberous root, and a major staple food of the Amerindians. The white flesh is used to make a flat bread, the *kasiri* alcoholic drink, and the *cassareep* sauce.

Castnet: A large hand-held fishing net with pieces of lead at the bottom which help to sink the net and entrap the fish.

Channa: Cicer Arietinum: Channa is known as chickpea and a legume which is high in protein. It is normally soaked and then cooked in several ways including as a curry, parched, or fried.

Chutney: As chutney music, it is a fusion of Indian folk music and *calypso* or *soca* and has a mixture of Hindi and English lyrics. The most famous chutney singers have been the Trinidadians, Sundar Popo, Anand Yankaran, and Drupatee Ramgoonai. The most popular Guyanese chutney singer is Terry Gajraj.

Chutney Soca: A combination of chutney music with harmonium, dholak, tabla and *dhantaal*, and soca with guitar, drum set, and keyboard. The duo, Babla and Kanchan, took popular chutney songs to Mumbai, re-recorded and enhanced them into chutney soca.

Coconut Broom: A broom made entirely out of the stems of the coconut tree branches.

Coconut Choka: A spicy side dish made of roasted and ground coconut and blended with spices, onion, garlic, salt and pepper.

Comfa: A term for anyone becoming possessed by spirits. However, Comfa is a folk religion with African origin and has links with Christianity and other beliefs in Guyana.

Cook up Rice: A rice-based dish which includes vegetables and spices. It is also called "peas and rice".

Cover Drive/s: A stroke in Cricket whereby the batter strides to meet the ball and hits it through the cover area of the field on the *offside*.

Crabwood: Carapa Guianensis: Crabwood is a tropical hardwood mostly used for furniture in Guyana. The seed of the tree produces a medicinal oil normally used by Amerindians. The oil is also used as a repellent against mosquitoes.

"Crappo": Rhinella Marinus: The world's largest toad. It is referred to as "cane toad" and was introduced to sugarcane fields to help control pests such as the cane beetle. It is also known as "mountain chicken". Crappo is derived from a French word crapaud meaning frog.

Creole/s: The term used to describe people of mixed European and African descent. It also refers to the language based on a mix of English, French, Spanish, and Portuguese.

Cuirass: Sciades Herzbergii: Cuirass is a non-scaled fish also known as the flapnose sea catfish. It inhabits areas of brackish or slightly salty water. It is popularly used in curries and stews.

Cutlass: The cutlass is a slightly curved instrument made of steel or iron and sharpened on one side. It has a protective short handle made of wood. It originated from the short sword used by sailors and pirates during the seventeenth century. It was adopted as the main cutting tool used to chop the sugarcane stalks by workers called "cane cutters".

Cutlass Fish: Aphanopus Carbo: This is a long black scabbard fish found deep in the Atlantic Ocean and is popularly known as the "cutlass fish" in Madeira. It is highly regarded as a delicacy due to its tender white flesh and being fat free. It is often served with banana and passion fruit sauce.

Daal or Lentil: Lens Culinaris: A type of legume normally used as a soup with Indian spices, and accompanies rice, roti, and *curry* dishes. There are several types of daal including moong (green), masoor (red), toor (pigeon peas), channa (split chickpeas), urud (black), and arhar (split pigeon peas).

Daalpuri Roti: A popular roti with a spicy split peas dry *daal* contained within the pastry. It is used to accompany various curry dishes.

Dhantaal: A percussion instrument made of a thin steel rod and a hand-held curved piece used to play the beats on the rod. The dhantaal is normally used to accompany the dholak drum and the harmonium used by local Indian singers.

Diwali: Diwali or Deepavali, is known as the Hindu Festival of Lights. It is a celebration of the triumph of good over evil. Within the epic story of the Ramayan, when Lord Raam and his companions returned to Ayodhya after their victory over the evil Raavan, they were greeted with lighted *diyas* or lamps lining the streets, in doorways, and windows. Diwali is also about the worship of three Devis or Goddesses, Lakshmi, Durga, and Saraswati. It is regarded as an auspicious day for the launch of new businesses with the blessing of Lakshmi, the Goddess of Wealth.

Diya/s: The diya is a soft warm light from a wick in some oil within a small clay dish. As with Diwali, the diya represents the virtue of knowledge over ignorance, light over darkness, and good over evil.

Downs or Ber: Ziziphus Mauritania: Downs or Ber (pronounced bear) is a tropical fruit with light green to brown peel when ripened, white flesh, and one hard seed.

Eddoe/s: Colocasia Antiquorum: The eddoe is a tropical root vegetable. Like the potato, the eddoe is roasted, boiled, or fried. The nutrition value of eddoe includes help with weight loss and stable blood sugar.

Eid-ul-Adha: An important Islamic observance to commemorate Prophet Abraham's (May Peace be upon Him) willingness to sacrifice his son Ishmael in obedience to Allah's (God's) instruction. It is regarded as the ultimate test of faith in God.

Eid-ul-Fitr: The Islamic festival of celebration at the end of Ramadan, the month of fasting, prayers, reflection, abstinence, and charity. The day begins with the communal prayer or salaat in the early morning and is followed by the sharing of food and gifts amongst families and friends.

Fajr: The first of the five daily prayers in Islam at dawn, followed by Zuhr (mid-day), Asr (afternoon). Maghrib (sunset), and Isha (night).

Farine: Farine is a type of flour made from *cassava* and is believed to have originated from the Amerindians who migrated from Brazil to Guyana. Farine derives from the Portuguese "farinha" meaning flour. It is the residue after the juice is removed from cassava and then dried in the sun for hours. Farine is used as a nutritious drink when mixed with milk and sugar. It is also used in making *cassareep*.

GLOSSARY

Five Fingers: Averrhoa Carambola: Five Fingers, or Shamrock, or Star Fruit which appears to be a star when cut through horizontally, is believed to have several health benefits including weight management, boost for the immune system, and the digestive system. It is best used when ripened to a dark yellow colour especially as a fruit drink.

Fried Bakes: Guyanese fried bakes which are also known as floats, are made of basic flour, baking soda, cinnamon, nutmeg, and salt. They are deep fried to a light brown colour and used as a breakfast accompaniment to fried salted fish.

Gilbaaka: Sciades Parkeri: A species of scaleless sea catfish which can grow up to five feet in length. It is popular in Guyana, and used in curries, stews or as fried snacks.

Genip: Melicoccus Bijugatus: A small tropical fruit with green peel and orange flesh when ripened. The genip is also known as skinip or Spanish lime and grows in bunches.

Gola: A small round pellet made of clay soil and used with the handmade *slingshot*.

Golden Apple: Spondias Dulcis: A tropical fruit with a green skin, yellowish flesh, and a prickly pith.

Gopi: A Sanskrit word meaning milkmaid. The gopis are selfless worshippers of Lord Krishna. Radha was the dearest and closest to him.

Grass Knife: A handheld small cutter with a curved blade and wooden handle. It is mostly used for cutting grass by hand.

Great Spirit: Makonaima: The Amerindians, as the First Peoples of Guyana, believe in the unseen Great Spirit which created the world and guides and shapes the way that the people live.

Greenheart: Ocotea Rodeii: The greenheart is one of the strongest hardwoods of the Guyana rainforest. It is commonly used in construction such as for marine bollards and piling for bridges and harbours.

Gugri: Another name for *channa*.

Guyanese Bakes: A small dough of flour, baking powder, sugar, salt, butter, and deep fried until light brown. Bakes are normally used with fried salted fish at breakfast.

Halaal: Refers to what is lawful or permissible for consumption in Islamic or Sharia Law.

Hassa: Hoplosternum: The hassa or cascadou is a freshwater fish found in slow moving waterways such as trenches, canals, creeks and streams. The scales are unusual giving the fish an ancient look. Hassa is normally cooked as a curry with a spicy masala, green mango, and potatoes.

Hoatzin: Opisthocomus Hoazin: The Hoatzin is Guyana's National Bird and is found in mangroves alongside rivers or swamps in Guyana. It is a large bird which attracts a local name of "stink bird" due to its digestive system which takes a longer time to break down food, and the excretion is unpleasant. The chicks have two claws under their wings which they use to climb back to their nests if they fall out. The claws are shred as the chicks grow older. The Hoatzin is also called "Canje Pheasant" but it is not related to pheasants.

Holi or *Pagwah:* There are at least three reasons for the Holi or Pagwah celebrations in Hinduism.
1. It signifies the advent of Spring, of harvest, or of a new life.
2. It celebrates the triumph of good over evil through the story of Holika a sister of the cruel King Hiranyakashipu who wished to kill his son Prahalad because he wanted to worship Lord Vishnu instead of his father. A bonfire was prepared, and Holika dared Prahalad to enter the fire as she had a magic cloak which would save her. But Lord Vishnu took away the cloak and granted it to Prahalad who was saved whilst Holika perished.
3. Lord Krishna, who was dark-skinned, wanted Radha's complexion to be like his, and smeared her with colourful powders. Radha then fell in love with him, and this playful smearing of powders became a regular celebratory event.

Holika: See *Holi* or *Pagwah.*

Holika Dahan: The Hindu festival where a bonfire is lit as a celebration of the burning of *Holika.*

Hooks: A hook is a Cricket stroke by a batter hitting a delivery into the legside either along the ground, or fully over the boundary for six runs.

Houri: Hoplias Malabaricus: A popular freshwater fish found in trenches, canals and other waterways in Guyana. It is a "sweet" tasting fish whether fried or curried but needs to be properly deboned.

Imam: The appointed leader of prayers or *namaaz* in Muslim Mosques. The Imam serves as a community leader and offers guidance on religious practices.

Jaaray: A Hindi term used in Guyana to describe the spiritual ritual to drive out evil spirits from someone.

Jahaji/s: The Hindi word adopted for the Indian Indentured Labourers who were taken on ships from India to work on the sugar plantations in Guyana and a number of other British Colonies in the 19th Century. Jahaji means a sea traveller or sailor. A jahaji bhai (brother) or behen (sister) is a fellow traveller and conjures up a sense of togetherness.

Jamaat: A congregation of Muslims offering prayers (Namaaz) together.

Jamoon: Syzygium Jambolanum: An oblong shaped small fruit of deep purple skin, pink flesh and a small black seed.

Jeewan Saathi: Hindi for a life partner.

Jumbie: A spirit of a deceased person, which can haunt or possess an individual.

Jumma Namaaz: A special Islamic prayer (Namaaz) on Friday (Jumma) afternoon replacing the normal Zuhr Namaaz.

Kaaba: The most sacred building in Islam regarded as the Bayt Allah (House of God), and located in Mecca, Saudi Arabia. It is the central point of worship for all Muslims during Namaaz (prayers). Muslim pilgrims circle the Kaaba which is in the centre of the Al-Masjid al-Haram Mosque during the Haj (pilgrimage) and stop briefly to kiss the black stone which dates to the time of Adam and Eve.

Kabukalli: Goupiaglabra: The kabukalli tree grows to about one hundred and thirty feet in height with a trunk up to about twenty-four inches. The wood is used in furniture, floor decking, wall panels, and mouldings.

Kasiri: A alcoholic drink made from fermented cassava juice by Amerindians.

Kukri: A type of hand-held short sword with a distinctive curved blade. The kukri is most associated with the Gurkha military.

Kurta: The kurta is a loose shirt that is collarless, and normally worn along with a pyjama.

Labba: Cuniculus Paca: A large rodent with horizontal stripes on a brown coat. The labba is nocturnal and is found in the rainforests. Its meat is popularly used as a curry.

Liming: A local term for small groups of friends standing around and idling.

Little Guyana: A name for part of Queens, New York City, in the USA in recognition of the presence and impact of Guyanese residing, working, and thriving there. The Guyanese population in New York City is estimated to be about 140,000.

Lukanaani: Chichla Ocellaris: A freshwater fish that is yellowish gold in colour with a red and black spot on its tail. It is considered to be the best tasting fish in Guyana.

Madras Roomaal: Contrary to the belief that the Madras Roomaal originated in Madras, India, this red and yellow checked cotton headwear was worn by enslaved women before Indentured Indians arrived in Guyana and the Caribbean in the nineteenth century. However, it was wholly adopted by Indian women as a regular headwear.

Makushi: One of the nine Amerindian tribes of Guyana. They reside mostly in Southern Guyana and close to the border with Brazil. They are about seven thousand in number.

Manicole Palm: Prestoea Tenuiramosa: A flowering palm found in Guyana, Brazil and Venezuela. It has many uses including the edible palm cabbage of the heart, making furniture from the stem, and roofing from the branches.

Maroons: The Maroons were escaped or runaway enslaved Africans who sought and established refuge and their own communities far into the hinterland of Guyana where they could not be re-captured. Maroons were known for their bravery, resilience, and strong sense of community.

Moongazers: The Guyana Moongazers are imaginary giants who gaze at the full moon. It is believed that if anyone passes between their legs they will be crushed.

Mora: Mora Excelsa: A robust hardwood which is used for interior flooring and externally for posts and building bridges.

Mukru: Chlorocardium Rodiei: A tropical vine which has many uses including the making of the Amerindian matapee which is used to squeeze the juice from cassava.

Namaaz: Islamic prayer, and one of the five tenets of the religion. Namaaz is performed five times each day.

Nibbi: Heteropsis Flexuosa: An aerial vine and root of the rainforest which is used by Amerindians in Guyana for furniture making, weaving baskets, and for tying the thatches of roofs.

Obeah: A traditional African based spiritual activity intended for good or for bad purpose. The ritual involves invoking ancestral spirit or spirits by chanting, the sacrifice of a fowl (chicken), and determination of the healing or curse requested by the client/s.

Offside: In Cricket, the half of the field faced by a right-hand batsman. The other half of the field is called the *Onside.*

Ole Hige: An ole hige in Guyanese folklore is an old woman who lives normally during the day and then manifests into a ball of fire during the night. Believers would keep a special broom to help fight off the demon.

On Drive/s: The On Drive is a Cricket stroke played by the batter hitting the ball off the front foot towards the mid on or long on positions in the field.

Pandit: The Pandit is a Hindu Priest who is a learned scholar especially of the ancient Holy books called the Vedas and Upanishads. A Pandit is of the Brahmin caste and a preacher who is fluent in the Sanskrit verses or Shlokas as well as the epic stories of the Ramayan and Bhagwad Gita.

Patamona: One of the nine Amerindian tribes of Guyana. They relate to the Pakaraima Mountain area in mid-west Guyana. The Patamona people call themselves the "People of the Heavens", and Kaieteur Falls is closely associated with the legend of "Old Kai" of this tribe. They are about five thousand in number.

Patwa: Cichlasoma Bimaculatum: A small freshwater fish usually used as a deep-fried side dish accompaniment to a main meal.

Pepperpot: A popular Guyanese national dish made of cassareep sauce and tough cuts of meat. The dish appears dark in colour and is enhanced by very hot peppers and spices such as cinnamon, thyme, and clove. Pepperpot is normally eaten with plaited bread.

Piaiman or Shaman: The Piaiman or Shaman is a spiritual Amerindian person who possesses special powers and great knowledge of natural plant-based medicines of the rainforest. The medicines are used for most ailments by Amerindians.

Piwari: A fermented drink made from cassava and sugar by the Amerindians. The alcoholic content is low.

Pork-knocker: An independent gold or diamond prospector who normally operates single-handedly or as part of a team. The earliest Pork-knockers were freed enslaved African Guyanese who chose to pursue wealth and a good living by prospecting for gold or diamonds in the hinterland. The name alludes to their fondness for pork and saying that they are going to "knock" (eat) some pork during their breaks from mining.

Poulouri: A small round deep-fried ball made of split peas batter including several spices and hot pepper. It is used as a side snack along with *acchar* or pepper sauce.

Psydium: Psydium Densicocum: A sweet berry with reddish flesh and a yellow peel.

Pull: A Cricket stroke where the batter hits the ball to the leg side of the wicket.

Purine: Or Puri leaf of the water lily which grows to be large enough to be used as a handheld "plate" for the serving and consuming of the famous "seven curries" of Guyana.

Purpleheart: Peltogyne Purpurea: One of the hardest and most durable woods of Guyana. It is purple in colour and the Amerindians use Purpleheart trunks for carving out canoes.

Rajao: A five-stringed musical instrument from Madeira and is similar to the ukulele.

Ramadan: Ramadan is the Islamic month when Muslims around the world fast between sunrise and sunset until the next new moon is spotted to declare the end of fasting and the advent of the *Eid ul Fitr* celebration. Ramadan is a time for reflection, abstinence, prayers, and charitable giving.

Rangwali: or Holi: The Hindu festival of colours in the season of Spring. See also, *Holi/Pagwah*.

Rap/Rapped: A rap or pass in a game of Dominoes occurs when a player is unable to match the "point/s" at either of the two ends of the game. The player says the word "rap" and/or hits the playing table with his/her knuckle or ticket.

Saada Roti: A thick roti made of whole wheat flour and used with curries and daal.

Saki Winki: or Squirrel Monkey: Saimiri Sciureus: A small-sized monkey of about twelve inches in length. The face is with dark coloured eyes and a white background. It feeds mostly on fruits and insects. The saki winki is a native of Guyana, Brazil and Venezuela. It is regarded as one of the cleverest monkeys due to its relatively large brain as a proportion to its body.

Salted Fish: Salted Fish is dried fish containing much salt for its preservation. It is washed thoroughly to remove as much of the salt as possible, boiled, and then sauteed with fresh herbs, peppers and other vegetables. It is the traditional accompaniment with Guyanese *fried bakes*.

Sanatan Dharm: Sanatan Dharm in Sanskrit means "eternal religion". It is essentially a way of life based on the teachings in the Vedas, Upanishads and other philosophical texts found in Hinduism. Sanatan Dharm ascribes to the idea of a One God (Bramha) and that the soul is everlasting.

Sapodilla: Manilkara Zapota: A brown round fruit with brown flesh when ripe and with a small black seed.

Sasparilla: Smilax Ornata: The sasparilla plant is a climbing woody vine which grows in the rainforests of Guyana as well as in Jamaica and other islands of the Caribbean. The plant contains many beneficial chemicals and apart from reducing inflammation and other remedies, it is believed to have aphrodisiac properties.

Shibadan: Aspidosperma Album: A hard and strong timber with a rose red colour. It is a good general purpose wood suitable for panelling and furniture.

Shorebird: A migratory bird which visits the muddy and sandy beaches of the coastland of Guyana. They are normally hunted and used as a food source.

Silverballi: Licaria Canella: A timber which can be divided into hard or soft wood suitable for exterior or interior carpentry including furniture.

Slingshot: A handheld catapult made of rubber bands secured to a fork-shaped wooden frame. The base is normally made of leather attached to the two pieces of rubber. The slingshot is fired by placing a *gola* in the leather base, pulling the rubber bands firmly, taking aim through the fork, and releasing.

Sloth: Choloepus Didactylus: The sloth is the slowest mammal in the world. It has a white and light brown face and a fawn body coat.

Soca: A local form of music invented in Trinidad through a combination of "soul" and "calypso". It is essentially dance music with some South Asian rhythms.

Sorrel: Rumex Acetosa: The red sorrel flower is used to make jams, sauces, and teas. The young leaves of the plant add flavour to salads.

Square Cut: A Cricket stroke where the batter hits the ball through square of the wicket on his/her offside.

Square Leg: A position on the Cricket field which is square of the wicket on the leg side of the batter.

Star Apple: Chrysophyllum Cainito: A tropical fruit of the sapodilla family. Its outer skin is purple when ripe and with pink, soft and sweet flesh. When cut through across the pulp and seed structure forms a "star" and hence the name.

Sweep Shot: A Cricket stroke whereby the batter crouches on one knee and hits the ball into the legside.

Taaga: A popular local game played in Guyana consisting of a small hand-held flat circular metal disc used to hit buttons set just beyond a line from the base a few feet away. Any button hit by a player is claimed by him/her until all buttons are won.

Taki-taki: A nickname for Sranan Tongo, the national language of Suriname, which literally means "talk-talk" or "say-say"

Tanagers: Thraupidae Passeriformes: Very colourful birds of several species found across South and Central America as well as in the Caribbean.

Tapir: Tapirus Terrestris: The tapir resembles the pig but with a longer snout and taller. The coat is short and reddish brown to black and is found mostly in the rainforest.

Tirio: One of the Indigenous tribes of Suriname and reside mainly in the border zone with Brazil.

Toshao: A democratically elected Amerindian village leader upon whom the residents depend for representation. Each Amerindian village or settlement in the hinterland of Guyana has an elected Council of members supporting the Toshao.

Toucanet: Aulacorhynchus Prasinus: The toucanet is a smaller version of the *toucan*. They are several in number including the emerald, crimson, chestnut and blue throated toucanet.

Trup Chaal: A local card game of Guyana where each player is dealt a number of cards and the first decides which suit he/she prefers to be the trump card. The player who selects the trump suit starts the game whereby the other three players must try to match or use a trump card to win the hand. The player winning the most hands wins the game.

Turu: Oenocarpus Bacaba: A palm which provides an oil which is used as a medicine or on the hair. The leaves are used as thatch for roofs. The palm heart is edible or can be cooked.

Twang: A way of describing an accent in Guyana.

Vaqueros: A vaquero is a local cattle herder who rides a horse to round up the herd. It is Portuguese in origin, and interestingly, the vaqueros of Guyana are mostly the Amerindians.

Vedic: Vedic related to the sacred Sanskrit texts called the Vedas. The vedic tradition is about the teachings and guidance provided by sages who were versed in the Vedas.

Wa Alai Kum Asalaam Arabic. A Muslim's reply to *Asalaam O Alai Kum* meaning "May the Peace and Blessings of Allah Be Upon You".

Wadara: Couratari Gloriosa: A large rainforest tree native to South and Central America. Wadara wood is used for both internal and external construction.

Wai-Wai: The Wai-Wai people are one of the nine Amerindian tribes of Guyana and reside in the dense rainforests of southern Guyana and northern Brazil. They are known for their deep connection to the rainforest and their traditional way of life, which includes hunting, gathering and horticulture. Their culture is rich in mythology, spiritual beliefs and intricate social structures. Their population of around two hundred is the smallest of the Indigenous tribes.

Wallaba: Eperua Falcata: It is a tropical hardwood tree which can grow to about sixty feet tall. The wood is durable and suitable for telegraph poles, and other construction uses.

Wapichan: One of the nine Amerindian tribes of Guyana. The Wapichan is also known as the Wapishana and reside mostly in South Rupununi and the Roraima area of Northern Brazil. They are a proud nation who continue to foster their ancestral knowledge of their environment and culture. There are about thirteen thousand Wapichans in Guyana.

Warao: One of the nine Amerindian tribes of Guyana. They reside mostly around the Northwest of Guyana, Northeast of Venezuela, Suriname and Trinidad and Tobago. The word Warao means "the boat people" due to their close connection with waterways. They are expert canoe makers. They number about five thousand in Guyana but just over forty-nine thousand in Venezuela. It is said that Warao babies learn to swim before they could walk.

Wayana: An Indigenous tribe of Suriname, Cayenne (French Guiana) and Brazil. They are Carib speaking and number about eight hundred in Suriname.

Wicket: A Cricket term for two sets of three stumps and two bails each which are set at twenty-two yards apart on the pitch upon which the ball is bowled towards a batter at the striker's end. The wicket also refers to the area upon which one or more pitches are formed.

Wiri Wiri: Capsicum Frutescens: A small round and red chili pepper with a hot tangy flavour.

Youman Nabi: This is the celebration of the birth of the Prophet Mohamad (Peace Be Unto Him), the founding Prophet of Islam.

CONTENTS

1. Invitation 23
2. One more trip 29
3. Rebels of West Demerara 34
4. JFK International to CJIA 40
5. Mutual love and respect 47
6. Direct flight 53
7. Welcome to Guyana 57
8. The old and the new 61
9. Of crossings and curses 68
10. The fighter, the educator and food for thought 73
11. The gathering and calling 80
12. Kaieteur – "Old Man Falls?" 88
13. Rest, reflection and recall 97
14. To Berbice: Of migrants, martyrs, mysteries and mind over matter 111
15. Kofi Badu, Babu John and Bholalal 123
16. A taste of things to come 132
17. Iwokrama: The Green Heart of Guyana 139
18. From Stabroek to Silica 150
19. Of monuments, meeting places and silent prayers 160
20. Of runs, runners and riders 167
21. Parika, Supenaam, Charity and Pomeroon's spirits 175
22. Identity 191
23. Rupununi rejuvenation 201
24. All that glitters 215

25. Shell Beach 222
26. The things we share 229
27. The Spirit of Paramaribo 239
28. Bartica: The gateway to riches 251
29. Of heroes and heroines 258
30. Santa Mission, Arrowpoint, Linden and the
    Blue Lakes 270
31. Domino! 277
Also by Khalil Rahman Ali 294

1
Invitation

The iPhone resting on the right arm of the brown leather settee rumbled as an incoming call was signalled via the pre-set ringtone matching a traditional telephone bell. The receiver picked up the phone and accepted the call.

"Hello! Hello! Who is calling?"

After a pause, the caller responded excitedly, "Hello! Am I speaking to Vishnu? Vishnu "Double Six" Prashad? It's Nazir. Nazir Khan from Anna Catherina, Guyana!"

Vishnu was momentarily taken aback as he was surprised to be called from Guyana situated in northern South America about two and a half thousand miles from New York, United States of America. It was six in the morning in both countries.

He coughed slightly to clear his throat and then said, "Yes, it is Vishnu. Man, this is a great surprise especially after so many years! How are you, my friend?"

Nazir took some ice-cold water as he leaned back into his neatly lacquered mahogany Berbice chair. He looked ahead through one of two large windows at his newly built six-bedroomed house in the village of Anna Catherina on the West Coast of Demerara in Guyana.

"Vishnu I am so glad to hear your voice since you left our village in Guyana way back in 1985. So many of you guys just got up and left the country and I lost contact with you all. How are you? How is your wife Parvati, your son Ramesh and daughter-in-law Sati? How is our dear friend Michael "Histry Maan" Brown and his wife Doreen? I wanted to call them, but I do not have their number. I hope that you can help me with this."

Vishnu eased his slim five feet and nine inches tall frame more comfortably in the settee and pressed the recliner button to provide support to his long skinny legs. He was still in his black, blue and red chequered cotton pyjama suit. He also stared ahead with his steely brown eyes through the one great window at the front of his modest New York family home.

"Nazir, my wife Parvati and I are as well as can be. We are in our eighties now. We left Guyana because our son Ramesh got a good job offer here in New York City in one of the big banks. He insisted that we must follow him and Sati. So, we took the plunge to come over since 1986. I do know Michael's number and will let you have it. How are you and your family?"

Nazir did not quite hear Vishnu's last response as a large truck rumbled noisily on the narrow Anna Catherina village road only about twenty yards in front of his house. It was the same start to the early morning rush hour traffic in Guyana and New York with the distinct difference between the two locations being the presence of vehicular traffic as well as cattle, donkeys, stray dogs, cyclists and pedestrians using the main road through the village in contrast to the usual slow-moving traffic in the street where Vishnu and his family lived.

He spoke a little louder into his phone, "Pardon Vishnu. I missed the last bit about why you and Parvati left Guyana. Can you repeat that for me?"

Vishnu instantly raised his voice, "No problem. I said that our son got a good job here in New York and he really insisted for us to be with him. So, we did just that. Otherwise, I for one had no plans to leave Guyana as we were well used to living with the problems there. I was more than happy to retire and enjoy all the fruits and vegetables we planted in our yard. But I noticed that more and more of my friends were either leaving or passing away. So, in the end, Parvati and I agreed to give New York a try, and to be with our family. We both could not bear the thought of being so far away from our grandchildren. I also said that I have Michael's contact number and will let you have it. He and Doreen live in Brooklyn."

Nazir nodded and responded, "Thank you. Man, I think that you guys did the right thing as Guyana was getting poorer and poorer. And tougher. I did go over to Suriname for a couple of years, but I could not handle their way of life and the local Dutch language they call *Taki Taki*. I also wanted to go to Trinidad to try my luck there. But I used to hear a lot of bad stories about how the Trinidadian people treated some Guyanese migrants very badly. So, I returned to Guyana and tried my hand at some hustlin'."

Vishnu sat up with surprise and asked, "Hustlin? What is hustlin? Don't tell me that you were smuggling contraband stuff?"

Nazir chuckled as he explained, "Oh no man! I meant to say that I did some retail buying and selling of household items. I used a small van to sell door to door. I did not deal in any banned stuff. That made no sense to me. If you were caught with such goods, you were punished severely. I always believed in making an honest dollar. Besides, I couldn't go round dealing with contraband goods when everyone knew me as "Snake Eyes"!"

Nazir, like Vishnu, was of Indian Guyanese heritage, and a few years younger than his friend. He was of medium height, slightly overweight and wore a white T-shirt loosely over plain blue cotton shorts. His eyes were of an unusual light green colour, and hence he was given the nickname of "Snake Eyes" by his childhood friends. The reference to snake was akin to someone who was deemed to be stealthy and thus not regarded as trustworthy. He never liked the name and the inference, and always tried to conduct his business honestly.

Vishnu appreciated his friend's situation, "That must have been very hard work, especially trying to find legal goods to sell. I guess that the people who were taking chances with contraband and moving drugs through Guyana were very brave as long as they were not caught. I agree with you my friend, it's always better to be safe than sorry."

Nazir looked around his room and then said, "Yes, I know a lot of people who did very well for themselves and started to build massive American style mansions here in the villages. At the same time the fools were drawing attention to themselves in two ways. One, the local criminals began to target their houses for robbery, and two, the other bandit, the taxman, started to ask questions about their sudden show of extreme wealth. I always say that showing off is a great weakness of some stupid Guyanese. In other words, if yuh coat yuself in sugar yuh ah bound to attract flies!"

Vishnu laughed as he said, "You were so right to chase the honest dollar, and now today you and your family must be very comfortable looking forward to the great wealth being brought by Guyana's newfound oil and gas. You must be very excited about this."

Nazir stood up, drank the remainder of his water and stepped across his large lounge room that led to a newly fitted and modern kitchen. He pressed the ice dispenser on the front of his upright American made fridge/freezer and then filled his glass with some freshly squeezed mango juice. He sipped the drink as he returned to his chair.

He sat back comfortably and then continued with the conversation, "Well my friend, from the moment it was confirmed that Guyana had oil out in the Atlantic Ocean in 2015, there was no great celebration as there were so many false promises about the discovery of oil before then. But the government at the time got over-excited and a bunch of Ministers and others went off to a big bash in America to sign up to a deal which we now know to be very unfair to our country. They got a nice signing-on fee, and you must have heard about how they tried to hide the eighteen million American dollars from all of us. I still can't believe that some people would be so tempted by such a relatively small amount of money when billions of American dollars were at stake. This is why I always avoided a "get rich quick" temptation and opted for honest and proper business dealings. Always give me a slow Guyana dollar than a fast American buck."

Vishnu frowned and shook his head as he said, "Man, you sound a bit disappointed. All I have been hearing is how Guyana will now become the next Dubai. Is this not true?"

Nazir gulped down some more of his mango juice and replied, "Look, since 2020 we have been witnessing a massive improvement in the economy alongside a lot of building and construction work. We have a very young and energetic President backed up by a lot of experienced operators as well as a bunch of much younger Ministers. Everywhere you look across the country you can see improvement. This is why I decided to call you guys and to invite you over to witness for yourselves what is happening here. As regards becoming the next Dubai, I don't agree with this nonsense. Guyana and all Guyanese need to build our own identity. We are a very different people and place with a lot more to offer the world. Besides, Guyana is a far more beautiful country than Dubai will ever be."

Vishnu sat forward in his settee upon hearing about Nazir's suggestion and asked, "Are you saying that you are inviting me and my family to visit and tour Guyana? I know that at my age I need to make at least one more journey to our home country and to see for myself what is really going on there. We get a lot of news from family and friends who have been there recently, and they talk about a lot of good things. We also get news on our local 'Little Guyana' TV and radio programmes, and we hear a lot of negative stuff from some disgruntled Guyanese about how the government is racist towards Afro-Guyanese and so on. I wish I can get to the real truth."

Nazir took a final drink of his mango juice and rested the empty glass on the beautifully designed coffee table with ornately carved mahogany legs and with feet in the shape of the paws of the jaguar. He then reached into a small drawer on the side of the table and took out a circular wooden coaster which he used to rest his glass upon.

He cleared his throat and responded, "Yes, my friend. That is the reason for asking you guys to come over and you can all stay at our place. I have enough room here and you will be well looked after. It would be nice to make contact with as many of the guys who played dominoes with us, and we can all do the trips together to see and experience our great and beautiful country. In addition to travelling to the country to see relatives and friends, I hope we can all visit and spend some time at one or more important sites in each of the ten Regions. Then you can all make up your minds about how things are for us ordinary Guyanese. We who stayed on in the country through the last few decades are now blessed with the prospect of a new Guyana on the rise!"

Vishnu smiled and asked, "And when do you think would be the best time to travel to Guyana? It's now April and thank God our winter has ended here in New York, and we are getting a lot of warm sunshine but with a lot of rain as well. The whole place is beginning to liven up and you can see how much happier we all are. I guess it's like being in Georgetown here in Jamaica, Queens."

Nazir looked across the road as if to confirm the local Guyana weather, "Man, as you know we only have two weathers: a long rainy season and a short one. But we get a lot of heat all through the year. I suggest that you come over in or around mid-May and spend a few weeks here."

Vishnu was warming to the idea and confirmed, "That is OK by me. What about the other guys in America and Canada? Would you like for me to contact them and get back to you as to how many of us can make the trip?"

Nazir was distracted by a kiskadee landing on a branch of a mango tree at the front of his yard. The bright yellow breast of the bird and its white and black head contrasted beautifully with its brown wing, back and tail feathers. The great kiskadee is only one of many colourful and wild birds of Guyana.

He smiled contentedly and replied, "First of all, I would dearly like to invite Michael and Doreen. Michael would be the right guy to have on our trips around the country and to tell us about our history and the people who have contributed so much to our nation. Please call him and our other friends and tell me how many will be coming on the trip. I will then arrange to pick you all up from the airport. I am offering the accommodation right here in the village as staying in one of the grand new hotels in and just outside Georgetown will cost you guys a fortune. The average price for a room in a decent four-star hotel here is as much as four to six hundred US dollars per person per night. The more high-end hotel businesses are cashing in on our sudden surge in demand by visitors as well as oil workers from abroad."

Vishnu was astonished to hear about the price per person per night at the top hotels, "That is crazy! There is no way that people like me can afford such prices!"

Nazir's generous offer was now irresistible, and a delighted Vishnu said, "My friend, your offer is simply great! I can't wait to begin this adventure to experience our new Guyana."

The kiskadee sang as if to say, "welcome home". Then it flew off to another tree in the distance. In New York, Vishnu was startled by the loud horn of a yellow cab as it passed by on the street outside his home.

2
One more trip

Vishnu did not waste any time as he set about planning for the Guyana trip. He broached the subject at the family's dinner table that same evening after allowing his wife Parvati and their son Ramesh and his wife Sati to finish their meal of gilbaaka and mango curry, long grain American brown rice, daal and saada roti. The entire meal was prepared by Parvati who had recently celebrated her eightieth birthday but continued to insist on doing most of the housework and preparing the family's meals whilst Ramesh and Sati were at work in Manhattan.

Parvati, who enjoyed good health, had always taken great pride in ensuring that her family continued to maintain as many of their Guyanese customs including the meals she prepared, the handwashing of clothes which were hung on a clothesline at the back of the house, and using a well-worn coconut broom to sweep the carpets and another for the concreted drive and pathway from the front to the backyard. Her daily routine was almost the same as she had practised in her home village of Anna Catherina. The only major hindrance to this was during the very cold and harsh winter months which restricted her outdoor activities. She was forced to accept the need to have a washing machine and dryer installed in the basement of the three-bedroomed home.

She saw her role as the main housekeeper looking after the family as Ramesh and Sati were too busy in their high-pressure jobs. The couple normally left for their commute to Manhattan just after a typical Guyanese breakfast of saada roti with baigan choka or with fried eggs and hot green tea brewed in the traditional way using a saucepan. Although Ramesh and Sati had installed many mod cons in the kitchen, Parvati continued to prepare meals using a gas stove as the nearest option to her earthen handmade fireside which was fired by wood chips back in Guyana. She insisted that food cooked in the traditional Guyanese way always tasted better than with the gas stove or any other modern cooking appliance. She was also delighted that the local Guyanese owned groceries and the vegetable and fruit vendors in Queens stocked many of the ingredients she preferred to use in her cooking than the frozen goods in the larger supermarkets. She was also very fond of wearing the red, black and yellow Madras roomaal which emphasised her appearance as a traditional Guyanese homemaker.

Parvati would normally wait for Ramesh and Sati to leave before rousing her two grandchildren to help them prepare for school. Now that they reached their late teens, they were away at college. Every time they rang to speak with their parents and grandparents, Parvati would enquire as to how they were preparing their meals. When at least once every two months Vishnu, Parvati, Ramesh and Sati would drive out up State to visit the scholars, Parvati would ensure that they were supplied with enough curry powder, dried salted fish, flour, channa and frozen daalpuri roti as well as cooked daal to supplement their mainly Guyanese diet. Parvati would always warn them against the more popular fast foods.

After the meal, Parvati and Sati brewed some green tea and took it in individual mugs to the dining table. Vishnu stood up and turned off the TV which was prominently placed in a corner near to the large bay window of the ample sized lounge. He returned to his place at the head of the table and said, "Parv, that was a delicious meal which reminded me of our time in Anna Catherina. So many times, especially after such a great meal, I just wished that we were there. Don't you agree?"

Parvati smiled to reveal a brace of well-kept white teeth and said quietly, "I am very happy to be here and that is why I have tried to make this our home from home. Now I do not wish to go back to Guyana. Besides, apart from only a few of our close relatives and friends, there is hardly anyone still around for us to meet. Most of the people in our age group we knew back in Guyana are either abroad or have passed away."

Vishnu's enthusiasm was curbed a bit, but he pressed on, "That is so true. But you know that we must make at least one more trip there as we are all getting on in age now. Besides, I cannot wait until I am too old or too ill to go on a long-haul flight and then cope with the Guyanese heat."

Parvati smiled as she looked into Vishnu's large brown eyes which appeared to be filling up with tears, and whispered, "Mosquitoes."

Ramesh laughed as he agreed with his mother, "Yes Dad, those mosquitoes would love to taste your fresh and healthy Americanised blood."

Vishnu continued to try to convince his family, "Of course we all know about the curse of the mosquitoes, but there are many ways to deal with them. First of all, many of the homes in Guyana have some air-conditioning and no mosquitoes or other insects survive that. And we can take all the travel vaccines and regularly use creams and ointments to keep them away when we are out and about. We just have to take precautions and all will be well. Besides, just look at how many people we know have been travelling back and forth to Guyana and say that they enjoyed their trips. Of course, there have been some who talk about how bad their experience was in Guyana. They must have been very unlucky or simply did not do the right things. You can't go to a place like Guyana and show off your wealth or pose like some bigshot American!"

Sati sipped some of her tea and commented, "Dad, it seems that you are very eager to visit Guyana. I do agree that you and Mom should make at least one more trip to see and enjoy our beautiful country. Perhaps Ramesh and I should also join you and to support you as you travel around the country. There is a lot to see and do in Guyana. So many beautiful houses, hundreds of miles of new and re-surfaced roads, shopping malls, hospitals, schools, hotels and holiday resorts."

Parvati was still not convinced and asked, "Why must I bother to go there when we can see all those things on the TV? I love watching that fellow who broadcasts so much about the country on his ARD "It's our life" shows. I love his down to earth style as he talks like a real Guyanese especially about day-to-day life."

Ramesh nodded and looked admiringly at his parents as he said, "Mom, I understand that. But it is far better to be there in person to really experience what they show on that programme. It seems to be a very good idea to make at least one more trip. Although Sati and I have not given this much thought due to the pressures of our jobs, perhaps we could at least go with you both for the first couple of weeks. Dad, when were you planning to go there and for how long?"

Vishnu smiled contentedly, realising that he had almost succeeded with his plan, "That sounds like a very good idea son. I was thinking of around mid-May before the schools and colleges close here and the demand for flights to Guyana go up and up and thus cause the airfares to rise. Of course, your children will still be in college, but I hope that they will also go on such a trip during their holidays or after they graduate. Ramesh, you and Sati could also have a look at what opportunities there are for jobs or investments in Guyana."

Parvati was still a little unsure about the trip and warned, "Let's do not get too carried away. Of course, Guyana is improving a lot, but I still hear stories about the crime rate there. People do not feel safe especially when they go to the big towns, and some are even afraid in their own homes. Violent robberies take place even in broad daylight!"

Ramesh reached across the table and placed his right hand onto his mother's, "Mom, you are right about feeling unsafe. But we also have a lot of crime right here in New York City and all around America. Don't forget that both you and Dad were once mugged when you came out at our local subway station. Sati and I have to be very careful and watchful when we travel to and from our offices. So, as Dad says, when we visit Guyana, we must act sensibly at all times."

Vishnu nodded, and with raised eyebrows, added, "That is true son. When we visit Guyana, from the time we land at the airport we will stand out as well-off foreigners. So, we must try to wear ordinary clothing, no jewellery and speak like Guyanese and not half-baked Americans. You know the saying, "When in Rome, do as the Romans do"? Well, I say when in Guyana, waak an' taak like a Guyanese!"

Ramesh drank some tea and leaned back on his dining chair as he spoke, "Well, it seems that Dad is very determined for us to make this trip to Guyana. If we are all in agreement, I am willing to pay for our flights and I will go online to check out the best deals on offer. Dad and Mom please check that your passports have at least one year to run otherwise we will have to renew them as quickly as possible. I don't think that we will need visas to travel to Guyana with our US passports."

Vishnu was very pleased that the family had agreed to go on the trip together, and gingerly stepped across to one of the drawers of an ornate wall cabinet which displayed a wide collection of ceramic ornaments, finely cut crystal glasses and other items collected over the years. He retrieved his and Parvati's US passports and quickly checked for their expiry dates. Then he placed them back in the drawer.

He turned to Ramesh and happily gave a thumbs up, "Our passports are in order with still at least two years before expiry."

Ramesh looked at his mother who was still wavering, "Mom, I can see that you do not appear to be happy about this trip. But Sati and I will go with you for at least the first two weeks and your friend will look after us. Isn't that right Dad?"

Vishnu continued to look and sound positive, "Yes, our dear friend Nazir and his wife Neesha will arrange to pick us up at the Cheddi Jagan International Airport and they will accommodate us at their home. I now have to contact some other friends here and in Canada to ask as to how many of them will join us. We should be able to feel safer in a bigger group as we travel around the country together."

Ramesh appreciated Vishnu's suggestion and commented, "Mom, that sounds much better and I hope that you now feel more comfortable about the trip. We may not get another opportunity like this in the future. I am sure that Uncle Nazir and his family will look after us very well. Besides, they know Guyana and how to move around there. Dad, who else will you be inviting?"

Vishnu opened a small notepad and mentioned, "I have been making a list of our friends we used to play dominoes with from the three villages of Leonora, Anna Catherina and Cornelia Ida. We had three rival teams called the LIONS of Leonora, the ACES of Anna Catherina and the COBRAS of Cornelia Ida. The first person I plan to call is my buddy, Michael "Histry Maan" Brown and his lovely wife, Doreen. Michael is a couple of years older than me so I do hope that he and Doreen will be up for this. They live in Brooklyn and I have not met up with them for many years now. Michael was our self-appointed coach of the ACES. He will be the ideal person to have on our trips around Guyana. I really do hope that they agree to join us."

Parvati finally smiled more re-assuredly and said, "I would love for Doreen to be there with us. We will then be able to keep an eye on you old boys. And remember, you will not be playing any dominoes and wasting precious time as you did back in the old days."

Vishnu grinned and confirmed, "OK. That's a deal. Welcome aboard!"

3
Rebels of West Demerara

Vishnu needed to look into an older address book to find Michael's phone number and waited anxiously as he dialled.

Michael answered, "Hello. Who is calling?"

Vishnu was excited to hear the voice of his old friend, "Oh my God! It's Vishnu here. How are you, Michael? And your lovely wife Doreen?"

Michael coughed slightly to clear his throat and answered, "Vishnu, it's so good to hear from you man. Doreen and I are both well. But we have a few niggles especially since we both caught that Covid thing. How about you and Parvati and your family? I hope that you guys did not catch that damn virus."

Vishnu settled into his sofa and responded, "Man, we were all very lucky and took all the vaccines we were offered. But those were scary times for all of us."

Michael shrugged his shoulders and solemnly said, "I was one of those people who believed what President Trump was saying although people were falling over like flies everywhere. I kept my faith in the Lord and prayed for the virus to go away."

Vishnu laughed and teased his friend, "Man I hope you didn't take the advice from Trump to use detergent to kill the virus!"

Michael frowned and replied, "Let's not go there. That man was crazy. Thank God we quickly changed our minds and took all the vaccines to help us. I think that we were saved by that, but we are suffering with what they are calling long Covid. Anyway, enough about the medical history. What's up?"

Vishnu grinned and answered, "Well, I am calling you to ask if you and Doreen would like to join myself, Parvati and our son Ramesh and his wife Sati, for a trip to Guyana in around mid-May this year."

Michael's eyes lit up as he lifted his spectacles to rest it on his head, "Actually only the other day Doreen and I went to a meeting here in Brooklyn to listen to a guy talking about how bad things are there in Guyana. How the government is only helping their own Party supporters and friends, how they are stealing the oil money, and how the ruling Party is racist towards us black people. We could not believe this, and we know the family of that young man from Leonora who is the President. His Great Grandparents Abdool Kadeer of Anna Catherina and Dost Mohamed of Leonora were decent hard-working businesspeople who helped everyone. So, Doreen and I decided that we should make at least one last trip to see what is going on for ourselves. I am not prepared to listen to politicians and some members of the media who use lies and no evidence to make ridiculous claims."

Vishnu was delighted to hear about Michael's intention and enthused, "Oh my dear brother, this is music to my ears! Ramesh is looking for the best prices for flights and dates, and it would be great if you and Doreen could join us on the same flight. Our old friend Nazir and his wife Neesha have promised to accommodate us and organise our transport to take us around the country. I am sure that they will allow you both to stay with them."

Michael smiled as he said, "Oh thank you very much. We will speak with Ramesh. Nazir "Snake Eyes" Khan and the lovely Neesha are the best people to look after us. I can't wait to get going. Here is Doreen."

Michael beckoned to Doreen and handed the phone to her.

She asked in a dulcet tone, "Hello Vishnu. It's Doreen here. How are you and your family?"

Vishnu smiled affectionately, "Oh Doreen it's so good to hear your lovely voice after such a long time. We are all well, and I am so happy to hear that you and Michael will be coming on the trip to Guyana. Parvati would love to have you as company. I can also promise you that us guys will not be playing any dominoes whilst we are in Guyana. How does that sound?"

Doreen laughed and said, "OK. I will hold you to that promise. I can never understand what you guys get out of playing that silly game and making such a racket! Take good care of yourselves until we meet up on the trip. Love to you all!"

She handed the phone back to Michael who continued his chat with Vishnu, "Well my friend, there you have it! As long as the boss says so, everything will be alright. Ever since I met her on that sandy beach in Anna Catherina, I have loved Doreen. She continues to be the great pillar of strength for me and our family. She has always insisted that no matter where we settle down, she will remain a simple down to earth Guyanese woman. It's people like Doreen and your Parvati who have kept us properly grounded in our culture, and this has been very important for our success here in New York. I am sure that this is true for all of our fellow Guyanese who are here in America and Canada."

Vishnu smiled as he asked, "So what do you think of our Guyanese people establishing our 'Little Guyana' here in Queens?"

Michael frowned as he replied, "Well, I think it's a great idea to show how we Guyanese can adapt well to any place we happen to settle into. I do have a problem though, as we in Brooklyn and the Bronx do not regard our presence here as part of Little Guyana. Whether we like it or not, we seem to have settled in these areas on a broadly racial divide with many more Indian Guyanese in Queens and African Guyanese in Brooklyn and so on. I like President Irfaan Ali's idea of a 'One Guyana', but we do need to work on this here in America and Canada."

Vishnu drank some ice-cold water from a glass tumbler and commented, "I do agree with you there my brother. I know that you have been a lifelong student of history, and it is people such as yourself who can understand why we as Guyanese of all backgrounds should respect each other's history, culture, religion and so on. Then we can see the future in a different light. Do you still research our Guyanese history?"

Michael smiled assuredly and said, "Yes, I do. You are right about us as Guyanese who are a people of six races including our First Peoples, the Amerindians, people of Indian heritage, my fellow African Guyanese, our Portuguese, Chinese and people of mixed races. We should all learn more about our past, understand where we are now, and then look at a future built around our unity and respect for our diversity. Only the other day I stumbled upon some information about enslaved Africans and the sugar estates where we came from on the West Coast of Demerara. It was about two slave revolts in 1772 and 1789 involving places we should know more about. They are from Zeelugt through to Hague, and all the way to Vreed en Hoop. We do not talk much about these revolts and many of us know much more about the great slave uprising of 1763 known as the Berbice Slave Rebellion which was led by Kofi who is Guyana's National Hero. In fact, the date of the 23rd of February when that revolt began, was chosen as Guyana's Republic Day."

Vishnu's eyes lit up with great interest as he asked, "Wow! Can you tell me more about this? Especially since it is connected with the villages we came from."

Michael fixed his spectacles onto the ridge of his long thin nose and continued, "The Dutch plantation owners had their command centre at Zeelugt where Dutch soldiers, some mixed-race infantry and several Amerindians were stationed. An uprising kicked off in Metzorg which we know as Meten-Meer-Zorg and spread to Uytvlugt. Note the original Dutch names for the estates. Then through to Vrees en Hoop which we know as Stewartville. Action also took place at De Leonora, Groenveld, Anna Catharina, Cornelia and Ida, and De Haag or Hague. I wish that some young researchers from the University of Guyana could investigate these revolts in much more detail and find out about this history which is so connected to us who were born and grew up in West Coast Demerara."

Vishnu was curious to hear more from the "Histry Maan", "Michael, those revolts were very important and showed the strength and willingness of the enslaved people to resist against their Dutch masters. But sadly, their protests must have ended in terrible brutality by the Dutch."

Michael took off his spectacles and wiped away some tears that welled up in his eyes as he said, "Yes, my brother, the 1772 rebellion lasted for about three weeks until it was over on the sixth of September. I found a list of the names of the rebels who were prosecuted and punished most severely and with a barbarism which emphasised the inhumanity of the Dutch slave owners. All of the rebels should be treated as our local and national heroes and heroines. Would you like to know who they were and what punishments were meted out on those suffering human beings?"

Vishnu also took some paper tissues and wiped away his tears as he responded, "Yes. Their heroism and memories must live on forever."

Michael carefully opened a small notebook and began to read out the information, "Well, amongst those who were captured and beaten whilst tied firmly at a wheel-shaped torture device and then beheaded, were Howard, Cobina, Louis, Neeltje and Gratia. Not only were they beheaded, but their heads were put on poles and their bodies burnt. The idea was to use these as examples to deter others from rising up. Other captives such as Hendrik, Bienvenue, Spadille and Vulcanus were severely flogged and then sentenced to lifelong work whilst permanently shackled in chains. Three women were also flogged and made to work whilst in chains, and they were Susanna, Claartje and Bella. One man who was known as the "English Negro" Felix, had his ears cut off and was banished for life to North America. Two years after 1772, a leader of the rebels named Callaert, was tortured at the wheel, then beheaded and burnt. There must have been many more who were punished for taking part in the revolts. Brother, I still feel their pain. All of us Guyanese should be feeling their pain!"

Vishnu continued to shake his head in disbelief as he said, "Michael, I do hope that we will be able to spend some time on our trip to Guyana to explore more of our past, look at what is happening in the present time, and hopefully we can envision a future that truly befits Guyana and Guyanese everywhere. Indeed, a future of which our heroes and heroines could not imagine. May God rest their aching hearts and souls."

Michael tried to regain some composure and then said, "Well said my brother. Whilst we are on the subject of slave rebellions in Guyana, you may recall that way back in 1985 during that final domino game of our last competition, I referred to unrest and disruptions by slaves which took place in Canje, Berbice in 1733 and which built up over many more years of brutal enslavement to the biggest ever revolt in 1763 which was led by Kofi, as I mentioned earlier. That uprising, although ending with the same type of barbaric punishments, must have inspired our own West Coast Demerara heroes and heroines in 1772 and 1789. More of such rebellions continued to flare up against the Dutch and continued against the new masters, the British, through to the 1823 uprising known as the Demerara Rebellion. Our African ancestors never gave up the fight for freedom even though it took hundreds of years until the British finally ended slavery in 1834. You know we call Guyana the 'Land of Many Waters'. Well, we must understand that our country's estates were built with the shedding of hurtful tears, the pouring of energy sapping sweat, and the floods of the blood of so many African human beings. It hurts me to say anymore."

Vishnu frowned, shook his head and said, "My brother, this is the kind of history which we as Guyanese must all embrace as we build our nation together. You have rightfully reminded me as to the real reasons for our quest. I only wish that you had become an educator to all of us both inside and outside of our beloved country."

Michael smiled and replied, "Thank you, my brother. This quest of ours will not only be about the history of our great country, but also a journey to find out more about ourselves and what the future holds for us all as Guyanese."

4
JFK International to CJIA

A very upbeat and energised Vishnu persevered until he was finally able to contact two more of his friends; Carlos "Reds" D'Souza, who had migrated to Florida, and Arthur "Speedy" Chung, who settled in Toronto, Canada. They both enthusiastically agreed to go on the trip to Guyana as part of the growing reunion of old friends.

Carlos had initially migrated from Guyana to the Bronx in New York, and over the years of very cold winters and extremely hot summers he and his wife Maria took a great dislike for the weather and the city. As soon as Carlos officially retired from his job as a security officer in Manhattan, he insisted that they should sell up their property and move to Florida. This mirrored similar moves by Guyanese who were increasingly retiring to Florida.

The price for a three-bedroomed family home in South Florida in the early 1990s was much lower than one of similar size in New York. So, Carlos and Maria engaged a good real estate agent to take them to view a few properties in the fastest growing city of Pembroke Pines which is situated within easy reach of the airports of Fort Lauderdale and Miami. They chose a house within the Pembroke Pines Village that was formerly owned by an American retired war veteran.

They found that they could buy the house outright from their life savings and thus wait for the best possible price for their property in New York. The financial gain provided them with a substantial amount to live on through their retirement years. They were very fond of going on cruises around the Caribbean and elsewhere.

Vishnu asked Carlos during their call, "So, how have you and Maria managed to cope with that persistent heat down in Florida? I know that Americans call it the 'Sunshine State' and it attracts a lot of tourists all year round from all over America and from abroad."

Carlos, sitting comfortably in his lounge with the air-conditioning switched on, said, "Maria and I do not have to go out and about in the hot sun. So, we wake up early in the mornings and do a bit of gardening before the temperature gets too high. Likewise, we wait for the sunset before venturing out. Besides, if and when we have to do some shopping, we just hop into our small car and cruise over to our local shopping mall. Over there we also have other facilities such as our local doctor, dentist and optician. Both Maria and I, like you, are in our eighties now and thank the Lord that we are still blessed with good health. And by the way, in our local mall we have a Guyanese owned and run restaurant and take-out establishment serving many of our well-known Guyanese and Trinidadian dishes, and at very reasonable prices."

Vishnu was impressed with Carlos's lifestyle and enthused, "Man, you seem to have your lives well sorted out. But what about those hurricane seasons? You must have had some scary times especially during the very big and dangerous storms. How do you cope with that?"

Carlos nodded and affirmed, "First of all, if the hurricane seasons were so terrible and destructive, how come so many millions of people still live here? Of course, we worry when we learn of a big one coming our way. So, all we have to do is to make sure that our house is well protected with the right roofing, shutters and of course, the right construction. We also calmly go out and buy all the right supplies of food, fuel and other things that we may need. We did something similar when we were forced to stay indoors during those fearful snowstorms we had in New York. We in Florida are very well prepared for the hurricane seasons and thank the Lord we have not had much damage to deal with since we came down to live here."

Vishnu nodded and smiled as he said, "I suppose that you are right as we know that Florida has long been the place where many Americans retire to. Maybe I should consider moving down there. But our son, daughter-in-law and their children are still having to build their lives and careers here in New York, and I know that Parvati will not want to be away from them. Besides, it would be like yet another migration for us. Maybe when the time is right, we will join you there, or perhaps even return to Guyana."

Carlos turned down the volume of his 65-inch TV and advised, "Don't leave that decision for too long as more of our fellow Guyanese move down here, the house prices have been on the rise. Mind you, that shouldn't put you off as your prices in New York are also increasing quickly. I know that you have your 'Little Guyana' there in Queens, but with more and more fellow Guyanese coming down this way we could soon have an even bigger 'Little Guyana' here. This one will feel more like our own big Guyana but without the flooding and so on. We get every kind of foodstuff here not only from Guyana, but from Mexico, other countries of South America and the Caribbean. Besides, Maria and I have a few fruit trees and plant our own vegetables and herbs in our backyard. This not only saves us a lot of money but gives us a lot of pleasure as well as some exercise. Come to think of it, we don't miss Guyana. But we are both looking forward to our trip with our old friends. We will fly directly from Miami to Georgetown and meet you guys there. Just let me know the date that you will be travelling from New York."

Vishnu's conversation with Arthur "Speedy" Chung who was residing in Toronto, Canada, was similarly animated as both friends were delighted to make contact with each other once again. Arthur was curious about Vishnu's request and desire for the friends to meet up and travel around Guyana. He was a regular visitor to the country and to Trinidad especially to meet his fellow Chinese relatives and friends who were steadily reducing in number through illness, old age, or migration away to America and Canada. The children and grandchildren were not keen on visiting or returning permanently to Guyana.

Vishnu asked his friend, "So tell me Arthur, why are you guys not interested in Guyana anymore? After all, your ancestors who were taken to Guyana as Indentured Labourers since 1853 had worked hard through the five years of their contracts, then used their savings to buy property and set up in retail and wholesale businesses all over the country. In fact, even your namesake Arthur Chung from Windsor Forest on the West Coast of Demerara became our country's first Governor of the Cooperative Republic of Guyana in 1970."

Arthur nodded and replied, "We Guyanese Chinese were never really interested in the politics there, and apart from how we all lived peacefully in our villages amongst everyone of different races and backgrounds, I for one did not like the racism between our African and Indian brothers and sisters. Besides, when the "buy local" policies were introduced, those of us in business were badly affected. So, gradually many of us sold out and left the country. As you know, my family and I stayed on in Anna Catherina for as long as possible until we decided to leave in the late 1980s. Our children preferred to take up their studies abroad and simply stayed on in America and Canada to pursue their careers."

Vishnu stood up and strolled around his lounge as he spoke, "I wonder why you and your fellow Chinese Guyanese will not now return to Guyana. I have heard that the country is of great interest to the Chinese from mainland China who are investing heavily in the development projects. They are very active in construction as well as wholesale and retail businesses."

Arthur moved out onto his veranda overlooking his well-kept garden and commented, "Man, I am not hearing good things about those Chinese people. I know that we have to be mindful about what we read in the local Guyanese press or see on the TV programmes coming out of the country. But I do believe the documentaries done by generally neutral foreign media reporting on how the Chinese run their contracts with their own people in the key positions. I hear that not many local people are being given good jobs on the projects. The Chinese people do not employ locals in their stores, and they tend to speak in their own language getting by with just basic English when they deal with Guyanese customers. I do not like that attitude. It tells me that they do not give a damn about our people and Guyana as a whole. Perhaps the government should be stricter on the conditions of their contract agreements and encourage Chinese businesses and contractors to show more support for local workers. Or else."

Vishnu interrupted Arthur, "Or else what? Or else we ask them to leave Guyana? Of course, we have to ensure the rights of our own people and stop foreigners from dictating to us. But, at the same time, it is important for the country to develop as quickly as possible, and then eventually reduce the reliance of foreign contractors in the years ahead."

Arthur noticed his next-door neighbour from South India tending to his plants in his garden and waved to him. He then continued his conversation with Vishnu.

"You see Vishnu, Guyana has suddenly become a place of great potential and interest for many countries. This is a very good thing.

But we cannot allow them to bully us right under our noses. This has been happening to us as a country and people from way back in the colonial years, and even after independence in 1966. Our natural resources such as gold and bauxite have been over-exploited by foreigners, and despite such wealth, we have never really benefitted as a people. Now I fear that our oil is attracting the same kind of attention from large global corporations. I only hope that our President and his government know this and will do their best to achieve the greatest benefits for our people. Anyway, I am on board for this great trip of discovery and of course to have a good time with you and the rest of our friends."

When Vishnu, Parvati, Ramesh and Sati arrived at the John F Kennedy International Airport in New York after a twenty minutes' drive by a local Guyanese taxi driver, they looked around the departure area of the Terminal 8, for Michael and Doreen. As they joined the short line to the check-in desks of American Airlines, their wait was over when Michael and Doreen arrived with their two large suitcases and smaller hand luggage.

The check in and security screening were completed in good time, and then the friends embraced each other before making their way to the departure lounge to await the boarding of their aircraft. They sat together as a group and established that their seats on the flight were in close proximity with each other. In the lounge, Michael sat next to Vishnu whilst Parvati and Doreen did likewise next to Ramesh and Sati.

Vishnu turned to his friend and said, "It is so good to see you and Doreen after so many years. I am really happy that we are making this trip together."

Michael adjusted his spectacles and replied, "Man, this has been long overdue. I can't help but notice that we are here at JFK and in about five hours of direct flight we will reach the Cheddi Jagan International Airport, or CJIA."

After chatting amongst themselves for about one hour, Michael drifted off into a deep slumber. Whilst he slept, Doreen and Parvati continued to converse as quietly as possible without disturbing him. When the expected boarding time approached, the airline's staff alerted the passengers by announcing the plan for boarding. This caused Michael to wake up suddenly. He sat up and turned to Vishnu.

"Man, as I was resting, a thought came to me about a kind of connection between this airport called JFK and the one in Guyana named the CJIA. The connection is really about a coincidence. You see, way back in October 1961, Dr Cheddi Jagan, the Guyana Premier, met with John F Kennedy, the American President, in the Oval Office at the White House in Washington DC. Cheddi was elected as the Premier of the then British Guiana after his People's Progressive Party, the PPP, won the August 1961 General Elections. His term of office was for three years to 1964. Earlier, in January 1961, JFK became the 35th President of the USA and served until his assassination in November 1963. Now, both the British and the Americans were not happy about Cheddi's Marxist leaning and they collaborated to try to remove him and the PPP from government."

Vishnu whispered, "I think that you should be careful about what you say here in the open. Walls have ears you know. And so do airport lounges."

Michael heeded Vishnu's advice and spoke in a more cautious way, "Yes, I'll keep this brief and quiet. So, Cheddi asked JFK for some financial help, and he was refused this. The Americans were much more concerned about having to deal with another potential communist state not so far away from Fidel Castro's Cuba. Of course you may recall about how in 1964, Cheddi unfortunately agreed to proportional representation or PR in the next elections which ended up with L F S Burnham's People's National Congress, the PNC, to form a coalition government with Peter D'Aguiar's United Force or UF Party."

Vishnu frowned, looked around the lounge and said, "I'm not sure where this is leading to. But please keep your voice down a little bit more."

Michael nodded, leaned across more closely, and whispered as low as he could, "Well, Mr Burnham later managed to secure a grant of two point six million US dollars from the new American administration in 1965 after JFK was killed in 1963. He wanted to build a new international airport terminal with an improved runway at Atkinson Field. Now, after Cheddi became President of Guyana in 1992, the same airport called Timehri International, became the Cheddi Jagan International Airport after his death in March 1997. I hope you can see a kind of irony with the names of the two airports we are about to use on our great trip to our homeland."

Vishnu glanced across to a very attentive Ramesh and Sati and commented, "Well, it is a very interesting observation, and we can see the connection and how history has played out for those two leaders Cheddi and JFK. But I hope that we have moved on now, and I understand that the current American administration is very supportive of the new Guyana government. Of course, the discovery of oil is a big factor, but stability in the region is of greater importance to the Americans especially with the latest threat from the Venezuelans and their claim for Essequibo which is about two thirds of Guyana's area."

Another shrill announcement over the tannoy drew the attention of the passengers who were advised to be prepared for boarding. Some of the more enthusiastic and impatient passengers quickly stood up and joined a growing queue to have their passports and boarding passes scanned or checked by one of the airline's attendants. Ramesh and Sati, being the more seasoned flyers, signalled to their more elderly companions to wait until the other passengers moved onto the aircraft. Then, after only about fifteen minutes, the two lines were sufficiently slackened to allow Vishnu and his friends to board as comfortably as possible and without the need to be unduly stressed.

Vishnu turned to Michael, Doreen and Parvati, and said, "This is how we will have to line up when we go on our tours in Guyana. Just a bit of patience will get us to wherever we have to go!"

Michael smiled and said, "I agree that we must learn to be more patient, but all I keep hearing from some fellow Guyanese is, "When are we going to see the oil money?"."

5

Mutual love and respect

Nazir "Snake Eyes" Khan and his wife Neesha who had remained in Guyana for most of their lives, had resisted moving to the USA where their four children had migrated to. When they returned from their short stay in Suriname, they decided to eke out a living in Anna Catherina and they were well supported by their children in New York who regularly sent them essential goods shipped in barrels and small amounts of remittances in American dollars. Nazir managed to supplement this through his business of buying and selling basic household goods and foodstuff to his customers door to door using a small van. Whilst his enterprise flourished, he resisted the temptation to expand it by establishing a large retail store. Instead, he along with his family, decided to build their substantial home in the village.

The practice of Guyanese in the diaspora, of sending goods and money back to their relatives, increased substantially in the years from the 1960s to the present as thousands migrated to the UK, then the USA and Canada. Remittances reached their highest in 2021 at nearly two hundred million American dollars with about eighty-seven per cent from the USA and Canada. This pattern significantly helped in the alleviation of poverty and hardship across Guyana particularly amongst those who were in receipt of such support from their relatives abroad. Nazir depended upon a regular supply of some of the items from the barrels his children sent from New York, and which he sold to his customers along the West Coast of Demerara. This type of trading was engaged in by many of his fellow Guyanese who tried to avoid dealing in any contraband goods. He delighted in saying that "the stricter the government, the wiser the population".

Nazir managed to contact his friend Afzal "Mule" Amin of Leonora who had also migrated to Suriname where he and his family were well settled in Paramaribo, the capital city. Suriname was a Dutch colony once known as Dutch Guiana and situated to the east of Guyana. Further east of Suriname is Cayenne, the former French colony called French Guiana. Guyana, Suriname and Cayenne were the only countries on mainland South America owned by the British, Dutch and French respectively. All of the other countries on the continent are either Spanish or Portuguese. Guyana is still the only English-speaking country of South America.

Afzal had tried his hand at several jobs in Suriname until he finally secured a well-paid fulltime position in a motor car repair shop. He attended night school to learn the Dutch language, and this became very useful to him whilst serving customers who mainly spoke Dutch or a Creole version known as *Taki Taki* or Sranan Tongo, a fusion of mostly English, Dutch, Portuguese and African languages. Many Surinamese of East Indian descent speak what is known as Sarnami Hindustani.

When Nazir called, he greeted Afzal with "Asalaam O Alaikum, brother Afzal. How are you? And your family?"

Afzal replied, "Waa Alaikum Asalaam, brother. Alhamdulillah, we are all very well. How are you getting on there in Guyana since you left Suriname?"

Nazir sighed and responded, "At first, I had a lot of doubts as Guyana was going nowhere and I could not get a permanent job. Even the Leonora Sugar Estate as you know, was closed in 1986, and that almost killed the area and caused many of us to migrate to Suriname and Trinidad as well as to America and Canada."

Afzal shook his head and said, "I guess you must have felt like you had jumped out of the frying pan and into the fireside. But now you must be a lot happier with Guyana finding so much oil. I am very happy to see that the two leaders of Guyana and Suriname are making commitments to work together on joint development projects. Suriname also found oil in 2020 within their part of the Atlantic Ocean."

Nazir peered through one of the large windows overlooking the verandah and observed a rain shower as he said, "Yes, these are exciting times for both countries but unfortunately, we are all getting too old to chase the new opportunities on offer. I guess that we have to leave that to our children and grandchildren if they are prepared to return to

Guyana. I called today to invite you and your wife to come over and join our friends Vishnu Prashad, Michael Brown, Arthur Chung, Carlos D'Souza and their wives who are coming to tour the country. Can you do this?"

Afzal was surprised by the request, and after pausing for a few moments, said, "Wow! I haven't seen or heard from those guys since we last played dominoes together way back in 1985. It would be great to meet up again at least for one last time. So, what are we going to do in Guyana? Play a lot of dominoes and have a good time?"

Nazir laughed and replied, "No, not to play dominoes. Sounds like you will come over with your wife. I hope that it will not be the last time you all come to Guyana. It was my idea for us to do this and I will accommodate most of you at my place and do the driving. Or we can hire a minibus and pay the driver to take us to as many places as possible. We will also use the other transport such as boats, planes and ferries as required."

Afzal warmed to the idea and confirmed, "Man it sounds as if you have already planned this thing out. Of course we must give you some money for the stay, meals and trips. Those things are very expensive there in Guyana. In fact, I will make arrangements to stay with some of my relatives in Leonora, but I will make sure that I pay for my share of the expenses. Who else will be making the trip? By the way, my dear and beautiful wife Nazmoon passed away a few years ago."

Nazir opened the windows he was looking through as the shower eased and breathed in some fresh air as he solemnly said, "Oh, I am so sorry to hear this. She was such a wonderful person and so well loved by everyone who knew her. Please accept sincerest condolences my brother."

Afzal spoke softly, "Thank you, my brother."

Nazir continued, "As soon as we end this call, I will ring Peter "Smokey" Ramdin who was from Cornelia Ida and the lead for the COBRAS domino team. He and his family are in Trinidad. I also have to speak with John "Black Buck" Charles who is still living here in Anna Catherina with his wife Muriel. I hope that they will also agree to join us. John knows the hinterland very well and he and Muriel have many fellow Amerindian friends and relatives there."

Afzal was pleased about the plan and pointed out, "That sounds great. Mind you, we are all now in our seventies and eighties and we will have to be very careful about taking on too much travelling in that heat. In fact, I have a heart problem and to make matters worse, I am afraid of flying."

Nazir frowned and noted, "Yes, we all have our long-term health issues such as diabetes, heart disease, hypertension and muscle and joint pains. So, we will have to take as much time to rest when needed and to look after each other. I will advise all the visitors to make sure that you have a good supply of the medications you use as well as those diarrhoea tablets, the vaccinations you require and some sprays to protect you against mosquitoes."

Afzal giggled as he said, "Man, this is sounding more and more like one of those major expeditions suitable for much younger people. Don't forget that us older guys in particular, have problems with our waterworks as well. We can't be seen going round and pissing everywhere. I think that applies to the ladies as well!"

Nazir laughed and advised, "Don't worry about that. We will have to make more frequent stops and there are good toileting facilities everywhere. Gone are the days of latrines in our backyards and over trenches. If on any trip to the interior we need to stop, then as you know, in any emergency, the bushes provide good cover. Besides, John and Muriel will show us how to cope with such problems and how to survive in that environment. In fact, we should all adopt the golden rule for each trip. That is, to have one for the road."

Afzal frowned and said, "I am not a staunch Muslim, but I have tried to stay away from alcohol."

Nazir raised the index finger of his right hand and pointed out, "No, I don't mean that we must have a drink before we leave. I mean that we must have a pee before every trip."

John and Muriel were delighted to hear from Nazir and were planning to visit some of their relatives in the hinterland within the period that Nazir had in mind. They agreed to meet at a local restaurant and bar in the village to discuss ideas for the tours.

Nazir and Neesha ordered fried chicken with hot pepper sauce and bottles of cold ice-cream soda. John and Muriel chose fried banga mary fish with some tomato ketchup and slices of lime. They opted to have small bottles of cold water. Muriel took a piece of the fish, dipped it into the sauce and ate it with relish.

"Hmm, this is so delicious. You cannot beat our local Guyanese snacks and foods. I will never have those foreign fast-food popping up all over the place."

Neesha took a bite of her fried chicken and said, "I do agree with you. I hope that all of these fast-food joints inspired and copied from abroad will never replace our traditional foods. I don't see this as progress."

John nodded in agreement, "Maybe our people are happy to try out things like pizzas and so on as a change from our local stuff. I hope that the owners of our restaurants can up their game and create more variety to offer to their customers. For example, I love our own mutton curry wrapped in roti."

Nazir nodded and said, "I love that idea, John. We Guyanese are very creative people and we can adapt to any kind of change. Don't forget that these fried chicken and fish were here since around the 1960s which must have been influenced by the Americans through their movies and music."

Neesha raised her right hand and spoke, "I agree with that, but we used to fry our chunks of fish in a batter of flour before cooking them as fish curry. I suppose we must move with the times, and that is what our younger generation is doing. The world is a much faster moving place now, and people are seeing so much about others in countries all around the globe in an instant."

John quietly asked, "So Nazir, why have you called us together? Any big news to share with us? Planning to open your own restaurant?"

Nazir placed the bone of a leg of fried chicken in a side plate, wiped his hands with a small paper tissue and replied, "I hope you and Muriel can join Neesha and I as well as some of our old friends Vishnu Prashad, his wife Parvati, their son Ramesh and daughter-in-law Sati, Michael Brown and his wife Doreen, all from New York, who will be visiting Guyana and staying at our place in mid-May. Arthur Chung is coming from Canada, Afzal Amin from Suriname, and Carlos D'Souza and his wife Maria from Florida. I am trying to contact Peter "Smokey" Ramdin who is living in Trinidad. It's meant to be a great re-union of old friends from Leonora, Anna Catherina and CI to experience how Guyana is developing so fast, and to offer our own views about the future of our people and country."

John looked across to Muriel and asked, "How do you feel about this?"

Muriel smiled re-assuredly and said, "It's a great idea. We can include them all in our plans to visit our relatives in Pomeroon and other places in the interior. Visitors to Guyana should go to look and experience our amazing hinterland first in order to appreciate the places and things which are the sources of our country's beauty, and why we must preserve this for future generations."

Nazir took a sip of his cream soda and said, "Thank you Muriel. We are looking at mid-May through to June so we can also celebrate our country's Independence Day."

Neesha frowned as she looked at Nazir and said bluntly, "This trip will be great. But as you know, I do not enjoy the celebration of Guyana's Independence on the 26th of May as I can never forget the brutal killing of some innocent Indian people in the Wismar massacre over Sunday 24th to Tuesday 26th of May in 1964. That was a very dark time in our history, and it is still very hurtful to me as to why Mr Forbes Burnham chose the 26th of May for Guyana's Independence knowing fully well how Indians were slaughtered, women raped and their properties destroyed by African Guyanese in Wismar, Christianburg and Mackenzie. I am sorry to repeat this, but I can never bring myself to celebrate Independence on the 26th of May. I know that this is over sixty years ago since that massacre and ethnic cleansing, but the hurt will never go away."

Muriel reached across the table and held Neesha's hands as she said, "I completely sympathise with you. I suggest that whilst all of our friends are here, we should get together and offer prayers for all of our peoples who have suffered such brutal genocide over the history of our country. Such healing needs to happen in order for us all to move ahead together."

John nodded and looked at Muriel and Neesha with great pride as he said, "That reminds me of the way that Nelson Mandela responded to the thought of revenge for the suffering and pain exacted by apartheid in South Africa. He chose reconciliation instead. We must not forget the wrongs that were done to us, but nation building starts with mutual love and respect for each other. Neesha, we share your pain and respect you."

6

Direct flight

Parvati eased herself into the seat nearest to the window of the American Airlines aircraft as Vishnu placed their hand luggage in the overhead locker. He then sat next to her, and his friend Michael chose to sit beside him on the seat nearest to the aisle. Apart from him being close enough to speak with Vishnu, the position provided him with an easier option to get up and walk to the nearest toilet. Doreen occupied the window seat behind Parvati, and Sati sat in the middle with Ramesh at the aisle seat behind Michael.

The flight was full of mostly Guyanese travelling back to visit the country and their relatives and friends. The chatter before the take-off was loud and animated with a mixture of the old Guyanese creole dialect and a combination with an American touch and twang. As soon as the main flight attendant who spoke with a mix of a Guyanese and American accents began with her announcement and safety instructions, the conversations were paused.

The take-off was smooth and efficient and as the aircraft gained height and speed, many of the passengers resumed their conversations whilst others sat quietly. Parvati was too nervous to look out of the open window, but Vishnu leaned across to peer through to observe the scene below which was mostly open and non-residential.

He checked to see that Parvati was more comfortable as he pulled down the shutter of the window. He then turned to Michael asking, "Well my friend, here we are on our epic trip. How do you feel?"

Michael adjusted his seatbelt to position himself more comfortably and replied, "I'm OK thank you. But I can't wait for us to reach Guyana. I do not really like long-haul flights lasting for so many hours."

Vishnu tried to reassure him and said, "This one should not be too bad as it is just under six hours directly to CJIA. It should be much better than flights of nine to ten hours. The captain promised us a good flight with no major turbulence ahead. So, let's sit back and relax. At least we don't have to stop and wait around in a place like Port of Spain, Trinidad as we used to do."

A relieved Michael nodded and commented, "Man, it's about time that Guyana and Guyanese people as well as others going to and from our country enjoy better travelling experiences especially by these new direct flights of the best airlines. I hear that even British Airways are now flying directly from London to CJIA with only one short stop in St. Lucia. That stop is only for one hour. This is why our main airport in Guyana has been extended and upgraded as a proper international facility. I won't be surprised to see that CJIA becomes even more expanded in the future as more and more people travel back and forth to the country."

Vishnu retrieved the inflight magazine from the holder in front of him and noted, "It's so good to see our country being promoted as a great tourist destination. There are so many hotels and other accommodation being built and becoming available so quickly. The hundreds of miles of roads, highways and new ferries for the river crossings are opening up the country faster than ever and in such a short time since 2020. Although I am not looking forward to too many long journeys in Guyana, it is still good to know that such improvements are being made to travelling and transport."

Michael leaned across to look at the magazine and said, "Man, gone are the days when we used to say "waan waan dutty ah bill daam". We will have to create new Guyanese sayings to describe what is happening there."

Vishnu smiled and suggested, "I think that I can offer a new one inspired by this flight. How about "movin' forward is like ridin' a bicycle"?"

Michael laughed and offered a high five as he said, "That sounds very good. Can you explain what it really means?"

Vishnu paused for a few moments and then offered, "Well, the only way to make progress is to keep pedalling otherwise the country will be at a standstill and going nowhere. Building new roads and repairing others as well as improving all types of transport provides for the faster movement of people and goods around the country. This will save a lot of time, and as you know, time means money in business."

Michael nodded and pointed out, "That is all well and good. But all such progress needs to be accompanied with helping the poor and needy along the way. No one should be left behind. And people must feel safe and protected. Just like we all are on this huge plane so high up in the sky."

Vishnu turned to face Parvati and asked, "Are you alright now?"

She reached out and placed her left hand on his right hand and warmly said, "I'm OK. I don't like flying, but so far it is good. I'm trying to think about what to expect in Guyana after being away for so long."

Vishnu nodded and said, "Yes, I have this feeling that as soon as we land there we will be spotted and easily taken for tourists. Plus, we will not know many of the people even in our own village."

Michael overheard Vishnu and said, "Man, I was thinking the same thing. I am going there as a traveller and not as a tourist."

Vishnu was not quite sure about Michael's comment and asked, "What is the difference between a traveller and a tourist?"

Michael leant forward and looked across to Parvati to have her attention, "You see, there is a difference between the two. As a tourist you go to a place and just look at the sights and listen to what your guide has to say. Besides, you walk around the places as quickly as the guide allows you. Then you take your pictures or videos. But a traveller is one who takes more time to research the place, learn more about its history and experience as many aspects of the culture and people living there. The tourist is constrained by allotted times, but the traveller arranges for more time to really appreciate a place and its people."

Vishnu smiled and commented, "I like that. And I agree that we should all go on this trip as travellers. This way we will get into the heart of Guyana and our people, and that will allow us to see the future of the country in a different light. Man, that is why I have always admired you as a friend. You are not just our "Histry Maan", but an inspirational guide for us all."

Michael calmly slipped his spectacles from his head onto the bridge of his nose as he said, "Mind you, at our age we have to be more careful about the traveller idea. For example, there are two ways to get to see and experience our magnificent Kaieteur Falls, the tallest single drop one in the world. It is about five times the height of Niagara

Falls in Canada. One way for the younger and fitter traveller is to go through the interior mostly on foot for a few days from Georgetown, and the other is to take a short flight from Ogle International Airport in a very small plane and get there to view the falls and the surroundings in only a short time. Two very different experiences."

Vishnu looked up ahead and then back to Michael as he said, "Well, I guess that most if not all of the people on this flight will opt for the easier although more expensive option of flying to the falls rather than taking the Indiana Jones adventure approach."

Michael was taken aback and asked, "Indiana who? I thought for a moment that you were talking about that mad preacher Jim Jones who was allowed to open up a large area of the jungle unknown to and not accessible by most Guyanese. The mass suicide of over nine hundred fellow American followers back in 1978 gave Guyana a very bad name. He and that story now form part of the folklore of our country. Indeed, that Jonestown massacre has unfortunately become too associated with the good name of our country. It left a bad stain and smell about Guyana. So, we have to paint a more amenable image of the beauty of our green land and our amazing people who had nothing to do with that nutcase from America. Of course, I will always have great sympathy for those unfortunate followers who perished for no real reason."

Vishnu chuckled and said, "Nutcase is the right word for him. Actually, we now have a saying not only in Guyana, but elsewhere about 'drinking the Kool Aid' referring to a person who believes in a possibly doomed or dangerous idea because of perceived or promised high rewards."

Parvati noticed two flight attendants offering a drink and snacks from their trolley and mentioned to Vishnu, "Talking of Kool Aid, I fancy a drink of lemonade or coke."

The first attendant overheard the mention of Kool Aid and smiled as she said, "Sorry ma'am we do not have Kool Aid on board, but we do have some Flavour Aid."

Michael and Vishnu laughed and Parvati politely requested, "Actually, only a coke will do for now, thank you."

7

Welcome to Guyana

The remainder of the flight from JFK in New York to the CJIA in Timehri, Guyana was smooth and uneventful as the captain had promised.

Parvati was nudged by Vishnu to look through her window as the aircraft began its descent over the coastland where the three largest islands of the magnificent Essequibo River appeared as almost virgin green carpets floating on the dark brown waters. The sky above was clear and blue apart from some pockets of white clouds appearing to serenely pass by.

Michael leant forward, peered through Parvati's window and pointed out, "Oh my God, just look at that fresh greenery on the three largest islands of the Essequibo River, of Wakenaam, Leguan and Hog. We will need to travel to those islands or at least one of them as they hold some of Guyana's history. Of course, we cannot see the other three hundred and sixty-two islands on that river which happens to be the longest in Guyana and the third longest in South America after the Amazon and the Orinoco Rivers. The Essequibo is around six hundred and thirty miles long. Actually, I read somewhere that there are around one thousand islands on the Essequibo River, but they stopped counting when they reached three hundred and sixty-five. I am not sure as to how true this is, but I like the suggestion. It emphasises just how magnificent the Essequibo River is. My treasured notebook has a lot of information about our great country and I am looking forward to sharing this with everyone."

Vishnu nodded and suggested, "It would be nice for the flight attendant or captain to just point out a few of the sights as we come in to land."

Michael agreed, "Yes, that would be a great help to most people on the flights coming into Guyana. Anyway, I think that I saw another great and very important place called Santa Rosa Mission. It is a small Amerindian village where you can visit to see and experience how some of our first peoples live. A day trip from Georgetown should be enough."

Vishnu nodded and asked, "By the way, as we head in towards the CJIA, what can you say about the airport's history?"

Michael, as always, was well prepared to answer, "I am so glad that you asked me about CJIA. First of all, it is the largest and oldest airport in Guyana and was first built in 1941 during the Second World War, by the Americans. It was named the Atkinson Aerodrome. Just around the end of that war from 1945, it became a commercial airport. It was then further developed and re-named the Timehri International Airport in 1969. Further on in 1997 it was given the name the Cheddi Jagan International Airport or CJIA in honour of our first Premier Dr Cheddi Jagan who died on the 6th of March that year whilst he was the President of Guyana. I am looking forward to seeing how much more has been done to make it a truly modern International Airport to reflect the needs of a more vibrant Guyana."

Vishnu acknowledged Michael's answer, and looking through the window, pointed out, "That was only a first glimpse of what our beautiful Guyana has to offer. I think that we are now moving across towards the airport which is only about twenty miles up the Demerara River. You can see the East Bank Road running just alongside the river. You can also see examples of the construction of housing and other structures as well as the neatly outlined rice and sugar cane fields with their Dutch built canals still functioning."

Michael continued to look through the window with Vishnu and said, "Yes, we have the ancient or very old ruins, the agricultural fields and now the modern buildings going up around the country. A great image of a country rising out of a long slumber and into this modern age."

Ramesh leant forward and touched Michael's left arm to draw his attention. Michael turned around to listen to what Ramesh had to say.

"Uncle Michael, I am putting your suggestions about the places to travel to around Guyana on a list and will send this to you and Uncle Nazir to help with the planning. I do wish that Sati and I could stay for more than two weeks as I am feeling more and more excited about this trip."

The captain announced his preparation for the landing, and the main flight attendant requested everyone to switch off their electronic devices and secure their seatbelts as the aircraft descended quickly and straight onto the main runway. Air traffic into and out of the airport was very limited each day and there was no need for circling around before landing. As soon as the aircraft touched down, many of the passengers applauded.

The aircraft taxied slowly and steadily towards the terminal where at the front the name Cheddi Jagan International Airport is spelt out in bold red letters. When it came to a standstill and the attendant gave permission for passengers to leave the aircraft, Ramesh stood up and reached for his hand luggage and then Sati's. He signalled to the group to remain seated.

"Let me take down all the hand luggage and hand each one to you. Then follow me off the plane and through the arrivals area. Make sure that you have your passports ready to show to the immigration people."

Ramesh patiently allowed most of the other passengers to leave before he guided the group through the aisle and the ramp leading to the arrival section of the airport. They each smiled at and thanked the attendants standing by the exit of the aircraft. The main attendant bowed slightly, and with a broad smile, said, "Thank you and do enjoy your trip to Guyana. See you on your return flight. Bye bye!"

Ramesh and Sati walked just ahead of the group and occasionally looked back to ensure that they were in close proximity. As they emerged from the ramp and entered the arrival section of the airport, they could see the bright and new space with a spotless floor and clear modern signage of the immigration checkpoints, through to the carousels of the baggage claim, the customs and then out through the main exit where family, friends and taxi drivers waited to meet and greet the travellers.

Michael paused to ensure that Doreen was coping with her small carry-on case as he guided their two large suitcases. Ramesh then secured two trolleys for the group and carefully stacked the six suitcases on both. Each laden trolley was then pushed slowly by himself and Sati. This greatly relieved the pressure on the four older members of the group as they ambled through and beyond the exit of the terminal. Vishnu and Michael as well as Parvati and Doreen, thanked Ramesh and Sati for their help and guidance off the flight and through the airport.

Michael, holding Doreen's right hand firmly as she stood beside him, remarked, "This is such a vast improvement and a very modern facility. I like it very much. I am also very pleased by the way the staff in each of the booths welcomed us and the very relaxed way that they operate here. I thought that I was being welcomed home and not under suspicion as you feel when entering the USA even though I am a citizen of that country. This airport is very quiet now with not many big flights coming in at the same time. This will change soon as a lot more passengers come through. I liked the big and beautiful map of Guyana and a great picture of President Dr Mohamed Irfaan Ali welcoming visitors to the country. What do you think?"

Doreen responded before Vishnu, "I agree. I was worried about the flight and did not know what to expect when we landed here. But I must say that both the flight and this airport made me feel very proud of Guyana and of being Guyanese."

Parvati nodded and noted, "Yes. This is a very good start to our trip. I feel a bit tired, but I am very happy with what I have seen so far."

Ramesh and Sati gently pushed their trolleys forward to an area where they could be easily seen and recognised by Nazir.

Within a few minutes, Nazir strode forward towards the group with outstretched arms and with a broad smile, "Welcome to Guyana!"

Everyone took their turn to embrace him.

Vishnu shook Nazir by his right hand and said, "Well my brother, here we are. Thanks for coming to pick us up. We are all looking forward to a great trip. This is a very good start to our adventure. I can't wait to see my dear sister Neesha and to settle in at your home. Thanks again for coming up with the idea of this trip."

Nazir smiled and said, "You are all most welcome. Let's get this show on the road!"

He turned and hugged Michael as he said, "Man, I am so happy that you came on this trip. I am looking forward to listening to what gems you have to share with us about Guyana!"

8

The old and the new

Nazir was pleased and relieved to have the help of Ramesh to load the suitcases and the other luggage in the boot of his eight-seater vehicle. He ensured that all of his passengers were comfortably seated and with their seatbelts securely fastened. He noticed that they were already perspiring from the humidity and put the vehicle's air-conditioning on as soon as he started the engine.

He looked around for a final check and said enthusiastically, "Well my friends thank you all for making this trip. As you can see, we are having a very hot weather spell at the moment, but we will also have some showers as well. Are you all ready for this great adventure?"

The passengers responded together with a loud "Yes!"

Vishnu sat in the passenger seat beside Nazir so that he could have a better view through the front windscreen and the window to his right. The vehicle was a left-hand drive due to its American origin, but the driving on Guyana's roads and streets are on the left side. He prepared his digital camera to film the journey from the airport to Nazir's home approximately thirty-five miles away. Michael sat just behind the driver so that he could speak with Vishnu as well as have a good view through the window on his left.

Vishnu turned to Michael and asked, "I have a trick question for you. Why is it that in most British and former British colonies such as Guyana, they drive on the left-hand side?"

Nazir chuckled and said as he glanced to ensure that the vehicle was fully charged through its hybrid system, "I bet that the Histry Maan cannot answer that one!"

Michael smiled with his usual confidence and looked around to ensure that everyone was listening to him as the vehicle eased out onto the main road, "Good question Vishnu. But in the UK a long time ago, when most travelling was done on horses, it was more convenient to mount and dismount from the left-hand side of the horse. So, this was easier and safer for riders to travel on that side of the road. This also helped to avoid collisions with other horse riders coming from the opposite direction. The authorities simply adopted that horse-riding system when cars were invented. Another reason is that in the past soldiers wore their swords on their left side, and mounting a horse from the left prevented any possible harm to the animal from the sword or other weapon. How is that for an answer?"

Ramesh, who sat beside Michael in order to allow Sati, Parvati and Doreen to use the three seats at the back, said, "Thank you Uncle Michael. You are truly a fountain of knowledge sir!"

Michael acknowledged the compliment and replied, "Well, there is more to this. In fact, using a vehicle with the steering wheel on the right is actually safer. It allows most drivers to have their dominant right hand always on the steering wheel and thus they are able to have better control of the vehicle."

Nazir smiled and added, "I have driven both types of vehicles and I can agree with you there. But I must say that it is also comfortable to have a left-hand drive. You can get used to this in a short time. By the way, we are approaching a beautiful sign on the roundabout ahead with a "Welcome to Guyana" greeting. Isn't that lovely ladies? It is just one of our First Lady Arya Ali's beautification of Guyana initiatives."

Doreen exclaimed, "Its lovely!"

Vishnu nodded and appreciated what Michael had shared, "Thank you, Michael. Even in your old age you are still gifted with such a good memory and so much knowledge. What is your secret?"

Michael nodded and briefly looked out of his window through which he could see the edge of the Demerara River on the left as Nazir made good progress on the East Bank Road leading towards the Demerara Harbour Bridge.

He answered with the assuredness of a College Professor, "There is no particular secret. But I do love to read and I am blessed with a good memory as well as a love for information. It is very important for me to be asked all kinds of questions about anything as this stimulates my memory and keeps me on my toes. Before this trip I made sure that I brushed up on my knowledge of Guyana. This little notebook is like a mini encyclopaedia, and I jot down a lot of new and old information. This will be my guide on this quest and no doubt I will find even more information to record and share with you all."

Vishnu turned to Nazir and commented, "Our Histry Maan is like a Guyana version of the thing they call AI."

Nazir was baffled, as he asked, "AI? What is that? Artificial insemination?"

Everyone laughed as Vishnu replied, "No. AI is for artificial intelligence. As far as I know, Michael has no experience of artificial insemination."

Michael turned to face Doreen, grinned and smiled sheepishly. She raised her right index finger to her lips and signalled to him to keep quiet.

Nazir slowed down to allow his guests to observe what he referred to, "This place we are passing through is called Soesdyke and you can see a lot of white sand around and beside the road. As you older guys know, the more you go into Guyana from the coastland, the land gets higher and there is a lot of white sand and dark, clear and clean water creeks. Ramesh do put this on your list as its worth visiting the Splashmin's Fun Park and Resort here. You can spend a day doing things like kayaking and even jet skiing on a beautiful lake. You can also spend some time on a farm there to sample some fruits and so on. It is quiet during the weekdays, but man it gets very busy and noisy at the weekends, especially on Sundays. I think that our group would prefer a quieter time at the site to really soak in the natural beauty of the surrounding environment."

Doreen shouted from the back where she sat between Parvati and Sati, "No jet skiing for me! A simple and quiet picnic will do nicely for us old people thank you!"

Nazir smiled and replied, "Don't worry ladies. There are a couple of other resorts near here. We have the Marudi Creek Resort where there is a no music policy so you can have a very calm and restful time listening to the birds. Another is the Pandama Retreat and Winery where you can sample many kinds of wines made from fruits and even baigan!"

Michael frowned and was taken aback, "What? Baigan wine? Never heard of it!"

Vishnu smiled and said, "Aha! Add that one to your AI. Michael, I think that we are all in for a lot of surprises in this amazing country. Ramesh, more possible trips and things to do on our great quest."

Ramesh tried to type as quickly as he could onto his iPhone, but remarked, "Yes Dad. I am just struggling a bit with some spellings. But I have the ideas covered."

Nazir continued to make good progress on the journey as the traffic on the East Bank Demerara Road was light and moved at a steady pace. Many villages were mostly created, populated and named by the Dutch colonists in the sixteenth, seventeenth and eighteenth centuries during their occupation of the then Guiana, and the others were added by the British when the colony was ceded to them in 1815 at the Congress of Vienna. The three former Dutch colonies of Essequibo, Demerara and Berbice were then established as British Guiana in 1831. The villages included Den Hueval, T'huist te Coverden, Caledonia, Sarah Johana, Land of Canaan, Garden of Eden, Friendship, New Hope, Craig, Golden Grove, Great Diamond, Little Diamond, Prospect, Farm and Herstelling through to Providence, leading to the Demerara Harbour Bridge.

Nazir slowed down and drew the attention of his passengers to the impressive structure of the Guyana National Stadium in Providence.

He proudly announced, "You must have heard about the new Providence Stadium which was built in 2006 just before the Cricket World Cup in 2007. I wonder if Michael can fill in more details about this."

Michael gladly accepted Nazir's invitation and said, "Yes, this whole area is being developed further with international standard hotels and the Amazonia Mall which is owned by the former Guyana and West Indies great batsman known as Ramnaresh "Ronnie" Sarwan. Not far from here is the location of a modern suspension bridge which is being built to replace the floating Demerara Harbour Bridge."

Vishnu pointed out, "I think that the stadium was designed by a firm from India and built with loans and grants from India. I recall a bit of controversy by some politicians in Guyana asking why India and not Africa, and the government's response was along the lines of which country in Africa would want to build a cricket ground and stadium in Guyana? Sorry for interrupting Michael. Do carry on."

Michael continued, "I heard that the stadium costed about thirty million US dollars at that time. The first cricket Test Match was played there in 2008, and sadly our great West Indies were badly beaten by Sri Lanka. Cricket fans had to wait until May 2011 for a local victory which came against Pakistan. By the way, the stadium is not just for cricket but is used for other major events. The greatest and most historic cricket ground in Guyana is called the Bourda, in Georgetown."

Ramesh typed more entries into his iPhone and pointed out, "We have only been for a short time in Guyana and already my list of places to see and things to do is getting longer and longer. Will we have the time and energy to cover these and much more over this entire trip?"

Vishnu shrugged his shoulders and replied, "You are right son. There is a lot more to add to your list. We will have to consult with the others in the group to agree on the best places to visit, especially given our age. Besides, we will have to take the most comfortable ones. We will still see a lot of the country and that will give us enough information to draw our own conclusions about where the country is and where it can get to. Michael, you mentioned the Bourda Cricket Ground just now. Do you want to say something about it?"

Michael sat more upright in his seat and readily obliged, "Yes Vishnu, I agree that we will have to pick and choose how we spend our time on this trip. I think that I am in fairly good shape, but I will not be able to handle too many long trips even though we will be in this comfortable car. Let's wait to hear from the others joining us."

Nazir nodded and asked Michael, "What can you say about Bourda?"

Michael adjusted his spectacles to the tip of his nose as he fixed his eyes on Vishnu, "Man, there is a lot to say about that historic cricket ground. Most Guyanese, especially in our age group and who love cricket, will have their own stories to tell about that place. It will take me hours to relate what I can remember about Bourda and the wonderful matches played there by so many of the all-time greats of the game. But for now, the first thing I want to say is that Bourda is the oldest major cricket ground in Guyana and was built in 1885. Not many people know that the eight acres of former sugarcane fields was once owned by a Frenchman named Joseph Bourda. Hence the name Bourda still being used for that area."

Vishnu's eyes lit up with surprise, "Wow! That is something I never knew about. Near that place is the Bourda Market, and that must also be one of the oldest in Guyana."

Michael nodded and looked at Ramesh who was busily typing into his iPhone, "That is correct. Bourda became an established Test Match venue and the first was played by the West Indies against England in 1930. I mention this also because of the remarkable batsman called George Headley who scored a century in both innings for the West Indies. Clifford Roach also scored a great double century for the West Indies in that historic victory."

Nazir smiled and proudly pointed out, "Oh, the great Sir George Headley who was known as 'the Black Bradman'!"

Vishnu looked up and said, "I do not like the term 'Black Bradman'. Sir Don Bradman was the best batsman in the world and he was a white Australian. Headley was his own man and set his own standards as a truly great stroke-maker with a graceful style. He was Jamaican."

Michael nodded and added, "Vishnu, I totally agree with you. This is only one example of how we as a people get compared to white achievers. Why don't we hear about a 'White Gary Sobers', the greatest all-round cricketer of all time from Barbados? Or a 'White Viv Richards' our Master Blaster from Antigua? Or a 'White Rohan Kanhai' our own Guyanese batting genius? Or a 'White Clive Lloyd', the brilliant captain of our all-conquering West Indies side? Or a 'White Brian Lara', the amazing record-breaker from Trinidad? We have to break free from such examples of colonial dominance. Don't you all agree?"

Everyone in the car answered with a resounding "Yes!"

Ramesh asked, "Uncle Michael, do you think that we will have to tour both the Providence Stadium and the Bourda Cricket Ground?"

Michael looked at Vishnu for some assurance and said, "I think that will be a good idea. It will give us a view of something that was important for us all historically and a flavour of how the country is moving forward from that past. We should preserve the best things of our history and remember our own heroes of Guyana and the Caribbean as the future unfolds."

Nazir increased his speed as the traffic eased, "Yes Sir! The street in front of Bourda has been named the Shivnarine Chanderpaul Drive in honour of the great little Guyanese and West Indies left-handed batsman who scored the second highest number of runs for the West Indies in Test Cricket, and just a few short of Brian Lara's record. Shiv also scored four Test centuries at Bourda which is equal to Sir Gary Sobers' record there. We are now heading up to the Demerara Harbour Bridge which is the fourth longest floating bridge in the world. It was built in 1978."

Michael smiled and noted, "Another piece of history is that the man who is credited with building that bridge was a Guyanese engineer named Joe Holder who was born in Bartica, Essequibo. Sadly, he passed away in 2022. He had given advice on the plans for the new bridge being built across the river."

Vishnu nodded, clasped his hands and said, "Let's hope that his vision will come through and live on for a very long time."

Michael acknowledged Vishnu's wish and said, "Yes Sir! A sort of bridge into the future!"

All the passengers responded with "Amen to that!"

9
Of crossings and curses

The drive across the floating Demerara Harbour Bridge was relatively smooth in some places but with a distinct clunking sound from the metal plates securely attached to form the single lane of the two-way drive. Sometimes the two lanes are doubled up for one-way traffic to help to ease the congestion from Georgetown to the West Bank of Demerara and vice versa. This involves a reasonably short wait. Drivers and other users are also informed each day as to the closing times to allow larger shipping to pass through the drawbridge section which is raised and lowered. The bridge is high enough to allow smaller vessels to pass under it at all times. The floating structure is held secure by cables attached to huge concrete anchors fixed in the river on both sides. The bridge also provides a pedestrian walkway and overhead streetlamps on one side from the Georgetown end. The replacement suspension bridge renders the floating bridge obsolete.

The original Georgetown and Vreed en Hoop ferry stellings located near to the mouth of the Demerara River, are still being used by small boats which are adopted as replacement for the ferry service. The water taxis are open on the sides with wooden seating and the passengers and two-man crew are required to wear distinct, orange-coloured life jackets. However, the journeys are only relatively comfortable when the waves of the river are less choppy. Other small boats are laden with farm produce and taken from the West Bank to the Stabroek Market located next to the old Georgetown stelling.

Michael stared out of his window to observe the deep blue sky with pockets of light white clouds floating serenely along and remarked, "I am sure that you will remember the time when we used to travel across the river by the large ferry to and from Vreed en Hoop. Do you remember the name of the first ferry used on this Demerara River?"

Vishnu looked around at the other fellow passengers and after no one volunteered a suggestion, he decided to offer a guess, "I think that the first ever ferry was an old ship called the SS Queriman. Am I right?"

Michael shook his head and replied, "No sir. The history of the ferry service goes back to around 1825. That was long before the SS Queriman. Now, can anyone else apart from Vishnu and Nazir, remember the name of the ferry which replaced the SS Queriman?"

Doreen and Parvati laughed and shouted, "Macouria!"

Michael turned to face the three ladies at the back and confirmed, "Yes, it was the MV Macouria, and it was one of three similar vessels with the MV Torani operating between Parika and Supenaam across the Essequibo River, and the MV Malali from Rosignol to New Amsterdam across the Berbice River. I used to enjoy travelling on those ferries. And ladies, I am sure that we all saw some flirting there!"

Vishnu giggled as he said, "Michael, you speak for yourself! I used to travel from Vreed en Hoop to Georgetown to attend High School and I can say that me and my friends were always well behaved."

Parvati shook her head in disbelief and said, "Nah! That is a lie! I heard that you and your school friends were always tackling the girls on the ferry. Right Nazir?"

Nazir was caught off guard by Parvati's question and momentarily seemed to lose control of the car. After steadying the steering of the vehicle, he replied, "I think that Vishnu and all the others who used that ferry should be able to answer your question. Besides, I heard that is how he met you!"

Michael laughed and said, "I think that Vishnu and Parvati met regularly on the West Coast train which ran from Parika to Vreed en Hoop. That was another journey which held a lot of memories for many people. It's a great shame that the entire railway system in Guyana was abandoned and never replaced. That West Coast Railway ended in 1974."

Vishnu rested his video camera on the dashboard and commented, "Great infrastructure such as ferries, stellings, trains and train tracks as well as train stations require a lot of funds for maintenance. If they are publicly run, then it is the taxpayers who end up paying for that through the government. It is reasonable to assume that when these services cost more to run than the revenues they take, they could easily run aground. The issue of good and affordable public transport is always going to be a big one for a country like Guyana."

Nazir continued to make good progress and prepared to turn left along the West Bank Demerara Road and onto the West Coast Demerara Road which led through many villages towards Anna Catherina. He pointed out the turning on the right which led to the Vreed en Hoop stelling and lamented, "Man, I know that having a bridge across the river is a great thing for the progress of the country. But it is sad to see how the historical stelling at Vreed en Hoop is falling apart. However, people are still trying to make an honest living by selling all kinds of goods in stalls they have set up inside the building where the ferry used to operate from. The small water taxis are very busy and are still providing a much-needed service for many people. You know I always say that we Guyanese can make a living out of next to nothing!"

Vishnu picked up his camera, panned it at the road and said, "Resilience and survival my friend! We have always been a hardworking people. Even when we left to go to places such as New York City, many of us took up two jobs to make a living and save. The same thing Guyanese have done in Canada and the UK. In fact, I should say that we Guyanese can survive and thrive in any country we decide to migrate to."

Nazir frowned and said with great concern, "Yes, my friend, we do work hard wherever we happen to be, but now we are asking our government for even more help from the oil and gas money. They are helping us a lot but many of us still feel that the rich guys are getting richer much more quickly than ever before, and I worry about the poor being left further behind. We need to close that gap between the rich and poor. I really do fear that if this situation is allowed to continue and more people believe what they hear, there could be some serious disruption even worse than we have experienced here in the past."

Just as Nazir spoke, a speeding car swerved out from behind him and cut into the short space ahead of him. He cursed as he pressed his horn in frustration, but the driver ahead ignored the warning whilst speeding further away.

Vishnu lamented, "Oh, how stupid! That kind of driving is what causes a lot of accidents and unnecessary deaths on these roads."

Nazir was still very annoyed when he replied, "Yes, I try to keep well within the speed limit and leave a safe space ahead, but the other jackasses on the road just ignore the rules and put themselves and others at great risk. We have already had over ninety road deaths in this year and it is getting worse. There is too much speeding and drinking and driving."

Michael smiled and observed, "I see that the only jackasses using the roads more safely are the stray donkeys!"

Vishnu looked across at Nazir who held the steering wheel firmly as he concentrated and said, "Nazir, I am glad that you are a very careful driver. I have noticed how the roads here are much busier with a lot more vehicles. Maybe this is a sign of how much more people are getting better off in the country. Coming back to what you said about the rich and poor I see that Michael wants to say something."

Michael turned to Nazir and asked, "Do you mean that you are worried about this thing called the oil curse?"

Vishnu nodded and said, "Yes, I think that it refers to resource curse where countries with plenty of natural resources end up with less economic growth and worse development than those with much less natural wealth. We only have to look at Venezuela and many African countries to see this."

Nazir shook his head and pointed out, "I don't care what kind of cussing you call it, but I know a lot of people want to see more fairness in our society. Just look at the huge mansions and other buildings on both sides of this road, and right next to them you see many rundown old wooden houses. I am all for progress and development. But we have to help our neighbours to come up as well. I am not talking about the grants and handouts alone. I mean more good jobs, better education and proper healthcare. I also want for all of us to feel and be safe!"

Michael opened a small bottle of water, took a sip and said, "Nazir, that is true. But rebuilding a country takes time, and from all the news I see on the internet, Guyana is on the right track in all the things you mention. The government is working hard to provide assistance and opportunities for the people. But there is a big shortage of skills and that's why you see more foreigners coming here to take up those jobs. I know that this can cause a lot of resentment from local people feeling hard done by."

Vishnu looked at Ramesh and asked, "What do you think son?"

Ramesh temporarily closed his iPhone and replied, "Well, people must accept that the jobs have to be taken up just like we as immigrants have done in America, Canada and so on. But I do believe that local Guyanese must be given more opportunities to train in the areas needed. Higher education scholarships is a very good thing, and so is the offer of training in the skills of building, plumbing, electrics and so on. Likewise, as the agriculture sector continues on its modernisation plans, then more specialist schools or institutes should be built especially closer to where the developments are."

Michael interrupted Ramesh and pointed out, "Yes, Dr Cheddi Jagan did establish the Guyana School of Agriculture way back in 1963. In fact, I should have gone to that college. Also, the University of Guyana has a Faculty of Agriculture and Forestry as well as research there. Is this not enough?"

Ramesh shook his head and suggested, "I am thinking more about an even higher level of institution linking up with the best in the world. This also applies to the fields of technology, engineering, science and so on. I hope that those in charge are well aware of such an idea and will be prepared to develop this level of education and make it an exclusive opportunity for our brightest young minds."

Sati broke her silence and pointed out, "Look, the government is really working hard for the people and in only four years we will see how Guyana is developing in every Region we will visit. But, as they say, Rome wasn't built in a day!"

Parvati shouted from the back, "Waan waan dutty ah bill daam!"

Doreen also ended her silence, and after clearing her throat, she suggested, "Look here. You are all talking about big things. But as a Guyanese woman, I want to see the people who are really needy get well looked after. I want to see Guyanese children given the best education. I want to see young people helped into the right jobs for them. I want to see families much happier and healthier. And I want to see older people well cared for and given a better quality of life in their old age. In other words, I want to see my fellow Guyanese at home becoming much more confident about themselves and their country. I rest my case!"

Parvati and Sati cheered Doreen and exclaimed "Amen to that!"

10

The fighter, the educator and food for thought

The drive from Vreed en Hoop over the nine miles to Anna Catherina on the West Coast of Demerara was relatively quick as Nazir continued to keep within the speed limit, and the traffic was less congested. His passengers began to show signs of tiredness from their long flight and the drive from the CJIA. He could see that Vishnu, Michael, Parvati and Doreen were having a nap whilst Ramesh and Sati were still keen to look out at the scenes presented by both sides of the main road as they passed through each of the villages which were well signposted.

Having crossed the Demerara Harbour Bridge, the sugar estates and villages including Goed Fortuin, Versailles and Plantation Walk, they had headed off to the left of Vreed en Hoop through long stretches of rice farms and lush green fields bordered by tall coconut palms and other, mainly fruit trees. The more populated villages along the route contained many grand houses, several types of businesses, restaurants and bars, rice mills, churches, temples, mosques, petrol stations, schools, supermarkets, drug stores and some local roadside stalls.

Nazir stopped the car, pointed out a complex in the village of Ruimzeight called the Kaashi Dhaam Hindu Crematorium and spoke in a hushed tone, "Ramesh, that crematorium may not be a place we will visit, but it has a very important history. Michael would know more of the details about this. It is the site of the first ever open Hindu cremation that was officially permitted in Guyana in 1956."

Ramesh took Vishnu's video camera without disturbing his sleep and recorded as he commented, "This must be the place where one of Guyana's greatest heroes, Dr Jung Bahadur Singh became the first person to be cremated in Guyana in the traditional Hindu way. He had fought for that right for many years up to the end of his amazing life.

I recently read a wonderful biography about that great soul written by the Guyanese historian and author, Dr Baytoram Ramharack. I must say that as a Hindu, I am disgusted by the way that the British rulers showed no care and respect for our religion and culture by not allowing cremations over one hundred and eighteen years since 1838 to 1956."

Nazir nodded in agreement and whispered, "Man, I also read that book. JB as he was known by most people, was actually born in Guyana in 1886. His father was from Nepal and his mother was a Bengali from India. From the age of sixteen up to twenty-eight, he worked on many of the ships which brought our ancestors from India, as what was called a compounder. That must have been really heroic, brave and amazing as it was bad enough to do only one such trip on those ships. What else can you remember?"

Ramesh paused his filming and said quietly, "Uncle Nazir, I wish that the others here could see and hear this story. Anyway, JB, his wife Alice and their children then went to Edinburgh in Scotland where he studied Medicine way back in 1914. That experience must have been another great challenge for him and his family until he graduated as a doctor, and they returned to Guyana in 1919. He became a Government Medical Officer and then he ran his own private practice as a doctor afterwards."

Nazir noted that all the other passengers were still asleep as he mentioned, "JB was also involved in fighting for workers' rights and then entered politics. He soon became the first Hindu to be elected to Parliament in 1931. That incredibly gifted man was also a leading light for *Sanatan Dharm* here and fought for the rights of both Hindus and Muslims. In fact, one of our own stalwarts of Anna Catherina, the late Haji Abdool Kadeer, the businessman and President of the Anna Catherina Mosque, was a great friend and supporter of JB when he campaigned for election. Haji Kadeer tried to convince the *jamaat* to vote for JB, and after a lot of arguing in the mosque, he collapsed with a massive heart attack and died later that day. By the way, I mentioned this also because Haji Abdool Kadeer was the great grandfather of our President Irfaan Ali."

Ramesh stopped filming and carefully placed the camera onto the dashboard in front of Vishnu who awoke and rubbed his tired eyes with his fingers before reaching into his back pocket for his white handkerchief to complete the freshening up. Michael also stirred from his short slumber as Nazir started the car to continue on their journey to his home in Anna Catherina which was just a few more miles along the coast.

Michael tipped his spectacles to rest onto his nose and stretched out his long lean arms like an old crow exercising its wings before taking flight.

Still a little drowsy, he asked, "I overheard something about JB. I happen to know a lot about that great Guyanese. Would you like to hear more?"

Ramesh sat back into his seat and opened his iPhone as he said, "No Uncle Michael. Uncle Nazir and I spoke a bit about JB and the crematorium we just drove away from. I am making some notes here to go with the video I took. We will all share this as another memorable event on the trip."

Michael appeared to be a little disappointed but said, "All I can say then is that there should be a great national memorial for that amazing man, or an important institution named after him."

Nazir asked his passengers who were all awakened, for permission to stop briefly at another site, the Saraswati Vidya Niketan Secondary School at Cornelia Ida, the village just past Hague. He gestured to Vishnu to do a video recording of the group as everyone stepped out of the car to stretch their legs. Vishnu duly obliged and then handed the camera to Ramesh to continue the filming.

Nazir stepped forward and began his introduction about the school, "First of all, I hope that we will find the time to visit this amazing and outstanding school. It is the brainchild of CI's own Pujya Swami Aksharanandaji, and it was opened since 2002. It is an independent Non-Governmental Organisation or NGO, and non-profit educational institution of the highest calibre not only here in Guyana, but also in the entire Caribbean. They have produced amazing results with their students embracing strong Dharmic principles and values. I am very proud that this school is right here in the middle of West Coast Demerara which is part of Region 3."

Vishnu was very impressed and said, "Thank you, Nazir Bhai. I have heard a lot about the Swami and his school. He and his staff run a highly disciplined institution. They encourage their students to work hard, develop respectful behaviour amongst each other, with their teachers, in the community and at home with their families. Learning is not just about cramming for exams but is strongly linked to character building. Do you think that this model should be adopted across the Guyana education system?"

Michael raised his right hand as is done by students in a classroom and suggested, "I think that the Minister of Education can adapt some of the best practices of this school, but the whole concept cannot be used as it really represents the teachings of one religion."

Nazir questioned this, "Hang on there Michael. What about all the other Christian schools? Is this really a Christian country? We have to find ways to unshackle ourselves from the chains of colonisation and promote the strength of our diversity. OK, the Swami's school is essentially about Hindu philosophy, but surely there is a place for this institution within the education system."

Vishnu intervened and said, "Well, of course we are a diverse society, but at the moment the biggest problem is a lack of easy access to high quality education and skills training for everyone across the country. I understand that the World Bank is supporting the building of more Secondary Schools in places where young people have little or no access to such high-quality facilities. That must be the right path to follow and to give more young Guyanese the right skills they need for the job opportunities being created now and in the future. A school like this is certainly a step in the right direction."

Parvati noticed some of the neatly attired students of the school passing by and she enthused, "Oh, just look at how orderly and well-presented those children are. I am sure that if you ask them, they will tell you that they love their school."

Doreen looked at the children with admiration and said, "I am sure that you will not find children misbehaving and being unmannerly in that school. I have seen footage on the internet of Guyanese children in other schools beating up each other in their classrooms. They are also very rowdy and out of control when in the streets. All of the children represent the future of Guyana and the quicker the authorities sort this out, the better."

Sati nodded and added, "I have no problem with the religious-based schools as long as the curriculum and other activities promote the best of Guyana's diversity. I also believe that this generation will have a huge role to play in Guyana's future, building on the foundations being laid now in the education system, the technical training institutes and other facilities. There has never been a more exciting time for young people in the history of this country."

Nazir clasped his hands graciously and said, "Ladies, you have hit the nail on its head. We do have a Minister of Education who listens and is working very hard to instil greater discipline and commitment from students, teachers and the co-operation of parents or guardians. This is what the Swami and staff have achieved here. Let's head home now. I did not plan to make these two stops, but I guess that we will be doing more of this as we move around our beautiful country."

In only a few minutes, the group arrived at Nazir's and Neesha's grand and imposing home in Anna Catherina. It was located off the main road through a side street and set alongside other individually designed properties. The approach road was much narrower than the main thoroughfare along the coast. It was newly tarmacked and with just enough space for vehicles, pedestrians, cyclists and other users. The drains on both sides were mostly open except for concreted or wooden entrances leading to different styles of fencing and gates. Nazir's driveway in front of a large garage was concreted as well and was decorated with a collection of floral plants neatly arranged in large pots.

Michael observed this and asked, "Nazir, thank you very much. You have a very impressive home and yard here. But why is there so much concrete everywhere?"

Nazir waved at Neesha who was standing before the large wooden entrance door to the house and then replied to Michael's question, "Thank you all for coming to our home. We have concreted around the property to help the water from the heavy rainfalls to flow away to a small trench running at the back of the houses on this side of the road. There is a similar irrigation system for the houses on the opposite side."

Vishnu stepped down from his seat in the car and looked around as he said, "You have a beautiful place here. I can understand why you need to concrete over so much. Besides, you are not far from the seawall and that Atlantic Ocean!"

Michael took the opportunity to offer an idea, "Nazir, I would try to route as much of the rainwater into large tanks for general use such as watering the plants as and when required."

Nazir thanked Michael for his suggestion and pointed to two tanks he had already set up to collect water from the rains via the substantial roof of the house. He then held the door of his car open to allow Doreen, Parvati and Sati to step out of the vehicle whilst Ramesh opened the trunk door to retrieve the suitcases. Everyone then took turns to meet and embrace Neesha.

Doreen held Neesha's small delicate hands and said, "It is so nice to see you after so many years. You have a beautiful home, and behalf of all of us on this trip, let me thank you and Nazir for hosting us. One thing I must tell you is that Parvati, Sati and I will be helping you as much as possible."

Neesha, a slight and short figure, with a broad and welcoming smile, said with a soft and gentle tone, "The pleasure is all ours. Thank you for offering to help me, but we have a very good housekeeper who will look after us. Nazir and I will give her a bonus for the extra work."

Parvati stepped forward and said, "Thank you so much. But the three of us will not be sitting around without helping. That is not the Guyanese way!"

Nazir led the way through the grand entrance door and into the smart, well-furnished sitting room with a white marble-tiled floor and large picture frames of portraits of members of the family, neatly set around the neutrally painted walls. The seating area was dominated by three large three-seater brown leather settees arranged to face an imposing sixty-five-inch TV resting on a sturdy mahogany stand. The centre of the room was occupied by a square-shaped coffee table with a well-polished mahogany frame and a decorated wooden top. This was resting on a red and black Persian-patterned carpet. A large crystal chandelier with modern candle style lights hung from the ceiling in the centre of the room. An air-conditioning unit located just below the ceiling on one wall furthest away from the seating area, was whirring and providing welcome and cool relief from the humidity on the outside. At each of the four corners of the room was a short wooden table where beautifully decorated ceramic plant pots of small ferns stood.

Michael's large brown eyes opened widely as he surveyed the room and said, "Wow! Brother Nazir and Sister Neesha, this is truly impressive! I guess that this is the type of interior we can imagine to be in all of those grand houses around the villages and across the country. God bless you guys for what you have achieved from your hard work over many years. The only thing missing here is your butler to take us around the house on a guided tour!"

Everyone laughed at Michael's quip.

Nazir proudly stood beside his charming and humble wife and announced, "Thank you, Michael. Let's all relax here for a while and have some light refreshment before retiring after your very long and tiring day of travel. Of course, we have some good ole' Guyanese dinner for later on. Meanwhile, do make yourselves at home."

Vishnu could not wait any longer as he signalled to Nazir his urgent need for the nearest toilet. Nazir showed him the guest bathroom facility on the ground floor and Vishnu muttered, "Damn airline food!" as he rushed for quick relief.

Michael chuckled as he exclaimed, "Domino!"

Doreen smiled and warned, "Don't you laugh, Michael. Your turn will come soon as well!"

Later on, the hosts and their guests enjoyed a sumptuous Guyanese homecooked meal of chicken curry, brown rice, daal, coconut choka, daalpuri roti and side dishes of poulouri, baara and mango acchar. Freshly squeezed orange juice along with ice-cold water from a dispenser within the fridge in the nearby kitchen, helped to soothe their mouths. Vishnu decided to limit his intake after his experience in the toilet and settled for some of the snacks and a glass of water.

He thanked his gracious hosts and pointed out, "Well, what a start we have had on this trip! If this is only the trailer, I can't wait for the movie! Nazir and Neesha, you have already taken us and shown us examples of what is making Guyana and Guyanese people proud of who we are, where we have come from and where we are going. Dr JB Singh fought all his life for our rights. Swami is using ancient Sanatan Dharm philosophy to bring out knowledge. And now, local cuisine to feed our souls!"

Michael smiled and said with great admiration for their hosts, "May our friendship last forever!"

11

The gathering and calling

The first evening for the travellers was comfortable and restful apart from Vishnu's visits to the toilet in the ensuite of the bedroom he shared with Parvati. The use of air-conditioning in the bedrooms along with mosquito netting over the beds successfully kept the blood-thirsty pests away, much to the relief of the visitors. As soon as the air-conditioning was turned off in the morning, the warmth was noticeable by the visitors who sought some respite from glasses of ice-cold orange juice or water which were placed in two large jugs on the dining table.

Nazir and Neesha had woken up at around five in the morning for the first *namaaz* of the day called *fajr*. They showered and then quietly performed the prayers in an ample space within their grand master bedroom, using separate and specially designed individual prayer mats which they laid out facing the direction of the *Kaaba* in Mecca, Saudi Arabia.

They then moved downstairs to the modern American styled kitchen and began to prepare breakfast for everyone. Their housekeeper, a young single mother of African descent, arrived shortly afterwards for her day's duties and took charge of the preparation of traditional Guyanese bakes, fried salted fish and pots of green tea. Neesha opted to prepare a bowl of chopped fruits including mangoes, bananas and imported apples and red grapes.

Most of the guests were up and ready by seven o'clock, and they made their way to the sitting room. They warmly greeted each other and Nazir asked whether they had a comfortable first night in Guyana. They all confirmed that they enjoyed the much-needed rest. Vishnu was also able to say that he had recovered from his stomach upset. He was concerned that Michael had not yet arrived, and Doreen expressed her usual disappointment about her husband's slowness in getting ready.

However, it was only a few more minutes before Michael made his appearance at the top of the grand winding stairway which flowed down from the first floor to a corner of the sitting room. Doreen looked up and covered her eyes with her hands.

She exclaimed, "Oh my God! Michael, why are you wearing that shirt and shorts? You look like you have just come out of a bird sanctuary!"

Michael as usual, ignored Doreen's questions and stepped down the stairs in a less than confident way, but with the broadest smile of a very proud, excited and happy traveller.

Vishnu took a closer look at his friend's outfit as he arrived in the lounge and commented, "Man, I love your shirt with so many different toucans, and those shorts which are exposing your skinny and ugly looking legs!"

Nazir laughed as he said, "Michael, my only worry about your outfit is that if any toucan sees you, they might want to mate with you! Anyway, I do love your spirit. After all you are on holiday in a tropical country!"

Sati stepped forward and gave Michael a hug as she said, "Uncle Michael, I love your style. You are cool, you look smart and are best prepared for our adventure."

Nazir stood just before the TV and announced, "Well, today Neesha and I have invited over our other members of our tour party to meet each other and to plan for at least some of the places we agree to visit and the things we would like to do. We can also agree for individuals to take time out to visit relatives and friends as you see fit. I hope that sounds OK."

They all nodded in agreement and Michael asked, "So tell us who else have come in to join us."

In answer to Michael's request, Nazir said, "Well, let me see. Before I talk about all those who have travelled from abroad, let me mention our great friends and neighbours here in Anna Catherina. John Charles and his lovely wife Muriel. I must say that out of proper respect for our Amerindian first peoples, we have stopped calling John by his false name of "Black Buck". This is a derogatory term and I hope we can all respect our friends by refraining from referring to them as "Buck" people. We do have some Amerindian people who are settled along the Coastland but most of them live in about two hundred communities or villages across the country and mainly in the hinterland. They are remarkable people, very intelligent and extremely friendly."

Michael nodded in appreciation of what Nazir mentioned and said, "I am very much looking forward to meeting John and Muriel. I gather that they never left Guyana."

Vishnu pointed out, "Well, why would they want to leave this place? Our Amerindian brothers and sisters understand this land and are more attached to it than we will ever know. Their views about life and living are quite different from ours, and I am looking forward to learning from them. Sorry Nazir, for interrupting. Please continue."

Nazir smiled and said, "Thank you for saying that, Vishnu. I know that John and Muriel do not like to talk about this, but I also know that for the first time in the long history of their people, they feel that they are now being treated with more respect in this country. I can see that Michael is itching to say something before they and our other friends come over to join us for a get-together to meet up and agree on our trips. Michael, over to you."

Michael duly obliged, "Please allow me to give you a little history for now, and I will share more when we go into the hinterland where most of the Amerindians or Indigenous peoples or First Peoples, live. The latest estimate of their population is around seventy-eight and a half thousands, or about ten per cent of Guyana's nearly eight hundred thousand people residing here. Excuse me, but I have this information here in my notebook which I will be referring to as I cannot remember everything."

Ramesh looked at Michael with admiration and said, "Nevermind Uncle Michael, you still know a lot more than many people. Can you tell us the names of the Amerindian tribes living in Guyana?"

Michael nodded and quickly found the notes he wished to use, "Thank you son. I was coming to that. There are nine tribes as follows. The Arawak, the Arecuna, the Carib, the Makushi, the Patamona, the Wai Wai, the Warao, the Wapichan and the Akawaio. As much as eighty-six per cent of the people live in their villages and communities in the ten regions across the country. It is very important for all Guyanese here and abroad, to appreciate these people and their history. I will pause here, as at the moment, I am feeling very hungry and can't wait to have some of that amazing breakfast being prepared. I promise to share more information about our Amerindian friends who even gave us the name of this country of Guyana meaning, the 'Land of Many Waters'."

Michael bowed gracefully to acknowledge a spontaneous burst of applause from everyone.

Nazir continued with his briefing, "Thank you my brother. Please look after that notebook of treasured facts that you will share with all of us. So, in addition to John and Muriel, we will meet Carlos "Reds" D'Souza and his wife Maria who have flown in from Florida. Peter "Smokey" Ramdin has come in from Trinidad, Afzal "Mule" Amin from Suriname, and Arthur "Speedy" Chung from Canada. They are all staying with John and Muriel right here in Anna Catherina, and I believe that Afzal will share the driving of another eight-seater with John. So, we will be doing most of the road trips with the two vehicles for as much as possible. Of course, we will have to use other forms of transport such as the river boats and even a small aeroplane to get to some places."

Ramesh did a quick mental check and noted, "So, Uncle Nazir, I reckon that on this now grand trip, we have fifteen people. That will be reduced to thirteen when Sati and I leave to return to New York in two weeks' time. Mind you, I am feeling so excited about this adventure that I will try to extend our stay. I can see that Sati is agreeing with me."

Neesha was anxious to have the breakfast served, and she signalled to Nazir to invite the group to their grand twelve-seater dining table situated in a separate area off the sitting room and nearer to the kitchen.

Later on, at around one in the afternoon, John and Muriel arrived with the other members of the tour party, in time for lunch and their first meeting together. They greeted each other enthusiastically and the house took on an air of a grand party. To ensure that it felt more of a traditional Guyanese get together, Nazir used his phone to select and play some old creole folk songs in the background, and others including *calypsos*, as well as hit songs of the 1960s to the 1990s by popular bands such as the Tradewinds and the Merrymen.

When the song, 'Not a blade of grass' by Dave Martins of the Tradewinds began to play, Michael asked everyone to pause and listen. The lyrics and catchy tune and rhythm commanded utmost attention until the end.

Michael, with great pride, commented, "I can see that you all remember that song written by our very own icon Dave Martins who was born in a large Portuguese family at Hague Village just a couple of miles from here. The family moved and he then grew up in Vreed en Hoop. Dave attended St Stanislaus College in Brickdam, Georgetown before migrating to Toronto, Canada. Our brother here, Carlos, can tell us a lot more about Dave Martins and his music in Toronto."

Carlos responded with, "First of all, on behalf of Maria and I, let me say how excited we are to be here and to join old friends for this great trip. Yes, Dave Martins and some friends formed the Tradewinds band, and they became very popular across the migrant communities in Canada, as well as across the Caribbean, and of course here in Guyana. We should all be proud of this Guyanese icon who has sadly passed away. I believe that Dave was a true Guyanese patriot, icon and legend. He was in fact granted an Honorary Doctorate by the University of Guyana."

Michael continued, "I agree. The song we just heard is a real rallying call for all Guyanese to be prepared to fight for and defend every bit of Guyana from any invasion by Venezuela. This is about the crazy claim on the whole of Essequibo by Venezuela. This territory was settled way back in 1899, and since then Venezuela has been repeating its claim which continues to be rejected by international bodies as well as countries such as the US, Canada and the UK. I have no legal knowledge, but I believe that President Nicolas Maduro of Venezuela and his government, need to back off! Essequibo is we own! Guyana is we own!"

Vishnu was quite animated when he said, "I see that they were even trying to stop the bids for eight oil blocks in the Atlantic. This is not only a case of not a blade of grass, but also not a drop of oil!"

Doreen kissed her teeth in anger, "Look, that madman cannot even run his own country and stop millions of the people from leaving Venezuela to look for basics such as food. Thousands of Venezuelans have come over to Guyana looking for jobs and to escape hardship. Many are Guyanese returning, but I hope that the other Venezuelan migrants are not here as some kind of advance party for an invasion!"

Parvati nodded and said, "I was wondering about that. I do hope that is not the case and they are genuine refugees. We Guyanese are caring people, and I am happy to see that they are getting help from the government."

Nazir stood up and pointed out, "I don't think that countries like America and Britain will allow an invasion of Guyana by Venezuela. Our oil means a lot to America, and they are still anti-communist. So, don't let this situation spoil our lunch and plans for this trip."

John had a worried look on his face as he said, "Of course oil matters, but I fear for the safety of my people living all over Essequibo. They are not happy about the appearance of so many Spanish-speaking migrants coming over the borders which are not guarded or controlled. On the other hand, many of the migrants are desperate hard-working people and a lot of them are highly qualified in various fields. We must also be mindful that many who come across are our Venezuelan Amerindian brothers and sisters who have been used to travelling between the two countries for hundreds of years regardless of the borders."

Peter Ramdin broke his silence and pointed out, "Venezuelan migrants have even ventured into Trinidad escaping the Maduro regime. They, like other migrants including us, are prepared to work hard, live peacefully and adapt to their new environment."

Sati warned, "There is an interesting issue here. Normally, when foreigners migrate to another country, they have to at least try to learn the main host language. So, you would expect that the Venezuelans must learn English. But in this instance and given the fact that most countries in South America are Spanish speaking like the Venezuelans, it seems that it is Guyanese who should be learning Spanish. When we migrated to America, Britain or Canada, we did not have such a problem as we all spoke English."

Carlos asked, "And what about the Brazilians coming into the south of Guyana illegally? Will we now need to learn Portuguese? I know that this is the ancestral language of Maria and I, but I am now too damn old to start learning a new language."

Maria smiled and said quietly, "Eu tambem. Me too."

Vishnu scratched his right temple and said, "Very nice, Maria. Sati, another issue we have is the fact that Guyana needs a lot of skilled people and if the Venezuelans and Brazilians have those skills, then we do need to accept them and help them to settle here."

Nazir put his hands on his hips as he stood before his friends and said, "I understand that we now have about thirty to forty thousand Venezuelans registered to stay and work here. I now wonder about if they get the right to vote, who will they vote for?"

Ramesh shook his head and pointed out, "Uncle Nazir, I don't think that we have to worry about that for now as I understand that if someone is not a Guyanese citizen he or she cannot vote in Guyana's elections. The migrants here have permits or need permits to stay and work. But I think that the government needs to tighten up its immigration policies and controls."

Michael pulled up his shorts and rubbed his hands as he said, "Talking about tightening up, my stomach is craving for that food I'm smelling from the kitchen!"

As soon as everyone had the sumptuous lunch and refreshments, they assembled in the sitting room to discuss and agree the tour plans.

Nazir stood up once again in front of his guests and announced, "John, Muriel, Neesha and I have been discussing some ideas for this venture. You are all most welcome to stay at our homes over the entire trip. So please feel free to use our kitchens and the facilities as you wish. In other words, treat our homes as if they are yours."

Michael put his right hand up and responded, "Thank you very much for the accommodation but I think that we should give you guys some money for this plus the food and drinks."

Nazir raised both his hands and said, "Oh no. We invited you all to come on this trip and we regard you all as family. So, we are not expecting any money for this. However, you may wish to pay for your travelling on the trips and tours you go on."

John interrupted Nazir and proposed, "Except for the gasoline for the two cars. Nazir and I have that covered."

Parvati asked, "Can we pay for the meals outside on our trips including for Nazir, John and your wives? That would be fair."

Doreen nodded and suggested, "Yes, I think that we should also pay for any entrance fees for you guys if and when you travel with us."

Vishnu smiled and noted, "I think that we can agree to do as suggested. By the way, what about washing and ironing our clothes?"

Nazir looked across at Neesha, John and Muriel, and as they nodded in agreement, he concluded, "The laundry will be looked after by our two housemaids. If you wish to give them some money, that will be no problem. But, as I said, we are giving them some extra bonus pay over the time of your stay at our homes. Now, for our first trip. Where would you guys like to visit?"

Ramesh picked up his trusted iPhone, and after turning it on, suggested, "Uncle Nazir, perhaps we can book a flight from Ogle to Kaieteur Falls and Baganara whilst we are fresh and ready for such a big one. May I suggest also that we mix it up with big trips between smaller local ones and those we will do to visit relatives and friends. How does that sound?"

Carlos agreed and commented, "That is a very good idea. Given our advancing years we will need a lot of rest in between any long trips. May I suggest a day or a couple of days trip to Rupununi by flight? Another idea for a long trip is up the Pomeroon River to visit an Amerindian settlement. Guyana also advertises trips to some eco-tourism sites and systems located in the hinterland."

Michael pulled his spectacles down onto his nose and looked at the group by lowering his head and peering over the rim of it as if he was a College Professor, "OK. It seems that we are already agreeing on some trips, and I am mainly interested in some of the historical sites. Given how many we are, perhaps we can agree for some to go on one trip whilst others go on a separate one. I would like to suggest that Ramesh, Peter, Afzal, Maria and Sati draw up a plan and schedule, and then let us get on with the adventure."

There was unanimous agreement to Michael's suggestion, and Ramesh proceeded to book the group's first major day trip to the magnificent Kaieteur Falls with a stopover for lunch at the Baganara Resort. Nazir, Neesha, John and Muriel opted out of the trip as they had already experienced it. This allowed Ramesh to book an exclusive flight for eleven people and thus avoid the problem of cancellation sometimes faced when there are insufficient passengers. He also managed to negotiate a reasonable discount for the tour.

12

Kaieteur – "Old Man Falls?"

The early morning of the next day booked for the trip to Kaieteur Falls was bright and warm. The tour party boarded Nazir's and John's vehicles and set out for the drive to Ogle on the East Coast of Demerara, about four miles from the east of Georgetown. The Ogle International Airport was renamed the Eugene F Correia International Airport in 2016 in honour of Guyana's most outstanding aviator who also served as a Member of Parliament and the first Minister of Communications and Aviation as well as the Minister of Works and Hydraulics. He was a pioneering gold and diamond miner and businessman who was involved in other ventures including quarrying, growing potatoes in the hinterland and running the Karia Hotel in Bartica. He was posthumously awarded the Guyana Golden Arrow of Achievement in 1973. The Baganara Island Resort was founded in 1989 and is owned by the Correia family business called the Correia Group of Companies.

The journey from Anna Catherina, across the Demerara Harbour Bridge, through Mandela Avenue and Sheriff Street and to the airport, took about one hour. Nazir drove the first car which included Vishnu, Parvati, Michael, Doreen, Ramesh and Sati, and John's passengers in his car were Peter, Carlos, Maria, Arthur and Afzal.

Nazir was very pleased with the progress that both cars had made, and upon parking at the airport, he said, "Well, that's a great start for this adventure. Thankfully, the traffic was much better through avoiding driving across Georgetown. Soon there will be a very fast four lane highway from Ogle to Eccles which will ease up traffic congestion by a lot more. That highway being built by an Indian company will be completed on time as those guys work very long hours."

Michael was pleased to step in front of the tour party after Nazir and John had seen them go through the security checks, and returned to their cars where they planned to wait until the flight took off. Michael wore a different T-shirt with a print of Kaieteur Falls in front, a pair of casual jeans and some comfortable sneakers. All of the other members of the group wore casual clothes and appropriate footwear as advised by Ramesh and Sati. Michael proudly led the group to the small waiting area as they awaited to board the Cessna Caravan aircraft which had a capacity for up to fourteen passengers. He casually took off his small rucksack and placed it on a vacant seat beside Doreen.

She looked at her husband who began to flex his arms and legs as if he was warming up for a football match or a long-distance run, and she signalled for him to stop clowning around and to sit down.

Michael pretended that he did not hear Doreen's instruction and said to the group, "Man, that security check was basic and simple. A friend of mine told me that when he came through here about ten years ago, the check was done by a female officer who just waved a battery-operated device over and around him. Unfortunately, there was no reading, and she apologised for the dead battery. My friend tried not to laugh and told her that he wished that he had some spare ones. The officer was not amused nor impressed and asked a male colleague to give my friend a brisk physical body search. He never said to me whether or not he enjoyed the manual examination. But when he finished telling the story he had a big smile on his face!"

The tour party, except Doreen, could not resist laughing as Michael bowed slightly before taking his seat. Within fifteen minutes, there was an announcement that the weather to and around Kaieteur Falls was fine and that the flight would be leaving on time. If the weather was unsettled, such flights would normally be delayed for safety reasons.

After a short walk in the open from the airport departure lounge to the waiting aircraft, they were greeted by the pilot as they boarded. Michael and Vishnu sat next to each other towards the front, and just behind the pilot. Everyone was comfortably seated and could see out of a window beside them. Afzal was perspiring profusely and Carlos leaned across to ask him if he was alright.

Afzal was mopping the sweat pouring down his face and began to shake, "Man, I don't like flying. Especially in these small planes."

Carlos tried his best to give him some assurance and said quietly, "Don't worry. Take some deep breaths and drink some water. The flight will be very short and soon we will be there."

The pilot, a young Guyanese appearing to be in his early thirties, announced that he was ready for the take off and that they would be flying for only about an hour over the one hundred and forty-seven miles to the Kaieteur International Airport. After a relatively smooth take off, the aircraft began to cruise and soon passed over the Demerara River on its straight flight path. Michael leaned over to Vishnu who was videoing the journey.

He spoke above the loud noise of the engines, "I am speaking a bit loudly so that your video can clearly record the information as we fly. I hope that you don't mind me saying something about the Falls before we see it."

Vishnu nodded in approval and gestured for Michael to continue speaking. Michael cleared his throat away from the camera and then leaned over nearer to it.

"The magnificent Kaieteur Falls is a real treasure of Guyana and is the largest single drop waterfall in the world at around seven hundred and forty feet. It is about five times higher than the Niagara Falls in Canada, and two times that of the Victoria Falls on the border of Zambia and Zimbabwe in Africa. There are two stories about the origin of the name Kaieteur Falls. I think that they are both interesting and credible."

Michael then opened his notebook, looked around the aircraft to ensure that everyone was listening to him, and then spoke loudly, "The first story is about Kai, the leader of the Patamona people of Chenau village who were regularly attacked by some Carib people from around the area. The Caribs would raid the homes for food and even kidnap some of the Patamona women. Kai, in wanting to save his people, decided to appease the great spirit Makunaima, took a canoe and rowed over the falls to his death. So, Kai went over, or teur, and thus the name Kaieteur."

Ramesh, on hearing Michael's account, asked, "Uncle Michael, that story sounds quite fascinating. Do we know if Kai achieved his aim for his people?"

Michael shrugged his shoulders and replied, "That is something I do not know. The second story is also interesting. In the Patamona language, the falls is known as Kayik Tuwuk or Old Man Falls. Charles Barrington Brown who was the first European to locate the falls in 1870, was told by the villagers that there was a very rude and unpleasant old man in the village. His relatives got fed up with him and they grabbed him, put him in a canoe and shoved him over the edge of the falls. Hence the term meaning Old Man Falls."

Doreen laughed and shouted across to Michael, "Now, you better watch your step when we get there before you suffer the same!"

Michael smiled and responded, "No chance of that happening my love. I am too scared of both water and height."

Parvati scanned around the cabin and said, "Now, that could apply to all of you old men here!"

Maria poked Carlos at his back and warned, "You better watch your step too old man!"

Afzal also laughed as the quips made him feel more relaxed about the flight. Peter stared through his window and regularly took pictures and short videos of the pristine greenery presented by the forests below.

Arthur sat back and simply stared through the window beside him fully absorbed in the scenes below and ahead.

The plane rumbled along having passed over the Demerara River above the village of Golden Grove and over Vriesland on the other side as it continued to head on its straight path towards the Kaieteur International Airport within the Kaieteur National Park. As the falls began to come into view, the pilot drew the group's attention to the first sighting of the legendary phenomenon. Vishnu, and all others taking pictures and videos focused their lens in preparation of a clear view of Kaieteur. Suddenly, the world's most spectacular falls appeared in the distance below. It was in full flow revealing the full length of its magnificent single drop of dark brown water at the top and with a lighter colour heading down to a white spray at the bottom. The passengers leant forward to get the best view from their windows and were stunned into silence.

The landing was slightly bumpy, and when the aircraft completed its taxiing to a final stop, all the passengers applauded the pilot. Afzal gave a great sigh of relief and joined in with the clapping and cheering. Carlos fist-pumped his friend. The pilot graciously thanked his passengers and wished everyone a great experience of the falls. They were all guided off the aircraft and used a short pathway leading to a rest house.

The showroom at the rest house included glass display cabinets with models of some creatures such as the golden frogs which were for sale as souvenirs. From the rest house, there was a short walk along a cleared pathway towards the first viewing point of the falls, with giant bromeliads being the dominant plant life. Michael spotted a golden frog perched on a leaf of one of the bromeliads and stood a safe distance away.

He pointed out, "Now please be careful here and don't touch this frog as it can poison you."

Vishnu aimed his camera at the frog and made sure that Michael was in the shot looking like a botany professor with his spectacles resting on the tip of his nose. He assumed a position of a half squat with his hands resting on his shaky knees. Other members of the group chuckled at Michael's posing.

Peter gestured to Michael and said, "Man, not only do you look like some mad professor, but also like the chief scout of this view of the falls they call the Boy Scout's View!"

A further gentle walk through an open trail took the group to the Rainbow View of the falls where there was a clearly visible sight of a rainbow near the bottom. They posed for pictures and videos taken by the guide and Vishnu. They then moved further closer through to the third spot to experience the full magnificence of Kaieteur. There were no safety rails and the guide asked everyone to go as far to the edge of the natural viewing points, but to be very careful. The thunderous rumbling of the falls was more pronounced and seemed to create a sense of intrigue for the visitors.

Carlos held Maria's right hand tightly as they both stepped cautiously to the open viewing ledge and they embraced and kissed each other whilst the other members of the group applauded and took pictures.

Peter smiled and enthused, "Man, you two look like a "Star bai an' Star gyaal" in a great romantic movie. Please be careful not to be carried away and fall over the edge!"

Ramesh, whose mop of black hair showed early signs of balding, stooped down at a spot where some of the river's water formed a small pool and cupped some in his hands as he said, "I heard that this water could cure baldness. So, I am trying some on my head."

Sati giggled as she stepped cautiously to the water's edge and advised, "Don't be silly. I don't believe that this water can cure anything!"

The tour party then stood as closely as they could get where the almost copper coloured water of the Potaro River reached the edge and tumbled over in full flow with a mighty and thunderous roar. Whilst Kaieteur had presented itself from the air as a silent and beautiful painting, now it revealed its awesome power and sheer majesty. Everyone, except Afzal, inched forward to look at how the huge volume of water tumbled downwards and created its own mist well before the water hit the bottom before making its onward journey.

Maria, still holding Carlos's left hand firmly, shouted above the roar of the falls, "I love the way the dark brown water at the top pours down and changes colour as if it is like a giant curtain gracefully flowing to the bottom. I love that rainbow at the end of the drop."

Afzal steadied himself and admired the view of the water moving in powerful white rapids away from the falls and into the distance. Arthur stepped forward and stood beside him in order to support him if needed. Afzal turned to his friend and nodded his silent approval.

He then turned to his other friends and enthused, "That must be an exciting stretch of the river moving on quickly towards meeting up with the great Essequibo. Am I right Michael?"

Michael held Doreen's left hand as he replied, "Yes my friend, Kaieteur flows as part of the Potaro River over this plateau and then tumbles another eighty feet and through those rapids eventually joining the Essequibo River."

Peter, who was standing next to Afzal, pointed to a flock of birds swirling around and asked about them.

Michael again referred to his notebook and said, "I think that they are the white-collared swifts which nest behind the falls towards the bottom. Man, our country is blessed with so many species of birds, animals, insects and plant life. And I am very happy that there is so much interest in these places by researchers from here and abroad. One note of sadness about nature is that the biggest enemy of the swift is an orange-breasted falcon you might be able to spot flying amongst their prey."

Vishnu continued to video the falls, the rapids below and the surrounding landscape of pristine forest.

He paused the camera and said with great pride, "This is a truly majestic scene which must be preserved for many generations to come. As far as I am concerned, and as a proud Guyanese, I regard this place as a true natural wonder of the world. I am also very happy that it is not invaded by too many tourists, and I suppose that the high price for a trip here helps to keep the numbers down. Michael, do you know how many people visit Kaieteur each year?"

Michael did not have to refer to his notebook and responded with, "I think that it is about six thousand people. I agree with you that this must be carefully controlled."

Doreen was eager to mention, "Personally, this whole site is a unique source of therapy to help with our health and wellbeing."

Afzal smiled and said, "Yes, I do feel a great sense of relief and calm despite the awesome roar of the falls. This place grows on you as if with some magical and mysterious power. I wish that I could spend much more time just sitting by this edge and soaking up the sensation and energy being generated by thousands of tons of that fresh and clean water pouring down from the mountains in the distance."

Everyone of the tour party stooped down or sat as near as possible to the edge to admire the way the river reached at the top of the falls and to observe in awe as the water seemed to take on a new urgency to tumble over and down to merge in the massive pool at the base before moving into the white-water rapids as the Potaro River continued its spectacular journey into the Essequibo River. The tour party savoured the stupendous sights and sensational sounds which the sheer majesty of Kaieteur and its surrounds presented.

As the visit to the falls neared its end, the guide agreed to use Vishnu's camera to record a final video of the tour party assembled in front of Kaieteur as it continued its magnificent and tumultuous display in the background. Vishnu asked everyone to join him in applause, and as the group did so, their sound was easily drowned out by the falls' awesome roaring. It was the perfect picture of welcome by Guyana.

The flight from Kaieteur to the Baganara Island Resort in the Essequibo River, was about forty minutes, and after a short walk from the landing strip on the island, the group prepared to have a buffet lunch. Just before they were invited to the meal, they were served with a glass of fresh ice-cold lime juice drink.

Afzal happily accepted his glass, and after he sipped some of the juice, he enthused, "Oh my God, this is so refreshing! The perfect start to our lunch. This not only quenches a thirst but has its own magical effect. That is how I feel right now."

Peter agreed with his friend and added, "This a great way to quench our thirst after imbibing the glory of that incredible waterfall. It was the greatest sight I have ever witnessed in all my life. Guyana is not just beautiful. It is full of wonders."

Arthur smiled as he said, "Kaieteur is just one of many stunning waterfalls across the hinterland of Guyana. Michael may wish to correct me, but I can think of a number of them including the Orinduik Falls, the Kumerau Falls, the King Edward VIII Falls, the Oshi Falls, the Amaila Falls and the Kamarang Great Falls. I can remember this from reading about them before I travelled over. I guess that with our limited time we may not be able to visit them. Taken together, I reckon that with all the magnificent rivers, waterfalls, mountains and so on, the Amerindians had the right name for Guyana as the Land of Many Waters. Truly spectacular!"

Michael waved to Arthur and gave him an approving thumbs up.

Carlos sipped some more of his soothing drink and pointed out, "I know that we have been very lucky to see Kaieteur in full flow. But I think that it will still be incredible even when it has only half the flow. The setting is the best stage that nature can provide to show us her awesome power and astonishing beauty. We have been very blessed today. In fact, I should say that Guyana is truly blessed!"

Michael nodded and said, "Well, to me it confirms why Guyana must never allow Venezuela to have not only one blade of grass, but not a drop of our waters."

Maria smiled and exclaimed, "Amen to that!"

Doreen nodded and noted, "I don't know about you, but there were times when I felt as if I was being drawn to the edge where the water tumbled over."

Sati stepped forward and held both Maria's and Doreen's hands and said, "Yes, there were moments when I thought the same. Maa, did you feel the same?"

Parvati joined the group and said, "Yes, there has been at least three people who committed suicide there by jumping off the edge. Tragic. A part of Guyana's big problem especially amongst the young people."

Vishnu acknowledged Parvati and said, "So sad. But I do hope that no barriers are put up at the site. Besides, if people are determined to kill themselves, they will do so regardless of any such protection."

Michael agreed and then led the way to the buffet. After the tour party chose their plates of the lunch on offer, they took up their seats at the dining tables. They were disturbed by the presence of some flies, and they set about trying to swat them away with their napkins. A staff member switched on the fans in the dining area and this allowed the group to settle down and enjoy their meals.

Following lunch, most of the tour party opted for a period of rest after strolling around the site. Baganara presented a welcome and tranquil experience ideal for reflection about the majesty and mystique of the magnificent Kaieteur. Ramesh and Sati chose to do some kayaking which they thoroughly enjoyed on the relatively calm waters of the giant Essequibo River. Soon, everyone was ready for the short flight back to Ogle sitting in the aircraft with their weary eyes closed but with their thoughts painting the best portraits of a once in a lifetime experience.

13

Rest, reflection and recall

The tour party was received at the Eugene F Correia International Airport in Ogle upon their return from Baganara Island, at about five in the afternoon by Nazir and John who took them back to Nazir's home in Anna Catherina. They were all given the opportunity to freshen up and then relax in the lounge until the serving of a hearty meal of chicken curry, daal, rice and roti.

At the dining table, Vishnu stood up and thanked Nazir, Neesha, John and Muriel for the exciting start to the visit to Guyana. The hosts acknowledged the gesture and Nazir asked Vishnu for his impression about their first long trip.

Vishnu looked around the table and then responded, "Well, let me speak on behalf of all of us who visited Kaieteur Falls and the Baganara Island Resort today. It was clearly the best sight to behold in this most beautiful country of ours. I read about Kaieteur and had seen a lot of pictures and videos, but to be there and to take in the sheer majesty and awesomeness of the falls in its setting was truly heavenly. I can still see the pleasure in everyone's faces through the smiles around the table. I will allow you all to express your own thoughts. Once again Nazir, Neesha, John and Muriel, thank you very much for your incredible hospitality, and let me say that this food caps an amazing day for us."

Peter, who was normally quite subdued, stood up to speak, "I must say that such a trip should be a must for everyone in this country to experience personally. I hope that for the benefit of our local residents, the price for a trip to Kaieteur should be much lower than over two hundred US dollars per person. Also, as you say, no photos or videos can match being there in person and having our senses opened by the sheer majesty and beauty of the falls and that amazing environment.

Even the noise of the falls was beautiful to the ears. I think that to experience the white-water rapids from the base of the falls through to the Essequibo River must be incredible and exciting to look at and those who venture to make their way through the jungle to the base of the falls over a couple of weeks would have a completely different perspective of Kaieteur as they look up from below."

Parvati nodded and added, "Yes, the most amazing experience ever! To me, that sight of Kaieteur and the stop in Baganara Island have already made my trip. Everything else from now on will be bonuses. Thank you, Ramesh and team, for choosing that trip as our first one. I hope that I do not spoil your impressions of our trip so far, but as you may or may not know, I do have a strong view about cleanliness. So far, I have seen some bright and clean environment around the airport and at the falls as well as Baganara. But I cannot stand the sight of so much trash beside the roads and in front of the housing here."

Doreen reached over and touched Parvati's left shoulder as she said, "Well said my dear friend. Guyana has so much to offer and now I am so looking forward to what follows. Today has been very special. Guyana is truly blessed. But you are right about the need to keep the country clean and tidy as this could be a big put off for tourists. Basic things like decent and clean toilets in public places must be improved and maintained."

Sati agreed with everyone who spoke and added, "I do hope that all fellow Guyanese living here and abroad will someday be able to afford such a trip to enjoy our own version of paradise on earth. Of course, such a wish will take a very long time to come through especially with only a few thousand visitors each year and the high cost of the package which seems to be geared towards us the tourists from abroad."

Carlos finished the remainder of his mango juice and pointed out, "I do agree with you all, but despite the high cost I do believe that the whole once in a lifetime trip was well worth the money. The falls were truly awesome. The stop off for lunch, and some rest at Baganara, was just the right thing for us to have after our senses were filled with so much natural beauty. Maria and I felt like we were in seventh heaven! It was quite romantic. You can see that she is still blushing!"

Everyone laughed at Carlos's quip, and Maria bashfully declined to comment. Michael looked across at Doreen and winked at her. She put her right index finger to her lips to warn him against saying anything that may embarrass her.

Michael, as usual, ignored Doreen's attempt to control him and he said, "Of course, Kaieteur is a romantic setting and I am happy for Carlos and Maria. I think that an early night might be just the tonic we need now to recharge our batteries and be ready for our next adventure. Ramesh and Sati, what's on the agenda for tomorrow? Of course we have to include our hosts in that."

Afzal intervened and said, "Before Ramesh answers that, I want to thank you all for helping me to overcome my fear of flying. I took a chance to go on the trip and I do not regret one moment of it. It was truly fantastic!"

Ramesh nodded and responded, "Uncle Afzal, you were very brave to do that trip. Tomorrow, we suggest more rest in the morning, and then in the afternoon we will check out one of the best shopping malls only recently opened right here in Leonora. We can have an evening meal there as well, and then end the day with an early night so that we could embark on another longer trip from early morning the next day. Is that OK?"

Nazir gave a thumbs up to Ramesh's suggestion and said, "I am so happy that everyone who went on the Kaieteur trip is so excited about the whole experience. It's a very good idea for us to visit the old and the new. The West Central Mall in Leonora is an exciting facility for local people. It brings a new experience of modern living for the village. It is one of the many examples of a growing trend of modernisation as part of the development of the country. John, would you like to say something before your guests retire for the evening at your place?"

John looked at Muriel for confirmation and commented, "I only wish to say that Muriel and I are really happy to have our friends here, and to share Guyana's ancient and natural environments with our histories of a diverse nation, and what is happening before our eyes for the whole world to see. I do hope that all Guyanese can enjoy these experiences, live this new dream and emerge from the nightmares of the past. Guyana is developing at a very fast rate and it is as exciting as watching Kaieteur in full flow. But it is really important that all Guyanese can go with the tide of progress and benefit from it."

Sati was very pleased to hear Nazir's and John's comments and said, "Thank you both. I could not have expressed that any better. I hope that our plans for the trip will give us all a good taste of that insight, and that we will tour at least one important place in each of the ten regions across the country."

Michael fist-pumped Ramesh and enthused, "Thank you and the others for your approach to this trip. I did my research on each of the regions so that I can offer some commentary on the old, the present and the future. You just have to ask and I will try my best to offer some information. I do not know everything, but if and when you want more you can just look it up online. I believe that this is how the young generation of Guyanese is learning about the country. There are lots of groups and individuals on social media who are posting mostly good information. But there are some who just indulge in mischief and post a lot of lies. Some may say "Oh dat's a Guyanese ting", but people need to be aware of the harm they cause to others who are trying hard to improve things here."

Vishnu agreed with Michael and added, "Yes, we have to be careful with what is there on social media. I don't mind good factual criticism about the country and those in power. In fact, I am sure that we can remember that we used to do this in our own way when we were growing up and *liming* although without thousands of people hearing our conversations at the same time. You know the old Guyanese saying, "Bush gat ears and dutty gat tongue"? Well, people need to be more aware of what they say and when to say it."

Michael smiled and offered, "I like that. It reminds me of the saying that goes something like this, "Clean yuh own house before yuh clean yuh neighba wan". In other words, sort out your own problems before trying to sort out others'."

The hosts and their guests retired early into the warm evening which was made very comfortable by the air-conditioning that was kept on for a few hours. Both Nazir and John had agreed that they would allow their guests to have an extra couple of hours of rest before breakfast. After that they drove the tour party to the West Central Mall which was only about one mile away along the main road from Anna Catherina to Leonora.

Vishnu turned to Michael and observed, "Well my friend, I think that these villages which were our playgrounds, are now almost unrecognisable. Many of the places we used to visit, to listen to music and to play our boyhood games such as 'taaga' and 'trup chaal' seem to have disappeared. Remember the old cinema called Monarch? I guess that you can tell us more about that place."

Michael glanced at Doreen, exchanged a smile and a wink, and then said, "Yes man. That cinema was the centre-point of our culture here in Anna Catherina. We used to lime at the sort of beer garden opposite the cinema and which was owned by a guy called Oscar Bam. The slot machine juke box used to belt out all kinds of music from soul, reggae, soca, calypso, rock, pop and of course, Bollywood songs. I must give credit to the man responsible for importing dozens of those machines we called "punch boxes" which played all of that music. He was known as Jack Mohamed the son of Dost Mohamed of Leonora. Mr Jack Mohamed also brought popcorn and ice cream machines and set them up in many villages around the country. He was a brilliant entrepreneur and just the type of businessman Guyana needs. As youngsters, many of us would show off our dancing skills around an open-air concreted floor in front of the premises, and we would pick up coins thrown at us whilst doing the splits and other moves. Mind you, some of us ended up with bruising on our knees from that concrete."

Vishnu commented before Doreen could speak, "Our dear friend Peter got the call name of "Smokey" because he used to challenge our guys as the champion dancer from Cornelia Ida and who used to "burn up" the dance floor at that place and at as many Indian wedding houses where he would challenge everyone to perform the kind of dances we see in the Bollywood movies. I guess that even at his old age he could still "smoke" the dance floor!"

Doreen could not resist poking fun at Michael and giggled as she said, "You doing the splits? If you tried you would just tear up your trousers and then when you got home your mother would dish out some licks on you! Anyway, carry on with your fantasy story!"

Ramesh laughed and commented, "Never mind Aunty Doreen, I can imagine Uncle Michael as a tall skinny kid doing those dance moves and picking up a lot of easy money in those days. I guess that Uncle Peter must have been a real class act and very popular especially at the wedding houses!"

Michael agreed, "Yes, Peter did smoke the dance floor! As for me, I became a rich kid and I was able to buy some baara, poulouri and gugri from a little food stall run by a lady we called "Beefie". The stall was located just below one of the two large advertising boards that dominated the wide entrance area off the road and in front of the Monarch cinema. The two advertising boards were pasted with the posters of the films being shown. We used to have the Indian films at one in the afternoons and eight in the evenings. The English ones were shown at five in the afternoons. It was only twenty-five cents to go in to the Pit but more for the Balcony at the upper level."

Nazir lamented, "Man, us poor kids could only afford to go to the Pit whilst better off people used to go up to the Balcony. Such was our social status then!"

Parvati put her right hand up, shook her head and said, "I don't agree with that. We girls were not better off, but it was expected that women and girls would go up to the Balcony to avoid mixing with you bad boys who were always teasing us."

Vishnu laughed and pointed out, "Well, some things that didn't care about who was poor or well off, were those bugs in the wooden benches and seats. Man, they sucked blood whether you were in the Pit or the Balcony. I remember the older guys who used to try to get rid of those bugs by using their lighted cigarettes or lighters to smoke them out."

Both cars slowly passed through the village, and Nazir and John stopped off the road in the middle of an area between Anna Catherina and Leonora called Edinburg. Nazir pointed out to where once stood the Leonora Cricket Ground, and opposite that, the Anna Catherina Anglican Primary School and Church.

The two groups from the cars gathered alongside the busy main road and Nazir said, "What you see opposite is one of the first statements of intention here in the middle of the West Coast of Demerara between Vreed en Hoop which means Peace and Hope in Dutch, and the growing town of Parika at the mouth of the Essequibo River. Part of the old Leonora Cricket Ground is now the new Leonora Secondary School, and behind that is the new Leonora Synthetic Track for athletics. Further back, where Michael just spoke about, and just across the Monarch Cinema, is the address of number five Anna Catherina which was once owned by the late Haji Abdool Kadeer whom he mentioned when telling us about Dr JB Singh. That general store was later run by his son Rayman Ali and his wife Sahidan who we used to call "Aunty Baba". She was the daughter of that great businessman named Dost Mohamed of Leonora."

Nazir paused for a few moments as a large truck sped by, and then continued, "In Anna Catherina, there were two rice factories with one owned and run by the late Willie Jodha and family, and the other, by the late Fazloor Rahman whose father Ratan, was the brother of Haji Abdool Kadeer. Those people were all pioneers amongst many others whom I have not mentioned. Every village or estate across Guyana will have great stories of such people who lived and thrived in them. Those people are amongst the real heroes who helped to build the country alongside the more recognised sugar, rice and mining industries. I love the way they conducted their businesses in the villages. They were demonstrating what we know as Social Responsibility by helping their customers and the communities. I was told that Haji Abdool Kadeer had some dwellings behind his house and store, and when customers travelled from far away, they would do their shopping and then be allowed to stay in the rooms if they were vacant, for no charge, until the next morning. They would also be given meals. Will we ever see such kindness and generosity now and in the future?"

Michael nodded and added, "Thank you Nazir for that very important piece of history. You are right. Every estate, village, town and settlement whether on the coastland or hinterland have the histories of the people who lived there and helped to grow those areas with their hard work and enterprises. I still say that they are amongst the people who laid the foundations for what we are seeing in the country."

Vishnu smiled with great pride as he mentioned, "Just behind us as Nazir pointed out, is the site of our Anna Catherina Anglican Primary School which most of us attended, and next to the church was the late Dr Wills Clinic. That Leonora Cricket Ground was full of great heroics in the past. I will let Peter talk about that as well as his own cricket club and ground at Cornelia Ida."

Peter, who was always very proud of local cricket in the area as well as Guyana and the West Indies, began by saying, "I will speak more about cricket as long as you are prepared to listen to me as we go around the country. But, as we are here opposite the former Leonora Cricket Club and Ground, there were many great players like Boodhoo Dwarka, a classy right-handed batsman who was similar in style to the legendary Rohan Kanhai of Port Mourant, Berbice, Guyana and the West Indies. Nabi Bacchus was a local exciting allrounder who would regularly hit big sixes out of the ground and across this road and some of the balls bounced as far as into the pond within the school yard."

Afzal pretended to hold a cricket bat and swing it as if he was Nabi Bacchus, "Peter, as a Leonoran, let me help you with some more names here. We had a fast bowler by the name of Godfrey Granger who was a Barbadian, and a couple of guys who bowled like the English spinners Tony Lock and Jim Laker, so we called them "Lock" and "Laker". There was the great Guyana and West Indies Umpire Tulsi Kumar and his brother, Hardat Kumar who was always well turned out in his bright white cricket shirt, trousers and boots. Leonora had another fine young batsman named Lildat Persaud who was also a right-handed player with the style of Rohan Kanhai. A few years later they had another good right-hander named Mahammad "Tonka" Ali."

Peter gave a thumbs up and added, "Please forgive us ladies for talking so much about cricket and cricketers. I wish to add another spinner by the name of Man Singh who was called "Benups" after the great Australian Richie Benaud."

Arthur frowned as he said, "As a local Chinese, I must say that I was never good at cricket, but I did teach myself how to play table tennis and became very good at it. There were some good players at the Cornelia Ida Cricket Club including a guy called Tamal Deo who was also a fine cricketer."

Vishnu thanked Peter and Afzal for their recollection of some of the great cricketers of Leonora and said, "I know, Peter, that you are a staunch CI cricket follower, and hopefully you will share some thoughts about the great cricketers from that place. Incidentally, when in 1964 we had the racial disturbance and conflict between African and Indian Guyanese, the British troops stationed at the site where we will be visiting, introduced football at CI and in a very short time the local team became very strong and competitive. In fact, the core of that team was made up of several members of the Mahadeo family of Anna Catherina. They were Walter, Neville, "Blackie", David and their cousin Henry the goalkeeper and who was also a good off-spinner for the senior CI cricket team. In the early days the British troops' football teams used to thrash the local lads until the last game of their stay in Guyana, they were badly beaten by ten goals to nil. It is always a source of great pleasure to beat our former British masters at all games that they invented, and especially cricket and football."

Carlos added, "Let me also say that we as Guyanese people of so many races and cultures, share a great ability to learn and master anything once we are given a chance. We need that passion right now to grab all the amazing opportunities on offer especially in the oil and gas industry and the many spin-off activities both offshore and onshore. The quicker our young people take up the training and development and go for those jobs, the better. We must not rely on foreigners for too long into the future. We must continue to grow our own!"

Maria reached over and hugged Carlos with great pride.

Parvati held Ramesh's left hand and Sati's right hand and lifted them up as if in triumph as she said, "These are the people with the right kinds of skills and experience you are talking about. Also, their children should be looking for opportunities to come back here and build their futures. The young President Irfaan Ali, who was born and bred right here in Leonora, has been literally begging Guyanese from abroad to come back home to invest and to help transform this country."

Nazir stepped forward and commented, "You are so right. Now that you mention President Ali, let me tell you a bit more about how he is personally connected here. You have heard of the late Haji Abdool Kadeer of Anna Catherina. Well, the President's grandma was Sakina, a daughter of Haji Kadeer. Also, the President's grandfather, the late Kaiser Mohamed, was the son of the late Dost Mohamed of Leonora. Of course, his other grandparents are from the island of Leguan in Essequibo. His parents, Osman Ali fondly known as "Sir" and Shariman known as "Miss", have served the communities of Hague, Cornelia Ida, Anna Catherina, Leonora and Stewartville, as excellent teachers for most of their lives. I, like the vast majority of Guyanese, love this young man's passion, energy, vision and hands on hard work both here and abroad. He comes from families of similar values, and we have never seen a President like him in this country. And I think that he and his government have already achieved incredible things in such a short time since 2020. I am looking forward to much more of the building and development of the country in the next few years and more. The current pace of change is breathtaking!"

Arthur nodded and affirmed, "We Guyanese now need to take away our prejudices and dislikes and get behind everyone who is here working round the clock to build the things that we should have had over the past fifty years. President Ali is reaching out to many countries and the response has been truly amazing. Some people say that the government is borrowing too much money too quickly to build infrastructure. But I am sure that Ramesh and Sati here who understand Economics, can shed more light on this."

Before either Ramesh or Sati could respond, Nazir pointed out, "Look, this government is not the one I voted for because of the things being said and posted on social media and the local press back in 2015. But I must say that I was badly let down by the last government whose people ended up doing worse than what they were accusing President Donald Ramotar's lot for. I regret ever switching my loyalty at that time, and now I know which party to vote for in the next elections. My conscience is clear."

Ramesh shook Nazir's right hand and said, "Uncle Nazir, you are clearly a man of integrity. Everyone in Guyana has the right to vote for whomsoever they wish to support for whatever reason. You are also free to change your mind. That is what democracy is all about."

Afzal joined in the conversation and rubbed his stomach as he mentioned, "Well, let's not dwell too much on politics now. I am really hungry and I hope that Ramesh booked a spot for us to have lunch at the mall."

Ramesh smiled and confirmed, "Yes Uncle Afzal. I did a booking for the Atlantis Cuisine restaurant there, and we have some time before we take up our seats. In answer to Uncle Arthur's question about economic debt, as far as I know, the amount of borrowing by this government is well within the pace of economic growth not only from the oil revenues, but also from other sectors. Guyana has the fastest growing economy in the world, and not all the developments we will see in the country are funded by the government. The West Central Mall as well as the Sheriff Hospital nearby are developments built by Guyanese investors. This government is actively encouraging such investments from the private sector and have a good progressive relationship with businesses and entrepreneurs."

John and Nazir signalled for the tour party to continue their journey to the West Central Mall.

Sati raised her right hand and said, "Just before we proceed, I wish to mention one more thing about the debt. By the time the new President Cheddi Jagan's government took office back in 1992, it was found that for every ten Guyana dollars earned, the previous government had to pay back nine dollars in interest. Guyana had become the second poorest country in the Western hemisphere after Haiti. I think that is something for us all to chew over."

There was ample space in front of the mall for parking, and the tour party stepped out of the cars into the hot midday sun. The ladies took out their hand-held fans and began to seek some relief from the intense heat. Ramesh and Sati asked everyone to follow the lead of Nazir and John as they all headed to the impressive entrance of the site.

Arthur paused and pointed out, "Man, I love the welcoming sign and images of green elephants at the front as we drove in. I also love the main colours of the Guyana flag being used for decoration."

As soon as they all reached inside the complex, Michael heaved a great sigh of relief.

"Phew! We need this coolness. Please let us take some time to stroll over to that restaurant and then look around here to see what is on offer for local shoppers. I notice a fair amount of people milling around, and they seem to be enjoying the place."

Nazir and John continued to lead the tour party up towards the Atlantis Cuisine restaurant on the top floor of the mall. A special assembly of chairs and tables was prepared for the group to sit together for their lunch. Vishnu took a video of the impressive and elaborate décor of the restaurant depicting an underwater scene of the ruins of the lost city of Atlantis.

Michael was the first to offer his personal impression, "This is a truly incredible venue, and it clearly has a high-class international feel about it. I love the décor and the fact that we can also sit outside on the terrace and take in a great view of the village which is clearly being transformed from the days of being a sugar estate. Leonora, along with other villages around the country, is becoming a small and more modernised town right in the middle of our dear West Coast of Demerara. However, I cannot resist noting that the idea of dining under a submerged ancient city does not bode well with the fact that here on the coastland, we are already a few feet below the level of the Atlantic Ocean which is so near to us!"

Afzal was anxious to look at the menu, and raised his eyebrows as he observed, "Well, I must say that this feels like we are in some high-class restaurant in America as Michael said. On the one hand, this is lifting up the choices for local people by the offer of a wide variety of international dishes alongside our more traditional curries, roti and rice. But, on the other hand, I have to question whether the locals are ready for this. No doubt, it is very impressive for us as tourists."

Arthur pointed out, "This restaurant and mall show how ambitious Guyana is becoming. It's like we are emerging from the depths of despair and poverty and rising to the top of the mountains. My question now is, how does this fit in with local peoples' taste, and more importantly, whether they can afford these prices."

Carlos looked across his seat at Vishnu and commented, "First of all I can see that this place and the many businesses on this site are providing lots of jobs for local people. Mainly young people. Secondly, I notice that whilst a lot of visitors are here, I don't see many of them with a collection of shopping bags filled with purchases. I do hope that the owners of the businesses have done their market research and are advertising their goods well."

Vishnu paused his attempt to select his meal from the menu and responded to Carlos, "Guyana needs to encourage more home-grown jobs, and this is only one example. As for local taste, I am sure that you can all remember that when we were young, we did enjoy foods from mainly America, like popcorn, ice cream and even the fried chicken sold by an outlet called Brown Betty. I recall that after practising our cricket we used to buy apple juice in cans at Oscar Bam's. As for the customers I see here, of course there are a lot of them who will come out and spend a couple of hours looking around for any bargains they could find. One worry I have is how much of this crowd pulling will take away business from local shops and supermarkets around the villages. Just as we have seen in America, Canada and elsewhere, the malls have destroyed many local businesses. I do hope that things will settle down and both can thrive here alongside each other."

Ramesh pointed out, "Don't forget that online shopping is already increasing here in Guyana, and that will pose a big threat in the future unless both the local businesses and those inside the malls can adapt and use that facility as well."

Doreen showed Michael the items she chose from the menu and then said, "I am sure that the ladies here will agree with me that from what we have seen so far, this is a shopping haven. They have such a great variety of goods here and more eating places with local and foreign dishes. The families all along the West Coast will be flocking here and hopefully some will also check out the local shops. Besides, I think that especially the local ladies and girls would prefer to shop here in Leonora than go into Georgetown where they may feel unsafe. As more malls are established around the country, I guess that the traditional business places in the big towns and cities will lose a lot of their customers."

The ladies around the table gave Doreen their thumbs up in agreement. Two uniformed young hostesses approached the table and took the orders for refreshment and the main courses.

Carlos made his choices and commented, "Well, I must say that I am impressed with the excellent variety of food on offer here. Can we also order some side dishes to share amongst ourselves?"

Michael and Doreen were quick to agree with Carlos's suggestions, and Michael added, "When we have all had our meals here, I would like for us to share the bill amongst all of us except for Nazir, Neesha, John and Muriel as our first gesture of thanks for all that they have done for us so far."

There was an immediate show of agreement by all the other members of the group. Nazir, John and their wives tried to refuse the offer by their guests but Vishnu in particular, was adamant that the bill would be shared as suggested.

Nazir was determined to contribute to the lunch and offered, "Well, thank you all very much. But please, I insist that John and I are at least allowed to do the tipping."

After their hearty and sumptuous meal, the tour party got up, thanked the manager and staff of the restaurant and began to stroll around the shops, boutiques, electronics outlets, children's clothing and other eating and refreshment establishments. When the tour ended, they gathered around near the exit and Ramesh and Sati noticed that the oldest members were tired. So, they suggested a short drive around the village of Stewartville and the remainder of Leonora before returning to relax at Nazir's and Neesha's home.

Michael reflected on the tour and mentioned, "I think that we have seen another glimpse of the direction that Guyana is heading towards. Whilst it was sad to see the empty site where our historic Leonora sugar factory stood, and the other places such as the train station and railway line gone, we are still relying on the Dutch built canals and *kokers* here and around the country. I am personally very happy that at least some of the largest sugar factories are still functioning. Same for the rice factories. I do hope that we will see some of the new Agriculture processing plants that I have heard about. Well, after such a lovely and interesting day, I am now looking forward to some more rest."

Vishnu added, "One thing I have already noticed whilst we were driven around or through the many villages is that whilst some of them are progressing well through the amazing new housing and other buildings, there are many others where the signs of real poverty are clear to see. Michael, you had pointed out this difference of richness and poverty. What do you think should be done for the people and those villages?"

Michael referred to his notebook and said, "First of all, I would like to see some real affirmative action by government and the private sector in going into those villages and working with the residents on the badly needed improvements. I would start with the villages which were initially purchased by the freed slaves including Victoria, Buxton, Belladrum, Golden Grove of East Coast Demerara, Golden Grove of West Coast Berbice, Plaisance, Den Amstel, Litchfield and Nabaclis. There are many more poor villages around the country and they should all be supported in their development. This would be a good way of showing the country and Guyanese everywhere how people and places are benefitting from the oil money!"

Everyone shouted "Hear! Hear!"

14

To Berbice: Of migrants, martyrs, mysteries and minds over matter

Bright and early the next morning, the tour party met for breakfast at Nazir's and Neesha's residence, and as they retired to the sitting room, Ramesh and Sati stood before the group to announce the plans for the day.

Sati began by saying, "I can see that we all had a well-deserved rest from so much strolling around yesterday. I am much younger than almost everyone here and I slept like a log. Even Ramesh's loud elephant-like snoring did not disturb me. Anyway, let's get down to business. We have chosen a trip to Berbice from where we are in Region 3 through Regions 4, 5 and 6. As you know, Guyana has ten administrative regions, and our intention is to tour at least one place or site in each of them. Each Region has something quite special about it and it is very important for us to explore as many of them as we can. This is in itself a great challenge for us all."

Ramesh, armed with his iPhone, opened it and referred to the plan. "Berbice is a very interesting place, and Uncle Michael tells me that there is important history he would like to mention as we travel over many miles from here. We will stop for comfort breaks and lunch along the way. Of course, if you feel that the trip becomes too tiring then we can agree to cut it short until another day. Uncle Nazir is happy to take on all the driving for our group, and Uncle John and Uncle Afzal will share the driving for their group."

Michael, wearing a white T-shirt with a print of the Kofi national monument at the front, and a pair of khaki shorts to go with his white designer sneakers, raised his right hand and said, "I hope that we will all be able to do the entire trip, and I propose to tell you more about the story of this man Kofi you see on my T-shirt when we stop for lunch or other break. I promise to keep it short whilst we wait for our meals."

Ramesh invited anyone else to comment, and Peter was the first to respond, "Well, I would like for us to stop at Port Mourant village in Berbice, and I wish to mention some truly legendary cricket heroes of mine from that area."

Muriel pointed out, "I have never travelled to Berbice, so I am looking forward to this trip. I know that of the Berbicians that I have met when they visited Georgetown, they are very friendly and hospitable people."

John was supportive of Muriel's comment and added, "Yes, I do agree about the nature of Berbicians. But that should not be surprising as they are like all Guyanese who are known for our kindness and hospitality towards others. I believe that whilst we in Demerara have had a history of more political and social unrest and upheaval over the last few decades, the people of Berbice have not had quite the same amount of turmoil. The same can be said of Essequibo apart from the events such as the invasion of Ankoko and that terrible Jonestown saga."

Carlos raised his right hand and said, "John, I can add the fact that we also witnessed an uprising in Rupununi in Southern Essequibo. I think I can see where you are going with this. Perhaps you are right about Berbicians not having to experience the kinds of conflicts we have seen elsewhere in Guyana including the riots and burnings in Georgetown in the 1960s. Berbicians have perhaps avoided a lot of the trauma as experienced elsewhere in the country."

Afzal could not resist the old taunt, "Man, we all know that the country's madhouse is in Berbice. That's where all Guyanese mad people end up."

Arthur frowned and asked, "Are you saying that because the Guyana National Psychiatric Hospital is in Fort Canje, in Berbice, that Berbicians "head na good"? That is very unfair. In fact, I think that most of the brightest of Guyanese people come from Berbice!"

Peter agreed, "Not because the madhouse is in a place, it means that the mad people come from there. In fact, it's our people with severe mental health issues who are outside of Berbice, who end up for treatment there."

Nazir shook his head and pointed out, "I think that Mental Illness is a very big issue for all Guyanese. It is not a laughing matter. It should be taken much more seriously and dealt with through preventative interventions. We are seeing a lot of our young people, failing to cope with problems such as unemployment, breakdowns in relationships and the temptations of illegal drug taking and too much alcohol. These things have been contributing to very high suicide rates. In addition, these pressures have also been leading to petty as well as very serious crimes."

Doreen kissed her teeth and advised, "These problems have been with us even in countries such as America, Canada and the UK. There is no magic wand to resolve them. But I agree that prevention is better than cure. I hope that the wealth that the country is beginning to enjoy will go a long way to helping the most vulnerable people in society to cope with their pressures, as well as fund the right kind of care that is needed when people fall through the net so to speak. However, there will always be a small core of people who cannot cope because of their disability. They should be treated with the best care and not left abandoned and unwanted."

Muriel agreed and added, "There is another quiet killer in our midst, and it is called dementia. As our fellow Guyanese of the older generation survive longer, we will see much more evidence of this terrible disease. Once again, it is very important for dementia to be spotted and diagnosed as early as possible and then for patients to be given the right support. I know that through our lack of understanding the symptoms of dementia as well as Alzheimer's diseases, sufferers can be subjected to mistreatment even by their own family members and some elements in society who think that the unfortunate sufferers are mentally ill."

Parvati nodded and said, "I know that we are on this trip to Guyana to enjoy the beauty and everything that is great about our country. But I can see that we cannot avoid speaking about some of the ills in our society. I think that you are all trying to emphasise that prevention will go a long way to solving these problems. I hope that the same can be done to help reduce crime from petty stealing to bigger things like violent robberies, and the curse of too much corruption as well as fraud."

Ramesh nodded and added, "As the country develops further, there is one very significant issue that will need to be tackled. It is called cyber crime. This can cause incredible damage to almost everything here in Guyana, and I am sure that the government is aware of this danger. I think that the way to tackle this is by more international support bearing in mind the need to avoid taking such help from certain countries which have been involved in cyber crime activity against other countries."

Nazir frowned and commented, "I am happy that you are all suggesting ways to deal with Guyana's problems and talking about how they are being approached in your own countries. But I still see that you have much bigger problems with mental illness and crime in America, Canada and the UK. We in Guyana also know how to tackle our problems, and hopefully there will be greater progress in all of these ills as the country develops."

Shortly after having their breakfast, the two cars with the hosts and visitors headed off eastwards along the nine miles from Anna Catherina to Vreed en Hoop and across the Demerara Harbour Bridge, through Georgetown and onto the East Coast Demerara Road alongside miles of the seawall defence. They passed through many villages with more evidence of massive constructions of elaborate mansion-like housing, large business premises, a huge mall and the construction site of the new highway from Ogle to Eccles on the East Bank of Demerara, designed to bypass Georgetown's growing traffic congestion.

The group paused for a few minutes to observe the popular and thriving Mon Repos Market comprising dozens of roadside stalls and the main site well known for the sales of fresh sea food, meat, vegetables and fruits. Nazir and Neesha took the opportunity to purchase some chicken, lamb and beef which were carefully packed in three separate "ice boxes" and securely placed in the boot of their car. They were pleased to note that the chicken, lamb and beef were *halaal* and they also bought a large gilbaaka fish as well as some shrimps to be kept in their ample sized freezer.

Vishnu asked Nazir whether he had managed to secure his items at good prices.

Neesha was pleased to confirm, "Yes, we bought our items at reasonably lower prices. In fact, you must have noticed that we stepped away from our group so that we did not end up with inflated prices."

Michael was perplexed by Neesha's reference to inflated pricing and asked, "Are you suggesting that we as foreigners would be charged higher prices?"

Afzal stepped forward and pointed out, "No Michael, Nazir and Neesha knew where to buy their foodstuff from. These vendors are very keen to sell off their products as quickly as possible, and they would be shooting themselves in the foot by trying to inflate their prices because you look foreign. Mind you, everyone could see how strange you appear in your outfit, and you can see some people staring at you and smiling. You might even be lucky to get some discounts just because of your looks!"

Ramesh and Sati asked the group about how they were feeling as the warm morning was giving way towards a hotter midday. Everyone agreed to continue with the tour through the villages of Annandale, Buxton and their next unscheduled stop at the Enmore Martyrs Monument. Michael requested the men in the group to allow the women to walk slowly up the path leading to the tall five-sided white structure. Each column bore a name neatly engraved below a cutlass rising upwards as a symbol of defiance and fight by the sugar workers who had lost their lives during a protest for their rights.

He then asked for a solemn minute of silence before relating the story behind the monument, "I must look into my notebook to make sure that I give you the right information about why this monument is here and why this event inspired greatness and the long fight for our independence and freedom. You see, way back in November 1946, some young people named, Dr Cheddi Jagan, his American wife Janet, a true hero Ashton Chase, and Jocelyn Hubbard formed the Political Affairs Committee or PAC to campaign for the introduction of universal suffrage, self-government, fair pay and land reform. Then the PAC merged with the British Guiana Labour Party to form the Peoples' Progressive Party or PPP in 1950. Incidentally, that BG Labour Party included Dr JB Singh."

Vishnu interrupted Michael and requested, "My brother, please don't go into the politics now and do tell us about the five martyrs whose names are on this monument."

Nazir commented, "Vishnu, I do not mind that Michael can refer to our politics. Everything in this country has some element of politics behind it. Please allow Michael to continue."

Michael turned a page in his notebook and proceeded, "Thank you. To cut a long story short, the sugar plantation workers here and at a few other estates nearby, went on strike in 1948 mainly about conditions of work on the estates especially about the issue of a very unfair change from the old "cut and drop" of the sugarcane by the canecutters, to a much more demanding "cut and load" system for the same money. Just think about this for a moment. It was bad enough to cut the damn sugarcane, and really unfair to all those hard-working people to then bundle them up, lift them and carry them to the punts waiting in the canals. Not only that, but the men never trusted the weighing system at the sugar factory, and always felt that they were being underpaid."

Doreen and the other women in the group began to feel more uncomfortable in the heat and put on their head coverings whilst using their hand fans to try to stave off the warm air from their faces. They looked at Michael anxiously, and Doreen signalled for him to speed up his talk.

Michael nodded and continued, "One other main grievance the workers had was a mistrust of the trades union called the Manpower Citizens Association and opted for the Guiana Industrial Workers Union or GIWU which later became the Guiana Agriculture Workers Union or GAWU. So, on the sixteenth of June 1948, about four hundred workers protested outside the Enmore Sugar Factory. When many of them breached the police defences, unfortunately they were fired upon, and five men by the names Rambarran, Lall known as Pooran, Lallabagie Kissoon, Surujballi known as Dookie, and Harry, paid the ultimate price with their lives."

Michael paused, as he and the others in the group began to wipe tears from their eyes as they slowly began to walk around the monument and stop briefly to look at the names of each of the five martyrs. They then assembled at the front to listen to Michael who was keen to conclude his talk.

He cleared his throat, lowered his spectacles onto his nose, and said, "The reason why I wanted for us all to see this monument goes beyond those events. What happened here in 1948 sparked the beginning of the long career of our late President Dr Cheddi B Jagan who was among those that joined the funeral procession all the way to the cemetery at Le Repentir in Georgetown. In his book, *The West on Trial*, he states, "At the graveside, the emotional outburst of the widows and relatives of the deceased were intensely distressing and I could not restrain my tears. There was to be no turning back. There and then

I made a silent pledge. I would dedicate my entire life to the cause of the struggle of the Guianese people against bondage and oppression.".''

Nazir pointed out, "By the way, the Enmore Martyrs' Day is an annual Public Holiday on the sixteenth of June."

Shortly afterwards, the tour party solemnly and quietly boarded their cars, and they headed back on the main road towards Rosignol passing through Mahaica, across the Mahaica River, Mahaicony, and where many other villages and plantations of rice, banana, plantain, coconut and cattle farms abound. As they passed through Mahaicony, Nazir reminded his group about the strange tree located in the middle of the road as if on an island.

He slowed down sufficiently to allow Vishnu to video the tree as he said, "I think that you must have heard about this tree. I do not know up to this day as to why this tree is still here. But there are all kinds of superstitious stories about it. Michael must be able to shed some light on the matter."

Michael readily answered Nazir's request, "Yes, it is a very old silk cotton tree which carries a lot of folklore amongst the peoples of West Africa as well as our own Amerindian people. They say that the roots go deep into the soil and the branches reach up to the heaven. So, people are afraid to cut them down. Even the Dutch settlers here were also fearful of the powers of the silk cotton trees."

Doreen was not convinced about Michael's take on the silk cotton tree, and challenged him, "Now tell me something. Why have such trees been chopped down elsewhere, and we never heard of any evil things happening to the people who did so? And why must this single old tree cast such a spell on sensible Guyanese people here? And for so long?"

Sati was also perplexed about the importance of the tree, and commented, "Well, I agree with Aunty Doreen on this one. To me, the stories have been allowed to persist so much over the years that people have become more afraid of the invisible power which they believe that it possesses."

Parvati added, "I could see both sides to this. I guess that John and Muriel will have a different view about the powers of not only one old silk cotton tree, but of all trees!"

Ramesh raised his eyebrows and remarked, "We haven't even reached Berbice and we are into martyrdom, mental illness and mystery. I can't wait to see and hear what else Berbice has to offer."

The two cars continued to make good progress towards Rosignol for the toll bridge crossing to New Amsterdam, Berbice. When they had passed the Mahaica River, Michael took out his well-known notebook and decided to inform the group in Nazir's car about a very important bird of Guyana.

He turned in his seat so that Vishnu, Ramesh and the three ladies at the back could hear him, "We passed the Mahaica River which flows from the hinterland to the coast, and if we wanted to view some more interesting bird life, I heard that a boat trip up the river is very interesting. So, let me ask you all a simple question. Which bird is known as Guyana's national symbol?"

Vishnu offered, "I think that the toucan is most associated with Guyana."

Doreen shouted from the back, "No! I would go for the beautiful macaw!"

Nazir raised his right hand from the steering wheel and suggested, "Ah, this is easy man. I think that our amazing harpy eagle, which is the world's largest, is the Guyana national bird."

Michael shook his head disappointedly and said, "I like all of your suggestions as they are very beautiful and interesting birds. But the answer is the hoatzin also known as the Canje pheasant or stink bird. It is a unique bird that is the only one of its sort of lineage and some experts say that it is connected with the bird species of the dinosaur age. It is a very large creature that cannot fly far and can be seen in the daytime up on the trees near to the water's edge. Another unique thing about it is that the chicks have a couple of claws on their wings which are used as defence and for climbing back up the trees if they fall out of their nests. In about three months, they then lose those claws."

Ramesh, like the others in the group, was fascinated, "So, why are they known as the stink bird? I have a picture here on my iPhone showing how ugly and clumsy the hoatzin is with its large red eyes set in its blue face and with mostly brown and red outer feathers. It also has very long tail feathers."

Michael acknowledged Ramesh's comments and continued, "The hoatzin eats a lot of leaves and takes a long time to digest them, and when they shit, it stinks like hell! That is why they are called stink birds. They are not related to pheasants, and the name Canje pheasant is misleading. So, there you have it. The hoatzin is Guyana's National Bird mostly for its uniqueness."

Ramesh observed, "Uncle Michael, thank you as always for your knowledge and wisdom. We have only been in the country for a few days now and have seen and heard some amazing and fascinating sites and stories. Regardless of the new oil wealth, I must say that this country is truly blessed with awesome beauty and mystery. If other countries have only half of our treasures, they would be boasting to the world. The majestic lift off and flight of the hoatzin is an appropriate representation of our Guyana on the rise!"

The two cars soon reached the crossing point of the floating Berbice River Bridge where the toll is paid one way only from the west. The bridge presented a much smoother and less clunky ride than the Demerara Harbour Bridge. Both bridges are quite long with the Demerara Harbour Bridge being just over six thousand feet and the fourth longest floating bridge in the world. The Berbice Bridge is just over five thousand one hundred feet long and the sixth longest in the world. It replaced the ferry service to New Amsterdam in 2008.

Nazir announced, "I have checked when this bridge will be closed for about one and a half hours today, and we will then plan our return journey for when it is re-opened. We will not be seeing the old ferry stelling in New Amsterdam, but I have to say that the area around the stelling has lost almost all of its former vibrance with lots of businesses and other enterprises closed down and with no sign as to what will or should be in their place. I put this down to really bad planning. I do hope that this is not being repeated in the rush for development around the country."

Vishnu agreed and observed, "I notice that at both ends of the bridge there is no real collection of small business enterprises as you normally see around ferry stellings where passengers mill around before boarding the ferry or boats. This attracts businesses, but the fast-moving vehicle traffic over the new bridges does not offer the same kind of commerce and of course, job opportunities."

Nazir's main focus upon arrival in New Amsterdam was to find a good restaurant for the tour party. He stopped in Main Street and invited John and his group to confirm their preference for lunch.

Arthur wanted some more local cuisine and suggested, "I like the look of the Lim Kang Restaurant and their offer of a good range of

Cantonese food. But I prefer to have my dinner there instead of lunch. So, I will go along with the majority choice."

Carlos listened to Maria's whispered advice and said, "Maria and I are both quite hungry and will settle for some simple curry, either vegetable or meat."

Afzal frowned as he mentioned, "After having such an emotional stop at the martyrs' site, I am also happy with something light and simple."

John and Muriel shrugged their shoulders and she commented, "We are also happy to accept the majority choice."

Vishnu nodded and offered, "I do not mind except that after hearing about the Guyana's National bird's habit, I would like to be excused from any chicken or duck dishes for the moment."

The other members of the party looked at Ramesh and Sati for a decision, and Ramesh suggested, "Well, I think that we can have a simple lunch with some good choices to meet everyone's needs. I can see that we are not far away from a place called The Halal Guy in Pitt Street. I checked it out on the internet and it has a good rating. And, yes Dad, you can easily avoid their chicken and duck curries."

The group enjoyed the restful and relaxed atmosphere at The Halal Guy restaurant and chatted amongst themselves in good spirit. After their meal, Ramesh ensured that the bill was split evenly amongst the group except for Nazir, Neesha, John and Muriel as was agreed.

He asked everyone, "Are you all OK? Its feeling a bit hotter now and we have to do some more touring here in Berbice. I must say that all the roads we have used so far have been really good and our drivers have made us feel safe and comfortable. Having a good road system as well as other forms of transport to move goods and people are critical for the economy and progress."

There was a resounding "Yes!" from the group and they spontaneously applauded. Ramesh and Sati acknowledged the cheering and pointed to the drivers with great appreciation.

Ramesh responded, "Thank you on behalf of our little unofficial planning team. I know that we had a solemn experience in Enmore, but now that we are in the heart of Berbice, we must stop to view the Indian Arrival Monument at Palmyra which is located next to the site for a new stadium there."

The tour party assembled briefly at the main gates to the monument site, and Vishnu stepped forward to speak about Indian Indentureship before they proceeded along the neatly paved walkway leading up to the imposing platform and sculpture of six bronze figures depicting images of Indian workers. The monument was envisaged and completed through a collaboration of the Guyana and Indian governments. The sculpture was designed and built by Guyanese artists Philbert Gajadhar and Winslow Craig.

Vishnu began, "I am sure that we as Guyanese know about the history of our enslaved African brothers and sisters who had to endure unimaginable suffering and hardship for hundreds of years right up to the end of slavery in 1834. Before we consider the arrival of just under 210,000 of our Indian ancestors from the 5th May 1838 through to April 1917 when Indian Indentureship ended, we must not forget that many of our Indigenous Amerindian brothers and sisters were also enslaved by the Dutch colonists. After the emancipation of enslaved Africans, the first Indentured labourers brought here to work on the sugar estates were our Portuguese brothers and sisters from the island of Madeira in the Atlantic Ocean from 1835. Carlos and Maria, we also honour your ancestors. Likewise, Arthur, our Chinese brothers and sisters were brought to Guyana in 1853 from Macao. Together, in this group, we stand in awe and in honour of our ancestors who toiled, struggled, shed their tears and blood so that we can come together as one in our beautiful country. I am not a historian, but I hope I have given you a very brief account of the people that make up Guyana, and how our ancestors laid the foundations for freedom and progress."

The group instantly applauded Vishnu's statement, and Michael added, "Yes, we must continue to strive as one people and resist any attempt to divide and separate us. I do not think that this should be down to our politicians alone, but by all of us from within our hearts and minds, our families, our communities and everywhere we live as Guyanese whether here or abroad."

Vishnu nodded in agreement with Michael and said, "I wish to add that there is another monument called the Indian Arrival Memorial Monument in Georgetown's Monument Gardens in Merriman's Mall off Camp Street. It is a replica of one in Kolkata, India, and has a bronze sculpture of the SS Whitby which was one of the first two ships that arrived in Guyana on the 5th of May 1838. It is perched on a black granite plinth and was unveiled by the Late Yesu Persaud in May 1997. Mr Ashook Ramsaran, the President of the Indian Diaspora Council played a key role in the establishment of the monument and museum there."

Shortly before the tour party boarded the two cars to continue their tour, Michael opened his notebook and wished to share some more information, "Whilst we are here in Berbice, I would like to mention a very little-known Guyanese by the name of Sir Edward Trenton "ET" Richards who was born here in Adelphi Village, in Canje. I can see many raised eyebrows, and that tells me that most if not all of you have never heard of this great scholar, teacher, lawyer, politician and civil rights fighter."

Vishnu smiled with great appreciation of his friend and remarked, "Ah! There goes our Histry Maan again! Always with some great surprise!"

Michael nodded and continued, "ET was the first non-white or black Head of Government in Bermuda between 1971 and 1973, and Premier between 1973 and 1975. He was born in 1908 and migrated to Bermuda at the age of twenty-one to teach maths. He then studied Law in London and was called to the Middle Temple Bar in 1946. He became leader of the United Bermuda Party or UBP, and in 1970 he was elected the first black person of Bermuda to be knighted by the late Queen Elizabeth the Second. He fought to remove the apartheid that existed in Bermuda, and sadly passed away there in 1991 at the age of eighty-two. What an inspirational Guyanese! Now, let us move on to another very important monument in honour of the great soul from Port Mourant, at Babu John."

Vishnu hugged Michael, and then the tour party proceeded towards Port Mourant almost drunk with an overload of martyrdom, fighters for freedom and a taste of some of the mystique of Guyana.

15

Kofi Badu, Babu John and Bholalal

The main road entrance to the sugar estate and village of Port Mourant is dominated by an extensive and long market with numerous stalls of fruits, vegetables, fish and other fresh meat, general household goods including clothing, utensils and other products. Both cars were parked alongside the road for a brief stay to allow Michael to speak about a significant event in the history of Guyana under Dutch rule in the eighteenth century.

He pointed proudly to the figure of Kofi on his T-shirt, and began, "We do not have much time for me to tell you all of what happened during what is known as the Berbice Slave Rebellion from the twenty-third of February 1763, and which lasted for around one year. Once again, I need to refer to my notebook and just give you some of the highlights of the rebellion. The Dutch plantation owners had established several sugar and coffee estates along the Berbice River with Fort Nassau as the main centre of defence and administration for the area. The enslaved people who were mostly from West Africa, were being treated very badly and harshly punished for the smallest thing. A group of the people attacked estates on the Canje River, and then many more joined in. By the end of March that year, they captured most of the plantations. The leader was Kofi Badu, and his two main captains were Atta and Accara. The Dutch Governor was Wolfert Van Hoogenheim, and he along with a small army took refuge at Fort Nassau. Kofi kept Sara George who was only nineteen, and the daughter of the plantation owner of Peerenboom, as his wife, and declared himself as Governor of Berbice."

Doreen's eyes lit up as she exclaimed, "Wow! He must have been a very brave man to do that!"

Michael nodded and continued, "You can all check out the whole story of the rebellion, and for now, I can say that whilst Kofi and his companions of around three thousand were very successful in the early weeks, the Dutch waited patiently and anxiously for reinforcements. Eventually, they defeated the rebels who became disunited and argued amongst themselves. Kofi tried to make peace with the Dutch Governor, but this did not work, and he eventually shot and killed himself. The Dutch caught most of the rebels with the help of some Amerindians, punished them severely with torture, and executed many of them most brutally. Sorry, but I cannot go on as I am feeling very upset about this."

Vishnu once again hugged his friend and solemnly said, "I share your grief, Michael. We all feel the same pain of suppression and it is right and fitting that Kofi Badu is Guyana's National Hero. I hope that we will visit the 1763 Monument in the Square of the Revolution in Georgetown."

Nazir pointed out, "Kofi Badu, also called Cuffy, was of the Akan tribe and many of the rebels were Muslim. I am so proud of them. Did you know that Muslim slaves were from the Fula tribe of West Africa? Well, that is why people like me, Neesha and Afzal are referred to as "Fulaman". Kofi means Friday and as you may know, this day is significant for Muslims as we do our *Jumma Namaz*. Many West African children who are born on Friday are given the name Kofi. One of the most famous people with that name was Kofi Anan of Ghana, the former Secretary General of the United Nations. He was also an Akan."

Carlos added, "I am also happy to recognise Kofi or Cuffy as our National Hero. The twenty-third of February 1970 was chosen as our Republic Day, and it is one of our national holidays."

John frowned before commenting, "As a member of our First Peoples here in Guyana, I would have preferred for one of my ancestors to have been called the National Hero. However, Muriel and I are happy to have the Amerindian Heritage month in September each year. This month was chosen as it was on the tenth of September in 1957, our first ever Amerindian parliamentarian, Stephen Campbell was sworn in. I hope that we will all visit the Umana Yana in Georgetown on one of our trips. The tenth of September is known as Amerindian Heritage Day."

The next stop for the tour party was at the Babu John cemetery.

Michael, who had regained his composure, announced, "Well, whilst we have been speaking of heroes, here we are at the cremation site commemorating the man whom many Guyanese regard as the "Father of the Nation". Let me say that I personally wished that both Dr Cheddi Jagan and Mister Forbes Burnham who were together to form the first really important political party, the PPP, had stayed together and worked for a united Guyana. This country would have been far more advanced by now. But in 1955, Burnham left the PPP and formed the People's National Congress or PNC. I am sad to say that it divided our country on racial Indian versus African lines. Most Guyanese know our political history very well, and I will not dwell anymore on this. Except to say that this country can do with some healing as we move forward together as One People, One Nation, with One Destiny. This vision is attributed to Mister Burnham."

Arthur raised his right hand and announced, "As a Chinese Guyanese, I do agree with you Michael. We cannot afford to go on and on talking about Indian and African Guyanese. We are not a nation of only two races, and whilst I am proud of my namesake Arthur Raymond Chung, who was our first President of Guyana from 1970 to 1980, I wish that more Chinese Guyanese could enter politics here and help to bring us all together."

Carlos nodded and added, "I know that as a Portuguese, we had Mister Peter Stanislaus D'Aguiar who was a great businessman and leader of the third most powerful political party called the United Force or UF. He became staunchly anti-communist and was supported by the US Government in the 1960s. He formed a coalition with the PNC under the system of proportional representation, or PR, in 1964. I am ashamed to say that he was found by an Inquiry, to be heavily involved in stirring up the riots in Georgetown in February 1962. I suppose you can say that he redeemed himself when he held Jagan's hand and they both walked out of the parliament in 1968 accusing Burnham of electoral fraud."

Peter smiled and raised his right hand pretending to drink, "Don't forget, D'Aguiar brought us Pepsi Cola and invented Banks Beer."

Carlos replied, "Yes, I wish that he had continued to be a great businessman like so many of my fellow Portuguese Guyanese."

Doreen stepped forward and pleaded, "Hey, please stop talking about men only! Right here is also a memorial to Mistress Janet Jagan who, although a Jewish American, was a true patriot of Guyana. She was side by side with her husband Cheddi, and became the first female Prime Minister, and then the first and only woman so far, to become President in 1997."

Parvati added, "I would like to remember Bachaoni who was the mother of the Jagan family here in Port Mourant. She, as a widow, who had come from India as a child, brought up her eleven children almost single-handedly until she passed away in 1970. These are the women we should also honour."

All the women of the tour party hugged each other in a huddle. The men stood back and applauded them as a small crowd of local people stopped to look at the group with curiosity whilst chattering amongst themselves.

Michael wiped away some tears from his eyes, opened his notebook once again and said, "One thing I did not mention here at Babu John is another remarkable coincidence. You see, Dr Jagan passed away on the sixth of March 1997. Now, whilst we rightly remember and praise the great women of our country, please allow me to mention that on the sixth of March 1964, another great martyr by the name of Kowsilla also known as Alice, was crushed by a tractor on the bridge to the Leonora sugar factory whilst protesting in a sugar workers' strike. The driver of that tractor, Felix Barr, was a "scab" worker who even got off for that terrible murder. Many other brave women were seriously injured in that senseless attack, and they must all be remembered and honoured on every sixth of March."

Parvati raised her right hand and spoke, "Thank you Michael. Amongst the injured were Jagdai and her friend Daisee Sookram who both suffered with broken backs and became disabled. Another of the most seriously injured was Kisson Dai whose hips were broken. The sacrifices of all of Guyana's workers must never be forgotten as we all now enjoy many of the benefits of their struggles. These are my heroines."

Neesha who was normally very silent but attentive, decided to say something, "Michael, there was another woman named Sumintra who was also martyred at Leonora in 1939. Two men called Robert Carter and Gunpat were also shot and killed by police in that incident whilst protesting and on strike."

Vishnu also decided to add to the conversation, "Well, we must also remember that the first ever strike by Indian workers in Guyana took place at Leonora way back in 1869. That protest was inspired by our female ancestors. Now, whilst we are here in Berbice, I must mention the Rose Hall Plantation Uprising of the thirteenth of March 1913 where during legitimate and justified protests by workers against unfair treatment and broken promises by the management, the action unfortunately ended with the massacre of fifteen innocent Indian labourers."

Michael once again offered to share some more information on such an important event, and read from his notebook, "The Rose Hall Martyrs' Memorial in Canje, was built by the Government of Guyana and unveiled by President Donald Ramoutar on the thirteenth of March 2013, in honour of the fifteen people who were killed. They were Badri, Bholay, Durga, Gafur, Gobindei, Hulas, Jugai, Juggoo, Lalji, Motey Khan, Nibur, Roopan and Sohan. The fifteenth person was another female martyr by the name of Sadulla."

The saddened tour party moved on to the Port Mourant Cricket Ground where Peter decided to ease the tension within the group. He invited everyone to look at the famous venue where the careers of some of the best known Berbice, Guyana and West Indies cricket heroes began. He appeared to be somewhat disappointed when he spoke about the sad state of the once well-kept and lush green ground.

"What you see here today is a sad, dry and parched cricket outfield with its short white picket fencing and a basic wooden pavilion badly in need of re-development. I hope that the authorities, Mister Charles Ramson the Minister of Culture, Youth and Sports, as well as business enterprises, can revive this place as homage to some of our greatest cricket heroes. I understand that a new stadium is being built at Palmyra, but something should also be done here in honour of those cricket legends."

Carlos pretended to play a cricket batting stroke with his hands, as he said, "Yes Peter, cricket has been a sport which has brought us Guyanese together, and this place must be treated as a site of reverence to the game and certainly to the names of the players you will no doubt mention. Sorry for interrupting."

Peter continued after noting nods of approval from everyone, "Let me start with the amazing Rohan Bholalal Kanhai. He was fondly known as the "Babulall". His approach with his slow and graceful walk to the *wicket* was itself worth the fees for a day's play. His open-necked shirt was complemented with a white handkerchief tied as a small scarf around his neck to mop up perspiration, but it looked more like he was one of those "badman Western outlaws" strolling into town. He would stand at the batting crease after a brief look around the field, take his favourite batting guard and stroll down a few steps patting at any spots on the wicket marked by the red cricket ball. Then, as he defended his first delivery, the crowd would shout "No!" and soon the entertainment would begin with blistering square cuts, cover drives, on drives, pulls, hooks and, if we were lucky, we would see his amazing falling sweep shot catapulting a spinner's delivery high over the square leg boundary and into the crowds for six runs."

John, standing next to Peter, commented, "I can see why people loved Rohan Kanhai. I never played cricket, but I loved watching the game at CI and Leonora. It would be great to see one or more of my people come through as star cricketers."

Peter was quick to put the record straight, and replied, "Well, the next great and brilliant batsman to play for Port Mourant, Berbice, Guyana and the West Indies, was Basil Fitzherbert Butcher, who was part Amerindian through his mother Matilda. His father Ethelbert was a Barbadian who had migrated to Guyana. A combination of Butcher, Kanhai and Joe Solomon was truly awesome. Add the left-handed opening batsman Roy Fredericks from Blairmont Estate to that group in the 1960s and 70s, and we saw something quite amazing. We do not have much time here but let me add a few more great names from this amazing village and club. They include Ivan Madray, Alvin Kallicharan, his brother Derek, and John Trim. I have one true story to share with you all. Would you like to hear it?"

Arthur intervened, "Hey Peter, before you tell us your story, I must point out that of the modern generation, there has been a player of Chinese origin by the name of Jonathan Foo who was born right here in Port Mourant. By the way also, another young player of Amerindian descent, Keemo Paul of Essequibo, has made it to the West Indies Test team. John and Muriel must be proud of this."

Peter thanked his friends for their comments and proceeded to tell his story, "On the first morning of a most important regional Shell Shield game between the mighty Barbados captained by Garfield Sobers, the greatest all-round cricketer ever, faced up to Guyana at the Bourda Cricket Ground in Georgetown on the twenty-eighth of

February 1966. The first four in the Guyana batting line up were Roy Fredericks, Joe Solomon who was promoted to open the batting, Rohan Kanhai and then Basil Butcher, who as we know were all from Berbice. So, in one of the stands was a large group of Berbicians there to support their stars. One fellow stood up and asked his friends to drink one shot of rum for every four or six hit by those four batsmen. The first wicket fell at the score of two hundred and ninety-two with young Fredericks making a brilliant one hundred and twenty-seven. Solomon made a patient sixty-eight and by the time he was out with the score at nearly four hundred, all the Berbicians were drunk! They never got to see their biggest heroes Rohan Kanhai blasting one hundred and forty-four and Basil Butcher slaughtering the Bajan bowlers for one hundred and eighty-three not out!"

Vishnu exclaimed, "That must have been carnage!"

Peter nodded and continued, "Guyana declared at six hundred and forty-one for five wickets, but Barbados put up a big fight with five hundred and fifty-two all out. Peter Lashley made a superb two hundred and four, and the genius Garfield Sobers made a fantastic one hundred and sixty-five. By the way, young Rex Ramnarace, another Berbician, took two wickets, and Roy Fredericks made another century in the second Guyana inning. That game presented the best batting I had ever seen in my life! Pity that those drunken Berbician fans only saw a bit of it!"

Michael was anxious to add to the conversation, "I believe that Rohan Kanhai made his highest Test score of two hundred and fifty-six at Calcutta in India, in 1958, and won the hearts of many Indian supporters. Indeed, Sunil Gavaskar, the Indian cricket legend, was so impressed by Kanhai that he named his son Rohan. Alvin Kallicharan did the same. We must not forget that Rohan and Alvin served as West Indies cricket captains, and Basil, Joe and Roy also served in various roles in the sport as well."

He turned to Ramesh and recalled, "I am sure that most of you will remember Alvin Kallicharan's outstanding attack on the great Australian fast bowler, Denis Lillee, when in one over he smashed twenty-six runs in the 1975 World Cup game which West Indies won against Australia. The West Indies went on to win that first World Cup at Lord's Cricket Ground in London in the final against the same opponents. The great Sir Clive Lloyd of Guyana stroked a magnificent century with Kanhai supporting him with a fifty in a decisive partnership. Sadly though, the Australians took revenge when the West Indies toured their country in 1975/76 by thrashing Lloyd's team by five Tests to one."

Vishnu put his right hand up, and when he was allowed to speak, he said, "Peter mentioned the two centuries by the young Roy Fredericks against Barbados. During that Australian defeat of the West Indies, he smashed a record-breaking fastest century in a Test Match when he scored one hundred and sixty-nine. That record stood for a long time before it was broken."

Carlos scanned around the ground once more and spoke with great pride, "Man, you fellas know your sports history and can talk about cricket so much. I hope that we will also talk about other sports and sportsmen and women who also represented our country with distinction. But thank you all for sharing so many amazing things about our people and our history on this trip. I am feeling a little tired now, and I hope that you don't mind if I ask for us to end today's trip here."

Ramesh and Sati acknowledged Carlos's request and asked the others about ending the trip and returning home. Everyone agreed, and Neesha stepped forward to speak.

"Thank you all for coming on this trip. I thought that we will just spend our time travelling to see places and enjoy a relaxing time. But this has been more like a non-stop history lesson. I have learnt so much in such a short time. Now let us relax on our journey back and be ready to enjoy a great meal being prepared at our home."

Nazir agreed with Neesha and pointed out, "I will try not to drive too quickly so that you can enjoy the sights. John and Afzal, do signal to me when you guys want to stop and switch drivers."

Michael anxiously raised his right hand, "Excuse me fellas. I need to use a toilet right now. Forgive me ladies, but nature doesn't use cellphones when she calls, but we gat fuh ansa she!"

Everyone stood by and laughed as Michael caressed his stomach and rushed off in search of relief.

When he finally returned to join the tour party, he wore a broad smile, and before boarding the car, pointed out, "You see, when we were growing up in our villages, and we faced cricket opposition who batted for a long time and scored a lot of runs, we used to say that was 'belly wuk'. But that was not the same compared to what I just experienced."

Everyone who heard him laughed out loudly.

He continued, "But seriously, all of our great sports icons we talked about have given us great inspiration to play cricket and so on, to gain fitness, to experience happiness, and most of all, to bring us together as Guyanese. I must say that these sports such as cricket and football were invented by the British and they form lasting legacies wherever they ruled. Nazir, please proceed!"

16

A taste of things to come

Before the tour party and their hosts finally retired for the night after their trip to part of Berbice, they agreed that they would use the next day for some further rest, and as Ramesh said, "To chill out and recharge".

John and Muriel decided to invite everyone to their home in the village as part of the period of rest they needed. They promised to provide Michael with the right traditional Amerindian cure for his stomach discomfort, and a lunch to help him recover his appetite. Nazir, Neesha and their guests walked across the short distance to John and Muriel's home after their lie in and late breakfast of salted fish and fried bakes. Neesha had prepared the salted fish using her own recipe including onion, garlic, tomato, pepper and some fresh herbs from her garden. Vishnu thoroughly enjoyed the breakfast and congratulated his hosts.

"Neesha, that was just what the doctor ordered. Could you please save some of the bakes for tomorrow morning? I love them even more when they are a day old or stale."

John and Muriel welcomed their visitors with open arms, and before they could settle down in their spacious sitting room, they invited everyone for a short tour of their backyard. John, with Muriel standing proudly beside him, began his commentary on the well-stocked display of mostly exotic plants and mature trees.

"As you can see, we have tried to bring some of our hinterland here to remind us of our environment we are more used to. Of course, we also have some of the normal fruit trees that you see everywhere along the coastland. Things like mango, genip, downs, psydium, golden apple, five fingers or shamrock, star apple, cherry, cashew, awara and some dwarf coconut plants."

Parvati was very impressed with the wide variety of fruits in the garden, and enthused about the vegetables, "I also like your vegetable patches you have here. I can see and recognise some of what dieticians are calling super foods. Things like caraila or bitter gourd, bhaji or spinach, bora, squash, pumpkin, different types of peppers, and I can also see a saijan tree in the background. Oh, I can't wait to have meals of these great vegetables fresh from your garden."

Muriel took up the commentary, "Yes, and we also have beds of cassava. We prepare our own cassava bread and farine, piwari, as well as cassareep sauce. We believe that our cassareep is the best, and we also cook the tastiest pepperpot which is on today's menu for our lunch along with some homemade pineapple juice."

Michael was very impressed with the wide range of plants, herbs, flowers and trees in the garden which extended to over two hundred feet in length and about fifty feet wide. He looked around to ensure that Doreen was not within earshot of him and moved closer to whisper in John's left ear.

"Do you have something for men's problems?"

John smiled as he replied in like manner, "Yes. We do not grow the vine here, but I have a small stock of the capadulla bark as well as sasparilla. I can prepare a special drink for you, and you can tell me tomorrow if it works."

Michael was very pleased about the prospect of having a traditional cure for his problem. He smiled and gave John an optimistic thumbs up.

Carlos was curious to learn more about the backyard and asked, "How do you find the time to do all of this? Have you got a gardener or a weeder to help you?"

Muriel opened her bare hands, stretched them outward, and showed them to Carlos, "John and I have taken many years to develop this garden. It was very hard at first, but we have set out the plants in such a way that they are now a lot easier to maintain. Due to our advancing years now, we are finding it more difficult to bend down to dig and to sow the vegetables and herbs. So, as you can see, we have built some raised beds closer to the back of the house and kitchen."

John eagerly added, "And, we don't have to fetch buckets of water to feed the plants. I had some help to instal a sprinkler system which a friend sent to me from Florida. All Muriel and I have to do is turn on or off one tap, and the garden gets what it needs."

Arthur pointed at two concreted drains running alongside the six feet high wooden fences on both sides of the yard, and leading down to the back of the site, and asked, "Where does the water flow to from those two drains?"

John invited the group to follow him and Muriel further into the yard and answered, "Well, we do get a lot of rain especially in the long rainy season between May and mid-July and then around November to mid-January. So, we try to avoid any local flooding and collect most of the flow in a large pond at the back end of the yard. We have some fish in that pond. But we do have to spray around the pond to try to control the mosquitoes which love stagnant water."

Ramesh commented, "Uncle John, you and Aunty Muriel have done a remarkable thing here. Instead of concreting and paving most of the land around the house and yard, you have shown us a more practical and sensible use of your environment. You have become self-sufficient with healthy produce, and at the same time, you are saving a lot of money. What do you do with all the extra fruits and vegetables through the year?"

Muriel was proud to say, "Well, we sell to who wants to buy, and we give away some to those who cannot afford to pay. Apart from eating healthily, we also save on basic medicines as we use a lot of our traditional "bush medicine" we have here or can buy in the market. We also bring back some stock when we return from visiting our relatives in the interior."

Arthur nodded and smiled in admiration as he said, "You and John are showing fellow Guyanese how to live comfortably off your land and are even helping some people in need. All of this adds up to a happy, healthy and harmonious lifestyle. In Canada, we try to do this at least in the Spring and Summer months each year, and it is truly therapeutic. It's a great pity that we cannot do the same over the very cold Winter months."

Afzal pointed out, "Well, we have a very young and energetic President of Guyana who understands the value of the soil and is encouraging fellow Guyanese to grow their own, eat healthily, and with a huge emphasis on modernising agriculture, Guyana will become the "breadbasket" of the region."

Michael leant over and picked a thyme leaf and smelt it with great pleasure as he said, "Hmm! Gone are the days when we were importing so much foodstuff. We have very fertile soil all over the country and I am really happy to see that the government is helping farmers to diversify and try out new crops without having to clear forests. Sugar, rice and coconut products have been good for the country over the last few decades, but we have the land and willingness to grow many more crops. It is great to see that this is already happening."

John agreed and added, "As Amerindians, we are also keen to see more of our traditional foods and plants become part of our country's staple diet and medical care across the regions. Muriel and I would like to see more emphasis on our Amerindian way of life which can help our fellow Guyanese to deal with problems such as anxiety, stress, depression and general ill-health."

He glanced at Michael, giggled, and said, "And of course, for our pleasure!"

Nazir was proud of John and Muriel's efforts to encourage the growth and use of local foodstuff, and particularly the Amerindian influences.

He asked his friends, "Whilst I am still fit and healthy, I think that Neesha will not mind but I would like to make a start on a similar garden at our backyard and hope that John and Muriel could be our mentors to help us achieve this kind of result. John and Muriel, would you be willing to help us?"

John immediately replied, "Of course, my brother. We would love to help you and Neesha design and lay out a garden with the plants and trees you prefer to have. I am sure that Muriel will not mind for us to help anyone else here with their garden."

Afzal promptly raised his right hand and said, "Oh thank you so much John and Muriel. I still have a big plot at my family home in Leonora, and unfortunately because I am so busy, the yard is overgrown. I do pay someone to weed and clear it up, but when the guy finishes at one end using his cutlass and grass knife, before he gets to the other end, the weeds and wild grasses just grow back. Sometimes I think that the man is just working slowly to keep himself in a job!"

John suggested, "Well, we would show him how to build up the garden and maintain it. We can also show him how to use a mower to speed up on the weeding and control the grass. Of course, you will also need to have a sprinkler system to make it easier to feed and maintain the garden."

Afzal was pleased to listen to John's offer and suggestion, "Thank you and Muriel. I am glad that you will keep him in the job and with proper training. In fact, I will give him some more money and look after him better."

Parvati thanked John and Muriel and commented, "Oh this is only one small example of how we as Guyanese can help each other to make a living. I am sure that Nazir and Neesha will also hire a gardener to maintain their garden."

Neesha agreed, "In fact, Nazir and I already have a housekeeper, and we will ask her if her husband would be willing to do the gardening. He is unemployed at the moment, and their family is struggling to make ends meet."

Muriel smiled and added, "I am so happy that from just showing you all our simple garden, we are now talking about making better use of our land and creating good jobs as well."

As soon as the group completed their tour of the garden, they sat around John's and Muriel's twelve-seater dining table for their special Amerindian lunch which was already laid out for them. The main item of the meal was the homemade pepperpot using John and Muriel's cassareep, some cassava bread as well as some home-baked rolls on the side. They chose to use halal beef in the pepperpot in keeping with the Islamic tradition of their Muslim friends. Normally, pepperpot would contain pork which is prohibited in Islam. Alongside the main dish there were two platters of boiled cassava, eddoes, sweet potatoes and green plantain. Although there were very hot scotch bonnet peppers in the pepperpot, the guests had the option to use more wiri wiri pepper sauce and acchar if they wished. Jugs of ice-cold water and pineapple juice were on offer to cool down their palates. John ensured that Michael had a glass of his special capadulla drink.

Maria looked across at John and asked, "Is that a drink to help Michael with his stomach upset? If so, can you also give some to Carlos please? He is now having similar problems."

Ramesh looked across at Sati and smiled as he said, "Don't worry. I will not have that drink as I feel fine."

Vishnu drank the last of his glass of pineapple juice and commended his hosts, "Thank you for a great taste of what we can expect when we do a trip to at least one of the Amerindian settlements. I am not sure as to which one John and Muriel will choose for us especially due to our age. So far, Parvati and I have coped very well with the heat and the many miles of roads, boats and airplane flights. What do you suggest John and Muriel?"

John did not hesitate to suggest, "I think that we should be able to drive over to Parika, take a ferry across the Essequibo River with both cars, travel on to Charity, and take a boat trip on the Pomeroon River to visit an Amerindian settlement just a few miles inland. That should not be too difficult for us all to cope with. I am sure that Michael will be able to share some more history with us along the way. Of course, Muriel and I will tell you more about our people."

Sati was delighted to hear John's suggestion and spoke as Ramesh typed in more detail into the plan on his iPhone, "I think that will be a great trip, and a good follow up from today's taste of the Amerindian culture and lifestyle."

Afzal appeared as nervous as a mouse as he responded, "I welcome the idea of such a trip and would love to see some of our interesting wildlife there. But I must warn you that I have never eaten things like capybara or watrash, and there is no way I will do so now. That animal is nothing but a giant rat! I cannot understand how people can eat giant rats!"

Carlos smiled and tried to pacify Afzal, "Do not worry my brother. We will not be using that meat in front of you, but I had tasted it in the past and it was very nice. They are not rats but are more closely related to guinea pigs."

Afzal was not convinced, and was more adamant, "Look, a pig is a pig no matter what you call it. And it is against my religion to eat it."

Michael added, "There is another animal in the interior which is indeed a large rodent. It is called labba and I have tasted it. The meat can be roasted, curried or stewed. Their diet is mostly fruit and nuts, so their meat is not harmful."

Afzal became even more convinced about not partaking in the wild meat, and affirmed, "As I said, there is no way that I am going to eat capybara, labba or any other bush meat. But I do not mind you all having it. I am happy just to see them in the wild and not on a plate."

Peter on the other hand, was already salivating, "Man, eating bush food is one of the great joys of this life here in Guyana. Don't worry Afzal, there will be a lot of other things to try in the hinterland. The best freshwater fish is there, and I am sure that you enjoy the best of them all, the lukanaani. I love that fish as a curry!"

Arthur rubbed his hands together enthusiastically and enthused, "You guys have whetted my appetite for so much more that our beautiful Guyana has to offer. My people love to have mountain chicken!"

Afzal was shocked and exclaimed, "Mountain what? Do you mean the giant crappo? Man, you guys are now completely putting me off that trip!"

Arthur shook his head and said, "Back in the old days when some of my relatives came over from Trinidad to visit the family here in Anna Catherina and Leonora, they used to offer a swap of iguanas for mountain chickens."

Afzal stared at Arthur and opened his eyes with a look of sheer disbelief.

Peter reached across to Afzal and tried to re-assure him, "Please don't worry my brother. I understand how you feel. In fact, why don't we prepare, or buy, some cooked food for everyone who does not wish to use the bush food, and have that on the trip?"

Nazir accepted Peter's suggestion, and with a nod from Neesha, he answered, "Yes, I am sure that we can knock up a simple cook up rice with some special fried chicken and take that with us. In that way we can kill two birds with one stone. Let's have the normal chicken instead of Arthur's mountain ones!"

Neesha, standing beside Nazir, suggested, "Well, now that we have all enjoyed a lovely tour of John's and Muriel's great haven, a delicious traditional Guyanese lunch and agreed on our next or future day trip, why don't we just relax for the rest of the day, or take a stroll around our old village? Maybe a short walk to the seawall to take in some fresh Atlantic air?"

Michael seized the opportunity to ask, "Or, maybe we can play some dominoes or cards?"

All the women immediately answered with a resounding "No!"

17
Iwokrama: The Green Heart of Guyana

The touring party enjoyed a very restful evening, and during the course of the conversations and reflections, there was a change of plan from a trip up the Pomeroon River, to a more adventurous one of the country's foremost forest preservation areas called Iwokrama. Due to the high cost of an overnight or extended trip, the group decided that those who had already visited the area would forego it and be excused from the adventure. Neesha, Maria and Doreen chose to have a day of shopping in Leonora including a short trip to Parika. Nazir acted as their driver whilst Afzal and Peter visited some of their relatives.

The group for the Iwokrama trip was thus reduced to Vishnu, Parvati, Michael, Ramesh, Sati, Arthur, Carlos, John and Muriel. It was agreed that John and Muriel would lead the group except for any activity they chose to do which required a local guide. The couple decided to hold a short briefing meeting with everyone on the tour as a way of highlighting some of the history of Iwokrama and the many opportunities to explore the incredible sights and sounds of the forest, waterways, and to appreciate the main purpose of scientific research, conservation and sustainability of that environment.

John and Muriel sat beside each other and faced everyone in their spacious and well laid out sitting room which included pictures of Amerindian life in the hinterland, and well-crafted figures made of mahogany placed on a central coffee table and on other occasional tables around the room.

John began by saying, "Muriel and I are really pleased that some of you will be making this trip to Iwokrama starting very early tomorrow morning. We will be staying over for one night only mainly because of our old age except of course our much younger companions

Ramesh and Sati. There is so much to say about Iwokrama, its history and the amazing work of local and international importance going on there. But first, almost anything we aim to do involving the hinterland, we must appreciate and understand the history of my fellow Amerindians in such places."

Muriel responded to John's hint and added, "Yes, our Makushi brothers and sisters have been living in Iwokrama Forest for thousands of years. In fact, evidence shows that there were settlements there such a long time ago through some stone markings near the Kurupukari Falls area."

John noted, "The stone markings are called petroglyphs. They show scenes of the lives of the people. Those markings are believed to be about eleven thousand years old!"

Michael once again, could not resist opening his notebook, and pointed out, "Guyana is within what is called the Guiana Shield of tropical rainforests which cover the neighbouring countries of Suriname, French Guiana or Cayenne and part of Colombia, Venezuela and Brazil which are countries in the North of South America. The Shield contains pristine rainforests, many rivers, wetlands, savannahs and tabletop mountains such as Roraima which marks a point where the boundaries of Guyana, Venezuela and Brazil meet. The Guiana Shield is nearly one million square miles in area, and the Iwokrama Forest within it is about one thousand and four hundred square miles. To fully explore Iwokrama Forest would take you weeks. Sorry John and Muriel. Please continue."

John thanked Michael for his input and proceeded, "Iwokrama has always been occupied by the Makushi people, and as the Europeans started to steal their lands and other unfriendly tribes from Brazil raided their settlements, they sought the safety of the Iwokrama Mountains. Iwokrama means "Place of Refuge" in the Makushi language. We are grateful to our former President Hugh Desmond Hoyte who offered to reserve Iwokrama in 1989 to be used as a research location showing how the rainforest can be managed effectively to allow the people to prosper without the need to destroy it."

Muriel was also anxious to share her knowledge and pointed out, "You will see examples of the many types of plants, animals, birds, fish and reptiles there. But we must all be prepared to avoid the mosquitoes which will be happy to taste your foreign blood. Michael,

I can see that you like to wear T-shirts and shorts. But on this trip, I advise that we all cover as much of our bodies as possible. I know that you all have sensible walking boots, and they will be more appropriate than sneakers."

Michael intervened once again, "Yes, I do have all the right gear. Hopefully, when those mosquitoes take one look at me, they will be pitiful and stay away. Anyway, after a few years of setting up and building the research centre at Iwokrama, it was President Cheddi Jagan who pushed through the Iwokrama Centre for Rainforest Conservation and Development Act. The place is organised and managed for research and is also geared up for the tourism business as well as other enterprises. So, on top of the cost for our short overnight trip, do spend some money in the shop. By the way, how are we going to get there and back?"

Ramesh raised his right hand to answer, "Uncle Michael, I know that the eight hours drive from here through the Linden to Lethem Road would be too rough for our older travellers and take away the real joy of the visit. So, we will take a flight from Ogle to the Fairview Village in Iwokrama and then a short drive to our base at the River Lodge."

The nine members of the Iwokrama tour party were up and ready for their eight thirty am flight from Ogle to the Fairview airstrip. The flight was comfortable and most of the view below was dominated by pristine forestry and the sight of the mighty Essequibo River. Several of Guyana's other great rivers such as the Cuyuni, Potaro, Rupununi, Siparuni and Mazaruni flow into the Essequibo.

The tour group was warmly welcomed by friendly staff at the River Lodge with a refreshing drink and then shown to their accommodation for the night. The group members agreed on how they should share the cabins which were with neat ensuite rooms. Vishnu and Parvati shared one, and the others were occupied by Ramesh and Sati, Arthur and Carlos, and John and Muriel. Michael enjoyed the relative luxury of having his own room. John suggested that they had enough time to walk down to the water's edge and look for a *giant black caiman* which was given the name, Sankar.

There was a strict notice prohibiting swimming in the river even though it appeared calm and inviting. Sankar became attached to the area after having been fed meat by the visiting researchers and staff at the centre. The creature, as a regular visitor, soon became a notable attraction for tourists.

John and Muriel took the lead and scanned the river with the aid of their binoculars.

As soon as Sankar was spotted, John alerted everyone, "Oh there he is! Wow! He's coming towards us! What a sight!"

Vishnu, alert as ever, aimed his camera at Sankar and began recording.

He took close up action and whispered like an intrepid explorer filming a nature documentary, "Well, this must be the popular attraction by the name of Sankar. He is a really cool character waiting patiently to be fed some raw meat."

After a few more minutes of observing and taking pictures of Sankar, the group was then led by an official guide onto a trail leading into the forest. John and Muriel strode beside the guide who was a young Makushi man and used their knowledge of the forest environment to point out and comment on the sights and sounds of the animals, birds, insects, trees and plants.

The first monkeys spotted were a small family unit of three red howlers that were perched up in a tall wadara tree.

John was anxious to ensure that Vishnu captured the three monkeys on his video and whispered, "There Vishnu. Take a close look at the male, female and their youngster who is probably only a few months old."

The guide endorsed John's assertion and began to mimic the sound of howling by cupping his hands close to his mouth and blowing steadily until the male monkey responded with very loud howling as if in animated conversation with each other.

Michael and the group were very impressed by the guide's ability to ape the howlers, and he commented in a hushed tone, "Man, that was awesome. If I tried to do that the male monkey would take me for some imposter and attack."

Carlos giggled as he suggested, "Michael, you may be too ugly for that guy to be attracted to you!"

The guide also chuckled as he re-assured Michael, "No sir. The howler would rant for a while and just move away with his family. Anyway, this particular family knows me and they are familiar with my bad howler accent and speech!"

Carlos looked up into the canopy and shouted, "There! There! Can you see the toucan? Wow, what a unique and beautiful bird! This could easily be our national bird, but I understand why the authorities chose the Hoatzin."

The guide stopped the group for a few moments as he spoke, "This is only one example of a variety of toucans here in Guyana and in other countries in the region."

John was keen to share his Amerindian view about toucans, "These birds have a special place in our culture and tradition. We have about nine types here in Guyana out of about forty around Central and South America. Some are called toucanets or aracari. But the one which we are most familiar with has that beautiful red, yellow and black beak and with the white throat. They normally gather in small groups and make different sounds. Some people keep them as caged pets. But I do not like this as they are sacred to our people and should be allowed to roam free as the Great Spirit intends."

The guide respectfully nodded and continued, "We will not see all the varieties of birds on this trail, but you can hear the calls of three types of macaws we have here. The blue and yellow macaw is different in plumage from the red and green macaw and the most colourful scarlet macaw with its white face, red head and breast, yellow and blue wings and a light blue at the base of its tail. There are more red, yellow and blue feathers to the tip of its tail. Unlike our toucans, our macaws can be trained to speak in captivity. I agree with our friend here and do not approve of the practice of keeping any kind of our beautiful birds including our many types of parrots and parakeets as pets. I prefer to see them in their natural environment."

Arthur agreed with John and the guide, "I know that the practice of keeping birds in cages goes back into ancient times and in places such as Egypt, Persia, Italy, India and China. Different birds were kept for different reasons. For example, the large cranes were associated with long life and good luck. Magpies were believed to bring wealth and happiness."

Ramesh pointed out, "I noticed as we were being driven around, that there were small groups of men who were mainly Indian Guyanese, parading their small birds in cages. This is a kind of unofficial sport where the birds spar against each other from within their cages in the so-called bird fights to prove which ones won the contests and became champions."

Michael shook his head and lamented, "I used to do that when I was a younger man, and every Sunday morning we would gather at a special meeting place in Anna Catherina, for the contests. Now, after all those years and listening to John and our guide, I have to agree that this practice should not be allowed to continue."

Parvati frowned as she expressed her displeasure with the practice, "I cannot see any reason for such a stupid and cruel sport. I think that it should be banned."

Vishnu nodded in agreement and noted, "I think that you are right. But there is some business attached to this practice involving the growing and selling of bird feeds and the making of the cages."

The guide confirmed, "We do have laws to protect our native birds, but they are not being aggressively implemented. One particular practice I do not like or approve of is the capturing of what is called shorebirds on the mudflats at the seaside on the coastland. You may have seen such birds for sale as meat at the Port Mourant market."

Parvati became more annoyed about what she was hearing, "Now that is truly disgusting!"

All the members of the group looked at each other in astonishment and Vishnu said, "To be honest, I did not see this. But man, I would not use that meat."

Arthur sighed and remarked, "I know that I mentioned things like mountain chicken and iguanas used for food, but I have to agree with you Vishnu and Parvati. I do not like what I am hearing."

Sati pulled a face of disgust and said, "I don't like such habits. All the more reason for me to stick to my strict vegetarianism. It is quite hypocritical for us to champion the survival of the rainforests and the creatures within and around them on the one hand, and at the same time, indulge is such cruel practices."

The short introductory tour ended just in time for the group to return to the River Lodge for their delicious Guyanese lunch served buffet style in the Fred Allicock dining hall. After lunch, some members of the group took the opportunity to lay in hammocks located around the circular verandah of the lodge to catch up on some sleep. Others enjoyed looking out onto the becalmed Essequibo River and taking in the light air wafting around. Michael decided to share more information on Iwokrama as he carefully sat in a hammock alongside Vishnu who was securely lying in his.

"This place is a unique and successful experiment designed to show the world how we as human beings can live in harmony with the environment around us. In this case, this beautiful rainforest where the resilient Makushi people still live and prosper. The new King Charles III loves this place and has had a hand in its development over many years."

Vishnu nodded in agreement and added, "King Charles has been a champion of the environment for decades whilst he was the Prince of Wales, and the world should be grateful for his work. Our former President Bharrat Jagdeo has also been a beacon light for the environment, and as a Guyanese, I am very proud of his work on this issue."

Ramesh strolled by and joined Vishnu and Michael, "Dad, I am glad that you mentioned President Jagdeo. He has been able to convince the international community to purchase some of the carbon credits held and stored within Guyana's vast rainforests. The Hess Corporation has signed an agreement to purchase about thirty per cent of Guyana's carbon credits for around three quarters of a billion US dollars over the next ten years. The Amerindian Toshao Council have agreed to accept fifteen per cent of such income for the people of the communities in the hinterland to plan and use their share of the money to develop their areas as they see fit. I understand that this share has been substantially increased to nearly thirty per cent."

Michael took out his notebook as soon as he saw more members of the group gathering around, and read from it, "Guyana has a Low Carbon Development Strategy 2030, or LCDS 2030 which spells out how the government and the people will continue to protect and sustain the rainforests and at the same time, demonstrate how they can make a living there without the need for wholescale destruction of this precious source of life. I am happy to note that this approach we are seeing here in Iwokrama continues to be endorsed and championed by all of our Presidents including the current President Irfaan Ali."

Ramesh nodded and then mentioned, "Thank you Uncle Michael. Now that most of us are here, and if you have rested enough, please let me and Sati know whether you wish to go on another important tour here today. If you feel too tired, we can put it off until tomorrow morning before we leave on our flight back to Ogle."

John suggested, "Personally, Muriel and I are happy to take on the trip to experience the canopy walkway now, or in the morning. We are happy either way."

Arthur stretched his arms out, yawned and then asked, "How long is that trip?"

Ramesh replied, "Only about one and a half hours or a bit more as we can pause for some rest when we take the steps up the hill to the top of the walkway."

Carlos nodded and suggested, "Well, I am happy to take this on now, and then come back for a nice dinner and a good sleep. I gather that there is also a boat trip in the night if anyone would like to do that. This place is truly amazing, and I think that if I was much younger, I would stay here for a few days and nights to really soak in the whole experience that is on offer."

Vishnu raised his right hand and responded, "You are so right Carlos. We have only seen a small amount of what's here, and it has been so refreshing and inspiring. I am happy to go up to the canopy now, and then come back to sleep like a log as Carlos says. I can see Parvati also agreeing to do this."

They all finally agreed to do the walk up to the canopy, and after using the toilet facilities at the lodge, they set off with the local guide taking the lead, and John and Muriel walking beside him. They soon reached the bottom of the walkway and began to take the well laid out steps whilst holding onto a wooden rail to protect them from falling. It was also a useful aid to the climb. As they reached a higher level on the steps, the group stopped to take a short rest before continuing upwards towards the first platform of the canopy walkway.

Michael was relieved to reach the platform which was covered by a protective roof and built around a living and growing tree. He held onto the rail and drew a strong breath. He exhaled in a slow and tedious way as he steadied himself before commenting.

"Oh God! That was a real test for my old heart! Let me take in some more fresh oxygen before we move on. I wouldn't mind if Mr Hess can give me some money for my carbon dioxide which I am adding to our reserves here."

The group all laughed whilst they also took a breather before inching their way along the first stage of the walkway. Michael looked around at the various trees making up the forest's canopy.

"Now, this is a view of a lifetime. This is like mother nature reaching out from the earth below and absorbing the sunshine and clean air we can breathe in at this height. To be so close to this canopy is a real Godsend."

The guide took the lead in showing the group how to use the yellow ropes with both hands as he strode slowly along the aluminium walkway which was supported by strong cables and protective mesh on both sides. When they all reached the first landing, he pointed out the sights and sounds of an array of birds and monkeys. He gazed at the outline of the Maipa mountains on the horizon.

John spoke to his fellow travellers, "As we stand here to rest for a few minutes, just look out and around closely at the top of the trees and at the scenery in the distance. Then take some deep breaths in and exhale slowly. Imagine that you are one of those harpy eagles or those macaws gracefully gliding along and looking for something that is on offer by the forest. The many sounds we can hear at this level are the conversations of the spirits of my people who have passed into the next world. Now, just close your eyes for a few moments and listen to those conversations. This is our paradise on earth."

After a short while, Muriel broke the silence, "Now please open your eyes, take another deep breath and slowly let the air out. Look around once more before we take to the next walkway. This is just a brief experience of our own form of yoga that John and I call "Living with the spirits"."

Michael acknowledged Muriel's and John's interpretation of the forest and enthused, "That was a most beautiful few moments of observing nature. You have made me begin to think differently about spirits because I am a man who is very scared of jumbies."

Parvati held Vishnu's left hand firmly and whispered, "This is a perfect place for some traditional yoga. It is so serene and soothing for the inner soul. I love this place."

When the group finally completed the canopy walkway, they arrived back at the River Lodge in good time to use the facilities in their respective rooms to freshen up and then go to the dining area for their dinner. Their meal was a sumptuous combination of locally grown and sourced fruits and vegetables. Most of the group opted for some spicy fried chicken and fish which were purchased from the Makushi residents.

John and Muriel decided to wrap up the evening by holding a brief session to discuss the trip and to ask whether anyone would like to do more of the tour options on offer.

Michael checked the entries in his notebook and mentioned, "There is a night boat trip from here up the Essequibo River where you can see some animals and birds in the dark. These include the large caiman, tree frogs and those large rodents we talked about. If you are lucky, you may spot the famous jaguar coming down to the water's edge. I feel too tired to go on such a trip as I really enjoyed our amazing day here. To me it has been a once in a lifetime experience."

Ramesh nodded and pointed out, "I suppose we could do a short trip tomorrow morning after breakfast where we can walk for about ten minutes and take a boat trip on the Essequibo to see the Kurupukari Falls and those petroglyphs we spoke about. I don't think that we will have enough time to do the longer trip via boat and then a trail for about ninety minutes up to the Turtle Mountains where you can have an amazing view around the Iwokrama forest."

John thanked Ramesh for his suggestions and added, "Muriel and I have done those trips when we were much younger, but I think that you guys can have your rest tonight and see how you feel tomorrow morning before we fly back to Ogle. There is one tour which is much more suited to young people looking for a more challenging trek deeper into the forest and with some tough climbs to get to the top of the Iwokrama mountain to enjoy a most spectacular view of the forests and mountain ranges. Along the way you can see many more howler, squirrel or saki winki and capuchin monkeys, agoutis, giant anteaters, sloths, armadillos, several kinds of tree frogs, incredible birds including the famous cock of the rock, herons, kingfishers, woodpeckers, the amazing harpy eagles and many others. Then, to cap it all, you can see many types of beautiful and rare butterflies."

Arthur's eyes lit up like one of the squirrel monkeys and exclaimed, "Wow! If only I was much younger, I would do that. Our country is a real paradise with so much still to be explored. Maybe the government should sponsor the schools to allow for careful and safe explorations like this for young Guyanese to experience places like Iwokrama. Informing people on social media and in classrooms of what we have here is one thing, but to be here in person is truly incredible."

Carlos agreed and suggested, "Well, in order to encourage future generations to protect this kind of environment, and thus the planet, all Guyanese here and abroad should learn more about our beautiful God-given country. I wish that I had taken much more notice of these beautiful places and creatures when I was younger. Now, all I can do at my age is to just have a taste of some of it."

John was quick to point out, "Carlos, I just wish to let everyone know that Iwokrama does outreach activities with schools."

Vishnu became emotional and looked at John and Muriel with admiration as he said, "Thank you both and all of your amazing people for your enduring passion and love for these incredible places everywhere in this hinterland. You continue to show everyone including the scientists, researchers, adventurers and others how to protect these places, how to preserve the very air that the world breathes, and how to use only what the Great Spirit has gifted to us all."

Michael smiled broadly, stepped forward and hugged John and Muriel, "My dear brother and sister, thank you for showing us the way to what Guyana is really all about. Iwokrama may be called the Green Heart of Guyana, but it is much more than that. This is what paradise must be like, and to think that it is so very near to us all!"

Ramesh nodded and smiled as he read on his iPhone from the official Iwokrama website, "I love the mission statement of Iwokrama. It says, "Our mission is to promote conservation and the sustainable and equitable use of tropical rainforests in a manner that will lead to lasting ecological, economic and social benefits to the people of Guyana and to the world in general by undertaking research, training and the development and dissemination of technologies."."

18

From Stabroek to Silica

The group agreed to have another day of rest. Vishnu, Parvati, Ramesh and Sati opted to spend some time with relatives and other friends they had in the villages of Leonora, Anna Catherina and Cornelia Ida. Michael and Doreen felt the need to reminisce and strolled around the village and the seaside at Anna Catherina. They found the location of the dark brown sandy beach nearest to where they had first met each other and chatted as they held hands looking out into the Atlantic Ocean. The tide began to return covering the dark green slimy mud flats and the remains of the first sea wall defence which was built by the Dutch and was destroyed by stormy waves which caused the first breach many decades ago.

Michael pointed to a small surviving clump of mangrove and remarked, "Doreen, you will remember the time when there was a lot of mangroves here. That was nature's way of keeping the waters of the ocean and rivers at bay. Looking back from this high spot, I am worried that those grand houses built so close and below the water level will be flooded out and destroyed if there is a massive breach of this seawall in the future. I really don't understand why people are building houses so close to the seawall and ocean!"

Doreen shook her head and replied, "Well, the people must enjoy living here and feel that this strong and high sea defence is more than enough to withstand any storm. Besides, living by the seaside is a very desirable thing in most countries around the world. So, Guyanese are no different. I love the cool sea breeze coming in with the tide. It's a great relief from the very hot and humid days and evenings."

Michael nodded and said, "Well I guess that you are right. This does not seem to be a concern of all the developers of the grand hotels and other structures along the coast as more tourists come into the country. It's a pity that the water of the Atlantic Ocean is not sky blue and our beaches are not bright white as you would expect in a seaside resort. But I suppose that our wild coast has its own mystique and attraction which fits in with the image of our beautiful and green country. Also, people will take up more opportunities to build homes further inland from the coast as more highways are built to open up the country. No wonder that our young President and his government are inviting us and our families to return here and to share in so many possibilities."

Arthur and Carlos also took the day off to visit relatives and friends still residing along the coast and in Georgetown. Peter and Afzal joined some friends to go to the backdam in Cornelia Ida to do some fishing in the canal or trench waterways which are used to take the cut sugarcane from the fields to the sugar factory at Uitvlught. They used three methods of catching fish such as the hassa whose black scales give the impression of a pre-historic type of sea life. The first method used was by a castnet which was made of fine strong string ringed at the bottom with lead clips which acted as an anchor to take the net down and to entrap the fish as the net is pulled back up the bank of the canal or trench. The catch could be seen struggling to wriggle their way out of the net. The second method was by a single fishing rod with bait and a patient wait for one fish to be caught. The third method was by one person holding his nostrils with one hand, diving below the surface at the edge of the waterway, grab fish from their nests, and in one action, throw them onto the dam for others to retrieve them and to place them into fish baskets. The castnet approach was by far the most successful way to catch some fish with each throw.

That evening the entire tour group was invited to dinner at Nazir's and Neesha's. They enjoyed some fried patwa fish as starters and a delicious hassa curry from the catch by Peter, Afzal and their friends. The meal was completed with daal and rice and a salad made with the produce of John's and Muriel's garden.

Having had a restful day away from a long tour, the group discussed and then agreed on a more comfortable trip instead of one involving a lot of travel or another adventure into the hinterland.

Ramesh commented on the final option, "The choice of a tour of some of the important sites around our capital city of Georgetown should not be too tiresome. There is a lot to see and appreciate in the city and I guess that we may have to plan another tour there to experience more of it. After all, Georgetown was once known as the "Garden City" in the past."

Michael frowned and shook his head, "Well, let's not raise our hopes of seeing such a thing. Poor management over decades has seen the city become more of a "Garbage City". I note that the President has led special clean-up operations there, and the First Lady is on a beautification mission. This alone will never result in a glorious Garden City without the people who live there and the visitors taking more pride in the city and working harder to keep it clean and beautiful. I think that the government, businesses and the city council should come together with the people and develop a plan to invest a lot more into Georgetown, New Amsterdam and other big towns around the country."

Doreen nodded in agreement with Michael and then asked, "So, how will we split the tour? Do we just take in a few sites on this first one and then pick up on the things we miss on a second one?"

Sati answered, "Yes Aunty Doreen. That will be a good way to cover the city which has a very interesting history. I am sure that Uncle Michael will fill us in with brief sketches of that history."

Michael smiled contentedly.

Peter raised his right hand and offered, "Of course, I will share information about cricket there in Georgetown. I'm sure that Michael won't mind if I do this on the tour."

Michael nodded in agreement.

Parvati looked at Neesha, Doreen, Muriel, Maria and Sati, and suggested, "I'm sure that the girls can be excused to do some retail therapy along the way!"

Vishnu's countenance was one of great surprise as he said, "I do not mind the shopping trips. But please tell me how are we going to take all of that stuff back home?"

Parvati brushed his question aside, "Two ways. Extra suitcases, or by shipping!"

Vishnu tried once more, "But most of the items you see here are made in China, and they are also in the stores in Little Guyana or in Toronto."

Parvati replied, "Well, we do know what to buy and what to leave."

Early the next morning, and after a light breakfast, the tour party began their journey to Georgetown using the two cars driven by Nazir and John. It was not long into the drive for Michael to take out his trusted notebook and to offer his thoughts.

"Ramesh, I hope that you will take some notes in your iPhone along with your dad's recordings of what I say, and we can all share. First of all, Georgetown was not the name of the capital city when the Dutch first started to colonise Demerara. In fact, let me say that Demerara is an Arawak name meaning "river of letter trees". It was in 1745 that the Dutch created or considered Demerara as a separate county and administered it from Essequibo. Whilst the Dutch colonials gradually began to establish plantations in Demerara, it was the English planters who were being attracted to explore opportunities here. The plantation owners wanted closer contact with the administration, and Borselen Island, which is about seventeen miles up the Demerara River, was chosen for that purpose. The Dutch built a small fort and a couple of other buildings there as a kind of defence set up. As the plantations began to expand and spread around the county, and Borselen was subject to floods due to high tides, it was decided to move the capital to Stabroek at the mouth of the river. The English were trying to take control away from the Dutch and built Fort St George. The French then got involved and took back control in 1763 naming the area La Nouvelle or "The New City" before calling it Longchamps. Later still the Dutch then started to develop the city by building the harbour and irrigation systems of canals and kokers to control the unruly tides from the Atlantic Ocean and the Demerara River. By the way, there are two other islands near Borselen called Biesen and Inver."

Vishnu and the other passengers in the car listened in silence and awe of Michael's information, and Ramesh turned off his iPhone.

"Uncle Michael, sorry for interrupting your flow. But I can't keep up with your amazing talk, and typing is getting more difficult for me with all the strange names you mention, and with the ride being a bit bumpy at times. I will look at Dad's video and hopefully use your notebook to fill in any gaps in the commentaries."

Michael continued, "No worries. In 1784, when the Dutch regained the city, they renamed it Stabroek after a fellow by the name of Nicolaas Geelvinck who was the Lord of Stabroek and Director of the Dutch West India Company. By the way, Stabroek, with all its canals and walkways, became known as the 'Venice of the West Indies'."

Nazir was not impressed and said, "Man, with all the flooding we get in Georgetown now I would call it a lake! If we are not careful that place could soon become a swamp! Since we are talking about

Stabroek, I think that the first place we should explore is the Stabroek Market and the stelling there."

Nazir and John dropped off their passengers at the front of Stabroek Market and then drove off to find parking. Michael gathered the tour party together and began his brief conversation about the history of the site after referring to his notebook.

"Although we know that this place has a Dutch name as if it was built by the Dutch, in fact it was constructed of iron and steel by Edge Moor Iron Company from Delaware, USA, in 1880. They built that iconic clock tower. But I must tell you that there was a market here since about one hundred years before that. These stalls are probably standing where our enslaved ancestors used to bring their provisions, fruits, poultry, eggs, fish and other goods to sell on Sundays."

Arthur noted, "With that kind of history, I think that the stallholders should be allowed to continue to do their trading here, and not charged for their space."

Michael nodded and continued, "By the way, that clock and tower was built by another company from America in 1880. There is a large iron bell which was made in England, and it used to ring out every half an hour, but it is not working now. You will also notice that the metal frame of the building is red and thus easily recognisable. Ladies and Gents, I should have mentioned before, but with this busy hustle and bustle here, we all need to hold on carefully to our belongings to avoid any pickpocketing."

Carlos shrugged his shoulders and lamented, "It is such a damn pity that both petty theft and more serious crimes continue to plague this country. I hope that with the right policing and law enforcement, this situation will improve. I cannot pretend that we do not have crime in Florida or New York, or London, or Toronto."

Arthur agreed and added, "I heard that London is now the knife crime capital of the world! It's sad to say that most of the victims and the killers are very young black men."

As the group strolled into the market, they were presented with lanes of small and large stalls of clothing, electronic goods and household wares through to the meat section including those with special provision of halal products. The food stalls were stocked with many local snacks and treats.

Michael paused and commented, "As you can see, there are hundreds of our fellow Guyanese who are working very hard to eke out a living. I guess that there must be a lot of competition between the larger and more established stallholders inside and the stallholders on the outside."

Arthur agreed with Michael and observed, "It certainly seems as if there is healthy competition going on here. But whilst I can see that most of the units inside are kept in a clean state, those on the outside are operating in dirty surroundings."

Carlos shook his head and was more critical, "I would go so far as to say that this whole area including the unique iron structure of the building should be re-developed with help for the small stallholders to have neat and clean units. At the moment, I cannot see myself buying any foodstuff here."

Michael pointed out, "I do recall that shortly after the new government took office in August 2020, the City Mayor and Council put forward a Stabroek Re-development Project. But so far, that idea has not moved forward. My feeling is that the government is not pleased with the way that the city has been managed for decades now, and perhaps they have other ideas for a re-development here."

Vishnu remarked, "It is quite obvious that this whole area needs to be given a different focus including all of the historic buildings such as the Parliament, City Hall, the Law Courts and other important sites. Of course, whatever proposals are made, the local people of Georgetown and in the surrounding areas as well as the people who come here to do their shopping and so on, must be consulted properly as they will be the main users of all the services."

Peter nodded and asked, "Do you mean a much bigger project costing many more millions of American dollars? As far as consulting is concerned, I think that the biggest opposition to any plans will come from these small stallholders. You see, they have been enjoying the benefit of having customers who pass by and notice their goods before they go into the market. If that advantage is taken away, there could be big trouble!"

Vishnu emphatically said, "Yes!"

Michael smiled, looked around, and noted, "Man, these days in Guyana, money talks! We have to look at these developments in bigger and better ways. I also agree with Peter. Any design for a re-development of the market will have to provide these vendors with the same opportunities whilst being given a cleaner and better environment. I think that they will want to continue to offer their goods a little cheaper than the stalls inside the market."

Carlos seemed to be unimpressed by the suggestions and commented, "Look, there is no doubt that Georgetown has a lot of important history and special sites. But I am still concerned about trying to re-develop the city when we have heard that most of it could be wiped out by one tsunami. We need a new capital further inland from here and not too far from the Cheddi Jagan International Airport. I see that the President is very keen on building a Silica City there."

Michael was happy to add his views, "Now I am very pleased that you have mentioned the Silica City. Preparation works are already underway, and consultations are happening with the local people living in or near the area chosen for the city. Especially with the people in a place called Kuru Kururu and Circuitville village. The government plans to build hundreds of houses in the Phase One of the development. The work to accommodate hundreds of young professionals who will operate in the city is already progressing rapidly. A master plan is being developed so that within the next twenty years, most of the city will be completed. Unfortunately, most of us here will not be around to see it."

Carlos pulled a sad face and lamented, "Yes, cities take a long time to build and to establish their own character and atmosphere, but this young President is not wasting any time to move this project forward. This is what you get with an energetic and ambitious young person showing inspirational leadership here, in the region and internationally. President Ali is not just a visionary. He is also an active hands-on leader. May God continue to bless him and his colleagues. Guyana is now rising out of a deep slumber."

Ramesh pointed out, "Whilst such a city can be built from scratch, there are many examples of new cities around the world to take ideas from. If Sati and I as well as our children are to return to Guyana, I think that we will opt for the new city as our home and work."

Sati immediately agreed, "Yes, that will be our best option. Of course, we will expect at least the same level of salaries we are enjoying now for our skills."

Parvati smiled, looked at Vishnu and said, "I will only return to live here in my retirement provided they have good hospital facilities and a decent care system for pensioners like us."

Vishnu picked up on Parvati's suggestion, "Well, I am now too old to cope with all the new technologies and artificial this and artificial that. I would be very happy with a nice comfortable home with my life partner here, our own fruit and vegetable plot and good fresh air. No more rat race for me!"

Parvati reached out and held Vishnu's right hand, "I left Guyana many years ago, but Guyana never left me."

As the tour party began to leave the market, a young man approached Michael in a menacing manner and mumbled, "Give me a raise."

Michael was caught off guard and replied, "Young man, why are you asking me for money? I can see that you are fit and well enough to do some work. Do I look like I am made of money?"

There was no response as the young man swore at him and began to move away.

Arthur shook his head and commented, "You see, if you were on your own, he would have just picked your pocket. Whilst we can all talk about the advancement of Guyana, we must be mindful that some people like that young man, will be left behind. Such people will need a lot of help. And I don't mean handouts. But more job opportunities and the right training and mentoring to build on their natural abilities and talent."

Vishnu stepped in, took out four one thousand Guyana dollar notes, and called out to the young man, "Here, take this money and use it to make more."

The stranger simply grabbed the notes and sauntered off through the crowd without acknowledging Vishnu.

Michael was annoyed and unimpressed by the young man's demeanour and attitude, and lamented, "I doubt whether he will use that money to start up something to help himself to make a living. We see a lot of this even in America and Canada. Such young people demand the best things in life but will not work for them. I do agree with Arthur. That young man needs a lot of guidance."

The tour party, still led by Michael, slowly walked across to the Parliament Building in Brickdam. They stood together at the main iron gates leading to the entrance of the two-storeyed building which initially housed the National Assembly at the right-hand wing, and the office of the Head of State in the left wing. At the centre, there is a dome and a balcony overlooking the front, and the Brickdam street.

The building was designed and built by the architect Joseph Hadfield and formally handed over to the British Administration on the fifth of August 1834. At the front of the building there are two canons mounted on stone plinths. The Guyana flag, known as the Golden Arrowhead, flies majestically over the apex of the portico at the entrance.

Michael stood back to take in the architecture of the building and drew attention to a bronze statue to the right of the canons.

He smiled and was full of admiration as he stated, "Now, I must mention a truly great Guyanese by the name of Hubert Nathaniel Critchlow who had dedicated his life to fighting for workers' rights through the Trades Union movement. This statue was unveiled by Dr Cheddi Jagan, the then Premier of British Guiana in 1964. Mister Critchlow is known as the Father of Trade Unionism in Guyana and founded the first Trades Union way back in 1919. It was called the British Guiana Labour Union, or BGLU. From the tender age of fourteen he took on many types of jobs to make a living here in Georgetown. He was also an athlete, footballer and cricketer. A truly amazing man! Maybe that young man who asked for a raise should be taught about this great human being."

Ramesh pointed out, "In case anyone is confused when you see Guyana's Parliament meeting in another place called the Arthur Chung Conference Centre in Liliendaal, that was due to when the Covid pandemic began."

Michael turned around to face the group, "Now, we do not have the time to visit the incredible and historic structures around Georgetown, but we can have a tour and see many of them from the cars. Let us go back and find Nazir and John and enjoy the drive around the city. It will be nice to get out of this heat and humidity and sit in the air-conditioned comfort of the cars. I suggest that after the drive we can stop at a great restaurant for our lunch."

Arthur immediately agreed, "Yes! After seeing and smelling so much foodstuff at the market, I would love for us to try out the New Thriving Chinese Restaurant on Main Street for our lunch."

Carlos smiled and cupped his right hand to his mouth, "Man, that sounds really good. I'm already salivating!"

Vishnu raised both hands in front of his face and pleaded, "Gentlemen, please let's not get carried away. Can we ask the ladies what they prefer to have for lunch?"

Parvati responded, "Thank you. I was wondering when you were going to ask for our opinions. I do not mind Chinese food, but I always go for our more traditional Guyanese curries and stews as we have been enjoying on the trip since we arrived."

Doreen shrugged her shoulders and said, "Same here. We have heard of many upmarket and fusion style foods in the modern restaurants. But, like Parvati, I prefer our traditional and simple food."

Muriel mentioned, "So far, we have shared a great variety of our delicious foods on our trip, and we are now seeing and tasting other types of cuisine coming into the country. That Chinese restaurant suggested by Arthur is not like our local traditional Chinese eating places with the usual chow mein, fried rice and so on. They serve a great mix of authentic Cantonese Chinese recipes in an amazing venue."

Sati suggested, "Well, we haven't tried any kind of Chinese food as yet, so I am happy to go with Arthur's idea. bear in mind that there are other types of food I would like to try on this trip."

Neesha nodded and added, "Yes, with all the building going on in the country and more people visiting and working here from abroad, things like hotels, guest houses and other facilities have to be in place. The Maharaja Palace restaurant in Sheriff Street serves more authentic food from India which is different from our local Guyanese curries. You guys from abroad will know more about that kind of Indian food than our local Guyanese people. But if this is progress, I am all for it."

Michael anxiously stepped forward, rubbed his stomach, and said, "Right. I think that I am hearing most of you in favour of Arthur's choice. So, let's get on with the drive around and then stop for lunch at the New Thriving Chinese Restaurant. As, right now I am feeling like on Old Starving Guyanese Man!"

Arthur smiled contentedly and said, "By the way I am assured that the restaurant does not serve mountain chicken."

Michael was relieved to hear this and exclaimed, "Thank God for that! I hope to taste their Cantonese Duck which is different from Peking Duck. Would you all like to know about the difference between them?"

Doreen smiled and replied, "No thank you. Please let's go for our lunch."

19

Of monuments, meeting places and silent prayers

The drive around Georgetown via Brickdam alongside the locations of a few of the official governmental buildings through to Vlissengen Road past the 1763 Monument, the city's zoo at the front of the Botanical Gardens, up to the seawall road turning left by the Bandstand, the Umana Yana, and into Main Street in front of the grand New Thriving Chinese Restaurant, took about forty minutes with the cars stopping briefly at chosen sites for pictures and videos.

Michael was well prepared to speak about the 1763 Monument and stepped out gingerly, flexing his arms in readiness for action.

"Now, you all heard about the 1763 Berbice Slave Rebellion led by Kofi and his generals against the Dutch. This statue here may appear to be crude and ugly. But it does not detract from the power and purpose of that great man. Just think back to about two hundred and sixty years ago and try to imagine how brave and strong was that man and the thousands who fought with him against the Dutch oppressors. Don't forget that Kofi even declared himself as Governor of Berbice!"

Ramesh looked up at the imposing statue, took a deep breath, and then commented, "Yes Uncle Michael. Kofi was a man with a vision. He and his companions were very successful in achieving the first part of that vision to be free from their suppression. The late President Forbes Burnham who unveiled the statue as part of the tenth anniversary of Guyana's Independence, was also a man with a vision for Guyana to become self-sufficient and not to depend on goods and other products imported from abroad. But unfortunately, both Kofi and Burnham could not achieve their dreams. This should be a warning to our current leaders. Having a compelling vision is one thing, but delivering it is quite another."

Arthur nodded vigorously and pointed out, "Hear! Hear! The vision for a new Guyana must be one of bringing our people together, saying where we are heading towards, and moving to that place hand in hand. This is not an easy thing to accomplish, and it will take many years, and even decades."

Michael lowered his head and said, "Yes, my brother. Let's hope that it will not take another two hundred plus years! OK, let's move on."

Nazir and John stopped their cars briefly in front of the Botanical Gardens and Zoological Park. They both stood beside each other at the entrance of the zoo and encouraged the tour group to gather around.

Nazir nodded to Michael as if to ask his permission to say something about the zoo, "Thank you Michael. Let me say that as a small boy I was always excited to be brought here for a visit to see some amazing animals and birds of our country. But today, I am ashamed to say that it is in such a bad state that I cannot bring myself or my grandchildren here. I will allow John to say a few words on this."

John took up Nazir's invitation, "Yes, I would advise against us going in to visit that zoo. Now that most of us have seen the Iwokrama set up and the wonderful work being done there to show how these creatures are supposed to be in their own natural environment instead of being caged up, I would strongly recommend that this zoo is closed down. I do not wish to even see this place upgraded or re-developed. I think that it is against the whole idea of the need to protect our animals and birds in their own environment. I hope that the government and the city council can rethink this place and come up with a more modern approach to provide information about our wildlife, the rainforests and so on."

Arthur thought for a moment and suggested, "Maybe they could set up a sort of host site for all the attractions in the hinterland showing films about the rainforests, places like Iwokrama, the Kaieteur Falls, life in the Amerindian communities, and so on to give people a flavour of the beauty of our interior and how it is being protected."

Carlos added, "Yes, show school children and our youths about how to travel to and survive in the hinterland including places such as the Rupununi. Of course, such things can be shown in all schools to encourage the next generation to learn how to respect and care for the environment. And this hub idea can allow tourists to come and get a good view of our country and to have the best advice about tours."

Michael frowned and said, "I have heard about some master plan for the zoo and the area. But I agree with you that whatever is done here there should be no cages or other systems to keep animals and birds in a country that wants to lead the world in preservation. We need to think differently here, and yes, I would abandon the zoo. Perhaps instead of cages they could build a rehabilitation centre for animals and birds with the plan to release them all back to their own environment as safely as possible. But no zoo for me."

The ladies gave a resounding approval by shouting "Yes!"

The tour of the city continued to a short stop at the seawall where they took in a grand view of the mighty Atlantic Ocean, and the colourful block pavings giving the area a new look that was part of the beautification project of Her Excellency Arya Ali, the First Lady of Guyana.

Doreen enjoyed the sights and said, "This place is now much nicer and well designed to give the people lots of opportunities to come here, relax, chill out and stay fit and healthy."

Parvati smiled contentedly and added, "It is now so beautiful here. I only hope that the people will take care of it and keep it clean. I am so proud of what our young people are doing in this country. I like the new snack outlets around the bandstand area. I also love all the colours of the paving stones, the buildings, the fences and the buntings. Beautiful Guyana looking even more attractive!"

The next stop on their Georgetown tour was at the Umana Yana. John and Muriel led the group slowly to the monument of five large tree poles on a white stone base and paused to read a plaque at its base. This is known as the African Liberation Monument within the grounds of the benab.

Muriel read the inscription out aloud, "Mourn not for us who died but for our brothers everywhere who live in bondage and in mourning turn away to act. The monument was erected in tribute to the Fighters of Freedom in Africa which was unveiled on Monday 26th August 1974 by President Forbes Burnham."

John was delighted to speak about the Umana Yana, "Thank you Muriel. The structure you see here is a circular shaped large room called a benab which is a meeting place you can see in our Amerindian villages around the country. Of course, the benabs are in different sizes but they serve the same purpose. Here, in the Umana Yana our people can come to meet or to exhibit our traditionally made products. As you can see inside, the space is dominated by the large conical roof made of thatch and wood. This benab has had to be rebuilt as it was completely burnt down in 2014. The open base with four entrances is designed to allow air to freely pass through the building and thus keep it cool."

Michael looked around the space and the roof, and asked, "Am I right in saying that this entire structure has been made without the use of nails? Also, was this built by our brothers and sisters from the Wai Wai tribe?"

John and Muriel replied together, "Yes!"

John proceeded to describe the main elements of the benab, "As you look up to the apex of the thatched roof made of the manicole palm leaves supported by some large and smooth wallaba posts, it is about fifty-five feet tall. Everything is firmly tied together with great skill and using the vines of the mukru, turu and nibbi plants. Actually, this benab happens to be the largest one in Guyana. So, the craftsmen and women had to scale up the building from their knowledge of the basic system of construction. This is a truly special place for all to see and experience."

The group had a closer look around the benab and its surrounds before boarding the cars for a final brief stop ahead of lunch. They were led by Michael when they arrived in front of the iconic Red House bearing its new name of the Cheddi Jagan Research Centre in bold red letters against a white wooden background. The three-storey building's dark red colouring including its roof and a tower at the top clearly contrasted with the white shutters of several tall windows. The entrance was dominated by two white rectangular posts and white staked fencing.

Michael retrieved his trusted notebook, and after briefly referring to it, announced, "This, as you will notice, is a grand wooden red and white house which goes back to the nineteenth century. It was the official residence of Dr Cheddi Jagan our first Premier of British Guiana in 1961. This building is a national monument, and from March 2000 it became the Cheddi Jagan Research Centre which is dedicated to the life and work of the great man, and of course, his wife Janet Jagan our first female Prime Minister and first female President. Anyone who is interested in the political history of this country and this couple's roles in it should use the facilities for research. If all is well, I think that our long-awaited lunch is at hand, or so my stomach is telling me."

Peter, Arthur and Carlos were also rubbing their stomachs in anticipation, and quickly headed back to their car. Nazir and John were more than happy to complete the short distance to park across the street and in front of the restaurant.

After their sumptuous lunch, the tour party decided to walk up to the large open terrace to relax and have some cold refreshment. Vishnu proudly put on his 'One Guyana' cap. Michael followed suit and the two friends posed for pictures beside Doreen and Parvati. The rest of the tour party then joined them for a group picture taken by one of the waiters who was then given a generous tip by Peter. As they continued to chat amongst themselves, Nazir and John hurriedly left the group and ran out of the building across the road and towards their cars.

A stranger stood near the driver's door of Nazir's car and stretched out his right hand demanding, "Give me some money for looking after your car!"

Nazir was momentarily taken aback, then asked, "Why?"

The man, wearing a black cap, an unclean white T-shirt, khaki slacks and an old pair of sneakers, said, "I been watchin' yuh cars."

Nazir snapped back, "Look. Just get lost! I was watching you watching the cars!"

As John stepped forward, the man desisted and quietly walked away muttering to himself. Nazir and John looked at each other, shrugged their shoulders and beckoned their passengers to prepare to leave the restaurant.

Further down Main Street, the cars passed more grand colonial style buildings including the residence of the Prime Minister, State House used by the President, and through to the National Library at the corner of Main Street and Church Street. Directly in front of the southern end of Main Street, Nazir in the first car pointed out the imposing Bank of Guyana, and to its left, the National Museum. He signalled for John to follow him as he turned left at the Avenue of the Republic and stopped briefly near to the magnificent St Georges Cathedral.

Michael enthusiastically stepped out of the car, and once again took out his notebook to refer to his information on the cathedral.

He spoke above the noise of the vehicular traffic, "I think that every Guyanese will recognise this magnificent, mostly wooden, building standing on this unique spot in our great city. It is, of course, known as one of the largest wooden buildings in the world, and has been here since 1892. I do not know much about architecture, but I note that this style is called gothic. As you can see, there is some restoration work being carried out both on the outside and the inside of the building. One of the most important timbers used here is the famous greenheart which is strong enough to last for hundreds of years. The beautifully carved woodwork inside, is mostly of mahogany."

Carlos interrupted Michael, "Sorry Michael, but I just wanted to say that I remember in my boyhood days going to high school here in Georgetown, when me and some friends used to come here on Sunday afternoons and ride around that circular track a few times. It was great fun until a policeman or woman stopped us."

Doreen looked up admiringly at the tall stained-glass windows which dominated the structure and observed, "That is truly beautiful, bright and must be full of meaning. I can't wait to go in and say a little prayer there."

Muriel looked across at Parvati and Sati and suggested, "Please feel free to join us if only for a few moments. Do sit with us as we do a short prayer on behalf of all of us as well as our beloved country."

Michael was pleased with Doreen's initiative, and he asked her to lead the group up the white concreted steps set out like a low pyramid shape through the main entrance of three doorways. Once inside, they all looked up and around at the grand wooden arches leading to the altar.

Michael turned to Vishnu as they took their seats along one of the solid wooden pews and whispered, "That brass lectern shaped like an eagle was donated by Barbados. I love how so much light pours through all of those beautiful stained-glass windows to provide such a calming effect. That amazing chandelier was given by Queen Victoria."

Doreen, sitting beside Michael with clasped hands to say her personal prayers, whispered to him, "OK. Let me say my prayers for the protection of this grand church, for all of us on this trip, and for the future of Guyana."

Michael also clasped his hands, closed his eyes, and whispered in reply, "Amen."

The tour party sat quietly for a few minutes of calm and reflection in a place of spiritual peace and sanctuary. The refurbished and renovated cathedral will no doubt continue to serve the people of Guyana amidst a growing collection of modern concreted, steel and glass structures reaching up around it over many decades to come. The charm and mystique of Georgetown is worthy of restoration and preservation to provide residents and visitors with a glimpse of its glorious colonial past, the sense of an emergence from difficulties and despair, and the signs of a relentless drive to modernisation.

20

Of runs, runners and riders

As soon as the tour party completed their trip to Georgetown and returned to Anna Catherina, they took turns to shower and refresh themselves using the modern facilities at Nazir's and Neesha's as well as John's and Muriel's homes. They agreed to gather at the formers' home for their welcome dinner. Neesha had asked for a simple main course of boiled sweet potatoes, eddoes, ripe plantains, cassava and slices of breadfruit which were boiled and then lightly fried. A special side dish of a popular Guyanese version of black pudding along with some very hot pepper sauce was purchased from a local snack stall. The meal was completed with fried saltfish. Each of the main items was presented along the middle of the grand dining table as Neesha spoke.

"Nazir and I felt that in such a short time, we have had a taste of so many types of our Guyanese as well as some foreign dishes. So, to help settle our stomachs down, we are offering some simple what we call local "Soul Food". We as a family have always set aside one lunch or dinner for this kind of food. It is tasty, wholesome and filling. I do hope that you enjoy the meal."

Everyone was invited to serve themselves, and it soon became apparent that one diner was missing. It was Michael.

Doreen raised her right hand, chuckled, and said, "Our Histry Maan is right now making new history upstairs in the toilet. He is having some severe "belly wuk". I do hope that he will join us soon. But there is no need to wait for him. Please start eating."

Carlos giggled and said, "Obviously, whatever John concocted for Michael hasn't worked!"

During the course of the meal, Peter took the place of Michael to talk about some of the great Guyanese sportsmen and women.

He began by saying, "Whilst our dear friend is having his marathon run, it reminds me of the local Guyanese legend named Moses Dwarka, the middle-distance runner from LBI. He was called the "Barefoot King". We also had other great runners such as Clem Fields, Harry Powell and George DePeana."

Carlos, who was a fan of Cycling, mentioned, "We had two great cyclists by the names of George "Boy Blue" Cumberbatch and David "Boogie" DeFreitas. Right now, we have a great young female cycling champion from Mackenzie, Linden. Her name is Suzanne Hamilton. We have also had some other female champions including Naomi Singh, Marica Dick and Claire Fraser-Green."

Doreen nodded approvingly and said, "I'm glad that you mention our female sportspeople. I recall a champion runner named Aliann Pompey who won a Commonwealth Gold Medal. You may or may not remember but I was a very good athlete in my schooldays. There was no training facility or track in those days, and I did not continue to improve. I am so happy to see that there is now a new track built between Anna Catherina and Leonora. That is one bit of progress that I personally appreciate. A healthy population makes a strong nation. Speaking of strength, just look at our own muscleman Afzal!"

Afzal flexed his muscular arms into the pose of a competitive bodybuilder and said, "I love weightlifting, bodybuilding, boxing and wrestling. Let me see, I can mention our best ever female bodybuilder by the name of Laura Creavalle who was born in Essequibo. She was outstanding, and is now living in Toronto. To me, the one male Guyanese bodybuilder who stands out is Kerwin Clarke with others such as Hugh Ross, Bruce Whatley, Yannick Grimes, Devon Davis and Emerson Campbell."

Carlos intervened, "Hey, don't forget some other females such as Rosanna Fung and Chandini Khan."

Arthur was hugely impressed and said, "Wow! I don't know how you guys remember all of those names! I am happy to hear the mention of at least one Chinese there!"

Vishnu looked at his arms disdainfully and added, "As you can all see, I haven't got any muscles to show off here. But I am sure that back in the 1960s there was a time when our local youths took up weightlifting and bodybuilding in our villages. I remember a couple of the Yhap brothers in Anna Catherina, Malcolm and Denis. Malcolm was a competitor for bodybuilding. Other youngsters like Afzal and his friends used to walk around in the villages sticking their bulging chests out like proud gorillas. Skinny guys like me and Michael could only look on with envy."

Peter laughed and added, "I don't know if you all will remember a lil guy from right here in Cornelia Ida who migrated to London and competed in weightlifting for Great Britain with a lot of success as a powerlifter. Sadly, he recently passed away in London. He had held a world record and was mentioned in the *Guiness Book of Records*. His name was Narendra Bhairo and known as "Naro". May his soul rest in peace."

The entire group was saddened to learn of the untimely demise of the local and British hero, whilst at the same time, they felt great pride about his achievements.

Afzal was now in his element as he recalled, "In boxing, Guyana has produced some great champions such as Andrew "Sixhead" Lewis who was the World Boxing Association, or WBA welterweight champion. Then we had Wayne "Big Truck" Braithwaite who was the World Boxing Council or WBC cruiserweight champion. Another was Ivan "Vicious" Vivian Harris, the WBA light welterweight champion in 2002 and 2005. Speaking of Guyanese who went abroad and did well in sports, I think that the one I admired the most was Denis Andries who went on to win the WBC light heavyweight title. He was the only Guyanese boxer who won a World title three times. Oh, and we had a guy named Motie "Kid" Singh who was called the "Fighting Rajah" and competed in the US way back in the 1920s!"

Vishnu chuckled and asked, "Afzal, I just don't know how you can remember all those names and facts about Guyanese boxers. I love some of the names they had, especially "Big Truck" and "Sixhead". I am sure that you can recall many more names from the sport."

Afzal raised both clenched fists and posed like a boxer as he continued, "I love talking about boxing just like how Peter can tell you so much about cricket. A few more boxing names are guys like Terrence Alli, Patrick Ford, Lennox Beckles and Kenny Bristol. Only one regret I have about Guyanese boxing is that we never produced a great heavyweight world champion. But then who could have stood up to my heroes such as Muhamad Ali, Joe Frazier, Mike Tyson and Lennox Lewis?"

Carlos suggested, "I am sure that if we have the right trainers, we could find the heavyweights. After all, Lennox Lewis is of Jamaican heritage. Anyway, enough about our boxers. Who do you consider to be our best-known professional wrestler?"

Afzal took a few moments to collect his thoughts and then mentioned, "Well, the one fighter that comes to mind is the great Ezekiel Jackson whose real name was, let me get this right, Parmar Ryckton Edward Stephens. He fought on the American World Wrestling Entertainment or WWE circuit. Do you all remember the great Dara Singh and his brother Randhawa Singh who were freestyle wrestling champions from India? Dara was famous for playing the strongman roles in Bollywood films. The brothers came to put on exhibition shows here in Guyana in the 1960s. That sparked my interest in wrestling, bodybuilding and weightlifting."

As the conversation progressed, Doreen noticed the long-awaited emergence of Michael who was inching his way down the stairs with great care.

She giggled and said, "Speaking about Athletes, here comes my own long-distance runner! Michael, I hope that all is well. Do come and join us for some solid food which will settle your tired belly and sore behind!"

Michael, still feeling the after-effects of his marathon spell in the toilet, rubbed his stomach gently, and cautiously took a seat at the table beside Doreen.

He spoke in a hushed voice, "Man, I can't handle any food at the moment. Just give me some more time to rest my ass. I could hear some of your talk about Guyanese sportsmen and women. Do carry on. This is an area I do not have much information to offer."

Arthur welcomed Michael and asked, "What about my favourite sport of table tennis?"

Peter was quick to respond, "Aha! Now, we loved to play table tennis in the cricket pavilion at CI and the other grounds around the country. One reason was that table tennis was good to keep our eyes, ball coordination and our reflexes very sharp. Our most famous Guyanese table tennis champion was George Braithwaite who lived most of his life in the USA and represented that country with great pride and success. In the modern era, we now have a brilliant young woman named Chelsea Edghill who became the first player from Guyana to compete in the Olympic Games in Tokyo."

Michael perked up after drinking some soothing warm water and asked, "What about football and football players from Guyana? I know that, as a nation, we have never been really strong in this sport like our neighbours Trinidad and Jamaica, and of course, the mighty Brazil. But Peter, you might know a lot about our football."

Peter nodded and replied, "Yes, back in the 1960s we played a lot of football at the CI cricket club ground and used to look at the black and white newsreels about the game played in the English Leagues and of course, Brazil. Guyana has had some good players with a number born of Guyanese heritage doing very well in England. Off the top of my head, I can mention guys like the Cort brothers, Walter Moore, Nigel Codrington, Matthew Briggs, Samuel Cox, Christopher Nurse and Shawn Bishop. The sport really needs a lot of investment here, and as with the other sports we mentioned, we should then produce even better sportsmen and women,"

Vishnu surmised, "I think that you are right about that. As our Guyana economy grows as well as our population with more ex-patriots returning here, we should see greater interest in sports and other leisure activities along with demand for more and better facilities including sports grounds, gyms and parks. A strong nation has to be built on a healthier population. I would go even further to suggest that the provision of such facilities and opportunities for our growing younger population must be one way of encouraging young people away from crime."

Carlos agreed and added, "You are so right Vishnu. In fact, as Guyana gets stronger, our young sportsmen and women from abroad may be tempted to return to represent the country like some of the footballers you mentioned. Perhaps, apart from having the right jobs here, they could even help to reverse the brain drain trend by advancing our higher education system to provide young people from here and abroad opportunities to do their college studies here instead of moving to America and Canada."

Parvati pointed out, "Well, if such facilities and opportunities were here in Guyana, our grandchildren could come to do their degrees at a much lower cost than in America, Britain and Canada. But we have to be mindful of avoiding any hint of resentment by locals against those who could be conceived as foreigners coming here to take advantage of the situation. Our young people should be in a position to learn from each other."

Doreen agreed with Parvati and added, "Yes, our country lost a lot of our finest brains over the last fifty years with people going away to study and then work and live in the UK, US and Canada. We need to buck that trend and turn it around so that our country can benefit from the best of our talent here and abroad working together. Sati, what do you say?"

Sati and Ramesh who were engrossed in listening to the conversations, took turns to offer their opinions.

Sati pointed out, "Clearly, we left Guyana at a time of great uncertainty and little progress since independence. We were lucky to get very good jobs in New York. But not everyone was so lucky, and they literally ran away from the hardships here, and sacrificed a lot to provide for their families abroad, and even send some help to those back home. So, it was not all about pursuing higher education. Our people worked very hard in very harsh conditions and in environments full of discrimination and racism. I hope that the conditions will be just right here in Guyana for that re-migration to take place over the next ten years and beyond. None of this will happen overnight."

Ramesh offered, "Again, I agree. We foreigners must tread carefully here. We must not speak and act as if we know everything, and thus cause our fellow brothers and sisters here in Guyana to feel in any way insecure. We must show them the utmost respect for remaining here and fighting for their survival against the challenges which made us get away from the country. I for one greatly admire the energy and hard work being shown by the young people in government, and we need to continue to support them."

Peter raised his right hand and enthused, "I do agree with you all. I had promised to talk a little bit about some great local cricketers from this village and CI who played their cricket at that club. Of the older names, you may recall guys like "Bussoo" Persaud, Tamaldeo and Seeram. Tamal was a very good left-arm spinner and competent table tennis player. The next generation produced some outstanding talent. First there was Sahadeo "Buns" Persaud, the younger brother of Bussoo, and an elegant opening batsman. He loved teaching, and after representing Guyana at the Under 19 level, he became a teacher and later, a headteacher. The next notable star from CI was Debichand Charran who played for the Guyana Under 19s as a left-hand batsman rated as potentially, the next Alvin Kallicharan back in the 1970s. He was followed by possibly the best all-round cricketer we ever produced in CI and the West Coast of Demerara. He was Babu Sankar who represented Guyana and the West Indies at Under 19 level. Later on, came Ravindranath Seeram who was a brilliant middle-order right hand batsman and who had a good stint for Guyana both at Youth and Senior levels."

Afzal added, "CI was a very strong club in those years. It was even stronger as some players such as Tribeni Ram, Frankie Joseph and Royston Brown a relative of Sir Clive Lloyd, came from Anna Catherina which didn't have its own club and ground."

Peter nodded and continued, "I have to mention two players who had roots here in Anna Catherina and CI but played most of their cricket in and for England."

Michael's eyes lit up as he asked, "Wow! Who were those players?"

Peter replied, "Well, there was Monte Lynch of Anna Catherina who is retired now, but had a great first-class career mostly with Surrey County and Gloucestershire County where he scored over twenty-six thousand runs and over forty centuries. He was a popular hard-hitting middle order right-handed batsman who also played for Guyana in the 1982/83 Shell Shield championship of the West Indies. He went with an unofficial West Indies cricket squad to South Africa and was given a three-year ban. He was later selected to play for England against the West Indies in three One Day Internationals but failed having been run out for a duck in the first one, and not having faced a ball."

Michael smiled with some satisfaction and said, "I think that he should have played more for Guyana and even the West Indies. But I guess that politics does come into play. So, Peter, who is the next player?"

Peter took a sip of cold water and continued, "The next player is Mark Ramprakash the former Middlesex and England player whose father is from CI and that is the connection. He was a classy right-handed batsman, very orthodox and with a good temperament. He scored over one hundred centuries in first class cricket including a few for England in Test Matches. But, for some reason, he never managed to carry the same heavy and consistent scoring in first class County Cricket into the Test arena. I wish he could have opted to play for Guyana and break into the West Indies side. But he is much more of an Englishman and even got national fame in the UK when he won the popular TV show called 'Strictly Come Dancing'! I would also like to mention another very talented all-rounder of Guyanese heritage, by the name of Chris Lewis who had a very successful career at Surrey and for England. Sadly, he was convicted in the UK for an offence involving illegal drugs and served time in prison for it."

Vishnu thanked Peter and the others who spoke about so many of Guyana's great sportsmen and women, and said, "This has been a real eye-opener for me. I have never heard of so many Guyanese and people connected with Guyana in all my years. I am sure that there are many more amazing achievers both here and abroad. But I think that we have had enough about this in this one sitting. It is very important for us as Guyanese to remember these people who have been such a big part of our nation's history and psyche."

Nazir agreed and commented, "Thank you all for yet another interesting day of touring and learning about so much of what makes this country greater than we think. I hope that we can have a restful night and be up and ready to see what tomorrow brings."

Michael excused himself quietly and ambled across to the stairway. He paused for a moment at the bottom of the stairs, waved to the group, and mumbled a "Goodnight" as he cautiously stepped up. Doreen followed closely behind him as the tour party laughed.

21

Parika, Supenaam, Charity and Pomeroon's spirits

The tour party had agreed to explore part of the Region 2 of Pomeroon-Supenaam in Essequibo at a more leisurely pace with the relatively short and smooth car ride from Anna Catherina to the small town of Parika on the East Bank of the great river. Normally, travellers would opt for the earliest ferry from Parika stelling at pre-dawn. However, the group decided to aim for a later ferry after having a light breakfast at John's and Muriel's home.

John and Muriel were nominated as the leads for the tour which they hoped would include a river taxi ride on the serene Pomeroon River, to visit an Amerindian village settlement. They had arranged, as is customary, for a formal visit through the local Toshao. Nazir and Neesha had opted out of the trip, and Afzal agreed to drive Nazir's car to take Vishnu, Parvati, Ramesh, Sati, Michael and Doreen. The other members of the tour party, Arthur, Carlos, Maria and Peter joined John and Muriel in their car.

Although Michael had announced that he was back to good health and was ready for the trip, John advised the group that they should opt to take the ferry from Parika to Supenaam as opposed to the quicker river taxi boat which would be much more uncomfortable for most of the tour party.

Before Michael could suggest otherwise, Doreen stepped in and advised, "There is no way that Michael could handle a rough river taxi ride across that river. Let's save his stomach for a more serene ride on a small boat on the Pomeroon."

Michael agreed with Doreen and tried to assure his fellow travellers that he was well enough to handle the entire trip.

Arthur intervened and asked, "I will leave all the decisions about things like where we will have our lunch and stop for rests, to John and Muriel. They must have done such trips many times in the past. I know that with so many miles of river travel we will need to relieve ourselves. I hope that we find clean toilets on this trip especially for the ladies in our group."

Muriel acknowledged Arthur's concerns and tried to reassure everyone, "Please don't worry about that. John and I know the right places to use. First of all, please make sure that you use the toilets at Parika before boarding the ferry. Also, when we arrive at Supenaam, please do the same before we go on our long drive to Charity where we will have our lunch."

The drive from Anna Catherina to Parika was relatively smooth and at a good pace as both cars passed through the villages of Leonora, Stewartville, Uitvlugt, Zeeburg, De Kendren, Meten Meer Zorg, Tuschen and Vergenoegen, through to Parika. Michael took out his notebook and provided a brief commentary for those in the car being driven by Afzal.

"I can just give you some of the highlights on this part of our trip. Of course, we all visited the new West Central Mall in Leonora. Before that, we saw the impressive Anna Catherina Mosque and the Leonora Stadium. We also passed the new Sheriff General Hospital in Leonora, the old Police Station in Seafield and off the main road near to the seafront, I can mention the Leonora Mosque, the private home of the President, and the new Leonora Diagnostic and Treatment Centre. Just opposite the Leonora Police Station is a well-established dry goods business and a new restaurant called Wolf's Paratha Palace. Afzal, could you please make a left turn into Uitvlugt Estate Road so that we could just have a brief look at the sugar factory. I know that we cannot spend much time there."

Afzal nodded, signalled for the left turn and ensured that John followed him.

Vishnu pointed out, "Before we talk about the sugar factory, I hope that we will spend some time to say something about our local cinemas around this coast and elsewhere in the country. Near here was the old Duchess cinema which was owned by the late Dost Mohamed from Leonora and run by his son the late Oli Mohamed. That cinema was bought by Robert Sookraj who named it Earlo after his son Earl. Whilst Anna Catherina had the Monarch cinema, and Leonora had the Roxy cinema, there were others on the coast such as the Tarla in Meten-

Meer-Zorg. Cinemas were the most popular form of entertainment for decades before being overtaken by TV and media such as videos and DVDs. I am very saddened to see the abandonment of our local Monarch cinema which was the focal point for our socialising especially in the early evenings. The whole area around the cinema including the bars and restaurants was a great attraction especially for us youngsters."

Michael was impressed by Vishnu's recollection and added, "Thank you Vishnu. I remember those days very well. There is one fact I have here about Uitvlugt which will surprise everyone. Now, I am not a drinker, but I bet that you do not know about a Demerara Rum that was made here called the Uitvlught 1988. It is now a rare collector's item, and one bottle of that rum is worth about half a million Guyana dollars!"

Vishnu was shocked, "What? That can't be true!"

Michael smiled and simply nodded.

Ramesh was also taken aback and commented, "Uncle Michael, you never fail to surprise us. I just don't know where you get these facts from. But this is surely another example about the greatness of our country."

The two cars arrived at the front of the Uitvlugt Sugar Factory which remained operational after the previous government had closed a few factories around the country on the basis that they were redundant in a failing sugar industry. Thousands of sugar workers lost their jobs, and their families suffered serious economic problems.

Afzal asked everyone to assemble in front of the entrance to the factory, and spoke about the noise of the heavy machinery, "You will notice how crude and rusty the metal structure of this factory is, but it is now being modernised to produce better quality of our famous Demerara sugar, and more yield. Our new government is trying to revive the sugar industry and hopefully, jobs will be recovered alongside new ones. Notice the canal passing through from the canefields bringing the burnt and cut sugar cane in metal punts which are lifted up to tip out the cane. That canal runs through to the exit koker to take the processed sugar out to the Atlantic and away to Georgetown. If you wish to come here to see the whole operation of the factory, we can try to fit that in the tours."

Ramesh nodded and took a note of the suggestion.

Michael referred to his notebook once again and informed the group, "Well, I mentioned the rare Uitvlugt rum. But I also saw on the internet, a bottle of El Dorado 50 Years Grand Special Reserve Rum for the equivalent of just over one million Guyana dollars!"

The tour group just stood in awe as Ramesh asked Michael, "Uncle, if cane sugar is struggling as an industry in Guyana, why are we still pursuing it? I am sure that Uncle Michael can verify this fact that Guyana is not in the top ten sugar producing countries of the world. I see countries like India, Brazil, the European Union, Thailand, China, USA, Russia, Mexico, Pakistan and Australia are way ahead of Guyana. Even Ukraine, before their war with Russia, was a bigger sugar producer than Guyana. Our neighbour Venezuela is also ahead of us. Even the island of Mauritius is a bigger producer, and they have also taken our Demerara name for some of their sugar. None of this makes sense to me."

Michael paused for a few moments and then responded, "Well, it is true that many other countries are ahead of Guyana in cane sugar production, beet sugar and in their exports. But we must never forget that this country was established by the Dutch and British to grow produce for their wealth creation and not necessarily for this country. Our ancestors were brought here to provide free slave and then very cheap indentured labour. Now, and quite rightly, our brothers and sisters still working in and around sugar cane must be paid fair wages. This plus the cost of energy to run those factories put a lot of pressure on potential profit. I do not know much about business and economics, but Ramesh and Sati here could cast more light on this matter. I think that there is still a place for a more efficient and productive cane sugar industry with much-loved by products such as the highly valued rum I mentioned. In fact, I hope that with the much more reliable and cheaper energy coming to the country soon, this will also greatly help run our industries more efficiently, and economically."

Ramesh nodded and added, "I agree with you Uncle Michael. A lot of families still rely on cane sugar for a living here, and I hope that there is still a place for this product in the emerging and more modernised and diversified agriculture industry."

Sati agreed and mentioned, "There was a good example of how cane sugar could be used to support another product. In Hawaii, the Del Monte company which made pineapple in tins, used their own cane sugar grown on one of the large islands where the company was based. You will be surprised to know that the labour force used to grow, cut and load the sugarcane was taken from Japan! I know that this operation ended in Maui Island a few years ago. Now the company has a huge pineapple operation in Costa Rica. We have a lot of really sweet pineapple here in Guyana, and we should be producing and marketing our own canned pineapples with the best and more authentic Demerara sugar in the world!"

Doreen chipped in with her suggestion, "Why not really extend production of our own Guyanese cakes and biscuits such as pine tarts, and sell them all over the world?"

Parvati agreed and added, "Look, we have so many beautiful fruits here, and we should be producing much more healthy versions of bottled or canned fruit drinks such as, mango, guava, jamoon, sorrell, sapodilla and sasparilla!"

Michael was keen to offer one more bit of information to the group, "Would you believe that rum and gunpowder had a connection way back in the seventeenth century? You see, gunpowder was being experimented with and produced in mills around England, and the sailors used to test their gunpowder by pouring some rum onto it and lighting it. If the gunpowder exploded, then they were able to say that the rum provided "proof" of its viability. Hence, we hear about rum and other alcohol having "proof". If a rum is one hundred per cent proof, then it is given a rating of fifty per cent alcohol. Sorry about this bit of trivia."

Ramesh interjected, "Uncle Michael, that is not trivia. I never knew about this. Your wisdom and knowledge make you sound like an oracle!"

Shortly afterwards, the tour party left the Uitvlugt Sugar Factory and continued on their journey to Parika.

Michael referred to his notebook and announced, "We will not be able to stop at any other site on this trip as we aim to catch our ferry at the stelling. But I must mention the establishment of a very impressive place of worship and learning for our young people in this district. It is called the Maharishi Dayananda Gurukula. I hope that I have pronounced that correctly. The man leading the group is none other than the enlightened soul by the name of Dr Satish Prakash who was born here in Uitvlugt, studied Sanskrit, the ancient Indian language, and conducts lectures on traditional *Arya Samaj* verses. The teachers and students there wear white *kurtas* and pyjamas and a simple white cap."

Vishnu nodded and remarked, "I have heard of Dr Prakash and the Gurukula. They aim to offer social, cultural and charitable work to help the community, and at the same time, promote *Vedic* philosophy and teachings. That is another place worthwhile visiting if we have the time."

The tour party arrived in Parika and headed directly to the stelling to await the boarding of either the MV Sabanto or the MV Kanawan river ferries which were donated to Guyana by the Chinese government. Doreen noticed that they passed by the famous Parika market with numerous stalls under the sheltered light blue rafters and roof, and many others established along the roadside.

She nudged Parvati and Sati and suggested, "Ladies, this place is worth a special trip to do some more shopping and spend a few hours looking around the area. I can see this small town growing into an even more important location, especially with the new and faster road link from the new Demerara River Bridge being constructed."

Michael turned around to face Doreen and gave her a thumbs up.

He added, "Yes, Parika has always been a thriving marketplace for the various vegetables and fruits grown in the three major islands we will catch glimpses of from our ferry to Supenaam. We must buy some of those very small and sweet fig "Parika bananas" to take onto the ferry. Doreen, you are right about this place which will no doubt develop further into a very important town. But there is more going on here with the Parika backdam and a nice recreational area at the Bushy Park waterfront. I do hope that entrepreneurs such as Mister Stanley Ming and the government will be able to take forward ideas for development in this area. He calls his plan "Guyana 2030". The banks of the magnificent Essequibo River have an abundance of natural resources such as good quality sand, timber and water which can be treated to serve much of Guyana. This is the kind of natural resource wealth that Guyana has alongside oil and gas. The new roadways being planned and built to Parika will open incredible potential, and the great thing is that these areas are above sea level and are not prone to flooding."

There was an eerie silence in the car as Michael closed his notebook and they moved closer towards Parika stelling. Most of the tour party, and in particular, Michael, took Muriel's advice and used the toilets at a local restaurant before making their way to board the ferry that was moored alongside the old wooden stelling. Afzal and John waited in the cars until their turn came to drive slowly onto the ferry's lower-level space reserved for vehicles. Muriel led the others up a gangway to one of the seating areas on the upper deck. Afzal and John securely parked and locked the cars and then used a stairway to go up to the upper deck.

John and Muriel took on their roles as the joint leaders of the tour and invited the group to join them at a good viewing area near to the front of the MV Sabanto. Shortly after all the passengers and vehicles had boarded the ferry, its powerful engine began to ease the vessel away from its moorings, and it began to head out across the vast mouth of the river.

John positioned himself to lean on a railing and face the assembled group, "If I am right, we will be travelling through a route which will offer us glimpses of the three largest islands on this great river. They are Leguan, Wakenaam and Hog Islands. I will ask Michael to tell us something about another island which we may not see, and it is called Fort Island. First of all, we will see the southern tip of Leguan. This is the smallest of the big three. It is about twelve square miles and with a population of about two and a half thousand people. The Dutch settlers named it Leguan after spotting large numbers of iguanas there. Now, you will notice how green the islands are, and Leguan is known for its production of mostly rice, sugarcane and some cash crops. The residents of Leguan usually travel by small boats or river taxis to Parika to do their shopping at the market and other stores."

Afzal interrupted John and mentioned, "I would just like to say that our President's mother, Shariman, who was a schoolteacher and affectionately known as "Miss", is from Leguan, and so are many of his relatives."

Peter leant on the wooden rails on the right side of the bow and added, "I have visited these islands in the past and I must say that the people living here are very friendly and hospitable. Of course, they are extremely hard-working. Same for the people of Parika."

Michael shrugged his shoulders and recalled, "Well, that is true. But I have some very unpleasant memories in Parika. Back in the 1960s, some of us came here as part of a wedding party, or baraat, and man we were treated so nicely by the hosts who offered us some daal, rice and vegetable curry as soon as we arrived at the bride's home where the Hindu wedding ceremony took place. We wasted no time in tucking into that delicious hot meal! The daal was amazing and hot and spicy with some homemade pepper sauce."

Arthur stepped back and away from Michael and said with a worried look, "Now, don't talk about that time when we ate that food and almost immediately the castor oil in that daal caused our stomachs to rumble like violent volcanoes! As we scrambled to find the nearest outdoor latrine, we literally shit ourselves. The locals had locked the doors of all their latrines!"

Peter was not amused and warned, "Guys, this is not the right time to bring up that story. We are now on a ferry, and if we have such an emergency, it will be very embarrassing, ugly and messy!"

John laughed as he said, "Now you can all understand why Muriel and I suggested that we should use the facilities in Parika before boarding the ferry. Of course, it will not look too good if we mess up on this beautiful vessel named MV Sabanto which is Amerindian for "beautiful one". The MV Kanawan is also named after the Amerindian word meaning "big canoe"."

Arthur leaned slightly over to observe the dark brown murky water of the river as the ferry picked up speed cutting through the waves moving against its path and emptying into the Atlantic Ocean. The much smaller river taxis and other boats carrying full loads of fruits and other produce steered well clear of the ferry, not only to avoid any collision, but also the roughened white foamy slipstream.

Suddenly, he lifted his head up and pointed excitedly, "Look ahead! Those must be dolphins heading out to sea. Oh, what a beautiful sight!"

Carlos scrambled around in his small rucksack and took out a pair of binoculars to inspect the creatures.

He exclaimed, "Wow! They are skipping over those waves so gracefully and putting on a great show! I have heard of the pink dolphins of the Amazon River, but these are more grey in colour."

Michael noted, "I have read somewhere that where the freshwater of the river meets the salty sea water of the Ocean, there are tiger sharks and whale sharks which feed off a rich supply of plankton and other food sources. We can see the red and black mangroves around the edges of the islands and the banks of the river. Look out for huge flocks of the scarlet ibis as well as other birds such as parrots, macaws, herons, tanagers and so many more. Guyana is a birdwatcher's paradise!"

Vishnu paused his video filming and turned to Michael, "Wow! The natural habitat and almost untouched environment across Guyana contain so much diversity in botany, birds and animals. This kind of wealth and beauty is incalculable and must be sustained and preserved for the current and future generations. Michael, before I forget, can you please tell us something about one of the islands we cannot see on this ferry trip. It is the Fort Island."

Michael gladly referred to his notebook and commented, "Fort Island or Fort Zeelandia is about ten miles from the mouth of this river. It was used by the first Dutch settlers and they named it Flag Island around 1679. In those days, the Dutch established Fort Kyk-Over-Al further up the river as the capital of their colony of Essequibo. On Fort Island, there is still a well-preserved building now being used as a museum, and it is called the Court of Policy. That building served as an important administrative office for the buying and selling of slaves who were both Africans and Amerindians. It also had a small prison and a church. The other main building there is more of a ruin, and that is Fort Zeelandia which was for the defence of the island. That Court of Policy was the first political institution in the colony. I do not like what was done there, but it is part of Guyana's history. Anyway, as I said, the Court of Policy is now a museum with artefacts and information about Dutch colonial activity. I must mention the Guyanese brothers Keith, Gordon and Michael Eytle who returned from the UK to Guyana and set up their Fort Island Resort there. The brothers belonged to the island."

As the ferry eased its way between the Leguan Island and Hog Island, Michael continued his commentary, "Hog Island is by far the largest one on the Essequibo River. It is about twenty-three square miles and thus bigger than some islands in the Caribbean! But it is sparsely populated with about only two hundred and fifty residents. People are more into farming such as rice, fruits and vegetables which they take by the small boats up to Parika to sell. The Dutch name for the island was Varken Eiland and due to the presence of many wild hogs it became known as Hog Island. There is one notable historic structure on the island, and it is a windmill which is the only one in Guyana. The windmill is a Guyana National Monument. Although there are no sugarcane plantations on Hog Island, the windmill was used by the Dutch to produce sugar. Hog

Island is crying out for development, and I hope that this could happen in the years to come."

Afzal commented, "Yes, this is another example of how much abundance there is in Guyana. Just imagine if this was an island in the Caribbean, it would be prosperous and thriving. The question is, who will be willing to go there and develop the island?"

Michael responded, "Good question. You see, the island has no real defence against flooding from high tides of the river, and needs proper power, water and sewerage infrastructure. Mind you, the next island on our right is Leguan, and although about half the size of Hog Island at about twelve square miles, it is thriving but is also in need of further development. Now, the next great island we will pass by is called Wakenaam which gets its name from the Dutch word meaning "waiting for a name". Wakenaam is also very large at about seventeen and a half square miles and with a much bigger population of about four thousand residents."

John mentioned, "The islanders' main activities are in agriculture, producing rice, fruits, vegetables and coconuts. Some people do small scale fishing, and cattle is raised for milk and meat."

Peter was anxious to add his comment, "Wakenaam is the birthplace of one of Guyana's and West Indies' finest batsmen. He is Ramnaresh Sarwan known as "Ronnie"."

Muriel frowned as she said, "These islands have lost a lot of their people who have left to go abroad or to the coastlands in Essequibo and Demerara in particular. But Wakenaam is still thriving. The locals call it "Paradise"."

The ferry finally arrived at the Supenaam drop off point and stelling. Supenaam is within the village of Good Hope and it has a group of restaurants, bars and general stores along the main road leading out towards Anna Regina and then to Charity.

Muriel pointed out, "Our main focus now is to get to Charity and have our lunch there. I know of an interesting spot not far from Anna Regina at a place known as the Lake Mainstay Resort in Mainstay Village. That is another good place to visit and to chill out."

Parvati nodded and said, "I like the way that in every region in the country we have places where the people can go to have some leisure time, have picnics, relax, swim in the cool freshwater creeks and rivers, and just get away from their days of stress."

Ramesh added, "Yes, along or just off this coast from Supenaam through to Charity are the Hot and Cold Lake Resort, the Capoey Lake Resort and the Lake Mainstay Resort mentioned by Aunty Muriel. By the way, although we mentioned the big three Essequibo Islands, there is another called Great Troolie Island. That is also a place where the local residents are into farming. Unfortunately, they also suffer from the high tide flooding from time to time."

The tour party boarded the two cars which disembarked shortly after the ferry moored beside the stelling at Supenaam. John and Muriel advised the group that they will be driven through to Charity and will only stop for their lunch and the use of toilets. They will pass through Suddie, Anna Regina and then stop at Charity.

Michael asked for the tour party to gather together as soon as they reached Charity. Once again, he referred to his notebook before addressing his friends.

"I wanted to mention another Slave Rebellion which began here in Essequibo on the ninth of August 1834. You see, the British had passed the Emancipation Bill and all enslaved people in the colonies were expected to be freed on the first of August. The Bill had an Apprenticeship System whereby house slaves had to serve a four-year period of apprenticeship, and all others, six years. Damon led about seven hundred former slaves in a peaceful protest at a local church using a white flag to signal their non-violence intention. Despite the peaceful protest and no fighting, Damon was arrested as the ringleader, tried and executed in front of the Public Building in Georgetown. Sorry that we did not pause to see his statue at Anna Regina. I do not wish to spoil our lunch, but a number of others who protested, were punished with one hundred to two hundred lashes on their backs. There is a tall white cross called Damon's Cross in the La Belle Alliance cemetery."

Arthur and Carlos were very pleased that the choice of the Club Purple Heart restaurant and bar was made for their lunch. Carlos was the first to walk through the purple and white painted gateway onto neatly set out multi-coloured floor tiles. Maria and Doreen stepped lightly and pretended to dance to an imaginary music beat.

Maria turned to her friend and noted, "I can see this place as a very busy venue in the evenings with locals and visitors having their meals, drinks at the bar and dancing to the music."

Michael stepped forward and tried to show some of his original dance moves, but was held back by Doreen who cautioned, "Now, now! Don't get too carried away before you get another attack of your belly ache! This place might be purple heart, but I don't want to see you lying down with purple lips!"

The rest of the tour party laughed as they settled down at their tables and ordered their lunch. They all opted for some light refreshments instead of any alcoholic drinks. After the lunch, John and Muriel led the group to the area where they negotiated special all-inclusive prices for two water taxis for their trip to Kabakaburi Village located several miles up the Pomeroon River. John and Afzal secured safe parking areas for the cars, and as the group assembled near to the two boats, John and Muriel addressed them.

Muriel began by saying, "John and I had applied for the permission to visit the Amerindian Kabakaburi Village in advance of this trip as is customary. So, when we arrive there, we will go up and briefly meet with the Toshao and some of their council members. We can offer some cash donations, and then we will be guided around the settlement. John can tell you more about the people who live there."

John stood beside Muriel and mentioned, "Most of our Amerindian people of our nine tribes occupy about twelve and a half thousand square miles of our country's eighty-three thousand square miles. That is just under fifteen per cent of this great and beautiful country. These lands are mostly in the northwest, the west, and southwest of the country, and there is a lot of gold mining activity in our territories. So naturally, our people work in those small, medium and large-scale mines. In fact, some Amerindians actually own small gold mines. Today, we will visit a beautiful village where the people are extremely polite and friendly. They are mostly of the Kalina or Carib tribe as well as Arawaks."

Michael could not resist adding further comment, "Just a small observation John and Muriel. The Caribs were known as more aggressive and warlike whilst the Arawaks have always been a more creative and gentle people. It is interesting to see how these two peoples have blended into that community. I think that this is an example for us all to learn from as we try to understand our differences and settle together as one."

John acknowledged Michael's observation and added, "Kabakaburi Village was founded by William Henry Brett in 1845. He was an English missionary who spent many years in Guyana preaching the gospel and converting the people to Christianity. Michael, here is an interesting fact for you. He wrote books about our Amerindian people, our legends and his experiences here."

Muriel continued with the briefing, "We are sharing this information now as we will not be able to do so whilst travelling on the boats. The boat trip will be quite noisy. Anyway, Kabakaburi means "place of the itching bush". It has a primary school, a health centre, a chapel, a sports field and a cemetery. You will meet at least one resident family, and you can speak with them and even pose for pictures. But please tread carefully and treat the people and place with much respect. I hope that you will enjoy this trip and experience. John and I also hope that you will learn a lot more about our people and our way of life."

The tour party boarded the two boats and put on the bright orange coloured life jackets as they took their places on the wooden seats straddling across the width of the vessels. On the first boat, Michael and Doreen, Vishnu and Parvati, and Ramesh and Sati along with Muriel, sat beside each other. John, Arthur, Carlos, Maria, Afzal and Peter did likewise on the second boat. The two boat drivers, both Amerindian men, started up their outboard engines, and after signalling to each other, they eased out and away from their moorings and straight into the gentle Pomeroon River. As the boats picked up speed, the bows lifted up and began to slap down on any higher waves thus causing some discomfort for the passengers.

Michael, holding on tightly to his 'One Guyana' cap with his left hand, reached out to Doreen and firmly grabbed her left hand as he said, "Man, I thought that this trip was going to be smooth!"

Doreen giggled, lifted her face, closed her eyes and allowed her long black hair to fly around uncontrollably as she revelled in the breeze that the boat was heading into. After a few minutes into the boat ride, the passengers became more settled and began to enjoy the views presented by both sides of the river. Many types of trees including coconut palms dominated the shorelines, and this was only broken by individual dwellings each with their own mooring for privately owned speedboats, canoes and others used as the only means of transport along the river and its tributaries.

Michael observed, "Doreen, I daresay that in a few years' time we will see much bigger privately owned yachts moving up and down this river!"

She smiled and responded, "Well, it's not too late for you to buy a place here and your own yacht! The Princess of the Pomeroon sounds nice!"

John and Muriel, being more familiar with the river, pointed out places of interest to their respective fellow passengers. The constant roaring of the engines along with the loud flapping of the waves onto the boats prevented much conversation throughout the trip until they eventually slowed down as they reached Kabakaburi. Upon disembarking with great care onto the wooden walkway with its light blue railing leading up to the higher ground of the village, they could see a prominent notice board with a "Welcome to Kabakaburi Village" sign. John and Muriel thanked the two boatmen and asked them to await the return of the tour party after their visit.

The group gathered together, and John and Muriel addressed them.

John pointed to the location of the office of the Toshao of the village and said, "Firstly, we must go across to meet the Toshao who is expecting our arrival for our permitted visit. Muriel and I know the people and the village very well, and we will wait here until you complete your guided tour."

Muriel added, "The Toshao is a leader who is democratically elected by the villagers, and so are the councillors who are there to support him or her. All the Toshaos meet as members of the National Toshao Council which is convened at least once per year, usually in Georgetown. I am very proud to say that our women are being given more opportunities to have their say in how our two hundred communities are run and developed. The Minister of Amerindian Affairs is the Honourable Pauline Campbell-Sukhai who is a very experienced politician and continues to serve all of our people very well. I am hopeful that many more of our brilliant young women will emerge as our new leaders in the years ahead. Our young men also have such a role to play as our communities develop further, especially economically and become much more self-reliant."

Shortly after the tour party met the Toshao, they followed one of the councillors who acted as the guide. She was middle-aged and of a slight figure about just under five feet tall. She held a homemade walking stick not as an aid, but more for pointing at objects and other items of interest during the tour. She introduced the party to the village priest, then the nearby Primary School, the playground, and the members of a family who were very friendly and welcoming. The male head of the family hastily put on a white T-shirt with the 'One Guyana' slogan and the golden arrowhead flag below the words. His young son reached over to take a red and yellow macaw from its perch and allowed it to stand on his left arm as he joined the family unit for group pictures and Vishnu's video.

The tour party then followed the guide to the entrance of the village cemetery, which was surrounded by tall, gracious and gently swaying bamboo trees. The guide muttered a short prayer before she proceeded to inform the group about the various aspects of the lives and environment of the people.

She raised her stick and pointed to the bamboo trees as she said, "If you listen carefully, you will hear sounds of the wind passing through. But that is no ordinary wind. I believe that it is the spiritual energy of the departed welcoming us all to this sacred place."

Michael appeared to be nervous as he held Doreen's left hand tightly, "Do these spirits stay here forever? Or do they wander off?"

The guide smiled reassuringly and replied, "Yes, they stay here with us to protect us from all kinds of problems. Don't worry. The spirits won't be following you home."

Michael rested his right hand across the left side of his chest and sighed with great relief.

Vishnu noticed a few recent graves and asked, "Did this community lose a few people recently?"

The guide bowed her head slightly and solemnly said, "Yes, we sadly lost a few people to the Covid virus. We did very well not to lose any more during that scary time. I also believe that these spirits did protect our community. We did of course, also pray in our church regularly."

Arthur commented, "Well, you can say that you had two types of spiritual interventions."

Carlos smiled coyly and said, "I think you must have a third, and probably the most important spiritual help. And that is your piwari!"

The group laughed along with Carlos as Maria prodded him on his left arm.

The guide graciously nodded, smiled and remarked, "Well you are right about that. Our piwari is soothing to our souls in such times. But the best defence we had was to ban any strangers from entering the village. That really helped us. Now of course, we are back to normality, and we can all enjoy each other's company on visits like this."

Ramesh pointed out, "Of course, you do need visitors who come here and buy products from your crafts shop. Sati is keen to look at your handcrafted baskets and so on."

The guide responded to Ramesh and said, "Well, let us go there now, and I do hope that you will buy some of our finest Arawak traditional designs which are the best you will find. By the way, you should also buy our local cassareep which I also rate as the best in Pomeroon, and I would go as far as to say in all of Guyana!"

Michael was more relaxed as he said, "Now, that is what I want to hear!"

The guide then introduced the group to the resident Christian priest, and he graciously welcomed the tourists. As he began to lead the group towards the front of the church, the guide paused for a few moments.

"As you can see, we are all Christians, but we also embrace our traditional beliefs in our Great Spirit and so on. I do love our traditional songs and music, but I have expressed a wish to our priest that when I die, I would like to have some Western classical music played at my funeral service. In fact, my choice is for Beethoven's Symphony Number 5."

Michael and the others stood back in sheer awe and spontaneously exclaimed, "Amen!"

22

Identity

The tour party returned from their trip to the Pomeroon in the early evening, and in time for a light meal at Nazir's and Neesha's residence before retiring for the night. Ramesh and Sati thanked John and Muriel for their guidance on the trip, and everyone agreed to spend the next day to rest and recover from their tiredness.

Vishnu was pleased with the decision and commented, "Man, this tour of our homeland is now proving to be harder for me in my eighties to handle. Let us take another break and also allow our drivers to have their rest. Why don't we meet up here tomorrow and talk about what we have seen and done here in Guyana so far. I must say that if our trip ended now, I would be very proud of our country and the way it is moving forward. But you know, the country continues to grow on me and the more I see just makes me want to soak up and experience more!"

Michael agreed with his friend and noted, "Yes, I was very excited when I first heard about the idea of us coming to see and experience Guyana so late in our lives. Now, despite my running stomach problems, I must say that this has been such an enriching experience for me and my lifelong partner, Doreen."

Carlos looked across to Maria who smiled and nodded as he said, "Maria and I have really enjoyed this trip so far. I wish that we were as young as Ramesh and Sati and having more energy to keep up with the travelling, and the heat. We always knew that Guyana is a big country, but now at our age, it certainly feels a lot bigger."

Peter leaned forward in his settee and pointed out, "One of the highlights for me has been meeting so many fellow Guyanese everywhere we visited. I can see that many of our people are doing very well, but there are those who are still struggling to make ends meet. When all is said and done, these are the people who must be supported to make their lives easier and better. Guyana and Guyanese are developing and improving rapidly, but no one should be left behind. I know that I may be sounding like an old record, but more needs to be done to reduce poverty across the country, and especially for people who are disabled and with mental health issues."

Arthur yawned through sheer tiredness, but managed to say, "I agree with you all. Let us turn in for the night and do as Vishnu suggested for tomorrow. Like Peter, I would like to know what you all think about Guyana and Guyanese now and in the future. This trip has already opened my eyes to all kinds of possibilities."

Afzal could not resist teasing Arthur and said, "Yes, my friend. I can see that your little eyes are closing as you speak!"

Nazir took a sip of his after-dinner coffee and advised, "OK, let's call it a night, and please let's have lunch over here and then we can continue with our discussion. We need the rest because we have much more to see and do in the days ahead."

Lunch on the following day was served a little later than the usual time of one o'clock as most of the guests had either overslept or decided to have a longer rest in bed. Michael was the exception as he was forced to get up and use the toilet due to another bout of stomach upset.

He finally appeared alongside Doreen for their lunch, and he made a special plea to Neesha, "Please can I have only some liquids? I will then try to use the saada roti and daal to see if I can get more relief."

Vishnu tried to comfort his suffering friend and said, "Michael, I can start up today's discussion, and if you feel any better, I would be happy to hand over to you."

Michael nodded and took a seat in a settee nearest to the ground floor toilet.

Vishnu duly began the discussion, "Today, we will speak about what we consider to be Guyana's identity. What are the ingredients of our melting pot of so many cultures? What are the values that Guyanese have or aspire to? What makes us into who we are? Who are the people or have been the people who have helped to shape our Guyana? Our writers, poets, politicians, historians, scientists, sportspeople, musicians, religious leaders, teachers, our myths, our heroes and heroines?"

Carlos was perplexed as he asked, "How can we answer all of those questions? Anyway, first of all I wish to suggest that there should be a change of the name of our country from Guyana to something else."

Vishnu frowned and asked, "Why?"

Carlos continued, "Well, almost every time I mention Guyana to anyone overseas, I would be asked about Ghana which is in West Africa! It is really important for our country to be easily and properly recognised by everyone."

Peter suggested, "Maybe we should rename Guyana as Kaywana, the name used by one of our greatest novelists, Edgar Mittelholzer who wrote a great trilogy covering three hundred years of our history."

Arthur nodded and added, "That sounds like a good idea. Another association with Guyana tends to be people abroad referring to the Jonestown mass suicide. Guyana certainly needs a more credible image. Something or things which can easily identify us and our country in a more positive way."

Michael leaned forward slowly in his chair, and without referring to his trusted notebook, offered, "If we were to go back to the time when our First Peoples came and settled here, the Carib nation called it "Caribana", and this was picked up by the Spanish as far back as the early fifteen hundreds. The English became more aware of the country through Sir Walter Raleigh's book titled, *The Discoverie of the Large, Rich, and Beautiful Empire of Guiana* in 1596. I think that if we reverted to Caribana it may then become confused with the Caribbean or even Cuba. I am happy with the Cooperative Republic of Guyana, known as the 'Land of Many Waters'."

John raised his right hand and spoke, "I feel compelled to come in here. The ancestors of Muriel and I were of many more tribes than the remaining nine we have today. Through the thousands of years our people found and named most of the places, rivers, mountains and so on long before Columbus and other Europeans came here. The Caribs were a dominant force, and I would prefer Caribana as a good name. The Spanish referred to Guayana. I hope that you don't mind, but I must mention the names of our nine tribes who now make up about ten per cent of Guyana's population. They are Akawaio, Arawak, Arecuna, Carib, Makushi, Patamona, Wai Wai, Wapichan and Warao."

Doreen smiled, and applauded, as she said, "Long live our First Peoples! They should be regarded, respected and treated as national treasures!"

Parvati echoed Doreen's comments and suggested, "Our Amerindian people must always be seen and regarded with great respect as you rightly say, and as the first Guyanese so to speak."

Afzal nodded in agreement and added, "I also read somewhere that the Dutch called this country 'De Wilde Kust' or 'The Wild Coast'. But such a name will not feel the same as the Gold Coast."

Neesha broke her silence and pointed out, "I think that Guyana is a good name. Don't forget that Dutch Guiana is now called Suriname and French Guiana is now Cayenne. So, there is no need to change the name Guyana as it has already been changed from British Guiana."

Michael was really pleased with Neesha's suggestion and concluded, "That's it! Well said Neesha! Let's now move this conversation forward. I think that we have very good symbols of what is Guyana, and who we are."

He took out his notebook and prepared to read from it, "We have our National Anthem, which is widely known by most Guyanese, and is still very much respected every time it is played or sung. It is called 'Dear Land of Guyana' and was written by Archibald Leonard Luker and set to music by Robert Cyril Gladstone Potter back in 1966 as part of the recognition and celebration of our Independence. The words of the Anthem tell us a lot about Guyana, our people, our history, and why we must serve and pay homage to this dear land of ours."

Nazir nodded in agreement and added, "I read somewhere that when there was the centenary celebration in 1931 of the unification of Berbice, Demerara and Essequibo into British Guiana, the 'Song of Guyana's Children' written by the Reverend Hawley-Bryant, was sung. Again, this song tells us a lot about Guyana, its beauty, its riches, and what all of Guyana's children can aspire to. After all our children and young people are the future!"

Vishnu was very impressed by Nazir's recollection of the song which they all sang whilst at school together, and added, "I think that most of us here will also remember how we changed the chorus from 'Onward, upward, may we ever go, day by day in strength and beauty grow'. to 'Onward, upward, Mary had a goat. Day by day she tied it with a rope. Till one day, de goat bus de rope. And Miss Mary had to run behind it'."

Everyone burst out laughing.

Michael waited until the laughter subsided and then pointed out, "Now, that is a very special quality of Guyanese! We are very creative people with a good sense of humour. In fact, we know how to use laughter to help us cope with our problems. We can laugh at anything! Vishnu, do you remember when we were at our Primary School and at the St John's Anglican Church, the priest used his huge thunder-like voice to announce, 'Ho Lee! Ho Lee!', and you and I used to point to our Chinese friend named Ho Lim and imitate the priest by saying, 'Ho Lim! Ho Lim! But not me!'"

More laughter filled the room.

Sati pointed to a brooch pinned to the left side of her white cotton blouse and said, "I think that a very unique symbol of Guyana is our beautiful flag called 'The Golden Arrowhead'. I believe that each colour means or represents something really important. Uncle Michael, can you tell us more about our flag?"

Michael was now in his element, and very excited to answer Sati's request, "Right. The five colours of the flag are green, red, black, gold and white. Each means or represents something of great importance. The green is for the pristine forests of Guyana. Red is about the passion of the people. Black represents the endurance of the people. Gold is about the wealth of the country and white highlights water. So, taken together, the name Guyana, the National Anthem, that children's song and the flag, tell us a lot about our beautiful country, its wealth, its peoples, its history and our aspirations."

Arthur raised his right hand and proposed, "There is something else which provides more clues about us and our country. Michael, what can you say about the National Pledge of Guyana?"

Michael paused for a few moments, adjusted his spectacles, opened his notebook, and began, "Yes, I do have a note of the pledge. Let me read it out. 'I pledge myself to honour always the flag of Guyana and to be loyal to my country. To be obedient to the laws of Guyana. To love my fellow citizens and to dedicate my energies towards the happiness and prosperity of Guyana'."

Carlos gave a thumbs up to Michael and enthused, "Thank you Histry Maan, for sharing and reminding us all about why we are Guyanese together as One People, One Nation, and with One Destiny."

Maria nodded and commented, "I love the last sentence of the pledge. Note that it says that we must strive for happiness even before prosperity. We have always been a caring, generous and hospitable people towards each other, and towards others. This is worth much more than any amount of money. I also endorse the notion of love for our fellow citizens. This reminds me of the proverb about "Love thy neighbour as thyself". This sounds simple, but when we look at each word more closely, then we will find a deeper meaning. Firstly, we need to understand what love is. Second, we must ask the question as to who is our neighbour. This could be the people living next door, or the person or persons who is or are closest to us. Thirdly, we need to know who we are, where we have come from, what we believe in, and how we see ourselves now and in the future. So, you see, this simple statement can be much more complex. If we in Guyana try to understand this and practice it, most of our problems will disappear."

Ramesh looked around the room and exclaimed, "Wow! Aunty Maria that is so sublime and true in every sense. I am so happy to be in this company, and to learn so much more about our country, our people and ourselves. I will make a special effort to read the Constitution of Guyana as I believe it must cover all of what we have been discussing here."

Michael quickly stepped in and added, "That is correct. In fact, I have here a quote from the Constitution which says that "It is the duty of every citizen of Guyana wherever he or she may be and for every person in Guyana to respect the National Flag, the Coat of Arms, the National Anthem, the National Pledge, and the Constitution of Guyana, and to treat them with due and proper solemnity on all occasions"."

Afzal nodded in agreement and then asked, "So, what do you all think of our President's new motto of a 'One Guyana'?"

Muriel immediately responded, "Let me say this on behalf of myself, my husband and even on behalf of my fellow Amerindians, that I agree with this idea. We as a people of nine tribes must try harder to support each other and come together as one. Of course, this also means that all Guyanese should thrive towards this idea of oneness. But, at the same time, we should also preserve, protect and promote our individual cultures. When we do this, we will become a much stronger nation. We must do everything in our power to avoid the old British tactic of 'Divide and Rule'."

Arthur sipped some of his mango juice and pointed out, "We are now in a situation where we all need to come together as one and stand up to the foreign threat which we are facing from that mad Maduro of Venezuela who is claiming almost two thirds of our country.

We are all in this struggle together, and even at my old age I am prepared to stand up and fight for my country."

There was a resounding "Hear! Hear!" around the room.

Ramesh acknowledged the heartwarming feeling of oneness and togetherness in the room, and his eyes welled up as he said, "I am so proud of all of you and for the passion you share for this great and beautiful country of ours. I know that those of us who are dual citizens with America or Canada have sworn our allegiance to either of those countries, but deep down inside we know and feel that we are Guyanese. I hope that there will be no need for a conflict with Venezuela as we are well outnumbered and ill-equipped to defend what is rightfully ours. Our young people in the Armed Forces will need all the support they can get from all Guyanese everywhere, and of course, from our strong international friends. If Maduro tries to do what Argentina did by invading the Falkland Islands, this time I believe that he will be facing up to the US, Britain and Canada."

Carlos pointed out, "I am sure that Brazil will also come to our aid. They have already warned Venezuela not to use their territory in any attempt to seize Essequibo."

Nazir stepped into the kitchen, and quickly reappeared with a large and sharp cutlass in his right hand and a grass knife in his left hand, wielding them in a threatening manner and proclaiming, "Man, I am ready for the fight! I also have my old slingshot and golas!"

Michael laughed at Nazir's comical but warlike stance, "Man, you look like one of those Gurkhas who terrified the Argentinians with their deadly kukri knives in that Falklands War!"

Everyone joined in with the laughter.

John then led a chanting of "Essequibo is we own! Guyana is we own!"

Michael stood up, walked over to embrace Nazir, and announced, "I am also with you, my brother. But let us hope that we as a peace-loving people will overcome any challenge to our sovereignty and continue to stay together and prosper as a united Guyana. All of our leaders have wanted us to unite, but this threat is helping us to achieve a 'One Guyana'."

Doreen was not entirely convinced by the show of unity and lamented, "Well, I don't think that it is only up to our leaders to unite us. They have all said the right things, but when they got into power, their actions resulted in dividing us even more. Now, we have a young President who is reaching out to all Guyanese both here and abroad like no other President had done before. I don't want to hear buzz words. I want to see action. I did like the idea that Mister Burnham had back in the 1960s which he called the "Meet the people tour" or something like that. He did meet a lot of people, but then when he banned so many basic foodstuffs, he really hurt even more of them."

Carlos shook his head and responded, "Doreen, I can see where you are coming from. The real difference with our young President is that not only is he meeting with and listening to the people all over the country and abroad, but he is also almost immediately trying to solve their problems. This is unprecedented. I can see why the people are showing him so much love in return. Of course, there will always be those who will continue to criticise, but we are in a democracy and free speech is to be allowed."

Afzal smiled and pointed out, "Carlos, this is true. But there are people here and abroad who just try to foment or stir up racial hatred and continue to show contempt for this President. I suppose that the only way for him and his government to deal with this is to continue to work even harder for all Guyanese."

Nazir nodded and added, "Afzal bhai, no matter what amount of good any leader or government does in most countries, there will always be people who show dissent and dissatisfaction. But that is the way of democracy. We can all see what happens when a country is led by a dictator where any hint of criticism is stamped out sometimes brutally! Thank God we are nowhere near to such a situation."

Vishnu nervously combed through his silver-grey hair with the fingers of his right hand and said, "Thank you all for helping to answer my questions. I think that we do as Guyanese and as a country, have an identity, and I believe that this is really defined by the people of our past and present."

Michael was pleased to hear that comment from Vishnu and he added, "Now we are getting closer to the answer as to who and what makes Guyana so special. I think that our great writers, poets, actors and actresses, singers, dancers, religious leaders, sportspeople and educators have all helped, and many continue to do so in spelling out who we are, where we came from, and where we are heading to as a new and vibrant nation on the rise. We have talked about or mentioned many of these great people over this short quest to date. There are many more we have not mentioned, but I also believe that ordinary people are the ones who can show us the way. Ordinary hard-working people who I call our "unsung heroes"."

Ramesh nodded and said, "Uncle Michael, you are so right. There are many Guyanese abroad who have also been contributing to this narrative, and again, they are too many to mention. No doubt, as we continue our tours, we may reflect on some more of these amazing people."

Maria agreed with Ramesh, and her face lit up as she said, "I am so proud of our Guyanese brothers and sisters both here and abroad who have accomplished incredible things in all walks of life. This by itself, is an incalculable wealth. How can a country produce so many achievers from such a small population?"

Michael opened his eyes widely when he heard Maria's comment, and replied, "Thank you Maria. It is indeed a remarkable fact that with a population of only three quarters of a million here in Guyana and a huge diaspora of about another half a million, we are still a very small country. About three hundred and twenty thousand are in America, eighty-five thousand in Canada, and around forty thousand in the UK. The remainder is scattered in all corners of the world. Now, with the new oil and gas wealth, I expect that if progress continues at the current rate, many will return here and our overall population residing in the country could increase considerably in twenty to thirty years' time. We have to remember of course and take account of the growing number of other migrants from Venezuela, Brazil and the Caribbean who are already adding to our great melting pot."

Nazir, always a little sceptical, frowned as he said, "Michael, to those of us living here, the issue of new migrants who are not Guyanese or of Guyanese descent, is a big worry. Already we are seeing Spanish being used around the country, and this could become a big problem where we as the hosts will have to accommodate these people by learning Spanish, Portuguese, and even French brought here by people from Haiti, in the years to come. Man, I am too old to start picking up these lingos!"

Neesha also agreed and pointed out, "We as migrants in Suriname knew that we had to learn Dutch and that was very hard for us. So, we gave up and returned to Guyana when things began to improve here. I think that the foreigners who need it must be given free help to learn English. Otherwise, we will be setting up many Spanish Towns and French Quarters as well as our own China Towns!"

Parvati pointed out, "Oh my God! Instead of a nation of six peoples we will become a nation of nine or more peoples! We struggle with uniting six peoples. How are we going to cope with nine?"

Peter sighed and exclaimed, "Now that is a whole new ball game!"

Afzal was more upbeat and commented, "I think that we as a country will have to learn from what we ourselves experienced when we migrated to another country and had to try to integrate with the local ways of life and their culture. Now the wheel is turning almost full circle, and we will have to accommodate and absorb our foreigners' cultures. It will be a good test of our maturity as a nation."

Michael was eager to point out, "My friends, Guyana has always had foreigners coming here to work. Don't forget that right here in our villages some people came from Barbados back in the 1950s and 60s to find work, and we welcomed them with open arms and minds. Of course, they were not as many as the thousands of Venezuelans coming here. Yes, all of this will be another test of our Guyanese kindness, hospitality and generosity!"

Arthur added solemnly, "And our patience."

Carlos smiled and pretended to speak like a Venezuelan, "Que sera, sera! Whatever will be, will be!"

Sati laughed and responded, "Si Senor!"

Ramesh nodded and added, "So this quest or search of ours becomes 'La busqueda!'"

Carlos grinned, and this time tried to speak like a Brazilian, "Or, 'a busca' in Portuguese!"

Michael raised both of his hands in the air and exclaimed, "Hey! 'el alto!' Stop! I can't cope with this anymore!"

23

Rupununi rejuvenation

Ramesh and Sati asked for a meeting of the tour party after they had their breakfast at John's and Muriel's home. They were keen to venture further into Guyana and wanted to assess whether and to what extent their travel companions were prepared for a three nights stay and tour of Rupununi in Region Nine.

Ramesh opened the discussion by asking, "Have you all had a good rest? Uncle Michael, how are you feeling today?"

Michael looked at Doreen briefly and then replied, "I am feeling much better now especially after yesterday's rest and meals. It looks as if everybody is up and ready for our next adventure. What have you and Sati got in mind for us?"

Sati smiled and responded, "I am really pleased that you all had a well-deserved rest. We have already done much more than many fellow Guyanese on their holiday visits to Guyana. Ramesh and I are really proud of you for coping with the travelling and for the knowledge you have shared with us. Now that we have had a taste of the interior through Kaieteur, Iwokrama and the Pomeroon, Ramesh and I wondered whether you are ready for a longer overnight trip to the Rupununi which is completely different from everywhere else in the country."

Carlos noted an approving nod by Maria and confirmed, "Yes, I think that we can cope with that, but I am not sure about any long overland trip."

Arthur also agreed on the trip and asked, "How long do you plan for the trip? Of course, we cannot do that in one day and night. Besides, I would like to see as much as possible of that region which I have not visited before."

Doreen held up Michael's right hand and cheerfully announced, "I am prepared for such a trip as long as my champ here is fit and ready and can cope with a longer tour and stay."

Michael simply raised a thumbs up with his left hand.

Ramesh nodded and replied, "Thank you Aunty Doreen and Uncle Michael. Sati and I were thinking of a stay of three nights in Rupununi so that we could see as much as possible. We do not recommend the overland road trip to Lethem and suggest that we take a flight to that place. How does that sound?"

Afzal suggested, "Well, from my experience, I think that you will need at least that amount of time in Rupununi, and due to our age, we should have another day of rest before leaving early tomorrow morning. I assume that you can book the flights and accommodation today."

Ramesh responded with, "Thank you Uncle Afzal. Sati and I had made some enquiries and provisional bookings and all we need to do is to confirm how many of us will be making the trip, our preferred dates of travel, and the amount of time we agree to stay there."

John and Muriel decided to opt out of the trip as well as Afzal who agreed to drive John's car with Arthur, Peter, Carlos and Maria as his passengers to the Ogle Airport. Nazir and Neesha also opted out of the trip, but Nazir decided to drive Vishnu, Parvati, Ramesh, Sati, Michael and Doreen in his car to the airport.

Ramesh managed to secure the return flights from Ogle to Lethem, and the tour party left for the airport as soon as they had breakfast at Nazir's and Neesha's home early the next morning. Nazir and Afzal returned to Anna Catherina as soon as they were assured that the tour party's flight had left Ogle.

Michael took a seat on the aircraft beside Vishnu who chose one next to a window so that he could video the scenery below. The flight over the two hundred and sixty miles journey took off on time on the clear sunny morning, and soon the landscape below came into view beneath pockets of soft white clouds floating gently over patches of greenery alongside neatly organised housing estates, commercial buildings, factories, sugar and rice fields, and local streets leading into main roads. The dark brown silty Demerara River wound its way through the populated East and West Bank. Further into the flight on a direct path towards Lethem Airport the lush green rainforests dominated the scenery below, reminding the tour party of their flight to Iwokrama.

Michael consulted his now famous notebook, and referred to an important development, "Vishnu and Ramesh, there is a plan to complete a big improvement of the Linden to Lethem Road into an amazing highway which includes forty-five bridges. That will certainly speed up traffic and the transportation of goods to and from the North and South Rupununi."

Ramesh asked, "Uncle Michael, will that also help Brazilian traffic through Guyana?"

Michael nodded and confirmed, "Yes, Lethem and that highway will become even more important for both Brazil and Guyana. I must say that whilst Venezuela is trying to bully us and annex the whole of Essequibo, the Brazilians have been coming through to Guyana, and many have established themselves in Lethem. I do hope that their new President Luiz Inacio Lula da Silva we know as "Lula", will continue to build stronger political and economic ties with Guyana. We do have to be mindful of ensuring that criminal gangs do not use the highway as a direct route for trafficking illegal drugs and smuggling gold through Guyana!"

Ramesh, with his iPhone at the ready, found a note about Guyana and Brazil collaboration, "Uncle Michael, it was the former President Jair Bolsonaro who had signed a very important agreement with President Irfaan Ali which includes some impressive ideas. They agreed to the full implementation of what is called the Guyana-Brazil International Road Transportation Agreement, a Technical Feasibility Study to install a fibre optic link between the two countries, as well as a railway link. Guyana is also in need of a deep-water harbour at Georgetown or Berbice within the next ten years and Brazil is keen to collaborate on that. These are very exciting times in the development of our country, and our relationships with our neighbours. And yes, both countries will have to work harder to stop criminals from trafficking through Guyana."

Vishnu paused his filming and frowned as he said, "To be honest, when I heard that Bolsonaro was interested in Guyana, I thought that it would not be acceptable to have South America's "Trump" anywhere near to our rainforests! I didn't think that he should be trusted especially due to the way he was allowing the destruction of the Amazon rainforest in Brazil. I was greatly relieved thank God, when he was defeated by Lula for the Presidency."

Michael also expressed his relief by saying, "Yes man. Now that Lula is there at least for the next few years, it is time to push forward and implement those important agreements and treaties between the two countries."

Vishnu smiled and noted, "Soon, Guyanese will have to pick up on the Portuguese language that Carlos is so worried about! Ramesh, I am sure I heard you and Sati speak about the Portuguese business culture based on building relationships. Am I right?"

Ramesh gave a thumbs up and replied, "Yes Dad. They believe that business must be built and done with people that they can get on with. We have seen how our own Portuguese people in Guyana are polite, friendly and do business in a calm and straightforward way."

Peter was very keen to offer his suggestion about the Guyana-Brazil collaborations, "I am all for good trading relationships with Brazil. But I would really love to have their football professionals come here to train and coach our men and women. We Guyanese have loved their style of play, and my own football hero was the legendary Pele whom I regard as the 'GOAT' meaning the 'Greatest of all time'! I love that World Cup winning team of Brazil's in 1970. Every time I look at the video of the final I see football being played by Brazil as sports poetry in motion. Truly beautiful!"

Michael was enthusiastic about Peter's suggestion and spoke as he shuffled his feet on the floor of the aircraft like a footballer, "I love the Brazilian style of football, but the thing I love much more is their Rio Carnival and the way those Brazilian women dance to the samba rhythm! I would love to see some Brazilian input to our own Mashramani parades. It would certainly liven things up!"

Vishnu laughed as he said, "Man, I have seen that our President Ali has some unique dance moves! But I'm not sure about Lula's!"

Parvati, Doreen and Sati looked at Vishnu, Ramesh and Michael with curious suspicion as the three men giggled.

The aircraft continued to make good progress, and the landscape below began to reveal another view of the dry, sparsely forested, and reddened trails and roads of North Rupununi.

Michael pointed out whilst Vishnu resumed his filming, "Our country is full of interesting contrasts. First, on this flight alone, we saw the flat heavily populated and agricultural coastland, then the white sands of the higher ground including areas of huge gold and bauxite mining operations, the beautiful greenery of the forests, and now the vast open savannah lands of the Rupununi surrounded by some mountains. This is truly stunning to behold!"

Soon after the landing on the small Lethem airstrip was successfully negotiated by the pilot, the passengers applauded in appreciation. They then stepped off the plane onto the pathway to the airport's arrival area. Ramesh and Sati ensured that all the other members of the tour party were in good fettle and advised them that they would be staying at Lethem for their first night of the trip.

Michael stepped forward, and after looking into his notebook, provided the group with some information about Lethem, "This place is a small town which is named after Sir Gordon Lethem who was a Governor of British Guiana in the 1940s. It was given town status only in 2017 and has a very small population of just over one thousand seven hundred people. It is next to the Takutu River which forms the border with Brazil. There is a new bridge across the river, which was built, and paid for, by Brazil. Lethem is roughly opposite to the Brazilian border town of Bonfim. Lethem also has a history of Brazilians coming over from their country to buy and sell goods. The town operates as the Capital of this Region."

Ramesh was proud to announce, "Uncle Michael, thank you for that. I have also done some research on Rupununi, and the Brazilian and Chinese influences here are very important for the area. There is not a lot to see and do here in the town, but we can stroll around for a while as long as we can bear up with the sun and heat. Then we can go to our hotel for our dinner and overnight stay. I hope that with a good night's rest we will all be up for a trip to Dadanawa Ranch where the Amerindians work as cowboys called vaqueros."

Michael pointed out, "You will notice that the business premises are signposted in Portuguese and English, and there are also some Chinese owned stores. At one time, Brazilian goods dominated until the Chinese came here to compete. Ramesh, I think that it is too hot for me to walk around to find our hotel. Can we hire a couple of local taxis?"

Ramesh nodded and suggested, "Well there are good choices of hotel accommodation here in Lethem. Both the Rupununi Eco Hotel and the Takutu Hotel and Bar are reasonable and comfortable. There are also the Kanuku Lodge Restaurant and Bar, the Savannah Inn, the Adventure Guianas Hotel Toucanna and Courtyard in the middle of Lethem and others. All of them within the same price range. We are booked in for the night at the Rupununi Eco Hotel and will have our dinner there."

At dinner, Michael took the opportunity to talk about an important historical event known as the Rupununi Uprising. He stood up at the head of a dining table he shared with Vishnu, Parvati, Ramesh, Sati and Doreen, took out his notebook, and found the page he wanted to refer to.

"I do hope that you will not mind me talking a little bit about an event which took place in this region in 1969. After Guyana became independent in 1966, the ranchers here feared that their rights to the land they occupied would be carved up and offered to outsiders. The Hart family, led by Valerie Hart who was a parliamentarian of the United Force Party, and other ranchers, led an uprising to create a Republic of Rupununi of about twenty-two thousand square miles. It was a daring attempt to take over such a large part of Guyana. I could not find all the true facts of the uprising, but five local policemen and two residents were killed, several buildings were destroyed, and the Guyana Defence Force, the GDF, regained control after the main rebels fled to Venezuela and Brazil. About one hundred Amerindian workers employed by the ranchers took part in the uprising, and although about twenty of them were arrested and charged, no one was convicted."

Vishnu's face was sullen with disappointment upon listening to Michael's account of the uprising, and added, "I understand that Venezuela had a hand in supporting the rebels with some training and arms. Thankfully, they were not a proper fighting force and could not stand up to the GDF. I also heard that the GDF went on to dismantle the ranches involved, and Rupununi's cattle industry never recovered from this episode in our history."

Carlos frowned as he posed a question, "So tell me. Do you think that Venezuela will invade Rupununi and take this region as part of their claim on Essequibo?"

Peter shook his head and replied firmly, "No way. I don't think so. The Brazilians have already warned against anyone trespassing across their territory at the border. Besides, they love Lethem and treat the town as if it is their own."

Arthur smiled and pointed out, "I guess that the Chinese will also not welcome Venezuelans here."

The tour group continued to chat about the uprising and latest threat of invasion for a while longer before finally retiring for the night.

Early the next morning, after a reasonably comfortable night's sleep, the tour party was keen to go on the road trip to the Dadanawa Ranch in South Rupununi. Ramesh and Sati had hired two vehicles for the journey.

Ramesh double-checked that everyone was still up for the trip and warned, "I must tell you that much of this ride will be bumpy. But I am told that the scenery is beautiful. Besides, we are now in the dry season and there will be no flooding to get through. One night and day in Dadanawa is the bare minimum and travellers prefer to spend a few days there to have a fuller experience of what's on offer. If anyone wants to stop for a comfort break, please say so and we will pause for that. Another thing to look out for is that the road is very dusty and that may not be pleasant."

Michael was missing from the group briefing for a few minutes, and he had a broad smile on his face as he finally arrived to join Doreen in their vehicle.

He gleefully announced, "Right. All is clear for this trip!"

Doreen nudged him with her right elbow and said, "No need to share that news with the rest of us!"

Ramesh completed his briefing, "By the way, I just wish to say that the accommodation at the ranch is normally only for about eight people at a time, so I hope that you do not mind doing a bit of sharing for the one overnight stay. Sati and I agreed this plan with the hosts there."

An excited Michael took up his usual seat next to Vishnu and proceeded to inform his fellow travellers in their vehicle, about Dadanawa.

"The man who founded and built up the Dadanawa Ranch was a pioneering Scotsman by the name of Harry Melville. He came to this area around 1891 and in about twenty years, he established what was believed to be the largest cattle ranch in the world. Sadly, for him, the job of taking the cattle from the ranch to the best place for the export of the beef was very tough and tricky through the trail, and many of the cattle simply disappeared in the forest. Melville had married two local Wapishana women and raised ten children. He eventually sold up the ranch, abandoned his family, and returned to England where he got married for a third time, and died there. The Melville family in Guyana were involved with the Hart family in the Rupununi Uprising."

Sati, sitting beside Ramesh exclaimed, "Wow! That Melville fella must have had a fascinating life here in Rupununi. But with so many colonialists, I do not like the bit about how he simply abandoned his family and left them to fend for themselves here. Thank you, Uncle Michael, for telling us about him. You never fail to surprise me with your history stories."

Michael proudly smiled and responded, "Thank you Sati. It is my pleasure. Thank you also for your patience in listening to me. Guyana has a lot of stories to reveal. We cannot say that we are Guyanese without knowing about our past and the people who helped to discover the places we are seeing, those who came in search of wealth, and those who built their systems to control and govern. By the way, the word Dadanawa is from the Wapishana word, dadinauwau which roughly means 'the spirit of the macaw in the creek hill'. The area covered by the ranch is about one thousand seven hundred and fifty square miles!"

Parvati turned to Doreen and exclaimed, "Wow! That is a lot of area to cover! No wonder travellers go to Dadanawa for a few days and nights at least!"

The two vehicles continued to move at a steady pace onto the road leading directly to the ranch. Initially, the ride was much smoother than expected, and the passengers quietly observed the unfolding terrain of plants and trees beside the dusty red roadway with the rolling Kanuku Mountains in the background. They passed through Amerindian villages with their low-level housing spread out across their own spaces unlike the more streamlined and linear housing lots of the villages on the coastland. The dispersed settlements provide a sense of independence of the people with the benab as the central point for casual community contact and formal meetings. The spaces between the houses allow individual families to grow vegetables and herbs and fruit trees such as mango, guava, genip and banana. Cassava is the most prevalent crop.

Michael allowed his fellow travellers ample time to look out over the journey and to observe the scenery until Vishnu turned around and spoke.

"Michael, I notice that some parts of this road have been very bumpy. It reminds me of a family trip we took to the rainforest region of Costa Rica in Central America. At first, the road was very smooth and comfortable. But when it became really rough, our tour guide said, "Welcome to the Costa Rican massage!" I hope that the rest of this trip will not be as bad as that! Our backsides were sore long before that trip ended!"

Michael screwed up his face, gently rubbed his midriff, and pleaded, "Man, we can all do without that kind of massage therapy! I hope that my delicate stomach will hold out for this one."

Ramesh reached out and placed his right hand on Michael's left shoulder, and with a comforting tone, said, "Don't worry, Uncle Michael. Just tell us if, and when you need a comfort break. I see that you have more notes on Rupununi. Please enlighten us!"

Michael wiggled in his seat, and when he felt more comfortable, he spoke, "Thank you, my son. The Rupununi name is from a Makushi word rapon which means black-bellied whistling duck which is common to the river. You know, I do love the names of places given by the Amerindian people. With each name you get a good picture about the place and the link to Mother Nature. Rupununi is also referred to as the "Land of the Giants". I don't know how many of the creatures we will see on this trip, but the giants are the jaguar, the puma, the giant anteater, the anaconda, the giant river turtle, the black caiman, the giant otter, the tapir, the arapaima and the awesome harpy eagle. Is this not incredible?"

Ramesh took a deep breath and enthused, "Yet more reason to celebrate the greatness of this amazing country! And to think that we have heard or seen only a few of the many incredible animals, bird life, fish, plants and trees, shows that for us to really experience more of Guyana, we will need many more weeks of touring around the country. The more I hear and see about our country, the more I am being drawn back to this land. I feel a deeper sense of belonging here."

Michael nodded approvingly and continued, "You see, there is so much about Guyana that we just take for granted. I am very happy that the government and more people are taking our environment seriously. I welcome every effort and expense to continue to show the world what a sensible and responsible people we are. We have an old saying that goes, "Yuh neva miss waata til de well run dry!" We need to double up our efforts to save, protect and cherish all the God-given wealth and beauty we have across this amazing country!"

Vishnu gave a thumbs up and commented, "Well said, my friend. The true wealth of Guyana is all around for us to see, use sensibly and sustain."

Parvati, Doreen and Sati responded with a resounding "Amen!"

Michael added, "Thank you, everyone. I shall always remember something which John and Muriel said to me the other night. In the Amerindian way, this land with all its riches is not ours. They believe that it is loaned to us to use and protect for the next generations. We must be at one with nature in all of this. Let us not leave any mess for them to clean up."

Both vehicles continued to make good progress despite the drivers having to pay closer attention to the road to avoid the large potholes and thus reduce the discomfort as much as possible. There was the need for only one comfort stop, and everyone in the tour party took advantage to step down and use the convenience at one of the villages en route to Dadanawa.

Arthur emerged from one toilet and had a look of great relief as he said, "Thank God we could find suitable facilities on such a trip. At least we are not in the depth of the forest where you have to find a spot, dig a hole, do your business and cover it up!"

Carlos giggled as he responded, "Man, sometimes you don't have time to indulge in such luxury!"

The rejuvenated and refreshed tour party was able to endure the remainder of the drive to Dadanawa, and they were very pleased to arrive at the main building where they were warmly welcomed by their hosts. They were offered some refreshing and ice-cold orange juice, and then shown around the accommodation which contained five rooms. The group agreed to share them for the night. Michael was overly keen to try out one of the hammocks on the veranda but struggled to steady it enough in order to ease his long slender frame into it. Doreen then offered careful assistance to ensure that he did not topple out and onto the hard wooden floor.

He closed his eyes, took a deep breath, and then opened them to scan the beautiful view in front of him, "Oh man! This is the life! I could just lie here and soak up this bit of paradise. Guyana is truly heaven sent!"

Doreen was not entirely impressed by Michael's selfish, single-minded option, and reminded him, "All well and good for you. What about me?"

A chastened Michael muttered, "Well, my precious, you are most welcome to join me out here, but in another hammock."

The others of the group looked at the couple and laughed.

Ramesh announced, "It seems like a good idea for us to spend some time to relax after that hard drive. Perhaps, if you so wish, you can join Sati and me for a tour around the ranch before we have our dinner."

The tour party heeded Ramesh's advice, and after an hour's rest, they were met by a vaquero who was a young Amerindian. He spoke to them about what a day in the life of a vaquero was like. He then led the group to look at some activity at the corral, the repair shop, the tannery and then browse in the small store at the ranch.

Over dinner, Michael once again took the opportunity to impart some more information about Rupununi to his friends, "We have only just had a small taste of what Rupununi is really like and has to offer to tourists. We do not have enough time to explore the whole place. For example, this ranch with its history, is still working and looks just like it was decades ago. If we were all much younger, we would have really enjoyed going out on horseback with the vaqueros to round up the cattle, do some lassoing and branding some of the young ones."

Carlos could not resist poking fun at Michael, and reminded him, "I like your enthusiasm. You were the first to volunteer to get on a horse when the vaquero offered us all a ride. All was well when you finally managed to mount the animal until we applauded you. Then the horse just reared up and galloped off with you holding on for dear life and screaming all kinds of words to stop it! Man, you were lucky that horse did not throw you off!"

Everyone joined Carlos in laughing at Michael who tried hard to swallow his pride.

Peter felt that he had an explanation for the hapless victim, "Michael, that horse noticed that you were wearing a T-shirt with a print of a cowboy riding a bucking rodeo horse and decided that it would teach you a lesson. Did you not see or hear how that horse snorted as you got closer to it?"

Doreen tried to conceal her mocking as she said, "Now, now! I am very proud of my hero! He looked like John Wayne as he walked up to that horse!"

Carlos laughed and said, "John Wayne? Man, when the vaquero pulled him off the horse, Michael's legs gave way, and instead of walking like John Wayne, he looked more like a 'Don Wine'!"

Michael tried to move the conversation on, "Man, at least I tried to have some fun. And none of you had the courage to even try! Anyway, as I was about to say, there are many opportunities both in the South and the North of this region, to experience tours and adventures. You can see just how much effort is being made to preserve a way of life and living in this environment by our Amerindian friends. For example, places such as Surama, Annai, Rewa, Karanambu, Yapukari and Nappi provide lots of opportunities to really appreciate what life is like here. I think that we need at least two weeks in Rupununi to have a good once in a lifetime involvement with this incredible environment. I know that Doreen and I are really happy that we have come here even though the rides can be tough on our bodies. OK, let's enjoy this great meal, and then have a restful night. Doreen, my sweet, I will need a gentle massage later on."

Arthur raised his glass of orange juice and offered a toast to Michael and the rest of the group, "Thank you Michael, Ramesh and Sati. As has been said, I wish that I was much younger to come here and spend much more time with you guys. Cheers also, to our hosts!"

The tour party retired early as soon as darkness fell and the night shift of birdsong, insects and other creatures filled the air with their unique opera as over-tiredness and sleep overcame the tourists. The thin walls of the rooms provided an ugly response of unmelodious human snoring paused only when mosquitoes that managed to penetrate the white bed nettings sank their stylets to quench their thirst for fresh blood, and successfully evaded the slaps and grunts from their victims.

Unusually for the tour group, the first person to get up early the next morning was Michael who wore a bright yellow T-shirt with a slogan "Essequibo is we own!" at the front and back. He settled for a pair of khaki shorts, white socks and sneakers. He then limbered up in front of the building and jogged around the perimeter of the site. When he finally joined the others at breakfast, he was panting like a tired jaguar after a failed chase to catch its prey. He took a deep breath, exhaled as if his life was leaving him and then slumped into his chair beside Doreen to his left and Maria to his right.

Arthur was very impressed to see his friend up so early and indulging in his exercise, "Man, that is what we should have been doing every morning on this trip, especially at our age. How about leading us in some warmup exercises to help us keep up with all this travelling, sightseeing, eating and drinking. I know some Chinese style exercises which I can show you."

Parvati sipped some cold water and added, "Wow Michael and Arthur! I can offer to show you all some yoga as well."

Peter laughed and advised, "Hold on everybody. I am always up for some group exercises in the mornings, but we have to be careful that we don't get our old muscles twisted and tied into knots from the different moves and stretches. I have some basic training exercises which my cricketers used to do before and after every practice session. I can adapt some of them to help us all keep in good shape."

Carlos was less enthusiastic than his companions and suggested, "I understand where you guys are coming from. But as far as Maria and I are concerned, we came to Guyana to do a lot more relaxing and chilling out rather than running around the place looking like old fools."

Ramesh intervened with, "I agree with the idea of taking things easy, However, I don't mind doing some limbering up in the mornings as I find that it does help me to stay reasonably fit through the day. One thing I do like in Guyana, is an hour's rest or siesta at around midday."

Doreen smiled and recalled, "I used to love my afternoon strolls at the seawall before the sunset, and sometimes on Sunday mornings."

Vishnu giggled and said, "Aha! I remember that it was a Sunday morning that when Michael saw you strolling along the seawall he tried to show off and impress you by running along in the sand. He didn't last long and then collapsed in an ugly heap. Luckily for him, you as a nurse, volunteered to give him the 'kiss of life' to revive him. Then shortly after that incident, you two fell in love, and as Michael will say, 'the rest is histry!'"

The tour party returned to Lethem for the third night of their stay in Rupununi by early afternoon, and after lunch and some more rest, they headed out for Moco Moco Falls only about half an hour's journey by road. As soon as they arrived at the falls area, they all followed the intrepid Michael's lead to take a dip in one of the naturally formed and refreshing pools. They had passed by the unused and abandoned hydro project which was built by the People's Republic of China but was rendered inoperative by several landslides in the area. The group was shown a concreted stairway behind the power plant building with nearly one thousand steps to the top. No one volunteered to walk up, and they all decided to visit the Moco Moco falls. The leisurely walk through the foot of the Kanuku Mountain to the tumbling waters from the falls bordered by a series of weathered rocks which were smooth enough for them to stand and absorb the scenery, was most pleasurable.

When Michael apologised to the women on the trip for removing his shorts, then he tip-toed to the edge of the crystal clear but darkened water, and immediately stepped back, and started to shiver as he exclaimed, "Man, that water is damn cold!"

Ramesh quickly decided to join Michael, and bravely stepped forward and entered the pool. He then encouraged everyone to step into the water. Sati did likewise and guided the other women into the pool and formed a group away from Michael and the other men.

Vishnu held his nostrils with his right hand, submerged himself below the waterline, and when he emerged with a flourish, he raised up his hands as if celebrating a victory.

"This is like being born again! Long live Guyana!"

24

All that glitters

The tour party arrived back in Anna Catherina with most members appearing and feeling very tired. Nazir, Neesha, John and Muriel welcomed their guests with open arms as they assembled at the formers' home. Jugs of fresh coconut water with bits of the soft white jelly from the fruit and chilled with ice cubes, were just the right tonic for the travellers. This was soon followed by a sumptuous meal of catfish and green mango curry, daal, rice, daalpuri roti and baara and poulouri with mango acchar as side dishes. The dessert was comprised of small bowls of fresh fruits including pineapple, mango, five finger or shamrock and sapodilla. The beverage was a special fruit punch made by Muriel.

Ramesh scanned around the lounge as the tour party eased themselves into the comfortable sofas after the heavy meal, and he announced, "Well we have had a very interesting three days experiencing a few of the amazing things on offer in Rupununi. Sati and I would certainly love to go back there and spend much more time exploring so many places of such incredible natural beauty. I suggest that we take another day of rest tomorrow whilst Sati and I along with Uncle Peter and others figure out what would be best for us to do after that. Perhaps after lunch tomorrow we can listen to what Uncle Michael would like to say about Guyana's other amazing sources of wealth."

Carlos nodded and suggested, "Before we do as Ramesh suggests, I think that we all owe him and Sati as well as our amazing hosts, a huge round of applause for guiding and looking after us older people on this incredible adventure around our beautiful and mysterious country."

Arthur agreed as he joined in with the cheering and mentioned, "This journey has taught me so much that I did not know about our country. If this quest ends for me now, I would be most satisfied. As has been said before, anything else from here onwards will be bonuses. Thank you all."

True to form, Michael, wearing another colourful T-shirt and shorts to match along with his 'One Guyana' cap, stood proudly before his audience after their breakfast. He did a fashion parade style of twirl to show off his passion for the bright colours of the Guyana flag and pointed to the yellow.

"Good morning my dear friends. Today, we will discuss how gold and other mineral wealth attracted Europeans to this country in their search for the mysterious city of El Dorado, known as the City of Gold. The story goes that the Spanish, after Cristobal Colon whom we know as Christopher Columbus, sighted the coast of Guyana in 1498, came looking for gold. Of course, John and Muriel will rightly tell you that Columbus was never the first human to discover what we know as Guyana today. The Arawaks and Caribs came here as far back as thirty-five thousand years ago. Roll forward to 1499, and a Spanish explorer by the name of Alonso de Ojeda along with Juan de la Cosa and an Italian map maker named Amerigo Vespucci, saw the local tribes living in houses with stilts over the water in the Gulf of Venezuela. Vespucci thought that they reminded him of Venice, and he named the area Venezuela, or 'Little Venice'."

Carlos exclaimed, "Wow! I am sure that there is a lot of history in all of this. So, when did the Spanish come through to Essequibo?"

Michael did not seem to mind Carlos's interruption and question as he replied, "Yes Carlos, the history of all the sea voyages to the Caribbean and here in South America will require a lot of time for me to explore and share with you. I can only give you all a little flavour of it. Whilst the legend of El Dorado seduced the Europeans, the Indigenous peoples had to fight long and hard battles against the invaders. I like the notion that the local people used the story of El Dorado to mislead their greedy and brutal tormentors. Sir Walter Raleigh failed hopelessly in his two missions from England to find El Dorado, and as we know, he literally lost his head at the Tower of London because of this!"

Vishnu was also anxious to find out more about Guyana's mineral wealth and commented, "We Guyanese do know that a lot of gold and diamonds have been mined in the interior. Mining continues to be a significant part of Guyana's economy, especially in the last few years of rising gold prices. Of course, our new black gold or oil, is now the dominant feature of Guyana's present and future. I think that as our people get richer here, there will be increasing demands for gold and diamonds locally, in addition to that of the export market."

Michael added, "I hear that there is talk of Guyana having our own gold refinery. If and when this happens, it will put Guyana's gold on the world map. Yet another example of the amazing quality of our natural resources."

Muriel looked at John and smiled as she noted, "Oh, I would love to have some more bling to wear. Of course, I love our traditional trinkets and creations, but nothing can beat our Guyana gold nuggets!"

Parvati joined in with Muriel's suggestion and cheerfully hinted, "Vishnu knows that one of the everlasting memories I want to take away from this trip, is a beautiful high carat gold and diamond set! I mean the whole works! Necklace, bangles, rings, earrings, brooches...."

An increasingly nervous Vishnu raised both of his hands as if in surrender and pleaded, "OK! I get the picture. I promise that I shall fulfil your wishes. I do think that you more than anyone else deserve this, and much more. It's the least I can do for you, my wonderful *jeewan saathi*, my life partner!"

Doreen, Muriel, Maria and Neesha all led a collective "Aah!", and then turned to face their respective partners as a warning for the same response for unforgettable jewellery. The men smiled nervously as they nodded.

Michael promptly continued after Doreen nodded approvingly, "Yes, of course our amazing wives deserve the right appreciation for their love for and devotion to us over so many years. Anyway, our story must continue. Gold has not only attracted the colonialists. When slavery ended, many of our ancestors headed for the interior to prospect for gold and diamonds. We know those ex-slaves as pork-knockers."

Arthur asked, "How did they get that name?"

Michael replied, "When the miners wanted a break to have a meal, they used to say that they were going to "knock some pork". This meant that they wanted to eat some pork. Hence the idea and name of pork-knocker. Gold mining in Guyana is at three levels. The small single-handed miner, the medium sized units and the large mainly overseas corporations' operations. Many Amerindians also work in the gold mining industry both as owners of their own operations and as miners working for others."

John felt obliged to comment, "Now that you have mentioned that Amerindians also work in gold mining, I must also point out that their land titling needs to be completed. A lot of progress has been made after the last government dragged its feet on this issue. Alongside land titling we also need to be supported in the protection of our rights to our land and in stopping illegal gold mining there. In addition, we demand that before any permission is granted to allow mining rights there must be full and proper consultation with the residents and their representatives."

Muriel was also keen to air her views, "We must be supported in the protection of our young women who face abuse and are often subject to violence in the mining towns. We are also seeing our young men being caught up in taking illegal drugs. This could all lead to terrible breakdown of our communities and disruption of our normal peaceful way of life. Of course, our young people are the future of our nation, of this environment and of this country."

Carlos nodded and solemnly said, "So you see, there is a lot of truth in the saying all that glitters is not gold! It's all well and good that we say the Amerindians are the best people to ensure the protection of our rainforests and at the same time we allow their young people to be harmed in such terrible ways. We as Guyanese must do more to support our First Peoples."

Arthur smiled, patted Carlos on his left shoulder, and added, "Well said my friend. We on the outside must not assume that all is well with our First Peoples and turn a blind eye on the things that harm them. Thank you, John and Muriel, for highlighting these issues. In all my years here and abroad I must admit that I had never heard of these problems. In fact, I am ashamed to say that I never paid any heed to the condition of our Amerindian friends. But, for me it is never too late to change."

Peter commented, "I am sure that our Minister and the Ministry of Amerindian Affairs are doing their best to tackle these problems. They must work very closely with the other Ministers and Ministries such as Education, Health, Home Affairs, Finance and so on to ensure that all of their needs are sorted out. No community must be left behind as our country advances."

Michael was really pleased to hear the comments and suggestions from his friends, and added, "Apart from our gold, diamonds and bauxite, we have the most amazing kinds of timbers here in our rainforests. We are sitting on locally made and beautifully designed mahogany furniture. But I must ask Nazir to tell us more about that elegant centre table in this lounge. The design on the top seems to be made of many types of wood."

Nazir stepped over to the low-level centre table and pointed to the multiple woods on the star design at the top, "Here we have examples of many of our amazing woods. I cannot remember all the names, but we have purpleheart, mora, crabwood, kabukalli, wallaba, shibadan and mahogany as well as others. This piece of furniture was actually designed by an Amerindian friend of John and Muriel. He is, indeed, a master craftsman and incredible designer! Our First Peoples are extremely bright and talented, and I am very proud of them."

Vishnu was impressed by Nazir's knowledge and enthused, "Nazir that was an amazing list of the woods used on that table, and most of them I have never heard of. The centre table is a wonderful piece of art, and I do hope that you keep it as it could become a very valuable antique in years to come. Each type of wood used is another example of the great natural beauty and wealth of Guyana."

John smiled and added, "My friends, my people were the first to find and appreciate such gems of our rainforests. In our home you must have seen many examples of Amerindian carvings, weaving, jewellery, balata figures and other items made by the local settlers in our villages and communities all over Guyana. I am happy that you bought some of the products at Iwokrama, Lethem, the Pomeroon and elsewhere."

Muriel pointed to examples of Amerindian embroidery on the cushions of the settees and commented, "Those are fine pieces of creativity and workmanship by our Arawak sisters, and I hope that you will buy such items to take back to your homes. That will certainly help the communities in their businesses."

Peter's eyes lit up as he said, "John, you mentioned balata, and it reminded me of the time when we were very young and did not have cricket balls to play our games in the villages. We used balata and rolled it into the shape of cricket balls, but they were heavy and hurt when they hit our unprotected legs. Later on, we were able to afford the imported rubber balls and other ones made of cork. We only saw and played with the proper official sized red leather balls when we joined the Leonora or the Cornelia Ida Cricket Clubs."

Afzal nodded and added, "Man, when we were young, we would make our own cricket bats out of coconut branches or any decent piece of wood and play our "bat and ball" games in any spare space we could find. We did this at the roadsides, the concreted spaces at the rice factory, and the sandy areas at the seaside when the Atlantic tide was out for a few hours."

Arthur laughed and pretended to bowl an imaginary cricket ball as he said, "Don't forget that we used to play for hours at an open piece of land in Anna Catherina called "Braacha Yard". We even played football games there until we were tired or were chased away!"

Carlos was keen to mention another activity and industry of Guyana, "Fishing has always been a big business here in Guyana. We are fortunate to have some amazing freshwater and saltwater fish and shrimps. We have already tasted some of the more popular fish like banga mary, catfish, houri, patwa, hassa, gilbaaka, cuirass, and the best of all, lukanaani. We Guyanese people love our fish and other sea foods. No wonder that most of us have benefitted from such brain food!"

Michael smiled as he warned, "Yes, we do love our fish, but we also have one fellow in certain waters who could attack people and strip our flesh to the bone! It is the famous piranha! The name means "biting fish" and it is a really fearsome predator!"

Carlos nudged Michael and told the group, "Maria and I visited the island of Madeira where our ancestors came from, and there is a fish which is quite ugly but very tasty, and it is known to the locals as the cutlass fish. We enjoyed that fish at more than one dinner at our hotel. Sometimes I wonder whether we could import and grow our own cutlass fish here. But I suppose that we already have enough to choose from. Besides, I understand that the cutlass fish is found mainly in the Atlantic Ocean just before Winter time."

Michael thanked Carlos for his contribution and then concluded, "Guyana's beauty and wealth fills me with great pride and joy. All of what we have talked about is just one part of this place. There is so much more to see and explore, and I hope that we will all have the strength and energy for more amazing experiences. Let us take some more time to relax and chill out before we take on our next trip tomorrow. Ramesh and Sati, what have you got in store for us? No doubt it will involve more travelling!"

Ramesh looked at Sati, nodded, and announced, "Well everyone, do have a good sleep this evening and be ready very early tomorrow morning for our next day trip. Right Sati? Let's all be prepared for more adventure!"

Before Sati could reveal the trip, Vishnu intervened, "Do tell us tomorrow. I would like to have a night of dreaming about El Dorado!"

Michael laughed, licked his lips and said, "Next time I go out I am going to have a shot of the rum with that name!"

Nazir smiled and said, "Sorry Michael. I cannot offer you any alcohol here due to our faith. But Neesha and I do not mind you having a tipple outside."

Michael nodded and replied, "Not to worry my friend. I was only joking. I do not drink alcohol for health reasons. Besides, I fully respect your abstinence on religious grounds."

Nazir bowed slightly, clasped his hands and said, "Thank you my friend. Do have a very good night's sleep everyone!"

25

Shell Beach

The early morning flight from Ogle International Airport to Mabaruma Airstrip was over the coastland across West Demerara, the Essequibo coast, and further northwest beyond Pomeroon. The weather was favourable apart from a brief shower during the flight. The length of the flight lasted for just under one hour.

Doreen, Parvati, Maria, Sati, Neesha and Muriel opted out of the trip, and Nazir and John left their vehicles at the Ogle Airport for the duration of the day. They then joined Vishnu, Ramesh, Michael, Afzal, Peter, Carlos and Arthur for the adventure to Shell Beach in the Barima-Waini Region One in northwest Guyana.

After a short drive from the Mabaruma Airstrip to Kumaka, the travellers decided to purchase some hot snacks including egg balls, baara and poulouri from a small outlet, and topped up their personal supplies of food and water for the day. They took a short walk to the small Kumaka wharf and boarded a motorised boat designed mainly for the transportation of goods.

The boat trip up the Arruca River directly leading to Shell Beach lasted for one and a half hours, and it was generally uncomfortable. They were surprised about their feeling of unease despite the visible calmness of the dark brown water of the river. Ramesh kept a close watch on how the older members of the group were coping with the travelling, humidity and discomfort. After a few minutes into the boat ride, he spoke to the group.

"I am sorry that today we are trying to take on this trip to Shell Beach which is normally over a longer period of stay. Anyway, are you enjoying this so far?"

Michael ensured that his One Guyana cap was secure on his head and replied, "I feel OK. But I think that this kind of trip should be for about three to five days in order for us to fully appreciate the sights at Shell Beach and the surrounding areas."

Peter, who was standing beside some metal rails of the boat, and alongside the other members of the group, noted, "This is the first time I have ever come so far to the West of Guyana. I have heard of Shell Beach and how the turtles go there to dig large holes in the sand, lay many eggs and cover them before returning to the ocean. We might not see this at this time of the day, but I am still very keen to visit the place."

Michael retrieved his trusted notebook from his small rucksack and referred to an entry before saying, "That's right Peter. There are four kinds of giant turtles which have been doing this every year for thousands of years. They are the green sea, leatherback, olive ridley and hawksbill turtles. There are about five hundred to seven hundred adults involved. I have seen videos of the newborn scrambling out and across the sand, and straight to the water's edge. It's so amazing to see them knowing exactly where to go without any guidance or help. How beautiful and remarkable is nature!"

Arthur was very impressed and asked, "So how far and for how long do they go in the ocean and then return to this same beach to follow what their parents have done?"

Vishnu offered an answer, "I read somewhere that the baby turtles go off thousands of miles to as far as Canada, and after several years they return to Shell Beach. I have no idea as to how the adult turtles do this year after year, and for so long."

Peter suggested, "Man, they must have the best navigation system in their brains! They must also possess powerful strength and a remarkable survival instinct that keeps them out of danger across such a great expanse of ocean. They are truly incredible!"

The boat settled into a good speed up the river passing by lush mangroves, coconut trees and other vegetation on both banks. Timber houses appeared every so often with their landings and moorings for personal motorboats at the water's edge. The constant whirring of the engine and the splashing of the bow onto the water ahead caused the voices of conversations to be raised higher than normal. This was a similar experience to that when they travelled up the Pomeroon River.

Michael, holding onto a rail with his left hand whilst referring to his notebook in his right hand, offered some more information, "I can share with you some of the more recent history about Shell Beach and the turtles. The one hundred miles of brown sand along the beaches are filled with thousands of broken shells and the remains of vegetation beaten down by the strong incoming tides over many thousands of years. Hence the name Shell Beach. This is now under great threat from the sea as well as people looking to poach the eggs and even the turtles. It is obviously a very large area to protect, but where there are wardens there is a better chance of survival. Maybe there is a case for the government to invest in funding many more wardens and additional protection against the high tides. Of course, this does not mean the building of high rocky sea defences, but perhaps growing a lot more mangrove."

Vishnu raised his voice to comment, "Man, those poor little baby turtles and the adults must encounter so many dangers out at sea with fishing trawler nets, plastics, propellers and of course, natural predators. Yet they manage to survive and return here. I hope that the authorities here in Guyana can do more as you say, to protect and sustain this amazing treasure that we are so lucky to have."

Michael frowned and added, "Yes, the four types of giant turtles are all endangered species. I wish to mention another remarkable thing about the turtles. You would not believe that each of the four species does not come ashore together but separately at intervals of about one month. The green sea are the first to arrive in the season. Then the leatherbacks, followed by the hawksbills and finally, the olive ridleys. Amazing! How do they know this? We humans have a lot more to learn from these amazing creatures."

John was eager to point out, "As with so much of our hinterland and natural spaces, we must be grateful for the efforts of our Amerindian brothers and sisters in trying to protect and sustain such sites like Shell Beach. They are from the Carib, Warrau and Arawak tribes. But we must give great credit to a conservationist named Dr Peter Pritchard who founded the Non-governmental Guyana Marine Turtle Conservation Society along with Guyanese, Romeo DeFreitas. Together, the people and the Society have tried to protect Shell Beach and its turtle activities."

Michael thanked John for his information and added, "Shell Beach is not only about the turtles there, but also of a wide variety of other wildlife such as dolphins, many species of birds and fish. The seawater fish include the barracuda, snapper and grouper. I am, however, very saddened to learn that due to global warming and increasing rising tides, Shell Beach is being eroded rapidly despite efforts to encourage more mangrove to help defend and preserve it from the ravages of the sea."

Carlos raised his eyebrows and warned, "I have heard of some concerns mentioned by environment activists that places such as Shell Beach and the entire coast of Guyana could be severely harmed by oil spills from offshore drilling operations. One major oil spill could devastate the entire habitat of Shell Beach, and so kill off the annual activities of the turtles and other creatures in the area. This issue must be taken seriously by the government and the oil corporations operating in the oilfields."

Michael acknowledged Carlos's comment, and he was beaming as he said, "There is one person who is a proud part-Amerindian Guyanese by the name of Annette Arjoon-Martins who grew up in Pomeroon. She has been a lifelong conservationist who is a qualified pilot as well. She is passionate about protecting and preserving our eco-systems such as in Shell Beach. One of the things I do admire about her is her belief that the people who are best placed to ensure environmental protection, are the Amerindians. I also believe that all Guyanese must be made more aware of this incredible place and be encouraged to support the protection of our environment here and across the country. We need many more Annette Arjoon-Martins!"

Arthur nodded in agreement and advised, "It is also very important for the new migrants from Venezuela as well as Brazil, to be educated about the need to protect the environment especially in the hinterland."

Vishnu took a final drink from his bottle of water and noted, "Thank you, Michael and everyone else for your insights about Shell Beach. Now we should be more prepared and better informed for what we will see when we get there. I feel much more excited about this trip!"

The boat finally entered the mouth of the Waini River, and the group disembarked at Almond Beach which is one of nine beaches or sections of the whole Shell Beach. They were warmly welcomed by a jovial Guyanese Turtle Warden who offered to act as their guide around the beach. The first advice given by the warden was for anyone of the touring group to ensure that they used the toilet facilities. Only a few including Michael opted to do so."

Due to the limited time for the trip, the group decided to use the beach to have their snacks and beverages. After their brief rest, the warden led them on a stroll along the beach which was dominated by many sizes of shells with some finely crushed over time. He located a giant leatherback turtle preparing to cover its eggs, and to inch its way down to the water's edge.

Michael was curious as to how many eggs were laid and asked, "Can you guess the number of eggs laid by this giant turtle?"

The warden, a young man in his twenties, stocky and about five and a half feet tall, spoke with a gentle voice, "Sir, I'm not sure. But I have seen around one hundred at times. It normally takes about one hour for them to be laid in a deep hole in the sand. This is then well covered up, and most times I cannot say for sure where they are until the little babies, or hatchlings emerge after an incubation period of between forty-five to seventy days. The newborns then take about one week to push their way up from the nest. Then to see them immediately scuttle down to the water, is truly remarkable!"

Arthur offered an answer to the mystery, "Maybe, as Peter said, the turtles' brains have some kind of inborn navigational system. All I can say is that it is nature's way which we are still trying to work out. By the way, the Chinese people call sea turtles 'haigui' to refer to Chinese students who go abroad to study, and then return to China after they pass their examinations with flying colours."

John nodded and enthused, "The turtle is held as a sacred being in some cultures. For example, it is a symbol of Mother Earth, and our native American brothers and sisters regard the giant turtle as supporting the Earth or world on its back. I love that image!"

Michael added, "I read that the turtle was even a fertility symbol in ancient Greek and Roman times. Arthur, in the Chinese system of Feng Shui, the turtle is considered to be a symbol of good luck and prosperity. Maybe we can say that with the turtles choosing to come here on Shell Beach, perhaps this has brought good fortune to our Guyana!"

Nazir, ever the sceptic, was not sure about Michael's reasoning and suggested, "Well, in my mind, Guyana has always been blessed with a lot of natural resources. Whether or not the turtles have brought good fortune to our country, I believe that we must do more to preserve this area and support the turtles and all the other wildlife here."

Ramesh nodded and lamented, "I now wish that Sati and I had booked for us to stay here for at least a couple of days. But we were not sure about the accommodation and other facilities. The large number of mosquitoes was another factor in settling for just this day trip to get a taste of the experience."

Carlos smiled and said, "I fully understand that decision Ramesh. Speaking of taste, I hear that turtle meat tastes a bit like chicken and beef, and the eggs are nicer than chicken eggs, but can have an aftertaste."

Peter frowned and remarked, "Man, I'm glad that you didn't mention this before we had our lunch! I can't understand how, on the one hand we want to see the turtles survive, and then on the other, we're talking about eating them. Terrible!"

Carlos bowed slightly and muttered, "I do apologise my friend. These amazing creatures should never be regarded as sources of meat or eggs for consumption."

The warden listened carefully to the conversation, and chose his moment to comment, "Gentlemen, the practice of stealing or poaching the turtles and their eggs has virtually ended since Dr Pritchard and Audley James got together back in the 1980s to buy the stolen items from the criminals. Nowadays, me and my colleagues patrol the beaches to make sure that the turtles and their nests are well protected. Audley James was himself a turtle hunter. Sirs, I must also say to you that we have much better foods and drinks here."

Michael, as vigilant as ever, opened his notebook and pointed out, "Yes, I have a note here that you have something called "Heart of Palm" from the Acai Palm tree. It is claimed to be a good health food which doesn't have fat and sugar and can help with managing cholesterol levels. This can be cooked as a vegetable, or added to curries, or used as a salad, or snack. The palm is found mostly around the edges of the Barima River."

The warden patiently and quietly continued, "Sirs, you may be able to spot members of around two hundred and fifty bird species here, including those beautiful scarlet ibis, kingfishers, greater flamingos, parrots, macaws, harpy eagles and many others. We also have jaguars, tapirs, red howler monkeys, squirrel monkeys, giant river otters, dolphins, manatees and many more. You need to spend a few days here to be able to truly appreciate the beauty and diversity of this vast area. Unfortunately, wherever we have so much water, you will get the dreaded mosquitoes".

Vishnu was quite appreciative of the warden's information and commented, "Thank you very much young man. We are all grateful to you and to your colleagues for watching over Shell Beach and this amazing eco-environment. It is a pity that our visit here today is coming to an end and as we have to get back to our boat and to Mabaruma in time for our return flight to Ogle."

John stepped forward, shook the right hand of the warden, and told him, "I am very proud of you and your colleagues, and all others involved in protecting Shell Beach for as long as it is visible and can withstand the angry tides of the Atlantic Ocean. These one hundred miles are truly a great treasure of Guyana, and we all hope that it will still be here for future generations. Whenever we talk about Guyana's natural resources, these are the locations which are with incalculable worth."

The warden smiled, bowed his head respectfully to the visitors, and waved as he walked away over the fragile shells of the beach.

26

The things we share

The tour party returned from Shell Beach in the early hours of the evening and were warmly welcomed by their partners and hosts. The men presented their wives with souvenirs they had purchased in Mabaruma, as well as small collections of some carefully selected seashells from Shell Beach which were well received. Parvati and the other women had spent the day meeting relatives and friends at their homes or at Nazir's and Neesha's and John's and Muriel's. Vishnu and his fellow travellers did not elaborate on their trip and promised to do so the next day. The entire tour party and their hosts agreed to use that day for some more rest from the travelling. The increasingly hot temperature during the day and only a small drop during the evenings were beginning to cause more discomfort for the visitors, and the rest days were helping them to cope.

Nazir and Neesha had invited some of their old friends from the coast to have lunch with the visitors and to reflect on the tours around the country. It was an opportunity for them to share their thoughts on their quest to find out more about Guyana and to consider the future of the country and its people.

Michael as always, was prepared for such a gathering, and he appeared with another white T-shirt with a motif representing the symbols of Christianity, Islam, Hinduism and Buddhism set out in a circle. On the back there was another picture of six different coloured hands joined together in a circular link. He proudly stood up before his friends in Nazir's and Neesha's lounge and pointed to the pictures on the front and the back of his T-shirt.

He announced, "You see, we are so fortunate to gather here as one people of our beautiful Guyana. We have our diversity, but we also have our mutual love and respect for each other. Our older generations had experienced a lot of division, disrespect and a hatred which exploded into a lot of violence back in the 1960s, and sadly, this lingered on like a sore that never healed. Many people had to leave this country that they loved, to get away from what was happening to them in all the decades to now. But thank God in whatever way we see him, for bringing us together at this moment in time when we have been given a chance to heal that scar in our hearts and minds."

Before Michael could continue, everyone stood up and applauded him.

Vishnu stepped forward, hugged his lifelong friend, and remarked, "What a way to start our conversation here today. Michael, you stand here like a beacon of hope, and this trip, this quest of ours, has already shown us how much we have in this young country to share amongst ourselves, and with the world. Yes, we do as a nation, have some deep-seated problems, but we also have the means to find the solutions to them. No country in this world is perfect, and even the most developed ones are still struggling with these problems in even greater measure."

Michael continued, "Yes, my brother. When the racial disturbance broke out in 1964, you may recall that we as friends in our villages, suddenly stopped talking to each other. Then, six months later, when things calmed down, at least we in Anna Catherina began to re-connect, but at first it was very strange, tentative, and there was a lot of trust lost in such a short time. Then many of our friends just left in the 1970s, to go abroad to study and work. Some of us stayed on to live through those years of great uncertainty and hardships until we left in the 1980s and 1990s. Now, here we are with so many memories and experiences, still looking to the future with the great hope that it will be bright for all Guyanese."

Nazir shook his head and said, "I love your optimism. You guys live thousands of miles away from our problems here in Guyana. It is very easy for you to bring such noble thoughts and ideas. But there are still too many of us living here who do not buy in to all this talk of a 'One Guyana'. There are some politicians who continue to peddle the racism card against the government. We still have a lot of poverty here, as well as crimes against the people and their property. There is also the stench of corruption still lingering in the air. Some people inside and outside of our country spend a lot of time in spreading their wild accusations about inequality and racism in our society. We see garbage thrown around by stupid and irresponsible people despite several attempts by even the President to clean up the place. You will have noticed how the prices for everything continue to rise making it worse for the poor. People talk about not seeing any of the "oil money" even though the government has given and continues to give so many grants, scholarships and have removed dozens of taxes imposed by the last government. I could go on and on about everything that is bad and negative about this country. But I also have to recognise all the good things that are happening here. I do hope that things will get better and better in the years ahead."

Michael appreciated Nazir's comments and responded, "Nazir, I do agree with you about us from abroad coming here with our views on the country and people. I also understand that poverty is still a significant issue. Ramesh and Sati will be more informed about the facts and figures about poverty in Guyana. I saw some information on this and despite the rapid rise of our economy due to oil and gas, the poverty rate here is over forty per cent! This is based on the measure of people living with only five US dollars and fifty cents per day. That is about eleven hundred Guyana dollars per day. With the cost of living going up and up, many more people are falling into that level of poverty whilst they see the rich getting richer. This inequality must continue to be addressed."

Arthur insisted, "There are many who talk about corruption and how the oil money is going only to the people in power and their supporters. It is very easy to make these claims on social media, but I am still waiting to see charges, evidence and judgements against alleged wrongdoers. As far as I am aware, the government has in place a strong system for the procurement activities. For example, a project for an infrastructure development will be properly specified, advertised, assessed, evaluated against strict criteria and then a choice will be made based on the best quality and price. I am familiar with such processes from my own experiences of managing large contracts. However, the problem we seem to have here in Guyana is to do with the sheer volume of contracts for so many projects across the country. I have heard that whilst the systems and processes are watertight, there is a shortage of skilled and experienced personnel to deal with the procurements in the most efficient and effective manner. This deficiency alone can create greater risks and thus give the impression of favouritism towards one group of contractors who seem to win many contracts. This then feeds into the allegations of favouritism and corruption."

Michael listened intently and then asked, "So, how can this problem be dealt with?"

Arthur suggested, "There are clearly at least two things which can be done. One is to ensure that the technical skills and capability of the personnel supporting the procurements are either bought in or acquired by training and development by experts. The second is to ensure that there is adequate capacity and capability to conduct audits on behalf of the government departments involved. If contractors fail to deliver on time and produce shoddy work, then they must be penalised severely. When this happens, the public will have more confidence and assurance about the processes. Accountability is a critical element of good governance."

Carlos took out his white handkerchief from his trouser back pocket and mopped his brow as he said, "Phew! It's getting too warm in here! Maria and I just don't take any notice of such allegations. We believe that the government must just get on with the work, meet the people, solve their problems, and let the world see this as the factual information and not, I repeat, not propaganda."

Doreen kissed her teeth, shook her head, and pointed out, "There will always be some people who see things differently, and when you add fake news to them, they believe in only the lies. It seems to me that the more you tell a lie to such people the more it becomes the truth to them. Then you find that you cannot argue with them."

Muriel acknowledged Doreen's point and suggested, "I think that the best way to deal with this problem is to continue to show how much is being done for the poor and others in need. Individuals and families are being helped and supported by several cash grants, the removal of many taxes, large pay rises greater than the rate of inflation and the creation of thousands of jobs. And yet some people can say that nothing is being done for the Guyanese people. I am sure that we will see much more help for the people in the months and years ahead."

Parvati intervened and noted, "I see that there are lots of jobs but not enough Guyanese with the right skills and experience to take them. That is why we are seeing more education and training being offered for free. It is not all about handouts."

John laughed and tried to lighten the mood in the room, "Talk about training? Man, I wanted some work to be done at the house and the guy I offered the job to actually turned up late on the first day and didn't have any tools! He even had the balls to ask me to buy some tools for him!"

Vishnu giggled and could not resist a taunt, "I bet that you must have fired him and given that job to a willing Venezuelan immigrant!"

Muriel nodded and confirmed, "You're right. That's what actually happened! The Venezuelan guy did a good job without any fuss, and with his own tools!"

Afzal warned, "If my fellow Guyanese don't try to help and improve themselves, these foreigners will soon bypass them. Then those same Guyanese will turn around and try to blame the government for their problems. I guess that you can't win with people like that."

Vishnu mused, "This is the kind of thing we see in many countries where the foreigners come in and take up all the jobs that the locals don't want to do or don't have the skills for, and when problems arise, it's the migrants who are targeted for blame."

Michael raised his right hand and said, "I can see that most Guyanese working on the construction sites and so on, are toiling very hard and I only hope that they are getting good money for their efforts. We mustn't let a few bad apples spoil the basket!"

Maria looked around the room and then commented, "Here in this room I can see a good cross-section of Guyanese people, and this is what the One Guyana idea is about. We must emphasise more on the things that bring us together. Our culture, our language, our food, our music, and even our religions."

Parvati agreed with Maria and added, "We as Guyanese must continue to build on the time when we showed much more respect for each other especially at times like Christmas and Easter. Whether we were Christians or not we all took part in the whole celebrations by decorating our homes with fairy lights and Christmas trees and bought presents for each other. At Easter, we all as kids used to make different types of kites to fly them at home and especially on Easter Sunday and Easter Monday, at the seaside. It never mattered whether we were Christian, Hindu, or Muslim."

Michael smiled and mentioned, "I remember that Vishnu was our best kite maker specialising in the ones which could "sing" the loudest and longest, and with the lethal tails with sharp razor blades fastened to encourage them to sweep across other kids' main kite string and cut them. That caused a lot of grief and tears as the poor victims ran after their kites trying to retrieve them as they flew away. I can see that Vishnu is smirking!"

Vishnu shrugged his shoulders and pointed out, "Well, we were all competing with each other, and in every battle, there has to be a loser, or many losers in my case. We also used to have great fun during the festival of Holi or Pagwah. Two days of real joy!"

Parvati intervened with, "Yes, the first day starts with the burning of the Holika and is known as Holika Dahan. Everyone just sang and danced around the fire in celebration. Holi is normally in late February or by Mid-March. The second day is called Rangwali when we get up early in the morning, offer our prayers, and then seek the blessings of our parents and elders. Pagwah is about the arrival of Spring and the triumph of good over evil. There is a great mythical Indian story behind Pagwah."

Peter eagerly put his right hand up and offered, "I can tell you about that! The story goes that once there was a powerful and evil king called Hiranyakshyap who saw himself as divine and wanted everyone to worship him. But his own son Prahalad preferred to worship the Hindu God, Vishnu. The king asked Holika to enter a big fire with Prahalad in her lap, but he was saved. Hence the burning of Holika."

Afzal smiled and noted, "Man, many of us Muslims and Christians join in with our Hindu friends to enjoy the fun of spraying each other with powder and especially the red abeer. We would go around the village and play Pagwah with everyone we could reach. Even those who didn't join in got a good soaking! It was about celebrating with great joy and happiness!"

Vishnu looked across at Michael and reminded him, "You ended up learning to swim very quickly as we lifted you up and threw you into the trench. As you flapped about calling for help, we all jumped in and pulled you out. Since that first time, you became determined to learn how to swim! Thanks to Pagwah!"

Everyone except Michael burst out laughing.

A chastened Michael sat up and proudly announced, "Of course, I forgave all of you. I see that you did not mention how I became such a good swimmer, and I beat all of you in our fight games in the water!"

Sati added, "Uncle Michael that is a bit like the legend Uncle Peter talked about. Holika was the sister of that evil king, and she wore a cloak which protected her from the fire, but it flew off her and covered Prahalad. She was destroyed and Prahalad was saved. I guess you can say that Uncle Michael was like Prahalad. Pagwah or Holi is celebrated all over India and everywhere there are Hindus. In fact, our Sikh brothers and sisters also celebrate this festival wherever we all meet."

Arthur asked, "Why do you use so many colours?"

Parvati replied, "Well, there is another story of our Lord Krishna who was dark-skinned and thought that all the fair-skinned gopis and Radha whom he loved, would not appreciate him. So, he playfully threw coloured powders on them."

Carlos giggled and noted, "Man, you have to go to Guyana's National Stadium to see how thousands of mostly young Guyanese of all races and religions turn up to listen to concerts, dance, play Pagwah and have an amazing time. Apart from the religious significance, I think that Pagwah is a great symbol of the merging of the colours of our nation and flag in one moment when we all show each other that we care for one another."

Everyone cheered Carlos who stood up and took a bow.

Michael, without looking at his notebook, spoke when the applause ended, "February is an important month for us. First, there is St Valentine's Day on the fourteenth, and our Republic Day and Mashramani celebrations on the twenty-third. Mashramani, or "Mash" for short, is a great carnival of parades, music and dancing as Guyanese get together once again every year. Last year the theme was about "Mixing and Mashing as One Guyana". I wish that we were here to take part in that great party!"

John nodded and pointed out, "Mashramani is very much rooted in our Arawak Amerindian culture, and it means a celebration after hard work. You may be interested to know that our cricket legend, Basil Butcher, suggested that an Amerindian word should be used instead of carnival. The parades include a lot of music and rhythm and masquerade characters such as "Mad Cow" and "Tall Lady" on stilts blend in with the amazing costumes and floats."

Muriel was beaming as she said, "Mashramani is about the birth of the Republic of Guyana. All kinds of our local music are played including calypso, chutney-soca, chutney and folk. I must say that it all started with an annual carnival in Mackenzie since 1966. Then it was agreed to have the big parade of Mashramani in Georgetown after 1970. So, Mash has been with us for over fifty years, and it's our greatest street festival bringing our people together."

Michael gave a thumbs up and added, "There is no doubt that we Guyanese are very fortunate to have so many festivals to celebrate together through the year. We go on from February to May when we have May Day or Labour Day which is a national holiday on the first of May. Again, the people take to the streets to parade with banners of the Trades Unions and wearing red shirts or tops and black trousers or skirts. The great Hubert Nathaniel Critchlow, the father of Trade Unionism here in Guyana is honoured and remembered."

Nazir smiled and said, "Soon after the May Day holiday, we have the fifth of May, the Arrival of Indian Indentured Labourers to work on the sugar plantations after the end of slavery. I would love to have this day as another special holiday, but whilst we commemorate the event it is not called Indian Arrival Day but a more general Arrival Day for everyone brought to work on the plantations. There is always some criticism of the government for this from some people of Indian origin."

Vishnu was animated as he said, "Yes, I see no reason why we should not have a special holiday for Indian Indentured Labourers' arrival. After all, we have a public holiday for the end of the enslavement of Africans called Emancipation Day on the first of August each year. I agree with that, but we need to recognise that our Indian population is the largest here in Guyana and I strongly feel that we as Indian Guyanese are being deliberately undermined!"

Carlos pointed out, "I get that Vishnu. But I can also call for a Portuguese Arrival Day holiday as my ancestors actually arrived here before the Indians, on the third of May 1835!"

Arthur ceased the opportunity to add, "And what about a Chinese Arrival Day holiday for the seventeenth of January? My ancestors first arrived in the year 1853."

Michael noted, "I can see why the government opted for one Arrival Day for most, if not all, Guyanese, otherwise we would have too many holidays in each year. In fact, I have never been able to identify the date of the arrival of my African ancestors."

John smiled and said, "Nor of mine."

Neesha frowned and mentioned, "I hope that we will not now talk about celebrating Guyana's Independence Day on the twenty-sixth of May for the reasons I mentioned before."

Michael acknowledged Neesha's concern and said, "In solidarity with you, I shall always mark that day in a low-key way. Sadly, this cannot be changed by us unless it is amended in the Guyana Constitution."

Vishnu also recognised Neesha's stance and added, "We do have the sixteenth of June as a commemoration of the Enmore Martyrs Day which we talked about during our trip to the memorial. Although it is a holiday, I suppose we can use that time to remember all the martyrs on our sugar estates since Sumintra in 1939, Kowsilla in 1964 and many others."

Afzal felt the sombre mood in the room and changed the discourse, "Of course, we also have holidays for *Youman Nabi* the Prophet Mohamed's birthday, on whom be peace. Then, *Eid- ul- Adha* or "Bakra Eid" as we know it in Guyana. The dates vary due to the first sighting of the new moon and dates in the Islamic calendar. We as Muslims fast in the month of Ramadan and when that is over, we have a great feast on *Eid- ul- Fitr*. On that day, we go to our local mosque for the Eid prayer, listen to some speech by our Imam and Islamic songs before visiting other families to taste their food until we eventually arrive at our own home. We give alms to the poor and exchange gifts amongst our family and friends. It's another time of caring for others and bringing people together."

Parvati clasped her hands together as if in prayer and stated, "I am really happy to have so many Muslim friends here as well as in New York. Vishnu, myself, Ramesh, Sati and our grandchildren are normally invited for the Eid dinner by our Muslim neighbours."

Vishnu nodded and added, "I am sure that everyone here could remember that when there was a Hindu wedding in our village, and the wedding house cooked strictly vegetarian meals such as the famous seven curries served on purine leaves, the hosts would normally cater for non-vegetarian meals by asking their Muslim neighbours to cook such dishes. Now Nazir and my other Muslim friends would take me to that house so that I could also enjoy some mutton curry!"

Nazir giggled and added, "Yes, we made sure that we called you by a Muslim name such as Akbar Khan! Then it was easier to sneak you into that house as one of us. Mind you, when we took you in, there was no need for you to go around saying "Salaam" to everyone you met."

Vishnu sheepishly looked at Parvati who pretended to scold him by wagging her right index finger at him.

Everyone laughed at the guilt-ridden Vishnu.

Ramesh smiled and said, "Thank you Uncle Nazir for bringing that to light. I guess that Guyanese Hindu homes must be adorned with hundreds of diyas and other festive lighting on the evening of Diwali or Deepavali known as the Hindu "Festival of Lights". Again, this represents the triumph of good over evil."

Sati added, "When Lord Raam, with the help of Sri Hanuman defeated the evil Raavan in Lanka, he and his companions returned to the City of Ayodhya in India which was lit up with thousands of diyas. Diwali gives Hindus a chance to welcome goodness and prosperity into their homes. It normally falls in October."

John stood up and commented, "It is truly amazing for us all to participate in, or observe, so many religious and other festivals. Of course, we Amerindians have the whole month of September to showcase our culture, our crafts, our music, dance and other aspects of our community. The events are always open to all of our fellow Guyanese."

Michael stood beside John and said, "Thank you my brother. This session has been so wonderful. This is the true face of Guyana and Guyanese, and long may it continue. All these events, festivals and celebrations have always brought us together, not only to enjoy ourselves, but also to allow us to show our mutual respect for each other and our customs and religions."

Doreen stood up and stepped across the room to where Neesha and Muriel were standing, and announced, "Can I ask all of you to join me in applauding these two amazing sisters? Their hospitality has been the best of what Guyanese can offer. Thank you, John and Nazir, for everything you have done for us all on this amazing trip."

27

The Spirit of Paramaribo

Ramesh and Sati duly informed the tour party that having visited at least one part of most of the ten regions of the country, the plan for the next morning was for a trip into Region Six including the area covered by Corriverton, the magnificent Courentyne River, and a short visit and tour of Paramaribo via Nikerie in neighbouring Suriname.

Michael expressed great enthusiasm for the proposed trip and advised that they needed to commence the journey as early as possible in the morning.

"I think that we should retire early this evening and be ready to travel from about seven in the morning. It will be a very long day on the road and across rivers through some well-known places to the Moleson Creek terminal for a ferry crossing to Nikerie in Suriname."

Ramesh agreed with Michael and added, "Yes Uncle Michael, we should catch the ten o'clock ferry from Moleson Creek ferry terminal, and then after the half hour crossing to Nikerie, we will have a three-and-a-half-hour drive to Paramaribo, the Capital City of Suriname. We will stop for lunch on that route, and hopefully we can have a tour of Paramaribo and get back in time for the return trip on the ferry."

Vishnu raised his eyebrows and promptly pointed out, "Ramesh, that is a very tight and challenging schedule over only one day, and with a hell of a lot of driving. I think that we will have to stay over in Suriname for at least one night before the return journey home."

Ramesh nodded and suggested, "Yes, the plan is for Uncle Nazir and Uncle John to drive us to the ferry crossing in Moleson, leave the cars there and hire a minibus to take us to Paramaribo and back."

Vishnu was not convinced by that plan either and asked, "So, what happens if we miss the return ferry?"

Sati answered, "Well, we will just have to stay in Nikerie for the night, and then return the next day."

Michael felt comfortable with the plan and commented, "I think that we should go with this plan. At first, I did not intend to visit Suriname, but I now feel that it is the right thing to do whilst we are in Guyana. I am very happy that the two leaders of Guyana and Suriname are willing to collaborate, and this is very good for the development of both countries especially since their discoveries of oil in the Atlantic."

Arthur agreed and added, "Yes, there is a plan to build a bridge across the Courentyne River from Moleson to a place called South Drain in Suriname. This will ease the movement of people and goods much more smoothly and quickly between the two countries. In fact, the three Presidents of Guyana, Brazil and Suriname are committed to a trilateral series of plans to work together on infrastructure development and the very important issue of security. Building such stronger relationships between these three countries will give Guyana the big benefit of greater strength against the continuing threat from Venezuela for Guyana's territory."

Michael smiled and gave Arthur a thumbs up, "Man, for a moment there you sounded like a very well-informed politician! I love the way that the three leaders are collaborating for the mutual benefit of the three countries and of course, the people. It is a great shame that Maduro continues to push for his mad dream about stealing Essequibo. I do hope that common sense will prevail and he backs off. I am really looking forward to visiting and touring Paramaribo. Mind you, I do think that common sense can be a challenging thing for many politicians!"

Afzal raised his arms aloft, had a broad smile, and proposed, "I am very happy to host you all in Paramaribo and wish that you can stay for a longer period. I am also thrilled about the stronger links between Guyana and Suriname, and of course, Brazil. If things progress well, I might change my mind about returning to Guyana and try harder to succeed in Suriname. Obviously, I am also very happy to see the way that Guyana is progressing, and this gives me good options on both sides."

Peter commented, "Well Bhai Afzal, as we say, the ball is now in your court. Perhaps you can stay in Suriname and set up in Guyana.

But of course, your decision will depend on how your family responds to your ideas. I don't envy you."

Michael was very pleased with Afzal's offer of the overnight stay, "Thank you brother Afzal. I agree that we should spend the night with you and your family there in Paramaribo, and then take more time on our return to possibly look at places such as Skeldon and so on."

Arthur agreed, "I have never been to Suriname, and I like the idea for us to spend most of at least one day and night there. We might even be able to help our brother Afzal to decide as to what he and his family should do in the future."

Carlos and Maria both nodded, and she said, "I would like to know more about Suriname and the Surinamese people. We have never been there. I am also curious to find out as to what extent the Surinamese people are like us. Or, how different they may be."

Very early the next morning and after a light breakfast, the tour party boarded the two cars driven by Nazir and John, and they made good progress over the West Coast of Demerara and the Demerara Harbour Bridge, through the East Coast of Demerara, and towards the Berbice River crossing. They stopped in New Amsterdam for a brief comfort break, and then continued towards Corriverton leading to the Moleson Creek terminal, just in time for the ten o'clock ferry crossing.

The men of the group carried their small rucksacks with snacks and refreshments as well as clothing for the change after their overnight stay in Paramaribo. They all awaited the slow but steady boarding of the maximum number of vehicles at the ferry terminal, and then they were allowed to walk along the gangway that led onto the ferry. There were not enough seating areas, and the tour party preferred to stand on one side of the vessel for the thirty minutes trip across the magnificent Courentyne River which formed the natural border between Guyana and Suriname.

The river was similar to those in Guyana and its water was the same silted light brown colour. River traffic across the route was relatively quiet. The ferry made good progress along the way until it finally eased into the harbour on the Suriname side.

As soon as the tour party disembarked from the ferry, Ramesh, Sati, Nazir and John sought out a suitable vehicle to hire for their drive through to Paramaribo which was about one hundred and fifty miles away. The driver was an affable African Surinamese who was of medium build, with broad shoulders, and a great smile exposing a gap in his upper front teeth. He spoke good English and welcomed everyone on board.

Michael, as usual, sat beside his friend Vishnu, and was quickly into his stride as the tour party's commentator.

"I hope that everyone is comfortable in your seats. I am advised by our friendly driver, that the ride will be straightforward and without any obstacles. If you look around, you will observe scenes which will remind you of Guyana. I do not have a lot of information about this journey, so I am leaving that to our driver. When we come to the end of using this vehicle, I hope that we will all give generously to the usual collection for the driver."

There was a resounding "Yes!" from the passengers.

Vishnu commented, "Note that we are driving on the left-hand side of the road as we do in Guyana. This is an advantage for people driving across both countries. I am now beginning to feel quite hungry, and I assume that our driver will find a good restaurant for us to have lunch before we finally arrive in Paramaribo."

The driver nodded and gave a thumbs up before driving off on the trip. The road was good apart from the occasional pothole. The tour party passed through many small villages, fields of sugarcane and other crops. The sun remained sharp, and the blue skies were only occasionally obscured when a threatening rain cloud crept across. However, there was no rainfall by the time the vehicle reached the restaurant chosen for lunch.

Ramesh announced to the tour party before they stepped into the restaurant, "Please use only about forty-five minutes to have lunch so that we can get to Paramaribo in reasonable time for a brief tour before it gets too dark after sunset."

After lunch, most of the tour party took a comfort break, and then returned to the vehicle, except for Michael who had to be retrieved by Ramesh.

Michael finally returned and stood in front of the vehicle. He announced, "I am sorry to take some more time as I wanted to get further information about Paramaribo and Suriname from the restaurant owner. He was very helpful and passed on a lot of interesting facts which I will share with you all."

Vishnu settled into his seat, and as soon as Michael sat beside him, he asked, "So, will you tell us more about Suriname? I know that we talk about our six peoples of Guyana, but I understand that there are many more in Suriname."

Michael quickly referred to his notebook and responded, "I am glad that you asked that question. Suriname has a population of only around six hundred thousand people, and with many thousands having migrated to Holland. The largest population group is the African Surinamese at about thirty-seven per cent. Of that group, they have Creoles who make up about sixteen per cent, and the Maroons at about twenty-two per cent."

Ramesh leaned forward from behind Michael's seat and asked, "Uncle Michael, what or who are the Maroons?"

Michael replied as the driver began the final leg of the trip, "They are descendants of enslaved Africans who escaped from the sugar plantations and settled in the forests. The second largest group is the descendants of Indian Indentured Labourers, and they make up about twenty-seven per cent. Then the Javanese Surinamese are about fourteen per cent, and mixed-race people about thirteen per cent. Suriname also has Chinese, Portuguese, Jewish and Lebanese people which makes the country much more than a rainbow nation. Note that they have a similar motto to ours and it is 'Wan Kondre, Wan Pipel' meaning 'One Country, One People'."

John, who like the other passengers, was listening carefully, mentioned, "Michael, please do not forget to talk about Suriname's Indigenous peoples. They are about four per cent of the population, and Muriel may correct me if I am wrong. The main tribes are the Akurio, Arawak, Carib, Tiriyo and Wayana."

Muriel smiled and confirmed, "John, that is correct. Well done!"

Vishnu asked Michael, "Can you remind us as to the name of the President of Suriname?"

Michael had to refer to his notebook and stated, "His name is Chandrikapersad Santokhi. I hope I pronounced that correctly."

Arthur noted, "It was very good to see President Ali and President Santokhi get together with some of their Ministers very early in their Presidency. In addition to the bridge across the Courentyne, I am looking forward to more joint projects that will benefit the people of both countries. Guyana and Suriname do have a lot in common with each other."

Afzal cleared his throat and commented, "I think that Peter is right regarding my situation. I am thinking of doing some kind of business which can support one of the joint projects between the two countries."

Parvati suggested, "Afzal Bhaiya, you need to find out what the people from both countries can use from each other. Something not thought about until now. That will place you and your business in a unique position."

Muriel pointed out, "Perhaps you can try to bring the two countries' Indigenous peoples together to exchange and trade the products that they make."

Doreen asked from the back seat, "Michael, what are we going to be doing in Paramaribo?"

Michael looked at Ramesh and Sati, and after getting a nod from them, he answered loudly enough for everyone to hear, "Doreen, the first thing we will do when we arrive in Paramaribo later this afternoon, will be to stretch our legs a little bit whilst on a short tour of the Fort Zeelandia site by the bank of the Suriname River. There is also the Suriname Museum. Now, if we feel too tired from the long drives on this trip, perhaps we can visit the Museum tomorrow morning."

Afzal added, "Well, as you suggest, let's stretch our legs at Fort Zeelandia, and then go over to my place for dinner and a restful evening. Then we will have an early breakfast and continue with our tour of the city before making our way back to Guyana."

Michael paused for a few moments and said, "Wait a minute there Afzal. I think that we have gotten this trip all wrong. I had not thought of this until now. We could have waited until we completed all of our trips in Guyana before coming over here to Suriname, to accompany you home. Now you will be returning to Guyana with us and then you will have to make another trip back to Paramaribo. That doesn't make sense to me."

Afzal nodded and confirmed, "Never mind, I prefer to be in Guyana with you guys for our farewell get-together."

Peter turned to Michael and enthused, "Man, this country is beautiful. I love the Dutch style houses we can see as we move along the main roads. I like the old charm of the place. I hope that Afzal will tell us more about Paramaribo and Suriname. By the way, I heard that when the Indentured Indians were being recruited in India, the people thought that they were going to "Sri Raam", the name they used for

Suriname. Our ancestors also used to call Trinidad, "Chinidad", and Demerara, "Demra"."

Michael smiled and was pleased to hear Peter's information, "Thank you Peter. I also heard that the name Suriname was picked up by the Spanish explorers out of an Indigenous name "Surinen". The Dutch of course named the country Dutch Guiana, and then it was changed to Surinam upon Independence in 1975, and finally to Suriname in 1978. By the way, the English called it Willoughbyland after it was founded in 1650 by Lord Willoughby when he was Governor of Barbados."

Some of the passengers drifted off to sleep as the minibus continued the long drive until just before arriving in Paramaribo. The driver alerted those nearest to him and told them that they were reaching the end of the drive.

Michael asked Afzal to take over commentary about the city and he readily obliged.

"Hello everybody. We are now coming into the city and you can see some beautiful older houses amongst the more recent business premises. We will soon arrive at the Fort Zeelandia site where we can stroll around for a while. The weather has held up and looks nice. We should be able to enjoy the sightseeing. The area will be feeling more comfortable with a cool breeze as the fort is next to the Suriname River."

Vishnu curiously asked, "Afzal can you tell us a bit more about what life has been like for you and your family here in Paramaribo?"

Afzal smiled and began, "When I brought my family here from Guyana, I was simply looking for work to look after ourselves. Besides, I had become disillusioned with my country when for example, our Leonora sugar factory was closed down and dismantled. Many people were moving out of Guyana and going abroad as we all know. And I just followed some friends who chose to come to Suriname. The local people were friendly, but I struggled to learn the Dutch language."

Vishnu asked, "Was it easy to find a job?"

Afzal thought for a moment and then replied, "Yes. Luckily, I knew someone who was able to fix me up. We even stayed at his home for a couple of weeks until we found a place to rent. It was hard work, but I had to bear up with the strain until I was able to find something else."

Michael nodded and pointed out, "That sounds very much like what many of us experienced in America and Canada. Such hardship and pressure do bring out the best in us. But, at the end of the day, we can look back and say that we have come a long way from rock bottom to where we are now."

Ramesh looked at Vishnu and then Parvati, and commented, "Of course, Sati and I as well as our children, are immensely proud of our parents for what they had to go through. Now, with all that support and our education, we are better off. But sad to say, nowadays there is so much unemployment amongst our young people around the world, and not much seems to be happening to secure good futures for them. For example, the competition for good graduate jobs is extremely high, and just like Uncle Afzal said, many young people find themselves relying on someone known to them or their family. It is very important to build up such networks, and I hope that we can all continue to build on this one that we have not only for ourselves but also for our children and future generations."

Afzal continued, "That is very sad to hear. We as parents always wanted the best for our children, and we do not hesitate to call in favours or speak with people we think could help. I agree that this group of friends should stay in touch and encourage our families to continue to build on this. That will be a great positive to come out from our decision to join each other on this tour of our homeland."

The minibus finally arrived near to Fort Zeelandia, and Afzal stepped off the vehicle, and then waited for everyone else to disembark. The tour party stood together and looked around the site in awe.

Afzal took up a position in front of the tour group and declared, "As you can see, I have been asked to lead the visits here in Paramaribo starting with the old Dutch fort. The remains give you a good idea as to how big it was, how near to the river it has stood to fight off any attacks, and how strong it must have been in protecting those within."

Michael was beaming with pride for his friend, "So nicely put Afzal. If Ramesh, Sati and I had known how good you are at guiding, we could have hired you for the entire Guyana trip. Do continue."

A very pleased Afzal shrugged his shoulders and adjusted his standing position as he said, "I have been watching and learning from you Michael. I have even tried to copy you, but I still cannot match your style and skills. You are much more than our Histry Maan!"

Afzal then led the group through the arched entrance of the fort which housed the Suriname Museum. There was a display of a Pharmacy with medicine jars and bottles as well as treatment tables. Many more displays of artefacts were on show on the upper floor with an opening onto the top of the building overlooking the Suriname River. Canons were in place at a lower level behind thick stone walls. Exhibitions about more recent history of Suriname continued on the top floor including sports and other cultural activities. Further into the building was representation of the Indigenous peoples of Suriname.

When the tour party emerged from the fort, they took a brief walk along several well-preserved wooden and brick buildings, including a sturdy former military prison. The well-appointed courtyards included exhibits and open-air benches for rest and talk sessions. They sat together as Michael took over from Afzal to say a few words about the history of the fort.

He referred to his notebook and mentioned, "This fort was first built by the French before the English took over around 1667, reinforced the structures and named it Fort Willoughby. Although the fort appears to be strong, by 1772 it lost its importance to the Dutch as a military defence system. The red brick building that Afzal pointed out to us that was used as a prison, is gradually falling apart. Visitors are not allowed to go in there as apparently strange things happen."

Carlos chuckled and exclaimed, "Oh no! It's not them Dutch jumbies again?"

Michael coughed before saying, "Man, just the sight of that building gives me the shivers. If there is any paranormal activity there, I would say that it by those poor enslaved people who were brutally tortured and locked up."

Afzal added, "Michael, I forgot to mention that the Museum shop is now located where there was a prison cell."

Doreen appeared concerned as she remarked, "Gentlemen, I think that I have seen and heard enough about this place. It may have been a safe fortress for the Dutch Colonists, but it must have been horrible for those poor enslaved people!"

Unperturbed by Doreen's comment, Michael proceeded, "I suppose you are right Doreen. These places tend to show the better side of the colonists. How well organised they were. The comforts they brought to provide them with a better life. And much less about the brutality they dished out on those poor souls."

Vishnu suggested, "Thank you Michael and Afzal. I think that we have had a very long day and I would like to retire soon. Perhaps we could return here tomorrow morning to have a look at the Presidential Palace, the Parliament and the Garden of Palms. Or we could drive by to some of the other sites before we head off to our ferry to Guyana."

Michael acknowledged Vishnu's suggestion and proposed, "OK. Let's do that. But before we head off to Afzal's place, I think that if we do more sightseeing in Georgetown, we may wish to look at similar institutions such as the Guyana National Museum, the Walter Roth Museum of Anthropology and the Guyana African Heritage Museum. They are all very interesting and certainly different compared to this museum. It is so important that our history and heritage are understood and preserved for everyone to see, appreciate, and learn from."

Arthur nodded and noted, "I remember visiting the Guyana National Museum. It is very different from this. There are many exhibits of skeletons and stuffed animals, birds and reptiles showing how ancient as well as diverse Guyana is. There are also many artefacts of human living through the ages. We may not get the time to visit the museum as well as the one called the Guyana African Heritage which needs to be upgraded. However, it is very informative about the lives of our African Guyanese brothers and sisters."

Carlos pondered for a few moments and suggested, "I hope that both the government and the private sector in Guyana can come together and upgrade and modernise these important facilities. The same goes for our National Library in Georgetown."

Arthur nodded and added, "Carlos, I so agree with you. We need to see much more about the histories of all our peoples in Guyana as they all add up to who we are, where we came from, and how we can move ahead as a stronger and more united country. You only have to look at how much emphasis is placed on such institutions in all the developed countries of the world. As Guyana heads towards becoming a more developed country, the government needs to invest a lot more into these things. In addition to the rare artefacts, I believe that it is also very important for all historical paper records about our ancestors and the colonists should be preserved in a digitised form and this will provide our children and grandchildren as well as other researchers easily accessible information to help to better understand where we came from, and what shaped our history."

The entire tour party gave a resounding "Hear! Hear!" to what was said by Arthur as he took a respectful bow.

The tour party was delighted to visit and stay at Afzal's home, and thoroughly enjoyed the hospitality of his family over a sumptuous dinner and a restful night. Although Afzal's home did not have enough rooms to accommodate everyone, his neighbours on both sides of his house offered their spare rooms to some of the visitors. The tour party, with the exception of Afzal, agreed to give their hosts some money in appreciation of their gestures.

Early the next morning, the tour party met together to have breakfast at Afzal's. The breakfast was typical for Suriname and consisted of a few separate savoury snacks of shrimp, fish, chicken, beans, rice and a choice of freshly baked rolls. Most of the guests chose coffee to accompany their meals. Shortly afterwards, the tour party boarded the minibus and left for their tour around Paramaribo. The driver paused for a few minutes at the most important sites including the unique presence of two beautiful and remarkable buildings standing side by side.

Afzal asked the driver to stop in front of the two iconic properties, "Here we have the beautiful Neveh Shalom Synagogue built since the early eighteenth century, and next to it is the largest mosque in our part of the world. It is so amazing and inspiring to see Jewish and Muslim people worshipping almost side by side. This is the sort of example that the world needs to see right now especially when we are witnessing the brutal killings and destruction going on in the Middle East."

The tour party then moved on to view the St Peter and Paul Cathedral-Basilica which is known locally as "the Cathedral". It was a sight to behold as the largest wooden structure in the western hemisphere. They also paused to view the biggest Hindu Temple in Paramaribo and had about half an hour to visit the Central Market where on the ground floor level there was a vast collection of stalls with meat, fish, fruits and vegetables for sale. The upper floor contained outlets selling clothing, household and other related items.

Afzal insisted that the tourists should see another special part of the market, "You are about to use this separate entrance to what is called the 'Witches Market' also known as the 'Maroons Market'. If you ladies find this difficult to look at, please go out and wait for a few minutes."

Michael was more direct, "I can see some stuff inside that will make you get a bit scared and upset. I don't think that after hearing so much about Dutch ghosts, you would want to see all kinds of concoctions including bones and herbs,"

Vishnu also joined the ladies as they stood well away from the building.

He looked at Parvati and said with an awkward smile, "This reminds me of a Zulu market in South Africa where they also had dead monkeys for sale amongst all kinds of ingredients for rituals. Parv, you almost ran out of there!"

When the brief visit of the city ended, and the tour party was on their way to catch the ferry back to Berbice, Afzal stood up at the front of the minibus beside the driver, Michael and Vishnu.

He clasped his hands, bowed slightly and smiled as he said, "Thank you all for this brief visit to Paramaribo. I am sorry that we did not have more time to see and enjoy much more of the city, but at least you can say that Suriname is worth visiting when people return from abroad to Guyana. Of course, I would love to see that bridge across the Corentyne River built as soon as possible. I hear that the design will cover a span over the river from the Guyana end and onto Lange Island or Long Island and then link to another span to the Suriname side. Now, did you all enjoy your stay?"

There was an instantaneous response of "Yeah!" followed by loud cheering.

Afzal acknowledged the applause and responded, "Thank you! Thank you very much! That's the spirit!"

Michael immediately shouted, "Oh no! No more spirits please!"

28

Bartica: The gateway to riches

The return trip from Paramaribo allowed for a brief stop at the Skeldon Sugar Factory which was opened in 2009 as part of an ambitious plan to re-invigorate the sluggish sugar industry in Guyana, at a cost of around two hundred million US dollars. Unfortunately, the state-of-the-art sugar plant did not deliver to expectation and was closed in 2016.

Michael stood at the head of the tour party and announced, "This my friends, is what people call a "white elephant" project, but it is more of a "blue elephant". I hope that with a new strategy for agriculture, this plant can still play a role in some kind of revival. Let us not lament on this and head up to the Number 63 Beach area on our way back home."

The Number 63 Beach which stretches for about ten miles along the Atlantic coast from Corriverton, provided the tour party a welcome opportunity to stroll down to the water's edge and allow their bare feet to be caressed by the soft ripples of the tide which was beginning to turn inwards. The two cars were parked nearby on the firm brown sand of the near deserted beach.

Carlos, with his trousers rolled up to just under his knees, stood in the water, and with outstretched hands, proclaimed, "My God! Just look at this amazing treasure! This place could become an incredible tourist site in years to come. This could be Guyana's answer to the great Copacabana beach in Brazil."

Michael smiled and pointed out, "I doubt that. First of all, the name of Number 63 Beach doesn't conjure up the same kind of romantic vibe and seductive mystery. Secondly, that Atlantic Ocean water needs to have a Caribbean blue colour we can see around the holiday islands like Barbados. Thirdly, I don't think that Guyana is really ready for an invasion of hundreds of thousands of sun worshippers way out here."

Vishnu nodded and added, "You are so right my friend. I like this place as it is. It has its own charm. There is no need to spoil this jewel. This is a place for respite and calm, and not calamity!"

Michael agreed and noted, "We all loved to see the amazing Shell Beach and welcomed the only visitors, the giant turtles. On the contrary, I don't wish to see this beach messed up by thousands of human bodies splayed out all over the place!"

The tranquillity provided by the beach was ample respite from the long road trip, and the tour party relished every moment of the experience. Later on, they settled down in the two vehicles and made good use of the opportunity to sleep for most of the journey back to Anna Catherina.

They were all invited for supper at Nazir's and Neesha's home and due to their late evening arrival, they settled for a light meal of chicken chowmein and a glass of mixed fruit juice, followed by tea and coffee. Ramesh and Sati briefed the group about the following day's trip to the Essequibo town of Bartica.

Ramesh stood up before the group, and with Sati beside him, announced, "Our trip tomorrow is yet another road and ferry run from here through to Parika and on to the unique town of Bartica which is the well-known gateway to the hinterland. Now, I must warn you that we will be crossing the mighty Essequibo River once again, but this time in the faster boats instead of the much slower ferry. It will be a bit uncomfortable, but it is important for us to spend as much time in Bartica and to consider the options for doing more in that Region 7, perhaps via the Mazaruni River."

Sati added, "Bartica is also famous for its annual regatta which is held over the Easter holiday weekend. In that short time, the place is packed with boat racers and fans. The variety of boat races on the river with the spectators on Golden Beach is incredibly exciting. The whole weekend is dominated by people having a great time with a lot of music belting out, alcohol flowing freely, amazing food and other events such as kite flying and dominoes."

Vishnu's and Michael's eyes lit up when they heard the word dominoes, but before they could say anything, Doreen intervened.

"Vishnu and Michael, let me remind you that you promised there will be no dominoes playing on this trip! So, don't think of starting this in Bartica!"

The two friends looked at each other, smiled, and then bowed to Doreen like two schoolboys being reprimanded, and Michael muttered, "Yes Miss!"

Doreen frowned and wagged her right index finger at them.

Nazir and John set out with their passengers very early the next morning and headed westwards to the Parika stelling. They parked their cars and joined the tour party on a motorised taxi boat wearing mandatory life jackets before taking their seats which were made of wood and accommodating only five passengers in each row. The front of the boat was open and not covered by protective windows. However, the passengers sat below a wooden roof and there were windows at the sides.

Ramesh and Sati had taken the responsibility to negotiate a good price for the tour party and succeeded due to the unusually large number of the group.

The boat was eased out of its mooring by its loud motor, and within a few minutes it began to cut its way through the strong current of the river. It gathered speed and headed westward in the direction of Bartica. Everyone looked out to the side that they faced and observed the tree-lined riverbanks. Occasionally, some people standing ashore would wave their hands, and the passengers felt obliged to do likewise.

When the boat passed near to a lone island in the river, Michael stood up shakily and faced the tour party, "We are passing an island called "Ring Bang". Now, that name is strange and doesn't seem to denote anything special in particular. However, the locals know that the island belongs to Guyana's greatest and most famous music artiste by the name of Edmond Montague Grant, or simply, Eddy Grant. He is an icon, an honorary doctor, and Guyana's most accomplished artiste who is well known around the world."

Carlos could not resist shouting from his seat at the back of the boat, "Electric Avenue!"

Michael nodded and continued, "Eddy is from a very humble background, and was born in the village called Plaisance which was bought by freed slaves since 1838, only four years after the end of slavery in 1834. I have here some of the names of villages bought by people after Emancipation. They are, Buxton, Golden Grove, Belladrum, Den Amstel, Agricola, Friendship, Beterverwagting, Barraca, Sisters, Lovely Lass, Anns Grove, Perseverance and many more."

Nazir exclaimed, "Wow! This is the kind of thing all Guyanese should know and respect. We have passed by some of those places on our tours, and I think that all of our governments should do more to help develop them and support the residents in any way they wish. If this is done, it will be a great example of the aim for a One Guyana. It will demonstrate that contrary to the fake news we hear on social media, the government is not racist and is trying to be fair to all Guyanese regardless of their background."

Michael was very pleased to hear Nazir's suggestion and continued, "Eddy Grant joined his family in London in 1960, and by 1965 he was a founder-member of a band called The Equals which became very popular. He left the band and was soon very successful with many hit songs earning himself fans from around the world. He bought this island here in the Essequibo River and built that magnificent colonial style mansion you can see glimpses of. Note also how well fortified it is as a protection against the river tides."

Nazir added, "And to intruders!"

Arthur was in awe of the sheer grandiose presence of the mansion and enthused, "Eddy Grant is a great example to all Guyanese who come from the humblest beginnings, learnt great skills, used his talent well and then came back here to his roots. I know that he loves the village where he was born, and his latest album is titled 'Plaisance'. May God continue to bless him, and all of our icons past and present."

Michael bowed slightly, and before resuming his seat, uttered "Amen!"

The boat trip from Parika to Bartica lasted for about one and a half hours. At the mooring, the tour party stepped carefully out of the vessel and onto the weather-beaten timber walkway. Ramesh had disembarked first and ensured that he helped his fellow passengers to climb unto the landing safely.

They gathered together after they handed the lifejackets to the boatman and his helpers. Then they followed Ramesh and Sati through the stelling and onto the First Avenue of Bartica. There was a "Welcome to Bartica" sign and a monument to commemorate the granting of the status of a town by the then President David Granger in 2016.

Once again, Michael stepped forward and informed the group, "I hope that we will have a good tour of Bartica Town, and to acknowledge all the effort being made to make this the first 'Green' town in Guyana."

Doreen suggested, "I think that the authorities should aim to make all the towns and cities across Guyana environmentally friendly, or as you say, green. That will certainly enhance the image of Guyana alongside the other wonderful low carbon initiatives, for the world to see and recognise."

Michael reached out and hugged his wife, "That was beautifully put my darling!"

John smiled and added, "Bartica will achieve its green agenda and image, but it will also be known for its red earth which is what Bartica means in one of our languages. You will see this redness everywhere you go."

Ramesh and Sati organised the hire of two comfortable taxis to take the tour party for a drive around the neatly designed grid system of the town's avenues and streets. They stopped for a brief view of the Grand Municipal Market with its many stalls including an area with fish and meat counters. The market was well presented and tidy. The walk through a narrow alley led to another view of the waterfront at the back of the site.

The tour party continued on their drive around the town and then stopped to stroll along the Golden Beach with its red brick paving, comfortable benches, multi-coloured shacks and beach huts including several food outlets. Palm trees dotted along and between the white and light green benches overlooking the brown sand of the beach and the Essequibo River where the Annual Regatta is held.

Michael stood up and leaned against the green railing in front of the benches where the other members of the tour party were seated. He referred to his trusted notebook and held it with both hands as a light breeze picked up.

"This beautiful beach is where hundreds of pork-knockers and their families and friends come to spend the day. They would participate in many activities including a bahir breakfast competition. A bahir is a cook. They call the event "Pork-knockers day" which takes place around the end of August. This day is part of the National Miners Week of the celebration of Guyana's Mining Industry. Pork-knockers are mostly African Guyanese as well as some Indians and Amerindians looking for gold and diamonds deeper into the forest from here. Now, more Brazilians and Venezuelans are into this small-scale mining. They are supposed to pay a rent to the Amerindian communities who own the land.".

Ramesh stepped forward and stood beside Michael as he said, "It would be great to go into the bush to see how the hardworking pork knockers mine for gold and live their lives. But that would be very difficult for us to do today. So, let's enjoy this fine weather and beautiful town. Chill out on the beach and then we will go to a restaurant for a late lunch."

The tour party took the opportunity to have some cold refreshing drinks and then strolled barefooted along the beach as close to the water's edge as possible. The gentle air freshened their faces, and the ripples of the incoming tide tickled their tired feet. After spending about an hour, they rejoined the cars and headed back into the town for a restaurant which was highly recommended by the drivers.

They were warmly welcomed by the host of the Mark and Elda Restaurante Brasiliero and Sports Bar on Second Avenue. They were invited to sit together and then go up to a hot and cold buffet serving a variety of grilled meats, Brazilian farine, salads and other dishes and drinks for a standard price.

Carlos and Maria were delighted with the mix of Brazilian and Guyanese cuisine, and Carlos remarked, "Our Guyana is rapidly becoming a nation of more than six races with the growing presence of our Brazilian and Venezuelan neighbours. I guess that if Maria and I and more of our relatives return to settle here in Essequibo, we may have to learn our Portuguese language."

Maria nodded and added, "And Spanish as well!"

John pointed out, "The presence of Brazilians from the South through Rupununi and up here into the mining areas has been one of concern for my Amerindian people who are not happy about the illegal gold mining that many of them do. I am also very concerned that we don't seem to have much security and policing in these areas."

Doreen was reflective and noted, "I am very happy with the massive amount of development going on across Guyana. My worry is that as our country goes towards becoming a developed economy, we will be attracting many more people from around the CARICOM area. I hope that our local people will be able to accommodate these migrants and tolerate them."

Michael adjusted his spectacles on his forehead and said, "Aha! Now, that is what migrants have to do here in our new, rich and beautiful Guyana. Adapt to our ways. Adapt to our customs. Adapt to our laws! And learn English!"

29

Of heroes and heroines

The tour party chose to have another day of rest after their splendid but tiring trip to Bartica. Nazir and Neesha as well as John and Muriel decided to allow their guests more time to lie in so that they could take advantage of some extra hours of sleep. Later that morning, after both households finally enjoyed their breakfasts, the guests assembled at Nazir's and Neesha's sitting room for a casual get together and to reflect on their trip to Guyana as it was nearing its end.

Ramesh and Sati stood before the group, and they noticed that Michael was not his usual exuberant and cheerful self as he sat quietly beside Doreen.

Ramesh stepped forward and asked, "Uncle Michael, are you OK?"

Michael looked up with some trepidation in his weary eyes and replied, "I am not sure son. Last night I was very restless. But after some time, I finally fell asleep. But man, I had the most terrible nightmare! When I woke up, my pyjama was covered in sweat. Nazir and Neesha, are you sure that you do not have any presence here?"

Nazir and Neesha were surprised and confused about the question.

Nazir frowned as he asked, "Do you mean jumbies?"

Michael was like a man possessed with his eyes kept wide open as he said, "Man, I felt like a whole group of 'ole hige', jumbies, baccoo and dead Dutch people came here to warn me to get out of Guyana!"

Vishnu laughed as he maintained, "No Michael. I don't believe in any of those demons, and all those things like obeah, comfa and moongazers! You must be over-tired. Has anyone else here encountered any of these things?"

John raised his right hand and said, "I don't believe in all of those folklore demons. But I do believe in our unseen and unheard Great Spirit who guides our people, and our Piaiman or Shaman has great knowledge about our environment and the powers of our plants and so on. They help us to ward off all evil."

Afzal smiled and moved over to hold Michael's sweaty hands, "Look, if you are possessed with any evil spirit, I know an Imam who could come and read some verses from our *Holy Quran* to you, and you will be back to normal. If the reading doesn't work, he will beat the devil we call Shaitaan, out of you!"

Michael winced at the thought of having any evil spirit beaten out of him. Everyone else giggled at their friend's dilemma.

Vishnu, trying his best to maintain a straight face, offered another suggestion, "Michael, we could arrange for a Pandit to come over and perform a jaaray ceremony and massage on you."

Doreen was not impressed by the offers to resolve Michael's problems and insisted, "Look, he is alright. All he had was a bad nightmare. It's all in his mind. Let us talk about some of the nicer things we have seen and have experienced in our beautiful country."

Maria was relieved to hear of Doreen's suggestion and added, "Yes Doreen. Carlos and I were discussing our trip so far, and we agreed that Guyana is full of surprises and amazing people and places. We have enjoyed this entire trip so much."

Muriel also agreed with her friends and pointed out, "On this trip, we have heard about some of the amazing Guyanese of the past and present time, and I do hope that they continue to inspire our younger generation to aim to do even better. I would like to mention here, our Minister of Amerindian Affairs, Mrs Pauline Sukhai who continues to serve our people very well across the country."

Parvati nodded in agreement and said, "Our women have played and continue to play their part in building our society with great values. I have seen a lot of our young women in particular, displaying good manners and a lot of respect for all of us of the older generation. Notice how quickly they refer to us as "Uncle" or "Auntie". Of course, there will always be the odd bad egg, but I hope that as our society continues to mature and get richer, they will also change for the better."

Michael listened with great interest and noted, "I think that we have also benefitted from having great families whose members have contributed as well. I am thinking of the Luckhoo family of outstanding lawyers and public servants. The Kirpalani family in the business world as well as the many other incredible entrepreneurs such as Toolsie

Persaud, the Gafoors including the writer and philanthropist Ameena Gafoor, the Gajrajs, the Mcdooms, the Sankars, the Yasins and so on. We also have what I call the "family" of lawyers who were, and are, in Croal Street in Georgetown."

Arthur was not entirely in agreement with Michael's suggestions of influential Guyanese, and pointed out, "Michael, don't get me wrong. I like the names you mentioned, but I notice that there are no Chinese on your list. I know that we talked about Arthur Chung, our country's first President. I am thinking of the dozens of Chinese businesspeople who have been into jewellery, restaurants, groceries and of course, many of our rum shops across the country. We Chinese have helped to build the economy of this country, but there is a sense of a lack of appreciation for this. Perhaps it's because we tend to be very quiet and keep a low profile."

Michael responded with, "Arthur, your people are too quiet and reserved. I can mention three great Guyanese Chinese, Robert Wong who became the first Chinese to be elected to the Legislature in 1926 and 1934. Then O Tye Kim who was a very successful church missionary in the 1860s. And there is Stanley Ming whom we talked about before. Now, the new Chinese investors and construction developers from mainland China are too keen to make big bucks and then return home. They show us no loyalty to this country, and I am very wary about them."

Afzal was eager to make a comment and mentioned, "Ladies and gentlemen, I have heard that the Chinese from China tend not to employ local people on their projects especially in higher positions and speak with each other in their own language. I say that we do not need such selfish people in our country. Don't get me wrong, the people they bring here do work all hours until they get the job done on time and in budget. But I dread to think what can happen when they all go away, and breakdowns happen. Our local people will not know how to solve such problems."

Nazir interjected, "Afzal, I can agree with you only to some extent. Crucially, Guyana needs to build a lot of infrastructure very quickly and we simply do not have the skills, or the numbers required to do the jobs. Right now, one of the most impressive of Guyana's new developments is the fantastic bridge being built across the Demerara River by Chinese contractors. They do hire local Guyanese workers.

The Indian company contractors also bring in their own people and they work very hard. They even stay on site until they finish their jobs. They are required to hire at least forty per cent of their workforce from local labour. We as Guyanese, can't sit on our backsides and point our fingers at foreigners who come here to work hard, earn fat salaries and then go away. We cannot afford to allow more foreigners to come here and boss us around. We need to take the training opportunities and work our way up the ladder. This is how the country can be fully developed."

Vishnu nodded and pointed out, "When people like me went to America, England, or Canada to look for work, that is how some of the host community in those countries looked upon us as only going there to take away their jobs, their housing and their social benefits. The difference is that we put up with that abuse, and just got on with our work and lives. We saved our money, bought our property, educated our children, and even sent money and goods back home to our relatives in Guyana."

Michael, feeling more relieved from his ordeal with demons, quietly said, "One of my worries about all of this, is that the development projects are happening too quickly, and I fear that mistakes in construction can occur. So, I do hope that our commissioners are keeping a close eye on the quality of the work, materials, equipment and engineering. I must say that I like how the President turns up to personally look at progress. He is a young man showing how much he really cares for this country and our people. He is a workaholic leading by example!"

Peter, who had been waiting patiently to add to the conversation, remarked, "Speaking about our people, I want to stress that our Guyanese men and women are amongst the most talented in many fields. Despite the many decades of struggle as a country, we still managed to produce famous writers such as E R Braithwaite, Edgar Mittelholzer, David Dabydeen, Martin Carter, Basdeo Mangru, Ryhaan Shah, Dmitri Allicock, Gaiutra Bahadur, Sharon Maas, Michelle Yaa Asantewaa, Maria del Pilar Kaladeen, Juanita and Rod Westmass, and Clem Seecharan, just to mention a few. I would also like to mention a poet and writer from Leonora by the name of Jai A Lall. I can add some more great cricketers such as Sir Clive Lloyd, Colin Croft, Carl Hooper, Lance Gibbs, Leonard Baichan, Faoud Bacchus, Veerasammy Permaul, Leon Johnson, Devendra Bishoo and some new stars such as Shimron Hetmeyer, Shamar Joseph, Gudakesh Motie and others. Michael should be able to add more great Guyanese people from all walks of life. I can see him opening his incredible notebook!"

A more energised Michael duly obliged, "Thank you Peter. My lists of famous Guyanese are much too long to mention here. But I can throw in some for you to appreciate on top of those we have talked about as we toured the country over all ten Regions! Some of the people I will highlight are from abroad and who carried or continue to carry our Guyana flag with great pride. I will include names which you may have personal issues with, but they are still worthy of mention. For example, let me start with Sir Shridath Ramphal, the former Secretary General of the Commonwealth. Dame Valerie Amos who is a member of the British House of Lords. Sir Trevor Phillips a broadcaster and journalist. Also, Odeen Ishmael, a great Diplomat, writer and historian. David Lammy, the new Foreign Secretary of the UK Government. There have been many more highly accomplished Guyanese in the US, Canada and elsewhere."

Michael paused in anticipation of comments from the audience.

Nazir looked around the room, and when no one responded, he spoke, "Michael, I like how you are trying to bring politics into the picture. I think that we are old enough now to understand that there will always be Guyanese who will have critical views in the world of politics and the media. Our country and people are on a path to greater tolerance and understanding now, and no one political party or supporter has a kind of divine right to have and exercise power over others especially in a democracy. To me, I have to salute all of those Guyanese who have achieved great things regardless of their politics, race, or religion. I think and hope that this is what the idea of a One Guyana is all about."

Michael smiled and continued, "By the way, I am not playing politics. Anyway, let me move on to some entertainment including music stars. Courtney Pine has been a great clarinet player. Sammy Baksh, Terry Gajraj, Cy Grant, Ken 'Snakehips' Johnson, Shabana the keyboard player, Keith Waithe the flautist, Sol Raye the Guyanese Nat King Cole, Ramjohn 'Porkpie' Holder, and the group called the Ramblers have all been excellent artistes. Back in the 1960s, we had the Indian Hotshots Orchestra with Bali Sankar, Neville Kallicharan, Tafazool Baksh, Noel Campbell and Seetal Gurprasad as some of the members.

There are some other artistes you may or may not have heard of such as Indian singers including Navin Balakan, Andrew Sookhoo and Dhanraj Persaud from London. Also, Ben Parag and Jeewan Chowtie from New York, and Robie Rampersaud from Toronto. Regarding Indian Classical Dancing I can mention Fidel Persaud of Guyana and his wife Isha from Trinidad, and their daughter Chandani, as well as Poonam Gunaseelan who are all performers and teachers based in London."

Arthur's face was etched with great surprise as he suggested, "Michael, I get the feeling that you have a lot more names in your notebook. Can we not claim the amazing Rihanna who is half Barbadian and half Guyanese? Or Leona Lewis who is half Guyanese and mixed with Welsh, Irish and Italian?"

Michael seemed to be taken aback by Arthur's question and said, "Thank you Arthur. I do not have those two amazing singers on my lists. But yes, Rihanna can be regarded as one of ours. Guyanese and Barbadians have always enjoyed good relations. Right now, we can see this with President Ali and Prime Minister Mia Mottley. I agree that we should claim Leona Lewis as her father is Guyanese."

Vishnu prompted, "I think that our country's music is as varied as our peoples. Our Amerindian brothers and sisters have their own tradition of music, song and dance. Enslaved Africans brought a rich heritage of traditional songs, music and dance. Indians brought a wide range of music, songs and even created the dhantaal locally as a percussion instrument made from steel rods. I can add some more great Indian singers such as Tillack, Mohan Nandu, Gobin Raam, Devendra Pooran, Peter Dass, Bhaskar Sharma, Kumar Kishundial, Yasmin "Queen Yasmin" Khan and Seeta Panday."

Carlos was keen to add, "Don't forget that Portuguese people from Madeira had instruments called the machete, rajao and brinquinho, and the ukelele came from the cavaquinho. I have a note here about this. This kind of music certainly found its way to Brazil."

Muriel smiled and noted, "You guys are incredible. Thank you for reminding us about so many of our great Guyanese men and women from so many fields. It is truly amazing to know that for such a small country we continue to produce such awesome talent. These, and many more are or have been our true nation builders. We have seen a lot of Guyana's natural beauty. How about some of our amazing Beauty Queens?"

Michael's eyes lit up as he turned to another page of his notebook and read out, "I have many names here, including the first ever Miss Guyana whose name was Umblita Van Sluytman. Then, Shakira Baksh, now Caine, Pamela Lord, Adriene Harris, Jennifer Wong, Nalini Moonasar and many others to the more recent beauties such as Nuriyyih Gerrard, Vena Mookram, Ambika Ramraj, Joylyn Conway and Andrea King. Amazing and very intelligent talents!"

Afzal stood up, looked around the room, flexed his arms, and then executed an impressive bodybuilder pose demonstrating his substantial biceps below the short sleeves of his tight-fitting T-shirt. Michael stared at him with astonishment as well as great admiration.

"Afzal, how have you managed to keep such incredible shape at your age?"

Afzal smiled and said, "Once I started to lift weights and do bodybuilding when I was so young, the bug and interest never left me, and I do some regular exercises to keep myself fit and in good shape."

Afzal then slowly relaxed his arms, and with a broad smile, announced, "Well, ladies and gentlemen, we have heard of those amazing Guyanese Beauty Queens. How about our body beautiful men and women of the sport of bodybuilding?"

Michael sat back in his seat and suggested, "Do tell us about the Guyanese stars of the sport that you are so fond of. But please save us from the sight of your own rippling but wrinkly muscles!"

Afzal chuckled at Michael's jibe and replied, "I have to say that my sport of bodybuilding is now on a healthy rising curve with great interest being shown in the men's physique and the women's Ms Bikini Class. It is now a cool thing to do this sport inspired by champions such as Kerwin Clarke, Emmerson Campbell, Hugh Ross, Bruce Whatley, Darious Ramsammy and others. There are some up and coming stars such as Nicholas Albert, Chandini Khan, Ashanti Conway, Rosanna Fung, Tariq Dakhil, Hannah Rampersaud and many others. Back in the 1960s we had a lot of local interest in bodybuilding in our villages, especially in Anna Catherina where Malcolm and Denis Yhap inspired others to do the training in their gym."

Vishnu nodded, and looking up and down at Michael's lean figure, commented, "Sadly, some of us did not manage to build any muscles on our meagre frames."

Doreen frowned and hit back with, "Well, I am very pleased with my Michael and his skinny frame. When you gentlemen succeed in flattening your big and ugly bellies, then you can talk!"

John agreed with Doreen and pointed out, "I do hope that the government and others sponsor bodybuilding and exercise as the nation is beginning to show worrying signs of obesity especially amongst the younger generation who are being seduced by so many fast-food outlets, and a growing lifestyle around many hours playing computer games. Obesity is one development in Guyana that needs to be quickly curtailed."

Muriel looked around the room and then suggested, "I suppose that as Guyana gets richer and the wealth spreads to everyone and all parts of the country, we will see many more cases of real resource health curse. That is more poor health habits, mental illness, drug and alcohol misuse, petty and serious crime, and all leading to a broken society. Sorry for sounding like a messenger of doom. But we can see all of this happening in Venezuela, and sadly for me, within our Amerindian communities. We need to tackle these problems now before we can say that Guyana is becoming a developed country."

Everyone applauded Muriel, and she stood up, smiled and bowed gracefully. John also stood up and hugged his wife.

Ramesh waited for John and Muriel to resume their seats and then commented, "We have talked about and shared the names of many more great achievers both here in Guyana and abroad. I would like to ask each of you to choose one or two of the Guyanese of the past and present whom you regard as being called an icon or hero or heroine who can inspire the change to make things better for Guyana. Let me start by saying that my own personal hero and heroine are my parents. They mean everything to me and my family."

Sati took her turn and added, "I accept Ramesh's choices, and I guess that everyone here can say the same about your parents and grandparents. I think that I will have to look towards my great grandparents for their bravery to take on the venture to come to this country to work and make a living away from the hardships they were facing in India. Likewise, I reckon that applies to everyone here except Uncle John and Auntie Muriel whose ancestors are probably unknown, but they were even braver than mine."

John took up the baton and acknowledged Sati's comment, "Thank you Ramesh and Sati. I agree with your choices. My icons are all the natural things of beauty we have seen around Guyana. These have been here long before humankind, and will I hope, still be here long after we are gone. Let us make Guyana to be better known for its natural beauty for the world to admire and take lessons from. Preserving and protecting our incredible God-given environment should always be our number one priority. Without our pristine rainforests and associated environment, we do not have a country."

Muriel was full of admiration for John and smiled as she added, "John, you have said it all. Your parents and my parents were great teachers. Not in the formal sense alone, but in passing on the stories of our people and the battles they had in order to protect themselves and their environment. We may be Christians now, but deep in our hearts we believe in our Great Spirit who continues to guide and protect us all. I also believe that this territory we call Guyana, and all its surrounding neighbours are just loaned to us for the benefit of our children, grandchildren and all others to come."

Carlos, like all others in the group, was in awe of what was said so far, and offered, "Oh my God. You guys have really opened my mind about this question. I was searching for someone or something to mention. But from now onwards, whatever we say or whoever we choose will not compare to what we have heard. As a Portuguese Guyanese, I was looking for someone in Madeira apart of course, from my ancestors. I thought of saying Cristobal Colon or Columbus who, by making a big mistake, headed near to our coast so many hundreds of years ago. But he and others who followed him from Europe, cannot be called my heroes, especially due to the way that they almost destroyed Indigenous peoples, indulged in the vile slave trade, stole everything they found and still enticed my ancestors to come here. Sorry guys, this is now a very difficult one for me. My conclusion is that I must embrace what John and Muriel have said to all of us. That is the more acceptable truth about Guyana."

Maria nodded in agreement with Carlos and added, "I was also thinking of naming a fellow Portuguese here in this country, and like Carlos, such a person cannot beat what was suggested by John and Muriel. So, I endorse what Carlos has just said."

Arthur took his turn to speak, "Like Carlos, I was thinking about a prominent Chinese such as Arthur Chung, but I am of the view that we, through our ancestors, have all brought something to help build this Guyana we are all talking about. But the question is now more about what is truly Guyana, and what it offers to the world. I think that people such as Dr Bharrat Jagdeo, who is a world champion of the environment, should be considered as an iconic guiding light for what John and Muriel have proposed."

When Arthur finished speaking, he pointed to Vishnu and Parvati signalling that it was their turn to speak about their icon or icons. Vishnu allowed Parvati to lead off with her thoughts.

"I agree with my son Ramesh and his wonderful wife Sati. But I am a very simple person who is mostly interested in looking after my family wherever we happen to be. I like the simple things in life, and I still cook the same meals in New York as I used to do in Guyana. You can say that you can take me out of my village, but you can't take my village out of me. So, my hope for Guyana and Guyanese is to keep to the simple life no matter how rich we become. Guyana does not need to be like other rich countries. We have our own culture, our own values and our own ways. We can't pretend to be like the Americans, British, or Canadians just because we now live in those countries and are picking up their habits. We can and must remain Guyanese. If I have to choose a heroine apart from my mother and grandmother, I will go for the late Kowsila or Alice from Leonora who was killed in 1964 whilst standing up for the rights of workers. She and her colleagues were incredible women!"

Vishnu nodded in agreement with Parvati and added, "My dear wife has been the real backbone of our family and so are most Guyanese women, past and present. Our women should be given more credit for their role in shaping us, our children and our society. I am a Hindu, and as far as religion is concerned, I think that the late Pandit Reepu Daman Persaud was a very important and influential Guyanese religious leader. But I am also mindful that we have to recognise the roles played by the great leaders of the other faiths that we have here in Guyana."

Nazir stood up, clasped his hands, and bowed slightly whilst facing his friends, and proposed, "You see, this thing we call friendship is a silent nation-builder. Most of you have come here from many miles away and we can reflect on how we were when we were growing up in these villages. We competed hard with each other in all the games we played, and at the end of the contests, we reverted to our friendships.

In fact, our grandparents and those before them used to talk about the Indian jahajis or fellow travellers of all backgrounds who clung to each other and helped each other through thick and thin. We are continuing to demonstrate that jahaji spirit, and I am very proud of this. If, as Vishnu has said, I have to pick someone as a hero, I think I can mention Abdool Majeed, a very successful businessman who along with others, helped the Muslim community to become more organised despite a lot of in-fighting amongst the various factions and jamaats. He and others established a secular high school called the Muslim Education Trust College or METC in Brickdam, Georgetown in 1960. That school soon became one of the best Secondary Schools in the country under the leadership of its Principal, Satya Jeewan Sawh, Vice Principal Haji Mohamed Yusuf, and incredible senior teachers such as Hasrat Haniff and a great science teacher, Halvidar Singh."

Neesha, normally very shy and soft-spoken, stood beside Nazir, and almost whispered, "My husband has said it all. I do think that our education institutions have played their part, and continue to do so, in producing many outstanding scholars who have gone on to even build which ever country they ended up in. I think of Queens College, Bishops High School, Central High School, the Indian Education Trust College, St Stanislaus College, Berbice High School and so many more."

Afzal agreed with Nazir and Neesha and expressed his view, "I think that you have all provided a lot of brilliant suggestions as to what and who makes Guyana. One of the things I would like to mention, is the role of our people who left this country for whatever reasons, and like us, are now looking back here to see what they can or should do to help our nation as it moves forward and upward. I think that all of us from abroad who have contributed to our relatives here over many decades, should be recognised as real heroes and heroines. We have to be mindful of a tension whereby all those who stayed and struggled through the really hard times may view us as cowards now looking to come here to take over. I personally believe that people from the diaspora should not come here and give the impression that we know best. This is a sensitive issue in my mind, and we need to be very careful as to how this is handled at least on a person-to-person basis. I think that the idea of a One Guyana for all Guyanese, is a good starting point. But we also have to recognise that even within the diaspora, there are issues of division which probably stem from our experiences of Guyana we have taken abroad. For example, I do not buy into the "Little Guyana" idea in New York when it refers mostly to Indian Guyanese living in Queens."

Arthur raised his right hand and spoke, "My brother Afzal, I agree with most of what you just said, especially about the relationship that we from the diaspora must seek to build with our brothers and sisters who are here. About the idea of a 'Little Guyana' in Queens, New York, I just wish to point out that there are places in some cities around the world where large settlements of Chinese migrants are known as "China Town" where they have created a mini replica of Chinese living. I agree that the "Little Guyana" is dominated by mostly Indian Guyanese, but they do show a lot about Guyanese and our lives there. However, it does not represent the One Guyana idea as far as I am concerned. I doubt whether we have any Guyanese Chinese people there."

Carlos noted, "Maybe no Portuguese Guyanese either!"

Ramesh closed the conversation by concluding, "Thank you all for so many rich ideas about our icons, heroes and heroines of Guyana. It is right to conclude that there is no one such person, but a myriad of all that reflect the beauty of Guyana and its peoples. Tomorrow Sati and I have planned for our final tour. Have a very restful day."

30

Santa Mission, Arrowpoint, Linden and the Blue Lakes

Very early in the morning of the final day of the tour party's trip to Guyana, there was a steady drizzle from a light cloudy sky along with a cool comforting breeze wafting in from the incoming tide of the Atlantic Ocean. The group had all agreed to have their breakfast over at John's and Muriel's home.

John stood up before his guests to offer a briefing about the intended trip, and to advise them that Nazir and Neesha had asked to be excused from the visit to Linden. They had expressed their unease about the place where the brutal attacks on the Indian population had occurred in May 1964. John and Muriel agreed to lead on the trip which included a short tour of the Santa Aratak or Santa Mission's Amerindian village up the Demerara River to be accessed via the Kamuni Creek. Afzal volunteered to drive Nazir's car for the road trip.

John looked at his watch on his left wrist, and began, "Today we will try to do two tours to the Santa Mission and to Linden. Both places would normally take more than one day to cover properly. You have had some experience of our Amerindian culture and way of life, but the Santa Mission offers us a glimpse of the vast potential we have across Guyana's hinterland for viable tourism which will benefit our communities. Besides, the Santa Mission is close enough to Georgetown and the Cheddi Jagan International Airport to allow for a short stay or an even longer one to enjoy most of the activities on offer. Linden Town is, like Bartica Town on the Essequibo, an important gateway into the interior. We hope to do both locations within the day and should get back here by early evening for our dinner over at Nazir's and Neesha's place. If there are no questions, let's hit the road!"

The two cars made impressive progress from Anna Catherina through to the point up the East Bank Road of the Demerara River near to Timehri where they were parked. The tour party then boarded a motorboat which sped across the river and through the Kamuni Creek to the landing dock of the village. The Kamuni Creek provided a close-up view of the dark, almost black, waters from the motorboat. The vessel's wooden seats were enough to accommodate all the passengers who were required to wear the luminous orange life jackets provided by the boatman. The creek was narrow enough for the group to observe a variety of trees and shrubs, including mangroves which were rooted at the water's edge and with their overhanging branches close enough to be touched. Occasionally, there were cleared openings with small landing points jutting out over the water and indicating small farm holdings or private residences.

The landing at the mission was simple and uncomplicated, and Ramesh stepped out as quickly as possible in order to lend a hand to his older fellow travellers and to ensure that they could safely climb onto the wooden open-ended terminal. A welcome sign to the Santa Aratak Amerindian Reservation was supported by two wooden posts which were firmly planted within the edge of the waterway.

John and Muriel gathered the tour party together and took the lead on a walk around the village which was spread out with the housing and other facilities including a school, health clinic and a local bakery accessible by cleared white sandy pathways. The village's three hundred residents took great pride in maintaining a tidy environment. The visitors soon arrived at the base of a magnificent cotton silk tree called the Kamaka which means the mother of all trees. The roots were believed to be spread around the village. Another attraction was a beautifully carved wooden monument dedicated to the village's past Toshaos. The tour party was warmly welcomed by some of the residents with the children keen to show the travellers around. John and Muriel politely declined the youngsters' persistent but polite offers.

The next stop for the group was the resort named Arrowpoint which was a further twenty miles along the Kamuni Creek offering more opportunities for relaxation, participation in the Amerindian culture, kayaking, canoeing, swimming, fishing, walking through the forest and mountain biking. The resort also provided excellent birdwatching of many species of Guyana's array of beautiful birds. The tour party gladly opted for the additional boat trip to Arrowpoint which was named from the tree which provide the stems used by the Amerindians for shaping by hand, their arrows used for fishing and hunting.

John and Muriel continued to act as the group's guides and were able to advise those who wished to purchase souvenirs crafted by the local community. Most of them decided to forego the activities on the creek, and after a short and enjoyable walk on one of the trails, they returned in time for a specially prepared lunch in the main resort building located a short distance away from the creek.

Ramesh and Sati took the opportunity to do some kayaking on the almost becalmed waters of the creek but had to curtail the activity when a light drizzle interrupted their playful fun.

They joined the others at the lunch, and were still excited as Ramesh enthused, "This is such a lovely place to come to for at least three nights and four days to take full advantage of so much on offer. Thank you, Uncle John and Aunty Muriel, for your great suggestion. This is a very nice way to round off our great Guyana quest."

The tour party took advantage of the remainder of the scheduled time in Santa Mission and Arrowpoint, to relax on the verandah overlooking the serenity of the creek and its surrounding environment. The stillness was a welcome respite from the many miles of travelling by the noisy powered boat, and everyone observed the silence to close their eyes and just listen to nature's conversation of birdsong, a cool breeze and the faint rustling of leaves in the trees.

After about half an hour of their repose, Carlos took a drink of his Banks beer and broke the silence by almost whispering, "I do agree with Ramesh. These places have so much potential to develop into more eco-friendly experiences to help visitors to wind down from their ongoing pressures of work in the city and elsewhere. Perhaps these are the places where the intended workforce of the new Silica City will come to indulge in nature's own form of yoga and natural care."

Afzal smiled, took a deep breath of the fresh air passing through, and added, "Of course, those new visitors will be the ones who would easily afford the prices for the stays and activities on offer."

Vishnu yawned, stretched his arms out, and commented, "That is a real prospect Afzal. I do hope that as the new city emerges, these resorts will become good partners in the provision of much needed wellbeing services."

Doreen looked around at the men in the group and asked, "Since each of you have such vision and good ideas, will you be looking to come together and invest your money in something like this here in Guyana?"

Arthur appeared to be enthused by the suggestion and proposed, "Well, to be honest, I have given such an idea some thought over the last few days of being with you on this trip. I am sure that collectively, we have a lot of skills and experience to form something like an investment group where we don't have to come here to do anything, but we can set up the enterprise, appoint the right people for the jobs and oversee the projects from abroad."

Michael acknowledged Arthur's suggestion and pointed out, "I know that there are such investors already here in Guyana with their business partners mostly from America and Canada. I don't mind putting my pennies to an investment project, but we must think of a proper niche enterprise away from malls, hotels, restaurants, resorts, housing and so on. At the moment, I cannot think as to what that can be."

Vishnu nodded and responded, "I do have a problem with the establishment of the things you mentioned Michael. Guyana has a lot less than a million people, and even if this population is doubled in a few years' time, there may not be enough people to make full use of those facilities. Perhaps a viable business could be one where we invest in the business ideas of young people living in Guyana and those from abroad wishing to return to establish their enterprises. Young people, especially the unemployed could benefit greatly from such financial backing along with our mentoring support."

Carlos gave Vishnu a thumbs up and suggested, "Now, that sounds more appropriate for us older people with some money not working enough for us in the banks. Such an investment fund idea will have some risks, but we can set it up and have the young people propose their bids and ideas to us either online or in person like we see on some TV programmes. Mind you, I am not too keen on the more aggressive names such as 'Dragon's Den' in the UK or 'Shark Tank' in India!"

Ramesh looked at Sati, and they both smiled. He then proposed, "I think that such an idea of a "Dominoes Investment Fund" is worth developing as soon as this trip is over. I am sure that Sati and I can take this on board and put the structure together. This could be a fantastic outcome from our amazing tour to Guyana!"

Shortly after, the tour party resumed their trip and headed towards the mining town of Linden. Along the way, they turned off the main road to view one of the most beautiful and serene Blue Lakes which was formed after the end of mining for bauxite in that area. They stopped at a spot where the landscape was carved out by decades of massive mining and quarrying activity. At the top, overlooking the deeply blasted and dug manmade terrain and the lake, there was a popular viewing spot where YouTube, TikTok and Instagram enthusiasts filmed their content.

Ramesh asked, "Uncle Michael. do you know how this water appears to be so blue?"

Michael did not refer to his notebook, but replied, "I am not sure. I do not have a note on this question. But I have heard that it is to do with the reflection of the clear blue sky above us. Also, there is a view that the white sand at the bottom of the lake causes the apparent colouring. Whatever is the reason, I think that it is beautiful up here. It is a most wonderful combination of a natural landscape and human activity."

Sati was perturbed and commented, "Uncle Michael, that may be so, but I do not like the look of those terrible scars made by many years of brutal destruction of the environment by blasting, digging and removing so much earth and rocks. I feel that all the mining activities here and elsewhere may be good for the economy, but the damage is too brutal and permanent. In my mind's eye, I do not see beauty here."

Peter smiled and pointed to a rock which was inscribed with a message, "I love the "Will You Marry Me" sign which seems to be popular with the visitors. Sati, I can see where you are coming from. If this place inspires a romantic outcome for people, I hope that it also reminds them that our natural environment holds more prospect for a better and lasting relationship with nature."

The tour party moved on through to Linden Town passing by streets named after the timbers of Guyana including, silverballi, greenheart, mora and crabwood. The Linden area is credited with supplying the woods used in constructing many of the colonial houses and administrative buildings in Georgetown. The group stopped briefly at the Linden Museum of Industrial and Socio-Cultural Heritage but did not visit due to the lack of sufficient time. Instead, they settled for a drive around Linden including a visit across the river to the other side of the town known as Wismar.

As the day began to close in with the sun setting in the sky appearing to be ablaze in different shades of red and yellow, the tour party began their drive back to Anna Catherina. Most of the passengers in the two vehicles took the opportunity to rest their tired eyes, or to sleep deeply. Good progress was made throughout the road journey, across the Demerara Harbour Bridge and through the West Bank and West Coast to the residence of Nazir and Neesha.

The travellers were all greeted by their hosts with warm smiles and fond hugs, and they proceeded to use the bathroom facilities to freshen up in preparation for their eagerly awaited dinner. Michael's prompt appearance caused quite a stir as he opted for a formal lounge suit and an attractive Guyana tie with the colours of the golden arrow flag. His fellow tourists looked at him in admiration and applauded him. Then they all tucked into a fully vegetarian array of curries, daal, roti and rice followed by some fresh fruits and ice-cold water.

Michael was the first to complement the hosts and stood up after the meal like a formal after-dinner speaker, "Ladies and Gentlemen, I am sure that you have all enjoyed this great seven curries meal which is so famous at wedding banquets here in the villages across our wonderful country."

Everyone said, "Hear! Hear!"

He continued, "We are now nearly at the end of our amazing trip, and on behalf of all the visitors, I wish to thank Nazir, Neesha, John and Muriel for their incredible hospitality, kindness, patience and great care of all of us over the three and a half weeks. It's normally bad enough to cater for much younger guests, but it must have been a much greater challenge for them to put up with so many older people, excepting of course, Ramesh and Sati."

The hosts stood up together and took a bow in gratitude for the kindness and appreciation shown by their guests. Ramesh and Sati stepped forward and handed gift-wrapped boxes to their hosts, and two bunches of flowers to Neesha and Muriel. The gifts were all graciously accepted.

Vishnu waited patiently and then took his turn to say, "My dear friends, it has been an immense privilege to be with you all. My wife and I as well as Ramesh and Sati will cherish these memories forever.

I only wish that most of us were much younger to be able to be more adventurous and to spend more time in the places we visited and those we only glimpsed as we passed by. Guyana is truly incredible, and I will go back to New York and encourage many more Guyanese and non-Guyanese to come here to see and experience this amazing country. We have wealth here in so many forms. The forests, the animals, the birds, the plants, the rivers, the creeks, the falls, the mountains...."

Michael put his right hand up and said, "Sorry to butt in my friend. But when you mentioned mountains, it immediately brought to my mind the magnificent and mysterious Mount Roraima which straddles across the border points of Venezuela, Brazil and Guyana. It was the location for Sir Arthur Conan Doyle's book titled *The Lost World* published way back in 1912. Of course, that was pure fiction as there are no dinosaurs on Roraima, but many exotic and ancient fauna and so on. Guyana is not in a lost world but is moving confidently into a new world of our own making."

Doreen smiled and looked at Michael admiringly as she enthused, "So well said my dear husband. I understand that we will all be gathering here tomorrow for our final day before we leave for our homes. I know that the ladies and I of this group had objected to a few of you itching to play dominoes. However, we have all agreed that you should play out at least one final set of games between your old rival teams of the ACES of Anna Catherina, the LIONS of Leonora and the COBRAS of Cornelia Ida."

The men gave a resounding "Hooray!"

31

Domino!

The day of the final domino showdown began with a late breakfast at both residences of the hosts of the touring party. It was a cloudy and windy morning in complete contrast to the bright, warm and sunny starts to the previous days of the visit to Guyana. Within minutes there was a burst of tropical rain which crashed onto the concreted yards of Nazir's and Neesha's as well as John's and Muriel's homes. Although the squally shower lasted for only about ten minutes, the volume of rainwater quickly created large puddles on the roads and caused overflows of the drains in front of both houses. When the rain stopped and the wind died down, the dark clouds gave way to soft white cumulus with a light blue sky in the background. Local people then emerged from sheltering, and many walked out to the main road to catch their minibus or taxi to head off to their workplace or to visit either Parika to the west or Georgetown to the east.

The tour party gathered at Nazir's and Neesha's home and settled down in the welcoming and comfortable air-conditioned lounge and the offer of glasses of freshly squeezed orange juice. Nazir and Neesha stood up alongside John and Muriel facing their guests for the last time before their departures booked for early the next day.

Nazir, with his eyes welling up, began the farewell session by saying, "First of all, I wish to thank my dear wife Neesha and our amazing housekeeper as well as our great friends John and Muriel and their housekeeper, for all their effort to make this visit to our beloved country such a great success. I am sure that we can say that we loved every moment of your stay with us as well as the trips to experience so much of the country in such a short time. When I first thought of asking Vishnu to come here to see for himself what is happening and to have a view as to where Guyana is heading towards,

I had no idea that the journey would be made by all of you at the same time. I felt that we would just come together, have some good times eating, drinking and so on as we toured around the country. Yes, and to play a lot of dominoes! But both Neesha and I have found the whole tour to be such an eye-opener for us, especially appreciating the incredible sights and listening to the stories about our history and our amazing fellow Guyanese who have shaped this country. Now, before we prepare to play some dominoes as members of our ACES, LIONS and COBRAS teams of these three great villages of Anna Catherina, Leonora and Cornelia Ida, I wish to ask each of you to come up here and share your views about Guyana without holding back. Please express your honest opinions as to where we came from, where we are, and what the future will look like for us as Guyanese as well as our country of Guyana. I think that the first person I must call has to be our incredible "Histry Maan" Michael!"

Michael sprung to his feet like a spirited jaguar, adjusted his glasses to sit near the tip of his nose, made sure that his 'One Guyana' multi-coloured T-shirt was tucked into the waist of his khaki shorts, and he then opened his trusted notebook.

He looked around the room, acknowledged his friends, and began, "On behalf of my beautiful wife Doreen and I, let me thank our hosts and companions here for a most memorable and enjoyable adventure, for your kindness and appreciation of typical Guyanese hospitality, and for your patience in listening to me sharing whatever knowledge I have. I have told you a lot about Guyana's histry, I mean history, the amazing heroes, heroines and martyrs who gave everything for the freedoms we are enjoying. Some of them are presented and remembered through monuments, statues and sculptures around the country. We have also been blessed with leaders who set out their visions, hopes and aspirations for us all despite facing local and international challenges, and a lack of money to put the plans into place. We heard about some of our ordinary Guyanese who came from less privileged circumstances, worked hard, used their brains and energy to build institutions, create businesses, excel in many fields, and shape the Guyana we know today. Now we have a young President and his government building on this strong foundation, our incredible heritage, and our strengths and weaknesses. The country is being taken towards new heights beyond our imagination. One word of warning here. I do not believe in the hype of Guyana becoming a "new Dubai". We are different from the people of Dubai. We are not influenced by one religion or people. But we have greater strengths in our diversity, and we will develop a different country with immense God-given talent, natural wealth and beauty. I predict that in twenty years' time, if Guyana continues to be built socially and economically at the current rate it will be the top country in this region, very well known internationally, and a great example for others to learn from. I have more to say, but for the moment, let me now ask our two representatives of our First Peoples, John and Muriel, to share their thoughts and ideas with us."

Michael bowed gracefully in response to warm applause around the room. John and Muriel took his place, and Muriel led their contribution.

"John and I are very privileged to be held in such high esteem by you all. We cannot claim to represent all the people of our nine Amerindian tribes, but we can share thoughts which you may hear from them. Firstly, we believe in this country, and love the fact that the most important plans being implemented called the Low Carbon Development Strategy 2030, or LCDS2030, is focused on our rainforests and the Amerindian people living there. It is vital for the development of the two hundred plus villages and communities to be determined and planned by the people themselves with support from the government if and when needed. Secondly, we must also continue to preserve our languages and culture for future generations to carry forward. In fact, both John and I hope that in twenty years' time, all of the young people across Guyana will be able to speak at least one of our languages alongside English starting at Primary School, continuing at Secondary School and through to our national university. I expect that Spanish and Portuguese will also be widely known in the country. Thirdly, I do hope that our Amerindian brothers and sisters will show our fellow Guyanese and the world that we can be trusted to help save Guyana from the growing dangers of the terrible effect of Climate Change. Finally, my fervent wish is for the girls and women of our communities to become empowered to take on more leadership in their villages and settlements across the country. Who knows, but one day in the not-too-distant future we will have an Amerindian woman as our President of Guyana! John can add to my thoughts."

John continued after the group cheered Muriel, "Of course we can all paint a rosy picture of the future of the people and the country. However, this can only happen if we deal with some serious issues affecting our young people and our women in particular. Muriel and I are very concerned about the growing incidences of drug and alcohol misuse by our youngsters, and their desire to move away from the hinterland to seek jobs and other opportunities elsewhere. Perhaps now and in the future, the people in the hinterland could become more self-sufficient and the entrepreneurs there being helped to set up and run various types of enterprises linked closely to the preservation of the environment. I also expect to see many more of our people embrace and succeed in higher education and produce our own doctors, lawyers and scientists needed in the hinterland. Our people are amongst the poorest in this country, and we believe that one way out of this situation is by education. We as a people, have invaluable knowledge about our culture and environment that is passed down to, and amongst us. This should be an integral part of the school curriculum across the country. Finally, I do agree with Muriel, and I dearly wish that one of our talented youngsters will become Guyana's first Amerindian President! Er, I mean female President!"

Muriel intervened with, "I think that our educators across the country should now introduce a new examination subject about dealing with the environment and climate change. Perhaps the subject can be called 'Environment Studies'."

Everyone applauded John's and Muriel's fervent desires as to the future of the Amerindian people and the country as they returned to their seats. Nazir then invited Ramesh and Sati to take John's and Muriel's places to speak to the gathering.

Sati stepped forward just slightly ahead of Ramesh, and she commenced with, "Wow! I love Uncle John's and Aunty Muriel's vision, and I would go further and hope that the first Amerindian President will be elected within the next twenty years!"

Doreen, Parvati, Neesha, Maria and Muriel expressed their approval by exclaiming together, "Yes!"

Sati continued, "In addition to eliminating poverty amongst the most vulnerable in Guyana, I agree that focus must be maintained on lifting most Amerindians who are the poorest group, out of poverty as quickly as possible."

John and Muriel applauded Sati.

Ramesh added, "If poverty is eliminated across Guyana, that will move our country much higher up the world ranking for development using what is known as the Human Development Index or HDI. This is a far more important measurement of development than the economic or wealth measure of Gross Domestic Product or GDP. I am sorry for mentioning these technical terms, but they are the ones currently being used to rank countries. I note that Guyana's HDI was increased by about twenty-four per cent from the year 2000 to 2021. In 2023, the World Bank classified Guyana as a high-income country due to the oil revenues and the fact that it is the fastest growing economy in the world. Importantly, the government is not just relying on oil and gas alone and is building the conditions to develop further our mining industry, timber, the agriculture sector with new crops, and in all areas of technology. Guyana is aiming to help the region achieve food security by 2025, and to sustain that in the years ahead. Achieving food security is another way towards reducing poverty not only in Guyana, but also in the region."

Carlos interrupted Ramesh and pointed out, "Man, we could not fail to see so many examples of rapid building, repairs or extensions of roads, bridges, hotels, hospitals, community clinics, schools, sports facilities, factories and so much more everywhere we travelled to. This is just incredible!"

Maria acknowledged Carlos's comment and added, "Don't forget the number of new housing for people desperate for decent shelter, the mansions and the impressive shopping malls and marketplaces. And, of course, the First Lady's beautification projects around the country."

Ramesh thanked Carlos and Maria and noted, "Of course it is great to see all the developments you have mentioned, but there are very many old structures and systems which are badly in need of renovation or even replacement. The heritage sites such as the St Georges Cathedral in Georgetown will always need careful preservation. And so will the drainage and other systems in the towns due to their age. We have also heard about the continuing threat to the coastlands by flooding and breaches made by the ocean and rivers. Moving towns or building new ones further inland could happen within the next twenty to thirty years. Silica City is a great idea and will set the template for such developments."

Afzal raised his right hand and was allowed to make his contribution.

"I am very happy to hear that so far you have given great importance to our people of Guyana both here and abroad. You see, the country can be built up and modernised in line with the wealth we are seeing. But Guyana can never be seen as a well-developed country without the people benefitting from the growth. No one should be left behind and the gap between the rich and the poor must be closed. Politicians have always promised to address this problem which is now getting worse. I love the fact that when resources such as the grants for school children are handed out, every person gets a fair share. I would also like to see more pay for the workers across the board for both the public and the private sectors. Taxes should also ensure that the rich pay a fair share and the poor and lowly paid are relieved of the burden of taxation. Our farmers, fishermen and women, must also be given the best prices possible for their produce."

Parvati was pleased to hear what Afzal suggested and added, "I have always been a simple country girl and woman. I would like to see that the people are able to get fuel at the lowest price possible, reliable and cheap electricity, clean water, better sanitation, more reasonable household equipment and utensils, air-conditioning, and support for growing their own. These are the things which will make me happier than having to look up at grand buildings and visiting fancy malls and such places."

Doreen did not wait for an invitation to speak and stood up beside Michael to say, "I love what our dear sister Parvati just said. I believe that most of our Guyanese brothers and sisters wish to live happy, comfortable, rewarding and secure lives. But they cannot have this without good health. It is very worrying to hear about ill-health issues from birth through to adulthood, and particularly the growing level of obesity. Guyana has plenty of good healthy food and drink options, and I am very concerned about the growth of so many fast-food outlets. We live in developed countries where such foods are literally killing the population through obesity, diabetes and heart disease."

Maria was eager to point out, "Yes, the people of Guyana need more support and help with the prevention of ill-health. Good food with fresh ingredients planted or sourced locally, plus healthy unprocessed fruit drinks, and a reduction in the use of beef, pork and mutton, should provide the kind of diet that can combat diabetes, heart disease and even cancer. There are so many amazing fruits and vegetables including ground provisions here so that the people can enjoy what is known as balanced diets. Of course, exercise and active sports are very important for better health and wellbeing. More dedicated parks should be created around and for the communities. I am just talking about this, and I am feeling a great sense of elation and happiness."

Peter added, "Speaking of exercise, I believe that regular and fairly brisk walking is a great way to gain fitness, lose weight and enjoy the outdoors especially early evenings before darkness. Riding cycles is also very good provided you are able to do so safely along the roads. I notice that people here do not use cycle helmets, and that should become compulsory. I suggest that good cycle and walking lanes should be built alongside the roads and streets. I think that there should be stricter controls on motor vehicles' speed with suitable penalties. This can help to save a lot of lives and reduce injuries. I would introduce and police the compulsory wearing of seatbelts in vehicles. Also, all vehicles must be subject to strict annual checks."

John nodded in agreement with Peter and added, "Prevention is always extremely important. Of course, the wearing of helmets may not apply to people in the hinterland forests, but I can see the need for the protection of people travelling by canoes and boats on the many waterways. Our Amerindian people know how to live and work in their environment, but they also need to adopt proper safety measures especially when they work as miners, in forestry, in fishing and of course when they come out to visit or work in the coastlands. Regarding diet, I think that they use only what is available to them, especially fish and ground provisions. But as Muriel and I have said, alcohol and drug misuse are serious problems for them as well as other Guyanese across the country."

Muriel took a sip of her coffee and pointed out, "I think that another problem for people especially in the hinterland, is quick access to health facilities near to where they live, and for people who are poor, the disabled and the elderly. I have no doubt that the current Health Minister is doing a great job and is well aware about the need to have people seen quickly, given the tests they need, and ensuring that everyone is offered the right vaccines to prevent viral attacks, and that people get their operations as quickly as possible. Of course, this includes the provision of the best aftercare in the community and in their homes as needed. Health and social care are still huge challenges even for people living in the richest countries such as America, Britain and Canada. I am so happy to see the building of new and well-equipped hospitals and clinics here in Guyana, and I hope that there will be more where they are needed. Of course, these services can only be effective if they have the right people with the right skills to treat and care for patients. I am so proud to know that many more of our young Amerindian women are taking up the offers to be trained healthcare specialists. There should also be more support for those of us who care for our family members, and for the people who choose to self-care. By self-care I mean that wherever possible, we need to be able to take more personal responsibility for our health and wellbeing. There is no sense in us neglecting our own health and then complaining that we cannot get treatment when we need this."

Vishnu, who had been listening to the conversation with great interest, took up the chance to air his views.

"I am so happy to hear all the comments and suggestions here. Muriel prompted me to pick up on another very important aspect of the development of the country. The amazing pace of change we have witnessed as we toured the regions actually highlights the problem of having the right education and training systems and facilities to enable our younger generation of Guyanese to be properly equipped to take on the sheer breadth of the skills and expertise required across the country. The government is aware of this and is trying to offer more training places in a range of skills such as for electricians, plumbers and so on. Guyana has always produced bright and very capable people, and I hope that with more investment in skills training and professional qualifications, there will be lesser need to depend on people from abroad."

Michael was quick to support Vishnu's and Muriel's suggestions about growing more local skilled personnel, and added, "The commitment to developing the local workforce will also help to slow down and perhaps stop the brain drain from this country that has been going on for decades. Guyana cannot afford to lose more talented people and then having to accept and pay for skilled people from abroad. But in order to achieve this, pay must be reasonable and competitive so as to also retain our best human assets."

Arthur looked at Vishnu and then at Michael before saying, "You two gentlemen have hit the nail on the head regarding this issue. All of our people have a role to play in the country's development. This in turn will give investors greater confidence to come here and help to build the country. But there is an age-old problem which no one seems to have answers for. That is the spectre of crime and criminals hanging over this country."

Afzal was quick to pounce, "I say hang them high!"

Arthur shook his head and replied, "Oh no! Guyana should never have the death penalty, but more resources must be put into hiring suitably qualified and experienced people to work with offenders and to try to turn their lives around. The Police also needs to focus on relieving criminals of their weapons and deal with the source or sources of them."

Michael was not as optimistic about how to deal with crime and criminals in Guyana.

"Crime and criminality will always be here to plague us. I cannot remember any time over the last sixty years that we were ever free from crime. Of course, we have to do everything to prevent crime and to deal with the guilty ones appropriately. But there will always be an element in our society who choose to live by crime. I believe that we can do much more to minimise or eradicate the curse in our society of domestic violence. We must work harder to appreciate and respect the girls and women of our country. I am not saying this to appease our wonderful wives and daughters, but I genuinely love and care for our girls and women. We need to promote love and understanding for this half of our population by education at home, our schools, our religious centres, our workplaces and also on social media."

Maria stood up and walked across the room to openly hug Michael whilst everyone else applauded his remarks.

Afzal waited for Michael to acknowledge that he wished to speak, and then pointed out, "This comes right back to the importance of encouraging our people to become more hospitable towards each other. We as a people are well known for our friendliness and warmth towards others. But we tend not to speak much about the growing intolerance towards people of the LGBT community. I am as guilty as anyone who as youngsters, used to tease and taunt homosexual men in our villages. I do regret such attitude and behaviour, and I am trying to come to a position of greater respect for and tolerance towards people of all genders."

There was a resounding show of approval for Afzal's comment. Doreen stood up, and after looking around the room, began to speak.

"Well, well, well! I did not expect to come to our beautiful country and to have a conversation such as this. I thought that I was learning quite a lot as we toured around the country, but now I am so proud to be here amongst friends who understand so much, and who care for this country and our people. I am convinced that when we leave here, we will look back and feel a greater sense of pride and hold higher hopes for the future of this land. Of course, there are lots of faults we can pick on but do tell me about any country in the world that is without faults. We will be going back to America, Canada and elsewhere in the so-called civilised world. But we know how broken societies are in those places. Long live Guyana! Guyana is truly on the rise!"

Ramesh acknowledged Doreen's wish and added, "Thank you, Aunty Doreen. I love the optimism shown here today. I would like to mention some more areas which need further development over the next ten to twenty years. Guyana has produced many outstanding scientists and now is the time to invest more into scientific research as well as new ways of doing things as we are seeing in the agriculture sector. Artificial Intelligence is also very important for all aspects of professional, business, leisure, sports and cultural activities. I note that the government is determined to take advantage of the benefits of what is being called a Digital Economy. There are many initiatives such as improving access to Information and Communications Technology or ICT in the hinterland and other areas, developing electronic health records, digitising historical records, creating "smart" classrooms, and working towards having all government services available online. We know that America, China and India are leading in these things, and Guyana will no doubt join such great countries in the future. But we must be very mindful of the danger and threat of cyber-crime, external and internal interference affecting the systems, our democratic processes, and so on."

Nazir smiled and asked, "This thing called AI could end up taking away a lot of jobs. I thought that this government wanted to create thousands of new jobs. So, what is the whole point of AI?"

Ramesh thought for a moment and then replied, "In my experience to date, AI has been a great help in dealing with lots of data and information and offering quick answers, but I am still in control. I use the AI information as well as my own experience and knowledge to make decisions. AI is also used in many surgical procedures and operations. I understand that AI is able to help detect certain cancers much earlier and more accurately than the human eye. These will all bring new job opportunities."

Nazir was still not convinced and asked, "All well and good, but will AI replace human beings in their jobs?"

Sati was anxious to answer and offered, "Uncle Nazir, the intention about the use of AI is not about replacing jobs, but on creating different opportunities and that is why our education system has to adapt to this, and so does our private sector."

Michael pointed out, "Many of us here will remember when robots and robotics were going to replace people in many jobs. But whilst jobs were being lost to robots, we are still seeing humans working alongside the technological changes. As far as I am concerned, I think that Guyanese have nothing to fear from a Digital and AI based economy. In fact, I would like to see that AI is used here to enhance the work of creating what is called a Green Economy as we lead the way in the fight to protect the environment and achieve below zero carbon."

Ramesh chuckled as he pointed out, "Uncle Michael, no science or technology can ever replace you!"

Michael fist-pumped with Ramesh and agreed, "Maybe my notebook, but not my personality! Never mind AI, I think that I have a lot of EI, meaning Emotional Intelligence!"

Vishnu smiled as he suggested, "Michael, I believe that you have offered the right kind of vision for this country. There is no doubt in my mind that Guyana can lead the way in showing the world how a Green Revolution can solve many of our problems, not just with Climate Change, but also helping to eradicate poverty and prevent vulnerable nations from the devastating impact of terrible destruction we are already witnessing. There are thousands of simple examples of how people are finding solutions to dealing with things like the pollution of our waterways and so on. Of course, mother nature will continue to present problems, but we have managed to withstand many of them. Guyana is very well placed to take this Green Revolution forward. Then that phrase "Green land of Guyana" will become a more recognisable and meaningful image of this country."

Peter raised his right hand, and Nazir gave him the nod to speak, "One of the ways in which the image of our country should be enhanced is through sports. Of course, you will expect me to champion the cause of cricket at all levels from schools to clubs, to regional teams, to national level, and of course, international. Not only this, but the people who participate in and represent our country in cricket and all other sports must be supported whilst they do this, and after they retire. Guyana, despite a myriad of challenges, still managed to produce incredible sportsmen and women, and promoted our country to the world. This can be significantly improved."

Michael nodded and felt that the time was right for him to highlight a different issue, "Peter, thank you for emphasising the area of all sports which I believe hold the keys to resolving one of the most difficult issues that has dominated the lives of Guyanese. We have talked about most things here except the spectre of racism. So, where do I start? Why has racism taken such a hold on many of our people? How can this be removed? I do not have all the answers, but I can offer my own perspective. I believe that from the moment outsiders from Europe landed here in Guyana, and they almost immediately imposed themselves onto the First Peoples they encountered, that was the birth of racial division and enmity. The Amerindians, although not united as one nation of many tribes at the time, fought hard to resist the intruders who came with their religion and their own view about civilisation. The Dutch for example, befriended some tribes and encouraged them to capture other Amerindians and enforce them into slavery. That to me was the first example of the divide and rule strategy of the colonialists. John and Muriel, is this how you see this issue?"

John took a few moments before responding, "There is a lot of truth in what you said. Before the first Europeans arrived in what we now call Guyana, there were many more Amerindian tribes than the nine we have now. And sadly, there was a lot of in-fighting and conflicts amongst the tribes. The Europeans also brought their diseases which killed many of our people. If there was one leader who could have brought most of the people together, then our history would have been different. So, the lesson here is for us to resolve our own differences in a peaceful way, and then we can withstand any challenges."

Michael nodded and continued, "The next challenge came when my enslaved ancestors were brought here to work on the plantations. Again, the seeds of mistrust and racial hatred were sown by the Dutch plantation owners who paid Amerindians to capture runaway slaves. The arrival of Portuguese Indentured labourers from Madeira after the end of slavery in 1834, added another element to the issue of mistrust and racism. The Portuguese tried to distance themselves from others in the country by claiming that they were White Europeans and should be treated equally by the British who refused to do so and insisted that they were just labourers."

Carlos was eager to comment, "Michael, I have heard about that approach by my ancestors. They did not waste any time to move away from the sugar plantations after the end of their contracts and pursued commercial activities from basic single-handed huckstering to large business enterprises. They also opted for better white-collar jobs in banking and retail. Over time, my people began to enter into mixed race relationships, and now this group is a significant proportion of the Guyana population alongside other mixes. Like everyone else, Maria and I are very proud of the achievements of our Portuguese brothers and sisters. I do hope that my fellow Portuguese can visit our ancestral homeland of Madeira which is about six hundred and seventy miles from the mainland of Portugal in the Atlantic Ocean. It is a beautiful island, and you can see where and how they grew sugarcane and produced sugar and rum. Nowadays, they are more into producing wines."

Vishnu took his cue and stood up to say, "When my ancestors from India arrived here in 1838 as Indentured labourers taking up the jobs left by others on the sugar plantations, they were subject to a lot of prejudice, discrimination and dislike from their white masters as well as the others who remained on the estates or lived in the villages. The Indians had to be more united as jahajis both on the sea journeys from India and whilst working on the estates. They had to resist any pressure to continue with the practice of the caste system that existed in India. It also took a long time for them to build meaningful relationships with everyone else. However, they inevitably faced more resentment due to their progressive ownership of land, property, businesses and substantial homes, especially after Indian Indentureship ended in 1917, and the vast majority of them opted to stay in Guyana. Like our friend

Carlos, I would recommend that descendants should try to find out where their ancestors came from and to visit those places. I am pleased that the government is committed to preserving the Indentured Indian and other records by digitising them and making them more easily available to researchers."

Arthur also picked his moment to comment, "Vishnu, the arrival of my Chinese ancestors from Macao in 1853 brought yet another dimension to the growing racial melting pot. They also preferred to leave the sugar estates after the end of their contracts, and like the Portuguese, they pursued business opportunities especially in the towns. As Chinese, we have managed to insulate ourselves from the racial conflict which has been experienced by our African and Indian brothers and sisters. But we now have another problem to deal with, and that is the new Chinese migrants from mainland China. I cannot see us coming together with them. In fact, my family and I prefer to embrace our new and dynamic 'One Guyana' of our own Guyanese people."

Doreen stood up once again, and with her hands on her hips, she pronounced, "Gentlemen, as a proud Guyanese woman, I think that this whole racism problem has been as a result of the hunger for power that men have. It was not European women who landed here to take away the land of the Amerindians, or who enslaved people, or brought other people here just to toil for the profits of the male plantation owners. So, in my humble opinion, this problem can only be solved by the minds and will of our Guyanese women! Maybe that proposition and wish by Muriel for a future President of Guyana to be an Amerindian woman could be an answer to our racism problem!"

All the women in the meeting applauded. Then, after a few moments, the men followed suit.

Michael, still smiling and looking at Doreen with great affection, opened his notebook for the final time, and said, "Thinking about all that we have said here today, Guyana is emerging from a position where our land was exploited by the Dutch and British in particular, used just for the purpose of deriving wealth from cocoa and sugar for centuries, drained of our natural resources through gold, diamond and bauxite mining, all by usurping the sweat and blood of all of our peoples, to a point in our history where despite more exploitation of our oil and gas by global corporations, we can still begin to dream. Dream of a future where every Guyanese can achieve the best of everything that will make us all happy. The best of health, education, opportunities, pay and safety. Our quest is not over. And I am very proud to be able to stand here in the village of my birth alongside the people whom I love and cherish so much, and to witness the beginning of that quest. I am a very happy Guyanese today. Long live Guyana! We are One People, One Nation, and with a Destiny within our reach!"

Everyone stood up and spontaneously applauded.

Vishnu acknowledged Michael's comments and added, "I fully accept everything said by everyone here today. But let me remind you all about a serious threat we touched upon earlier. It is to do with how we as Guyanese deal with the Maduro claim for Essequibo. Clearly Guyana cannot match his military strength. So, the only way is to maintain and strengthen the support we have from our international partners, and for us as Guyanese to come together and stand up as one to that madman! I say, Essequibo is we own! Guyana is we own! Long live Guyana!"

After the applause for Vishnu's comment ended, everyone took their seats, and Nazir reminded them, "Thank you all so much. I think that now is the right time for that set of dominoes by our three rivals, the ACES, the LIONS and the COBRAS. Gentlemen, please take up your positions around the table and three chairs we have in the middle of this room. You will play three games, and the person winning two will be our champion."

Michael was quick to question Nazir's plan and asked, "So, what happens if each of the three players win one game?"

Arthur suggested, "Well, just play a fourth and final decider game, and whoever wins that one will be called the champion."

Carlos asked, "So, what happens if that fourth game is a draw? Do they play a fifth and final game?"

Nazir acceded to the suggestions and asked the players to commence playing.

Michael raised his right hand and asked, "Who will be our referee? Can I suggest John?"

Nazir nodded and asked John to oversee the play.

The first three games were played very quickly as Vishnu for the ACES, Afzal for the LIONS and Peter for the COBRAS each won a game. It was the first time that Neesha, Doreen and all the other women in attendance eagerly supported their favourite player, and they became increasingly excited as the three players banged the domino tickets so hard that the sequence of the play was disrupted causing John to step in and reset them. Game one was won by Afzal who got up from his seat and did a victory dance around the table much to the onlookers' amusement. Peter won the second game, and simply raised his hands in the manner of a cricket bowler dismissing a batsman. Vishnu won the third game, and did not display any emotion, but looked intently as John shuffled the dominoes for the fourth game.

Vishnu was quick to play the double-six domino to start the game. Afzal raised his eyes and stared at Vishnu sternly.

"Referee! I object to that play!"

John was perplexed by the intervention and announced in the manner of a judge in a Law Court, "Objection overruled!"

Afzal was not pleased by the refusal of his objection and pleaded, "Your Honour, Vishnu is known as 'Double Six' because he steals an advantage in the game by his habit of picking out this particular domino when he really needs to."

John stood firmly by his decision and ordered the play to continue. It was Afzal's turn, and he rapped.

Michael could not resist commenting on the game, "You see John, that is why Afzal complained. He doesn't have any sixes in his hands. Now, our ACES star player is on top. A bit like Guyana heading towards victory as the most progressive country in the region!"

John pointed to Michael and requested, "Please Michael, no talking during the game. OK gentlemen, play!"

The players, appreciating that it was the final and deciding game, slowed down considerably from their usual excitable slamming of the dominoes with each play. Tension filled the air, and John weaved around the players like a boxing referee peering at each move and ensuring that each domino played was positioned neatly and correctly.

During the game Afzal managed to recover from not having any sixes, and skilfully put Peter under pressure by posting dominoes that finally caused him to rap. But Vishnu kept a calmness like a serious professional Poker player in a game of high stakes. Michael, his unofficial coach and adviser, obeyed John's instruction and desisted from trying to drop any hints to Vishnu as he used to do in the past.

Finally, Vishnu was on the brink of utilising all of his seven dominoes, and held the last one securely covered to avoid his opponents from catching a glimpse of it. The game came to a standstill as everyone rapped, and John declared that it would be decided on which player had the least number of points on their domino.

Afzal frowned as he declared a ten point double five and slid it across the table in frustration. Peter then smiled with the air of a victor, and calmly placed his two points domino in front of him.

Nazir could not contain himself, and nervously shouted, "Oh no! The COBRAS have won! Well done, Peter!"

Vishnu waited for the excited murmuring of the onlookers to subside, and stood up slowly from his chair, and with one flourish, slammed down his domino which caused those on the table to bounce around.

"Domino! This is for One Guyana! Ace blank for One Guyana on the up! One Guyana on the rise!"

END

ALSO BY KHALIL RAHMAN ALI

DAUGHTER OF THE GREAT RIVER
Published in 2020

Daughter of the Great River is a story based on the struggles of Indigenous Peoples in the fictional country of Kayana, "Land of Many Waters".

Onida is the eponymous daughter of the great river who emerged more than five hundred years after her ancestors were brutally suppressed by invading Europeans and were forced to flee to the safety of the rainforests of Kayana.

Her tribe of Kayanese is made up of several Indigenous Peoples who prefer to live in the hinterland of Kayana's vast rainforests. She is the 'chosen one' to lead her peoples out of their challenging circumstances where the natural resources of gold and timber are being exploited by local and foreign interests.

Within the world's current population of 7.8 billion people, there are an estimated 370 to 500 million of Indigenous origin. They are defined as having a historical continuity with pre-invasion and pre-colonial societies that developed on their territories, consider themselves as distinct from other sectors of the societies now prevailing in those territories (United Nations).

They continue to suffer from disproportionately high rates of poverty, health problems, crime and human rights abuses (UN).

Paperback, 244 pages, ISBN: 978-1-912662-18-0
Price: £11.99 (UK only) / US $18.00 (RoW)

Ebook: £5.99
ISBN: 978-1-912662-28-9 (Epub)
ISBN: 978-1-912662-27-2 (Kindle)

ALSO BY KHALIL RAHMAN ALI

IN PURSUIT OF BETTERMENT
Five Stories from the Indian Diaspora
Published in 2017

A collection of stories of families from India, Guyana and the Caribbean, Mauritius, East Africa and South Africa. The five families share a compelling desire and drive to achieve betterment through education, work and business, against the backdrop of the histories of the countries from which they originate or leave.

The first story is set in India and London as the Shivwani family grows from humble beginnings to international business success.

Little Guyana is the story of Inshan Khan who was sent to London to study Law. His extended family also had to leave Guyana due to a decline in the local economy, and became part of the emergence of "Little Guyana" in New York.

Murali Dharam from Mauritius, arrived in London to study psychiatric nursing. His romantic liaisons created family tensions both in Mauritius and England.

Manubhai Patel and his family were forcibly expelled from Uganda in 1972 and were faced with new challenges in Leicester, England, including racial harassment.

In Durban, South Africa, where the largest population of Indians have settled outside India, Professor Yusuf mentors two young PhD students seeking answers about their country's emergence from apartheid.

Paperback, 392 pages, ISBN: 978-1-910553-76-3
Price: £11.99 (UK only) / US $18.00 (RoW)

Ebook: £5.99
ISBN: 978-1-910553-80-0 (Epub)
ISBN: 978-1-910553-81-7 (Kindle)

ALSO BY KHALIL RAHMAN ALI

THE DOMINO MASTERS OF DEMERARA
Published in 2015

It is the 6th of August 1985, and the final and deciding game of dominoes between three rival teams from the sugar plantation villages of Anna Catherina, Leonora and Cornelia Ida, in Demerara, Guyana, is underway. Michael "Histry Maan" Brown, the selfappointed coach to the Anna Catherina ACES, reverts to new tactics to pass sublime tips to his captain, Vishnu "Double Six" Prashad.

The game is played out at a time when Guyana and its peoples were still emerging from a history of struggle through African slavery, Portuguese, Indian and Chinese indentured labour, political independence, racial unrest, mass migration and economic downturn.

Michael, Vishnu and their friends use every means available to continue to survive, and to build their lives in their multi-racial, multi-religious and multi-cultural society.

The game of dominoes provides them with the opportunity to demonstrate their competitiveness, their search for unity, and their resolve to face up to their challenges.

Can they succeed as One People, One Nation, with One Destiny?

Paperback, 188 pages
ISBN: 978-1-910553-07-7
Price: £11.99 (UK only) / US $18.00 (RoW)

ALSO BY KHALIL RAHMAN ALI

SUGAR'S SWEET ALLURE
Published in 2013

It is 1843, and Mustafa Ali, an eighteen year-old Muslim Indian labourer from a village near Kanpur, Uttar Pradesh, India, is forced to run away through the discovery of his forbidden love for Chandini Sharma, his Hindu childhood sweetheart. His dream was to find work, save his money and return to ask for his beloved's hand.

This dream took him further afield into the promise of good work, pay and conditions as an indentured labourer on one of the sugar plantations, thousands of miles away in the colony of British Guiana on the mainland of South America. His experiences on the Grand Trunk Road across Uttar Pradesh to Bengal, and on the treacherous sea voyage from Calcutta to Georgetown, tested his resolve to the limit. Then, when he and his companions were allocated to their sugar plantations, they had to endure and overcome more challenges of racial, religious and cultural differences, in addition to the unrelenting and punishing workloads in extremely harsh conditions.

This is a story that is shared by millions of the descendents of indentured Indian labourers who are spread across all parts of the world. Will Mustafa succeed in his quest?

Paperback, 312 pages
ISBN: 978-1-906190-66-8
Price: £11.99 (UK only) / US $15.00 (RoW)

Ebook: £7.79
ISBN: 978-1-906190-76-7 (Epub)
ISBN: 978-1-906190-75-0 (Kindle)